Outstanding praise for the novels of J. J. Murray!

A GOOD MAN

"In this deceptively light but ocean-deep sendup of dating and reality television, Murray takes a fun, reflective look at interracial relationships. . . . The religious elements are always uplifting and never overbearing, and readers should brace for a three-hanky finale."
—*Publishers Weekly*

"Murray orchestrates another smart, entertaining interracial romance. . . . Murray's wonderful characters, caring perspective, humor, and the story's fabulous ending make this a winning read."
—*Booklist*

"J. J. Murray uses the reality TV show and the behind-the-scenes machinations to launch a romantic comedy between well-developed characters with a unique introspective style. The burdens of interracial love are interwoven without a squeamish approach. On the flip side, the blessings of interracial love are celebrated with a masterful touch that rings true with genuine respect and consideration. *A Good Man* earns a place at the top of the to-be-read pile."
—*USA Today*

I'LL BE YOUR EVERYTHING

"A sexy story of love, romance, and getting even."
—*Upscale Magazine*

THE REAL THING

"Murray tells a sexy story of interracial love that's long on charm, romance, and humor."
—*Booklist*

ORIGINAL LOVE

"Thoughtful and well done."
—Library Journal

SOMETHING REAL

"*Something Real* is about a woman finding herself and finding her voice in a community too quick to judge. *Renee and Jay* was a promising debut. *Something Real,* which is a more mature and richer work, is even better."
—The Roanoke Times

"Delightful! Sexy! Touching! *Something Real* is like a burst of sunshine. This release is definitely something special and something real! This is a story that readers must experience for themselves."
—Romance in Color

until I saw your smile

Books by J. J. Murray

RENEE AND JAY

SOMETHING REAL

ORIGINAL LOVE

I'M YOUR GIRL

CAN'T GET ENOUGH OF YOUR LOVE

TOO MUCH OF A GOOD THING

THE REAL THING

SHE'S THE ONE

I'LL BE YOUR EVERYTHING

A GOOD MAN

YOU GIVE GOOD LOVE

UNTIL I SAW YOUR SMILE

Published by Kensington Publishing Corporation

until I saw your smile

J.J. Murray

KENSINGTON BOOKS
www.kensingtonbooks.com

KENSINGTON BOOKS are published by

Kensington Publishing Corp.
119 West 40th Street
New York, NY 10018

All Kensington titles, imprints, and distributed lines are available at special quantity discounts for bulk purchases for sales promotion, premiums, fund-raising, and educational or institutional use.

Special book excerpts or customized printings can also be created to fit specific needs. For details, write or phone the office of the Kensington Special Sales Manager: Kensington Publishing Corp., 119 West 40th Street, New York, NY 10018. Attn. Special Sales Department. Phone: 1-800-221-2647.

ISBN-13: 978-0-7582-7728-2
ISBN-10: 0-7582-7728-8
First Kensington Trade Paperback Printing: June 2014

eISBN-13: 978-0-7582-7730-5
eISBN-10: 0-7582-7730-X
First Kensington Electronic Edition: June 2014

10 9 8 7 6 5 4 3 2 1

Printed in the United States of America

For Amy

Chapter 1

Matthew Mark McConnell, self-employed Internet lawyer, opened the door of his apartment above Mittman's Pharmacy and Jesse's Plastic Covers at South 3rd and Havemeyer Street in the shadow of the Williamsburg Bridge in Brooklyn, and he didn't smell *baleadas* cooking, nor did he get his usual spicy kiss from his girlfriend, Joy.

He stepped inside and sniffed the air. *Oranges? I haven't had an orange in months. I wonder where Joy found them.*

"Joy, did you get us some oranges? Where'd you find them? Santos? Alegria? I was just at Melo's and didn't see any." He had seen grapefruits in abundance but only because someone had decided February should be National Grapefruit Month. *The shortest month for a sour fruit.*

He opened the closet door and hung up his dripping trench coat, its lining loose and flapping. He then set his laptop case and a plastic bag containing microwave popcorn on the pockmarked walnut kitchen table.

"I got the popcorn," he said in the direction of the apartment's only bedroom. "Are we eating out tonight?"

He heard the usual buzzing of the refrigerator, the drip at the sink, the steady hum of traffic on 3rd Street, the hiss of the radiator in the living room, and the ticking of the clock above the stove.

Perhaps Joy is hiding under the covers, he thought. *So my sweet Honduran* princesita *wants to cook in bed tonight instead. This week is going to end in style.*

"*Tu eres muy sexy,*" he called out. "*Tengo ganas.*"

And that was almost the extent of Matthew's grasp of Spanish. Joy was *very* sexy, and he was horny. *What else is necessary to know on a Friday night?*

Before he joined his *belleza chiquita* warming up in the bedroom, a flash of pale yellow paper caught his eye. Affixed to the refrigerator, just below the "World's No. 1 Teacher" magnet Joy's elementary students had made for her, was a Post-it:

Off to the DR with Carlo.
Key on nightstand.
Adios, anciano!
PS: Sorry! ☺

Matthew blinked at the Post-it.

He reread the Post-it.

He continued to blink.

He looked at the kitchen counter, an empty space crawling with dust and bread crumbs. *Where's the microwave? Did it die already? It serves me right for buying a used microwave with a thirty-day warranty—*

He read the Post-it a third time.

Anciano*? I'm not an old man. I'm not ancient. Thirty-five isn't old. Joy says it doesn't matter that I am ten years older than she is. She says she likes a man with a little extra mileage on him. And she says she's sorry? Doubtful. I have never heard her say, "I'm sorry." I have never heard either of us say "I love you" either, but we're working on that. And what's with the smiley face? Who puts a smiley face—*

He closed his eyes.

Who puts a smiley face on a breakup Post-it?

Matthew briefly wondered if "the DR" was a new restaurant somewhere in somewhat trendy, hip Williamsburg.

Only briefly did he wonder this. He knew his hometown and all its eateries like the back of his now shaking hand.

He tried valiantly to take stock of his situation.

Joy is off to the Dominican Republic with Carlo.

Joy has left *me for Carlo while I sat at the Atlas Café all day sponging off their free Wi-Fi and electricity, trying to solicit clients. Okay, okay. I only played marathon games of Internet spades, ate pear chocolate turnovers, and drank sour coffee.*

Joy, my girlfriend for a year and my giggly, sexy roommate for the last six months, has left me . . . for Carlo.

Who's Carlo?

Oh, right. The short, hairy guy I met at Tabaré a few weeks ago. "You just have *to meet him," Joy had said. "Carlo is* so *amazing. He has* so *many stories to tell about his beautiful country."*

Matthew reread the Post-it.

It still ended with the smiley face.

An exchange teacher. Carlo di Ponti or di Pointy or something like that. Joy has run off with an exchange teacher. He's only here for a few months with his students from the Dominican Republic. "I love your country," Carlo said to me. "It has so many possibilities." I suppose that's Dominican code for "I'm taking your smoking hot girlfriend back to my country, ha ha, you stupid anciano!*"*

An exchange teacher. Who runs off with an exchange teacher? Isn't it supposed to be the other way around? Isn't Carlo supposed to get Joy to marry him here so he can get his green card and stay here? What color card will Joy get down there*?*

Out of habit and not knowing what to do with the breakup Post-it now crumpling in his hand, he opened the refrigerator door and looked inside.

It was empty.

Except for a smattering of spills and congealed, red blobs clinging to the wire metal shelves, it was completely empty.

Joy took the leftovers.

She took the leftover tortillas. She took the bean soup and the fish soup. She took the yogurt, celery, cheese, butter, bacon, bottled water, and all the condiments, too.

What kind of disturbed, psychotic woman takes a man's condiments? What, are they traveling on the slow boat to the Dominican Republic and they're not sure where their next meal will come from?

No, Carlo and his students originally flew into JFK.

How are they going to get all that onto the plane?

He opened the bottom right drawer of the refrigerator, the one usually reserved for alcohol. *She took the bottle of Krug Grande Cuvee, the champagne we had been saving for a special occasion. I guess today was a special occasion for her.*

He looked at the top of the refrigerator and saw more emptiness. *She took the box of stale Ritz crackers* and *the last bag of Bachman's pretzels. She and Carlo must be flying coach. I hope those pretzels are so salty she has to drink Caribbean water and gets the runs while she's in the air! Maybe the blue water in the plane's bathroom will splash up on her—*

He checked the freezer compartment. All the Lean Cuisines and even the last Trader Joe's Chicken Tandoori and Celentano lasagna were gone, too.

Joy left one ice cube tray containing half of one crusty, frostbitten cube of ice.

He left the kitchen for the bedroom and looked at his bed, now a collection of rumpled bed sheets, the comforter thrown back to the headboard, the pillows mounded suggestively in the middle.

I made the bed this morning, didn't I? I always make the bed. Joy says she can't reach all the way across and that it hurts her shoulders to pull up the comforter. And why do I smell more oranges? Carlo smelled like orange juice at Tabaré, but I thought it was because of the screwdriver he was drinking. This room smells like eau de exchange teacher. And Joy. She bathed in vanilla, always vanilla. Candles, lotion, perfume. The combination is toxic.

He cracked a window and considered tossing the Post-it into the night. He shoved it into his pocket instead before gathering the pillows and bedding carefully, rolling it all off the bed and onto the floor.

Burn them or wash them? Wash them, then *burn them? Joy picked out the comforter and the oversized pillows, but I paid for them. Yeah, I'm paying for it, all right. Michael warned me not to date a younger woman. He warned me not to hook up with a woman who smiled at me while cursing in a language I didn't completely understand. Joy taught me a great deal of Spanish, but I have enough trouble with English. "She'll cost you in the end, my friend," Michael had said. "There's something about her eyes. She has crazy eyes, Matthew. They don't ever quite focus. Never trust a woman with crazy, unfocused eyes."*

I hate when Michael's right, but then again, Michael's been right about nearly everything since we skated through NYU law and survived six years together at Schwartz, Yevgeny, and Ginsberg, where he's still cranking out billable hours and suing the world. Michael owns a walk-in Sub-Zero refrigerator while I have a completely empty, blood-red, 1950s Philco V-handle refrigerator.

And a package of microwave popcorn.

With no microwave to cook it in.

He stared at the bedroom floor, the hardwood scuffed and bruised, and for the first time he missed Joy's ratty slippers, slippers he tripped over nearly every night getting into and out of bed.

I can't use this bedding again unless I get it cleaned at Giant Laundry Mat, but they might lose it all. They already lost four of my shirts. "Call three-one-one," the counter guy said. Having to call a number to report shirts missing—what is this country coming to?

Matthew sighed.

Then I must burn it all. Where do you burn your soiled bedding without calling attention to yourself in Williamsburg? I could wait until the Knicks, Mets, Nets, or Jets win a championship and burn it out on South Third in the eventual "victory riot," but then I'd probably be stuck with it all for a long time. I could throw it off the Williamsburg Bridge, but it would probably wash downstream to the Statue of Liberty, where the entire world would see my bedding on CNN as Homeland Security checked the pillows for bombs using one of those robots.

He tried to remember Joy's last words to him that morning. Was it "This isn't working out, Matthew"? Or "I'm going to work out, Matthew"? It might have been "I'll give you a workout when you get home."

He had been hoping for the last one. Joy was good at working him out.

He looked again at the mound of sheets, pillows, and comforter.

And, evidently, she was good at working out Carlo, too.

What a mess! This kind of thing only happens in bad French movies where I would be lighting up a cigarette, smiling some enigmatic smile while looking out the window, and opening a bottle of wine right about now. I could be throwing things—like the pillows—but I don't want to touch them ever again.

He sighed again.

Joy could *have said, "Matthew, I think we should see other people," that reasonably mature though trite and trusted way to break up with someone without saying the actual words.* I *didn't see other people.* I *only saw Joy.* I *thought Joy was The One.* I *thought we were on the same page.* I *thought we were two hearts beating as one.* I *thought . . .*

I thought wrong.

Maybe I wasn't thinking at all.

We were together an entire year, the last six months here in this claustrophobic apartment, and I didn't even look—

Okay, there was this waitress once who had a round, firm booty at Bar Celona, and Joy caught me staring and didn't speak to me for the rest of the evening, but—

He looked again at the heap of bedding on the floor. *So while* I *wasn't seeing other people, Joy was on the prowl. And what do I see now as a result? I see soiled bedding crawling with Carlo's and Joy's DNA.*

I also see my immediate future. I have the joy of reliving the last year of a relationship that I *took seriously while my only bottle of champagne, the entire contents of my refrigerator, and a bag of pretzels flies off to the Dominican Republic!*

He kicked the bedding into the hallway.

A short exchange teacher with chest hair, a thin moustache, and an accent. "I love how tall *you are,* mi macho *Matthew," Joy had said. "I love how* smooth *your face is,* mi amorcito,*" she had said. "I love your accent,* mi cariño,*" she had said.* Joy had even called Matthew *quequito,* her "little cupcake," even though he was twice her size.

Hairy. Joy evidently liked hairy, which is ironic. She always told me to shave and "tidy up down there, por favor*" and "ooh, there's a* cabello *in the sink" and—*

He didn't see the key on the nightstand.

He really didn't want to touch the nightstand.

He decided that if he did burn the bedding, he would add the nightstand to the fire.

Joy forgot to leave the key. Why waste a line telling me that on the Post-it then?

He dropped to his hands and knees and looked under the bed.

He found the key.

He also found a pair of Victoria's Secret leopard-print ruffled panties he had bought Joy for Christmas.

That she had been wearing *this morning.*

He warily tossed the panties into the hallway.

I growled at her this morning, didn't I? I always growl at her when she wears those. Why else would I buy that particular print? You buy animal print underwear for your girlfriend so you can growl at her.

But if they're *here and* she's *on an airplane . . .*

I hope she's cold.

No. They're flying to *the Caribbean.*

He stood and leaned lightly on the edge of the bed before easing toward the dresser. *I can't sleep in my own bed until I get a new mattress. It's a Kluft, and it's only two years old! I suppose I could flip it—*

No.

Spray it with Lysol? Use a bottle of Scrubbing Bubbles? A container of Ajax? A mixture of all three?

What . . . a . . . mess!

He closed his eyes.

What would Jesus do?

He would probably do the laundry, flip the mattress, and forgive the panty-less Joy.

Jesus never had anything like this happen to Him.

No one I know has had this happen to him.

What do I do now?

Besides burning the laundry.

Do I call her? She wouldn't answer.

Do I call Michael? No. He'll laugh at me and tell me, "I told you so."

Do I get back on the horse? Do I put myself back into circulation? I'm sure I'd get some sympathy tonight. "She took my microwave! She took the tortillas! She even took all my condiments! Can you believe that? My condiments! All my leftover ketchup packets are gone on an airplane to the Dominican Republic!"

He went into the bathroom, splashed water on his face, and washed his hands. He turned to dry them.

Where's the—

He braced himself on the sink, gripping its cold white edges as water dripped off his chin.

She took all the towels *and left me a thin, almost see-through white washcloth. Don't they have towels in the Dominican Republic? I'm sure they do. Those towels weren't that special, and they weren't even a matched set!*

Who takes the freaking towels *after a breakup?*

He looked at his reflection in the mirror, seeing familiar lines sneaking away from his eyes and creasing his forehead, his brown hair still thick though beginning to recede. *You're not getting any younger. In fact, at this moment, you look older than thirty-five. Maybe you* are *an* anciano. *Joy aged you. She's* still *aging you. You* are *older.*

But not wiser.

Matthew thought he was a good judge of character. He thought he knew Joy inside and out. He thought he had a lasting relationship with Joy. He thought that all dedicated teachers at P.S. 319 stayed in their classrooms until well after midnight to work on their lesson plans and grade papers, even on Saturdays and Sundays.

He also wondered how he could possibly dry himself without the benefit of a towel.

As these random thoughts collided in his head, he abruptly remembered what Joy had actually said this morning: "This isn't working out, Matthew. Where's my passport?"

"Where's my passport?"—the global village's ultimate breakup line. It's not a bad line as lines go. The next time I break up with someone, I'll say, "I'll just get my passport and be off then."

And to think that I told *her where she could find her passport this morning before she left for school.*

And for the Dominican Republic.

With Carlo, his orange scent, and his chest hair.

He returned to the refrigerator, as if looking inside would magically make leftover *baleadas* and his condiments reappear.

They didn't reappear.

The red blobs hadn't moved. They even seemed to glisten more brightly.

Despite his anguish and tangled thoughts, Matthew had a sudden lucid moment. *How could Joy even afford the plane ticket? She barely paid one-third of our bills. Luckily, we had just paid all the bills . . . this . . . month . . .*

He dropped his chin to his chest, whispering, "*I* will pay the rent this month, *mi quequito*. Do not worry about a thing. You give me the money, and *I* will take care of it."

Joy has been planning her escape from me for a while, maybe even from the moment she saw Carlo step off the plane.

He checked his old-fashioned answering machine on the kitchen counter and saw two messages. One was from PS 319: "Miss Rios, you do not have any sick days left, and if you don't come tomorrow, you will be out of a job." The other was from Matt's landlord: "You're late with your rent . . ."

Joy didn't pay the rent.

That's how she bought her ticket.

And then some.

It can't possibly cost eighteen hundred dollars for a one-way plane ticket to the Dominican Republic. She probably had to buy a cooler for all the food. I'll bet she had to ship the microwave, too. She probably stuffed the bathroom towels inside to keep the glass carousel tray from breaking. That's what I would have done.

He wondered how much he would have to dip into his IRA again to restock his refrigerator, get a new microwave and towels, and pay his rent.

And the ten percent late fee.

He wondered if there were women in the world who were single, sane, and wouldn't run off on him to the Caribbean bare-assed, packing towels, and carrying salty snacks, condiments, and a bottle of champagne.

He also wondered if he should go ahead and defrost the refrigerator since it was already empty.

It'll make the job easier. That ancient thing is a beast to clean.

He shook these foolish thoughts from his head.

I don't need to clean the refrigerator. A man does not defrost and clean out the refrigerator after his love has left him.

He sighed yet again.

If she ever were my love at all.

No more sweaty, caliente *nights. No more long, black hair. No more tan-as-sand skin.*

No more bean soup.

I need to find a woman I can have fun with, a woman I can laugh with, a woman who has the proverbial heart of gold, a woman who doesn't smell like vanilla ice cream twenty-four hours a day, a woman who doesn't talk to herself in Spanish all day. I need a woman who doesn't listen to Garifuna music as "the only music worth listening to," who only dances the punta *while flapping—not snapping—her fingers, and who can't be bothered at all whenever she watches* Ugly Betty *because* her *girl America Ferrera, of Honduran descent, is her favorite actress. I also need to find a woman who doesn't say she's at the school grading papers when she's shacked up somewhere with an exchange teacher, who doesn't take raiding the refrigerator to the extreme, and who would have the decency to leave at least one usable towel behind!*

I also need to find a woman who doesn't have an ironic name. Joy never truly brought me any. "Pain" would have been a more appropriate name for her. "Pain Rios," middle name "Full."

He slumped into his easy chair, certainly the oldest living easy chair in Brooklyn, its lumpy cushion comforting, its springs moaning, each coffee, pizza, and food-stain marking his progress from NYU undergrad to successful litigator to occasionally paid Internet lawyer. He had originally wanted a love seat, but even that wouldn't fit into his tiny apartment.

Whom do I know who is fun and has a heart of gold?

No one.

Matthew decided to take it one little step at a time.

Whom do I know . . . who is fun?

No one.

Matthew posed a better question. *Whom* did *I know once who I* once *thought was fun?*

Monique.

He smiled.

Monique Delicia Freitas.

Yes.

He closed his eyes and saw the sculpted calves, thighs, and hips of one of the many paralegals carrying case files and rushing through Brooklyn Legal Services Corporation, his most recent "real" employer. Eventually he moved up her slender body to her face and found a smile and a pair of smoking-hot hazel eyes. As a matter of personal policy, Matthew didn't date anyone at Brooklyn Legal, but if he had, it would have been Monique. She had done her best to entice him with her long brown hair, her huge hazel eyes, and her too-silky long legs she never hid even if it were ten degrees and snowing outside.

She told me her people were from Bushwick by way of Trinidad. She said she loved to dance, loved to party long into the night, and loved to let it all go. "Any time you want to lose it with someone, Matty, just give me a call," she has said. She called me Matty "McConaughey-hey" because I have a, well, passing resemblance to the actor. If you squint. And if you don't compare his picture too closely to me. I think I'm taller. He has a chin. I have more facial hair and a dimple on my left cheek. He has a hot Brazilian wife and two adorable children. I have Joy and Carlo's DNA on my sheets. The real Matty "McConaughey-hey" has millions.

I have . . . to mine my IRA again.

Monique Delicia Freitas had been the Brooklyn Legal seductress, the paralegal every male lawyer and several female lawyers had wanted to work with.

She was always flirting with me, her eyelashes reaching out from her perpetually dark eyelids to tickle my—

I am seriously *hungry. I can't think straight. Eyelashes do not reach out and tickle anything.*

He looked through rain-streaked windows into the Williamsburg night and saw La Espanola Meat Market, the graffiti memorial for Lil Rich, the now closed and graffiti-splattered New China Restaurant, and garbage bags piled as high as the parking meters casting their shadows over cracked and festering concrete.

Matthew was sure there was a metaphor out there somewhere on that chilly night before National Freedom Day.

Since he seemed to think more logically whenever he sat in his easy chair, he took complete stock of his present situation.

I'm a free Willyburg man now. I'm free. I am single again. I am unattached to anything but this easy chair, where I will be sleeping until I can remedy the bed and bedding situation. I'm thirty-five, relatively handsome, currently healthy, and occasionally self-employed. I have a profession considered honest and ethical by a whopping eighteen percent of the American public in a city that once sued itself *a few years ago, and I have no towels.*

I should call Monique so I can have some fun.

And I can get something to eat.

But would I do that so soon? Joy left today. I should be having a pity party fueled by copious amounts of alcohol. I should be calling Michael to come comfort me in my hour of need. I should be writing a malicious Internet blog about the dangers of dating Honduran schoolteachers who smell like vanilla. I should be removing that malevolent mound of DNA from my apartment.

Matthew knew that it was necessary in this human condition to be miserable every now and then because misery made the rare good parts of life seem even better. He knew he should simply stay in his comfortable easy chair and listen to his stomach rumble while worrying if he had enough *paper* towels in the apartment to dry his body if he took a shower.

But why would I want to put myself through all of that misery?

It's Friday night, and I am a man in the prime of his life.

I live in a somewhat hip and trendy section of Brooklyn.

Joy has just dumped me in the most blisteringly bizarre way.

I need a blisteringly bizarre night to complete this absurdity.

I also need to see if Monique's middle name is accurate. If my grasp of Spanish is correct, delicia *means "pleasure or delight."*

I could use some pleasure.

And something to eat.

Chapter 2

But Matthew didn't have Monique's number.

He couldn't call a Trini Bushwick babe without her phone number.

This is why someone invented WhitePages.com.

There were eleven online listings for a "Freitas" but only one Monique.

Will she even remember me? Let's find out.

To save his dwindling cell phone minutes, he used the apartment phone.

"Hello?" said a sexy voice.

"Hi, Monique. It's Matthew McConnell."

"Who?"

The sexy voice sounds confused. What did she call me? "Matty McConnell. I used to work at Brooklyn Legal about three years ago."

"Okay."

The sexy voice is still confused. "You used to call me Matty McConaughey-hey."

"Oh yeah," she said. "I remember you. What's up? You coming back?"

"No. I have my own practice now." *Not really. My Web site isn't even on the first five pages of Google or Bing if you type in "cheap lawyer." I never should have named my Web site CheapBrooklynLawyer.com.* "Monique, are you doing anything tonight?"

"Are you asking me out?"

Wow. Her sexy voice can get even sexier. "I guess I am. If you're not too busy."

"I'm not busy at all, Matty."

I like the way she says my name. Hate the name. Like the way she purrs it. "We could get some dinner and then . . . see what happens. Does that sound good?"

"Yeah."

Now where can I afford to take her? If I had a microwave, we'd share some popcorn. "Can you meet me at Lovin' Cup Café on North Sixth?"

"Oh, I love their tortilla soup," she said. "When?"

I'm hungry. I had no baleadas *tonight.* "How soon can you get there?"

"In maybe an hour."

"Great. See you soon."

"Bye, Matty McConaughey-hey."

Matthew used *the* washcloth and some Dial soap to freshen up, drying his arms, chest, and face with several paper towels. He didn't shave.

I shall be hairy from now on. Is the "rough look" still in? Williamsburg has plenty of Dominicans. I have to keep up with the competition.

He opened the bedroom closet expecting to see a row of empty hangers and the floor.

The hangers were full. Joy's shoes covered the floor, crowding his shoes into a corner.

Joy didn't take her clothes or her shoes. Why didn't Joy take any clothes or her beloved shoes? What am I supposed to do with them? Is she going barefoot and naked?

He stepped over to the dresser and opened the drawers on her side. *She took all her Burberry and Longchamp purses, her underwear, and her bras. I hope the Dominican Republic has an epic cold snap for the next few months.*

He returned to the closet and thumbed through a row of skinny jeans. *Why did I ever agree to wear these? They put my package in a bunch.* He found a pair of baggy Levi's and ironed them on the kitchen table. He rummaged through his dresser drawers until he found a heavy red wool sweater that only had a few pulls. Finally, he stared at his shoes.

It's all about the shoes. It's important that I wear something that says "fun." The gray and white suede Adidas? No. My black Clark desert boots? Well . . . The black Dugo slip-ons are nice, but . . . The brown Cole Haan loafers and a. testoni Oxfords look a little too classy. My gray Alfie's?

Why do I have so many shoes?

Then he saw a pair of black and white high-top Chucks. *These will work. These say I have old-school style and I know how to have fun.*

Donning an old, cracked, brown-leather bomber jacket, he left the apartment and stood among the garbage on Havemeyer—Greenpoint to the north, Bed-Stuy to the south, Bushwick to the east, the East River to the west.

Hello, Billyburg. You miss me? I'm back from my hibernation.

As he walked north and somewhat west, he smiled at his increasingly multicultural neighborhood. On a four-block chunk of Havemeyer, he could eat Vietnamese at Nha Toi, Mexican at Buffalo Cantina, Venezuelan at Arepa Arepa, Japanese at Sumo Teriyaki and Sushi, and Italian at Mezza Luna Pizzeria. His neighborhood was an eclectic mix of Hispanics, Italians, Puerto Ricans, Jews, Catholics, hipster artists, and Dominicans.

Carlo would have felt right at home here. He smiled. *We might have even become friends.*

Well, maybe not.

If Cornelius Vanderbilt could see his supposedly hip hometown now. Billyburg is hip, or at least that's what real estate agents are telling people thanks to the plague of artists around here. You can add just about anything to Williamsburg, and it will never truly be hip. All the indie rock in the world won't change this place for the better—or for the worse, for that matter. Williamsburg just is, *take it or leave it, and some people can't handle that.*

People are always leaving Billyburg. Corning Glass Works went upstate and created its own city. Pfizer, once the largest producer of penicillin in the world, left Brooklyn first for Manhattan and now has plants in New Jersey and Pennsylvania.

Oh, and Joy, originally from Staten Island, is off to the Dominican Republic.

And to think Williamsburg used to be wealthy. Times have sure changed.

He looked west toward the area bordering the East River, where ten percent of the entire nation's wealthy people once built mansions and the plants that made them wealthy. The Domino Sugar, Esquire Shoe Polish, and Dutch Mustard warehouses were now overpriced factory condominiums ordinary Williamsburgers couldn't afford. When the Williamsburg Bridge opened in 1903 and let Manhattan's Lower East Side spill across the river, Williamsburg became the most densely populated city in the United States. It was so dense that when the novel *A Tree Grows in Brooklyn* came out in 1943, Williamsburgers could pass around a single copy of that book hand-to-hand without moving more than a few steps in any direction.

And a few years ago, someone counted all 1,588 trees in Williamsburg. That must have been a fun job.

Matthew crossed Driggs Avenue, where supercop Frank Serpico was shot before Matthew was born. *Yeah, this place can be dangerous. Some community development group called Billyburg "the most toxic place to live in America." Red Auerbach, Joy Behar, Peter Criss, Zoe Kravitz, Barry Manilow, Henry Miller, Gene Simmons, and Barbra Streisand didn't seem to mind.*

He looked toward the bridge, shaking his head, wondering why *Coming to America,* supposedly set in Queens, was primarily filmed on South 5th Street in Williamsburg. *It made me laugh to see Billyburg in that movie. Eddie Murphy is really trying to find his queen in Williamsburg, not Queens. Billyburg has always been cheaper, I guess.* He rolled his eyes. *We may be cheap, but we're not easy. That CBS TV show* 2 Broke Girls *allegedly takes place here. Only* two *broke girls? CBS should have called it* 170,000 Broke People Who Can't Afford the Trendy Condo Upgrades. *Try fitting that title in* TV Guide. *The only reason anyone in Williamsburg watches that show is to see how badly we're misrepresented.*

But I love Williamsburg. It's what Manhattan used to look like before Manhattan went suburban.

When he saw Monique standing outside Lovin' Cup Café, his heart skipped several beats. Monique was brown as coffee with cream and two sugars. She was tall, with a pierced navel shining out from under a loose purple top, silver bracelets and necklaces glinting, and a pair of the tightest jeans allowed by law almost painted on above a pair of stiletto heels. She had long straight black hair, thin black eyebrows, red lips, and a smile that filled her somewhat wide mouth. When Matthew considered Monique from head to toe, he immediately thought of sandy beaches and skimpy bikinis.

I have chosen my fun date wisely.

Monique skipped over to him, her heels clicking on the sidewalk. She clung to his arm and whispered a single word: "Matty."

Matthew decided at that moment that he didn't mind her calling him "Matty" at all.

"Hi," he said.

"Are you hungry, Matty?"

He looked into her hazel eyes. "I'm ravenous."

Monique batted her long eyelashes. "Not as ravenous as I am. Let's eat."

Lovin' Cup Café had a long bar on one side, a collection of small tables with two chairs on the other. Matthew looked forward to their knees doing the cha-cha-cha in this crowded, intimate restaurant.

As soon as they sat looking over the menu, Monique's calves rubbed against his.

"Oh," she said, "they have drunk brunch specials. Maybe we can come back tomorrow for brunch."

Matthew thought this was a wonderful idea. "I haven't been here in quite a while. What's good?"

"Oh," Monique gushed. "You have to try the tots."

Tots. A grown woman has just said "tots" to me. "I think I will."

They ate Whole Lotta Lovin' Tots. They savored tortilla soup. They split an order of Jalapeño Mac 'n' cheese.

And Monique drank.

A lot.

In less than half an hour, she knocked back two strawberry tequilas and a Parlourita, a spicy margarita with jalapeño tequila, Cointreau, and lime.

Twenty-five bucks for our food, twenty-five bucks so far for drinks. There's something symmetrical about that.

Matthew soon discovered that although Monique had absolutely nothing to say as she ate, her body never stopped talking and whispering, "Take me, Matty!"

As Monique sipped her second Parlourita and Matthew his original Sam Adams, Matthew tried to get a conversation going. "So, how's Brooklyn Legal?"

"The same. You know."

I don't know. That's why I asked. "Still busy?"

"Yeah."

"Still crowded?"

"Yeah."

"You obviously like working there if you're still there."

"Yeah."

"How long have you been there now?"

Monique groaned. "Five years."

That was a sexy groan. I hope she groaned because of my question and not the effects of all that alcohol. What's she weigh, one-twenty? She has an unusual tolerance for alcohol.

"Is Mitch still there?" Matthew asked.

"Yeah."

"I remember when I started and Mitch was doing some Greenpoint rezoning case and fighting developers," Matthew said. "That was a mess, wasn't it?"

Monique blinked at him, frowning.

Did her eyes just roll? They did. "But that's past history."

Monique's smile returned.

I talk, and she rolls her eyes. I stop talking, and she smiles. I will stop talking. "The night is young. Do you want to go somewhere, maybe play some Brewskee-Ball at Full Circle Bar?"

Monique blinked.

Not her idea of fun. "Or maybe we could catch a movie at the Nitehawk. I think they're doing a series of Kung Fu flicks with live music. Or is it *The Princess Bride* with waffles and chicken? Either way, it will be really . . ." *Monique is frowning. This is not good.*

Monique sighed. "I'd rather go to The Cove." She pointed out the window and across the street. "I love to dance."

She has a body built for dancing. But at The Cove? That's a mini aircraft hangar, a veritable firehouse that masquerades as a nightclub.

It's always so crowded, but if she wants to dance, we will dance. I want to see her dance.

"It used to be called Hugs," Matthew said.

"Yeah?"

Monique can also turn "yeah" into a question. She has an incredible vocabulary. "Let's go dancing." Matthew stood and threw three twenties on the table. "Ready?"

"Yeah."

They crossed 6th Street and passed people standing outside talking on cell phones and smoking. A strong whiff of urine washed over Matthew. *They still haven't solved their bathroom problems. If I have to, I will use the upstairs bathroom.*

As they waited to be carded, Monique grabbed Matthew's driver's license from his hand. "Do you have a car?"

I would have picked you up if I had a car, right? "Not anymore. I used to have a BMW when I worked for Schwartz, Yevgeny, and Ginsberg."

"Who?"

You can't turn on the radio or TV without hearing their abrasive, in-your-face ads. "The 'Know Your Rights or You're Nowhere!' guys."

Monique blinked.

She has no idea. And she's a paralegal? SYG is the scourge of the legal world from coast to coast. "They're the lawyers who sue the known and unknown world, the living and even the dead, the law firm with all those loud ads on TV."

Monique squinted then broke into a dazzling smile. "Oh, *those* guys. I didn't know you used to work for them."

"Past history."

Monique shrugged. "Matty, if you don't have a car, why do you still have a driver's license?"

"It's mainly for ID, so I can get into clubs like this."

"Oh." She held the license in front of her nose. "It says you're a donor."

"Yes," Matthew said. "I'm leaving all my organs and my eyes to someone who needs them when I die."

"But won't you need them?" Monique asked.

Wow. Is she trying to be funny? Her eyes are serious. “Yes. Now. I need them now.”

“So why are you a donor?” she asked.

Oh boy. I need to go inside so I can stop talking and she can stop trying to think. “Are you ready to get your dance on?”

Monique shook her head. “Get my dance on? You’re so old-fashioned.”

“I guess I am.”

“No one says that anymore, Matty,” Monique said, handing her ID to the guy at the door.

“Okay, how about . . .” *Keep it simple.* “Are you *ready* to dance?”

Monique smiled. “You know it.”

Matthew handed his ID to the guy. “Still no cover charge?”

The guy nodded and handed his card back.

Monique grasped Matthew’s arm, and in they went as DJ Full Time Fun was playing a reggae song that had the crowd bobbing and Matthew’s ears ringing.

One hundred twenty decibels at least. It’s as loud as the subway in here. I hope he plays some old-school hip-hop and R&B tonight. Those don’t seem as loud for some reason. And I hope I don’t have to use the unisex bathrooms. It’s extremely disconcerting to open your stall door and face a woman waiting for her turn.

“There aren’t any places to sit!” Matthew yelled.

“What?” Monique shouted. “I’m thirsty!”

Monique dragged him straight to the bar, where Matthew wasted thirteen bucks on a gin and tonic and a Brooklyn Black Chocolate Stout, as green lights flashed and glowed, giving the place a post-Christmas and pre-St. Patrick’s Day feel.

Notorious B.I.G.’s “Juicy” thundered from the speakers, and Monique raced to the packed dance floor, leaving Matthew to bob and weave his way next to her.

I will not talk much here. Therefore, Monique will smile at me often. I’d have to put my tongue in her ear for her to hear me anyway.

He looked up. *Such low ceilings. This is more a cave than a cove. If you throw your hands in the air and wave ’em like you just don’t care, you could chip your nails, bruise your knuckles, or dislocate your fingers.*

Monique gyrated and writhed, sweat beading on her forehead, her gin and tonic high in the air.

And she hasn't spilled a single drop. She obviously has her priorities in order.

Within a few minutes, Monique was only a flash of bare midriff and some tight jeans three dancers away.

She has forgotten that I exist in the span of one song while I'm bathing in other people's sweat. Hey! Watch the toes! Is that a man or a woman? Or both? Matthew took a closer look. *Or neither? Is that being even human?*

He saw Monique's hands waving in the air, no sign of her drink. *She needs to hydrate more during the day. There's a guy a millimeter from her booty. Flavor Flav? Here?*

I am getting too old for this scene.

Matthew wormed closer to Monique as the song changed.

No, no! Not Katy Perry's "The One That Got Away"! This is Joy music. If they play Britney Spears's "I Wanna Go," I'm leaving.

He stood next to Monique and shouted in her ear. "Such a cheesy song, huh?"

"This is my *song,* Matty!" She grabbed his hands. "Dance with me!"

To this?

Monique put his hands on her hips.

Well, maybe it's not such a bad song. Look at her hips go. My hands are getting dizzy. They'll be buzzing for days.

Matthew looked around at the other dancers. Most were doing no more than wiggling and writhing in place. Hung-over and high hipsters, some wearing the Samurai "Man Bun," shook themselves near tanked bankers and hot ripped vixens in ripped jeans. Some gin-sipping gay and straight fashion divas of both sexes bumped elbows with thugs armed with beer bottles and tattoos, while wasted frat boys wearing worsted sweaters ogled some seriously overserved European women with bad accents and even worse dance moves. It didn't matter a bit that Matthew really couldn't dance. He could barely move, surrounded by a kaleidoscope of Latinos, Jamaicans, and assorted white people bumping chests and thumping toes.

And surrounding his date.

It's the attack of the leeches, Matthew thought sadly. *Joy hated men to be "all up on her," so I only brought her here once. Monique doesn't even seem to notice.*

One huge guy wearing a William Paterson University sweatshirt grabbed Monique's booty from behind, and Monique only smiled at him.

I guess that's how they say hello in New Jersey. He's gone. I should have said something like, "You could have shaken her hand."

While Monique swayed to Mary J. Blige's "I'm Goin' Down," an old Jamaican wearing a Rasta cap stood shouting a millimeter from her left ear while a Latino shouted into her right. Matthew found it bizarre that strangers became territorial over people they had just met.

They're being more territorial than I am, and I'm her date!

Matthew tried to get in front of Monique, but the Jamaican boxed him out as the Latino asked to see Monique's phone.

Don't give it to him.

Monique gave the phone to him.

Matthew watched him put in his number.

He watched Monique save the man's number, pressing several buttons to give him a name.

I should have said something like, "Dude, she's with me," but I want Monique to smile. The less I say to her, the more she smiles.

Matthew felt more like a security guard than a date. *Actually, I feel more like a* typical *security guard, one that only watches and reports and doesn't actually keep anything secure. It's not as if we're dating, though this is technically a date. I think. What passes for a date these days is up for debate.*

What bothered Matthew the most was that Monique didn't seem to mind any of the groping or the grinding, as if she actually expected to be groped and ground. *She loves the attention. Maybe getting felt up by strangers in public is her foreplay.* Matthew was sure Monique rode the train from Bushwick to Brooklyn Legal so men could get a handle on her before and after work.

The song changed to "Holiday," a prehistoric Madonna song, while Matthew was more than three sets of hips away from Monique. *She's moving way too fast for me and twice as fast as the song. What's she doing? What's it called,* soca, *chutney, calypso,* zouk?

Matthew noticed a crowd of appreciative men inching closer to her.

No one can do the limbo at The Cove. You'd be trampled to death. Hey! Does she have to lock her groin with that guy?

Matthew was about to give up and find a place to sit when Monique appeared in front of him. She finished his beer and set it on the ground. She smiled, turned around, and grabbed Matthew's hands, placing them on her front pockets.

Okay, now we're dry humping on the dance floor. Joy told me about this. What's it called? Daggering? Cabin stabbing? Whatever it is, I like it very much.

And so did about eight other guys before me.

The Jamaican man crouched in front of Monique.

Hey, we're dry humping over here! She's busy.

"Did a magician give birth to you?" he shouted loud enough for Matthew to hear.

"No!" Monique shouted, laughing.

"But you are so magical!" the man yelled.

I've had enough of these interruptions. Matthew pulled Monique's booty tight to his groin and looked down on the man. "She's with me! She's my magic tonight!"

The man backed away.

Monique straightened up and turned. "I'm your magic?"

I'm buzzing from her breath! "Can I get you anything?" *A gallon of coffee, perhaps? Some breath mints?*

She stood on tiptoes and shouted, "You can get me out of here, Matty!"

Matthew took her hand and led her outside, a few men straining their necks to watch Monique's booty bounce by.

Outside in the crisp, fresh air, Matthew wiped the sweat dripping from Monique's forehead with his sleeve. "Should we get a cab?"

Monique nodded. "You hear that guy in there?"

Which one of the dozen *who talked to you?* "Yeah."

"He said I was magical."

Matthew smiled. "You are."

Monique stepped closer and kissed his chin. "Ooh, salty."

They took a cab to her apartment in Bushwick near Miguelito Grocery on Central Avenue. After entering her cozy ground-floor apartment, Monique didn't turn on a single light, pausing every few feet to light a candle.

It's romantic, but come on! There have *to be other kinds of scented candles. Vanilla again? Why not cranberry or apple pie or something?*

"Are you ready for me, Matty?" Monique whispered.

"I think so," Matt whispered.

As Monique moved through a tiny kitchen, she kicked off her heels, shimmied out of her jeans, tore off her blouse, and dropped her bra and thong onto the kitchen floor.

She has obviously practiced that. She has dispatched all of her clothing on less than ten square feet of linoleum in less than ten seconds.

Matthew noticed several tattoos above, below, and in between her magnificent booty as she opened her bedroom door and threw herself face down on the bed.

"Mmm," she cooed. "See anything magical, Matty?"

Matthew nodded. *That is not a body. That is a living sculpture. That's some serious booty art.*

Monique turned over and ran her hands over her breasts. "Are you ready to get busy, Matty?"

Matthew nodded, watching one of her hands sliding down between her legs.

"I'm getting ready, Matty," she whispered. "Any time you're ready."

Well, yes and no. Yes, I am ready to enjoy your body and read all your tattoos, especially the largest one: "Je suis trop sexy." *I didn't take French, but I can guess what it means. But no, I'm not prepared for this. At all.*

"I didn't expect we would do this, Monique," Matthew said. "I mean, on a first date. I mean, I hardly know you, you know? We haven't spoken in years, right? So I'm not . . . I don't have any—"

Monique's other hand slid down her stomach to join the other. "Top drawer of the nightstand . . ."

Matthew had to duck under a ceiling fan to reach the nightstand. *That fan isn't up to code.* Opening the drawer, he saw the largest collection of condoms ever assembled in one nightstand drawer on planet Earth.

In every color, flavor, size, and texture. I live over a pharmacy, and I've never seen anything like this in there. Jex Menthol? Scotch-flavored McCondoms? Vanilla-flavored Glyde Ultra, which are one hundred percent Vegan? Coffee-flavored Moods? Most people put some gum or some mints in their nightstands for those late-night cravings. Monique has these.

He watched her slender fingers for several long moments.

"Hurry, Matty . . ."

"Monique?" he whispered.

"I'm almost *there,* Matty."

Matthew looked into the drawer and noticed that all but one of the XL condoms was missing from a box. In fact, most of the boxes were nearly empty. *That condom wrapper is already open, and it's glowing.*

Monique's hips rose and fell, her booty rising a foot off the bed. "Matty, come *on.*"

"Um . . ."

Hit the brakes! I know she's probably a nice girl. Okay, maybe not. She's definitely popular. She likes to dance, right? Horizontally, too. She is far too fast for me. I'm sure she's a gymnast, intense, insatiable, free, an exhibitionist, loud, and most likely a scratcher from the looks of her nails, but the cornucopia of condoms in her drawer is a definite stopper.

"Matty . . ." Monique's booty dropped to the bed, her hands returning to her breasts. "What are you waiting for?"

A certificate from the health department? No, that's a mean thought. She is practicing safe sex. Often. But she is too wild, too flirtatious, too sexual, too . . . loose. Does anyone use that word anymore? Monique is fast and loose. Or maybe she just likes to have a lot of sex. There's nothing wrong with that, but that makes me only another hookup to her. She'll probably be calling Latino man later this week.

"Matty, what are you doing?" she asked.

I'm not doing . . . anything . . . or anyone. I wanted to go on a fun date that led to more fun dates. I didn't want a one-night stand. I didn't want a hookup. I didn't want to see the contents of this drawer either.

"Monique," Matthew said, "I had a great time, I really did, but I . . . I have to go now."

Monique rolled off the bed in a flash, standing dangerously close to Matthew. "You're kidding, right?"

She is so fine. "No. Thanks for dinner and . . . dancing." *And a show I will never forget.*

Matthew slipped to the side, ducked under the ceiling fan, and left the bedroom, stepping carefully over Monique's clothes on the kitchen floor. By the time he reached her door, Monique was beside him, wrapped in only a whispery thin sheet.

"You're leaving?" she shouted. "Now?"

She doesn't have to be so loud about it. "Yes."

"Did I do something wrong?"

"No, Monique," he said. "You are gorgeous. I will regret leaving you the second I shut this door behind me."

She moved between Matthew and the door. "Then don't leave," she whispered.

Matthew sighed. "I'm not ready."

Monique slid a hand down his leg. "You looked ready."

I was wearing baggy jeans. How could she tell? "I should have told you this earlier. My girlfriend left me today."

Monique blinked. "You have a girlfriend?"

"I *had* a girlfriend until this morning. At least I think she left me this morning." *That was a lot of food to move, and the microwave is bulky.* "We were together for a year."

Monique's lower lip drooped. "You poor man."

How does she know I'm poor? "She got on a plane to the Dominican Republic today."

Monique frowned. "Oh, so she only left on a plane somewhere."

"With someone *else,*" he said. "A man named Carlo."

Monique's sexy eyebrows became one. "Oh." She blinked. "Oh. What'd *you* do wrong?"

"I'm not sure. I either wasn't hairy enough or I didn't smell enough like oranges."

Monique continued to blink.

"Whatever it was," Matthew said, "she chose him over me, and I went out tonight to try to forget her. I hope you understand."

Monique pulled the sheet tighter around her chest. "So I was your get-over date?"

Yes. "No, not exactly. I just wanted to have fun tonight, and I thought of you. You're fun. I had fun tonight."

She tugged at his hand. "Then let's go back and finish this fun date."

"Monique, I have these interior brakes, and they . . . they're locked up tight right now." *I have even set the emergency brake for the first time in my life.* "I don't want to rush into anything so soon. Do you understand?"

"No."

I didn't think she would. "Okay, let me explain it this way. Monique, I'm not that handsome."

"I think you are," Monique said.

Because you're drunk and horny. "Women as beautiful as you rarely look at me for more than a second unless they absolutely have to, and in most relationships I've been in, I never had sex on the first date, or even the second. I guess I'm a little old-fashioned."

Monique leaned forward, rubbing her body against his. "So . . . let's have some old-fashioned sex."

There is nothing old-fashioned about this woman. "What I'm saying is . . ." *I wish her body didn't feel so nice!* "I don't want this to be a get-over and get-lost date that ends once I leave your bed. I want to begin something that will last. Don't you want something that will last for more than one night?"

Monique stepped back.

She is stunned. I have asked her a loaded question, maybe a question no one has ever asked her before. Should I withdraw the question?

"How do you know that we won't last after tonight?" she asked.

"I don't know, I mean, how *can* I know, right? But, seriously Monique, that . . . drawer . . . in there . . ."

Monique squinted. "What about it?"

Whoa. That had some attitude. "It gives me the impression that . . . what I mean to say is . . ." *I can't say that I won't be the last man in your bed this week or maybe even this evening.* "Most of the condoms were missing, Monique, which means you have an extremely active sex life, and, well, I'm not—"

"You calling me a whore?" Monique interrupted.

"No, no, Monique, nothing like that." *Well, maybe something like that.* "You have an obviously healthy sexual appetite. I respect that. I am in *awe* of that. I *worship* that. Most men would find your preparedness *extremely* appealing. But I'm the kind of guy who has to ease into a relationship, you know?"

"You think I'm a whore!"

"No. That's so far from the truth."

"What, because I was prepared and you weren't, I'm the whore?" Monique asked.

Her hazel eyes can sure catch fire fast. "I never said you were a whore. I have *great* respect for you, Monique."

"For a whore."

"You're not a whore." *Why'd I say the word?* "I'm just not, how do I say this, as *fast* as you are. I wasn't prepared to have sex tonight because I didn't *expect* to have sex tonight. I didn't go on this date expecting to be in your bed. Do you understand?"

"No."

I didn't think she would. "I respect you, Monique."

She's stunned again. Words are forming on those delicious lips, but I hear no sound.

"I respect you as a person," Matthew said.

She's still stunned. Am I speaking English?

"And anyway, Monique, I'm more of a snuggler, a cuddler, you know, the guy you snuggle up with while watching an old movie playing on the TV, one we both have seen a dozen times," Matthew said. "And we'd be eating popcorn and drinking some hot chocolate and saying all the lines—"

Monique jerked opened the door. "No *wonder* your girlfriend left you. She was bored to death. Good-*bye,* Matty."

Matthew stood on the other side of Monique's door, wondering whether he should apologize. He also wondered how fast Monique would pick up her cell phone.

He heard a series of beeps.

He heard silence.

He heard, "Hi, yeah, we met at The Cove a few hours ago. What are you doing right now? Yeah? Want to come over? I *knew* you would . . ."

At least I warmed her up. Sort of. She was awfully good at warm-

ing up herself. She really should restock the XL boxes before her next visitor, though.

As the sun rose weakly behind him, Matthew wandered back to Williamsburg in a northwesterly direction, amazed that he hadn't stayed with Monique. In the old days, he wouldn't have put on the brakes. In the old days, he would have stayed all night and taken her out to breakfast, brunch, or lunch the next day. In the old days, he could handle being up for twenty-four hours without feeling exhausted.

He yawned several times.

These aren't the old days anymore.

He turned south off Metropolitan onto Driggs Avenue, following the intoxicating aroma of coffee to a red-brick building housing Smith's Sweet Treats and Coffee, a coffee shop he hadn't been to since he was a child. Across the street, a construction site sign boasted: "Coming Soon: La Estrella."

Ah. La Estrella. The Hispanic Starbucks. Why'd they pick this block where there's a landmark coffee shop across the street? The leeches.

He read the sign on the door: "Cash only."

Old school. I like that.

He dug into his pockets and found a crumpled five-dollar bill.

Here's hoping an old-school coffee shop has old-school prices.

Chapter 3

Though it was only a little after six AM, there were already two people in line. Matthew sneaked to the front and snatched a simple paper menu from the top of the glass case before returning to the back of the line. Smith's Sweet Treats and Coffee served breakfast, not brunch, offering eggs, waffles, toast, pancakes, and sausage, all at reasonable prices, and all made-to-order. The glass case and counter forming an L on the right side of the shop boasted croissants for less than three bucks, pastries and turnovers in every fruit flavor, cupcakes, bagels, muffins, and cookies with more chips and nuts than dough. As he basked in an agreeable collision of scents and aromas, he read the largest sign on the wall behind the counter:

I AM <u>NOT</u> A BARISTA.
I BREW AND POUR COFFEE.

Only a few kinds of coffee were listed on a dusty chalkboard hanging over the register: Jamaica Mountain Blue, House Blend, and Breakfast Brew. Matthew checked the menu for prices. *I can actually afford a large cup and something sweet.*

Floor-to-ceiling windows at the front for people-watching, lots of small, square wooden tables and matching chairs, three lights dangling from a wood-beamed ceiling, black and white checkerboard pattern on the floor, five spacious booths covered in brown vinyl, lighted sconces on the walls, mostly black and white pictures of old Williamsburg spaced around the shop—*this place has class and ambience. And it's so quiet. No music, indie or otherwise.* He smiled at the old-fashioned sugar dispensers on the tables.

"Happy National Freedom Day."

Matthew looked at the black woman behind the counter. "It's not Groundhog Day?"

"That's tomorrow," she said with a smile. "I'll bet we get six more weeks of winter."

She has a nice smile. "I hope not."

"So do I," she said. "What can I get for you?"

As Matthew scanned the sweets in the glass case, he also scanned the only worker at Smith's Sweet Treats and Coffee. She was dark brown and wore no makeup or jewelry; her eyebrows were somewhat bushy, her dark black hair pulled back. "There are so many choices," he said. Squatting, he looked past a row of turnovers to her nicely proportioned, curvy lower body. He stood and took in her bright smile, large brown eyes, medium-length hair, cute ears, snug jeans, and snugger black sweater under a crisp white apron.

Matthew smiled. "There are too many choices."

"Late night?"

She has awesome eyes, a mixture of dark and light brown. "Does it show?"

"A little. Your . . ." She patted her hair.

"I'm having a bad hair morning, huh?"

She smiled.

He squinted at the chalkboard. "What's in your house blend?"

"It's a secret family recipe."

Matthew leaned on the counter. "I won't tell."

The woman stepped closer and whispered, "Brazilian, Colombian, and Sumatran dark coffees with a hint of cinnamon and some other special ingredients."

She's has just described herself. Try not to stare too long at her cinnamon lips. How does the brown skin around her lips blend so perfectly into cinnamon? And all of it is set off strikingly by bright white teeth. Beautiful.

"Does that sound good?" she asked.

And it looks good. I mean, she *looks good. Say something.* "Yes."

"Large?"

"Yes, I will need a large," Matthew said.

"I hope you don't mind waiting," she said, "I'll call you when it's ready. I brew the house blend longer, so it's not quite ready to serve yet. Another five minutes or so. Are you in a hurry?"

"No." He sniffed the air. "What else do I smell?"

"Blueberry and cherry pastries," she said. "They'll be out in about seven minutes. You interested?"

In your beautiful eyes? Yes. In the pastries? Yes. "I will wait."

"Thought you might."

Matthew wandered to the front and noticed a flyer taped to the window advertising a block party tonight near King Park in Queens. *Why would anyone throw a block party in February? Okay, it's National Freedom Day, but really. Hmm. No one will know me in Queens, however. It might be fun to be incognito on a Saturday night. If I don't freeze my ass off. I'd have to dress—*

"Coffee's ready."

He returned to the counter.

"How do you take it?" she asked.

"With lots of caffeine."

She smiled. "There's plenty of that. No cream, no sugar?"

I just left her. Monique was all cream and too much sugar. "Give it to me straight."

"Okay," the woman said, "you need to shave, take a bath, and do something about your hair."

Matthew laughed. *She's sharp.* "I do, don't I? I'll move farther away."

"It's all right. Which pastry do you want?"

Such a sweet voice. She could sell me anything. "One of each."

"Couldn't decide, huh?"

Maybe I like to keep my options open. "I like variety." He pulled out the five, smoothing it out. "What do I owe you?"

"Four-fifty. Tax is included."

A large cup of coffee and two pastries for less than five bucks? In Brooklyn? No, in New York City? Maybe she's hooking me up. He handed the five to her. "Keep the change."

She plunked two quarters into a jar marked "Angela's IRA."

Her name is Angela. "Thank you, Angela," he said.

She poured and placed the cup on the counter. "You're welcome, um . . ."

"Matthew."

"Matthew." A buzzer sounded from somewhere in the back. "The pastries are ready. If you have a seat, I'll bring them out to you."

"Thanks."

Matthew collected his coffee and took a sip. *Wow. Real. Rich!* He sat in the middle booth, the vinyl whining slightly. A moment later, Angela brought the pastries to him on a small china plate before returning to the counter. Matthew watched her move, her black walking shoes moving swiftly, her legs—

"How are they?" she asked.

Your legs? Sexy in those jeans. "I haven't taken a bite yet."

"Let me know."

He took a bite of the cherry pastry. *Light, fluffy, sweet. What do people sometimes say? This is bangin'.*

"How is it?" Angela asked.

"Angela, this is the first real cup of coffee I have had in years," Matthew said. "I will be awake until Monday, and these pastries . . . wow. Real blueberries and real cherries."

"They're the only kind I make," Angela said. "You could take some to go."

And I wish I could. I blew close to seventy-five bucks on Monique last night. "Maybe next time."

She wiped the counter with a white towel. "You promise?"

That woman has the soft sell down pat. How could I refuse her kind face, sexy eyes, bright smile, and sweet voice? "Yes. Thank you."

He wolfed down the pastries and sucked down the coffee in less than five minutes.

"You want a refill to go?" she asked.

I can't tell her that I'm broke. "One cup of this coffee will last me all day."

"Okay," she said. "Don't be a stranger, now."

"I won't." He slid out of the booth. "Are you open tomorrow?"

"Every day of the week from six in the morning to eight at night."

"I may see you soon." He nodded. "Good-bye, Angela."

"Good-bye, Matthew."

Fortified by sugar and caffeine, Matthew walked a few blocks to Bedford Avenue to see his landlord about the rent. As he entered the cramped office, Carly the receptionist barely looked up from a copy of the *New York Post*.

"I'm a little late with my—"

Carly rolled her eyes. "See Larry."

Matthew walked around several desks to an open door and Larry Long lounging behind his desk. "Hey, Larry. Matt McConnell. Over on Havemeyer."

Larry shuffled a few manila folders, opening one. "You're not normally late. Tell you what. I'll waive the late fee if you sign up for another lease." He spun the folder around. "It will, of course, include a rent increase."

Matthew scanned the document. *Two hundred more bucks a month. Is he crazy? My lease is up in seven weeks, and I can't afford two grand a month for a one-bedroom.* "I'll pay the late fee, Larry. Nineteen-eighty, right? You still take debit cards, right?" He held out his scuffed debit card.

Larry sighed and took the card. "You're not going to find a better deal, Mr. McConnell. Unless you want to move to Bushwick."

I'm avoiding Bushwick for the time being. "I'll manage."

Larry left the office and returned a few minutes later with the receipt. "Trust me, Mr. McConnell. For what you're getting and that location, I'm being reasonable with the increase. You'll be getting an official notice in the mail next week."

Matthew took the receipt. "Sure. Great."

He spent the rest of National Freedom Day restocking and cleaning his apartment. He hit an ATM to get cash to buy cheap towels, cheaper bedding, and the cheapest microwave he could find at C & H Appliances over on 4th Street. He replenished his condiments and bought some actual food at Melo's. He carefully crammed the soiled bedding into garbage bags and put them in a Dumpster.

He stood in front of his closet for the longest time. It hadn't really been his closet since Joy had moved in. *Look at all those colors. Joy liked color. I liked her colorful body, the way her knees and elbows were just a little darker than the rest of her smooth, shapely legs and arms, the way her eyes seemed to change color according to her moods, the frisky way she'd wake me every morning. I wish she were back here with—*

No. Let's be rational about this. I don't wish she were here. She left me. It's over. Throughout our relationship, I was the rational one. Joy is the irrational woman who wouldn't speak to me after she *had an erotic dream where she "caught" me making love to another woman. "You cheated on me," she had said. "It was a freaking dream* you *had, Joy," I had said. "You* still *cheated," she had said, and she had kept her silence for a week.*

That still has to be a record for a Honduran woman.

He sighed.

At least I get my closet back.

He bagged Joy's clothes and shoes. *I'd hate to have these sit outside until garbage collection on Monday, and I don't want them to sit around here either. I really shouldn't throw them away anyway, so . . .*

He took them to the Salvation Army Thrift Store on Bedford.

It took him three trips, each trip feeling shorter than the last. The bags themselves even seemed to get lighter.

When the worker at the thrift store asked if he wanted a receipt for tax purposes, Matthew shook his head.

"This is some nice stuff," she said.

"It's okay," Matthew said. "You are doing me a *big* favor."

Good-bye, color.

Back at the apartment, he took a long nap.

He didn't dream of Joy.

He woke in darkness, showered and shaved, put on some jeans, a black sweater, and his bomber jacket. Then he walked to Marcy Avenue and took the J Train to Jamaica Center, counting twenty-three stops. He sat among Italian girls flashing their nails, Latinas shouting into cell phones, Chinese ladies placing their children on seats in dense-pack formation, Hasidic Jews gripping poles, and hipsters swaying even when the train stopped. *These are real New Yorkers,* Matthew thought. *This is the New York everyone should experience.*

As he left the platform and walked toward King Park, he heard shouting to the east. He wandered a few blocks to 153rd Street and saw barricades manned by police and a man screaming, "Stop and frisk has got to go!"

Oh no.

This isn't a block party.

It's a protest.

Chapter 4

Matthew moved closer to a boisterous crowd, with signs proclaiming, "No justice, no peace!"

For whom? For what? Aside from a few Occu-parties a few years ago, Williamsburg has been deathly quiet. Nothing has happened in Queens since some Sikhs fought with cricket bats and a sword at a Sikh temple. Wasn't the last "Stop and Frisk" protest back in 2011?

He stood next to a short black woman standing on the edge of the crowd. "Excuse me, but what is he protesting?"

"The usual," she said. "Police brutality. Stop and Frisk. Racial profiling. He'll be done in a minute. He's already wrecked and wants to get his drink on like the rest of us." She smiled up at Matthew. "Just another excuse for someone to throw a block party, huh? I ain't complaining, though." She held up her cup. "You should get you some."

"I will. Where . . ."

She pointed to a keg in a garbage can filled with ice, and Matthew filled a red cup to the top.

"Stop and frisk ain't worth the risk!" the man shouted, and then he stumbled off the little stage as a DJ started playing some loud stomp music.

Matthew returned to the woman and sipped his beer. "Is that the end of the protest?"

"The protest never really ends around here, but yep." She squinted up at him. "What brings you over here from Brooklyn?"

She has a good ear. All those earrings studding her ears must amplify speech. "How do you know I'm from Brooklyn?"

"I can hear, can't I?" she said. "You ain't from around here. Why you really here?"

"Adventure."

As he drank, he drank her in. She had brown skin, short reddish hair, and a few tattoos leaking out from her arms, neck, and chest. *She's definitely thick in those jeans, but why is she wearing sunglasses on her head? This is another fashion statement I don't understand.* Matthew did, however, like what he saw. *This is one rugged yet feminine woman.*

"You came to the right place for adventure." She peered around him. "You ain't with anyone?"

"No. I'm a free man."

"Every man here is a free man once he gets his drink on." She licked her lower lip and smiled. "Why you free, Brooklyn?"

"My girlfriend left me yesterday for a man named Carlo, who took her on a plane to the Dominican Republic."

"Damn," she said. "That's harsh."

Do I mention the condiments? No. Maybe later. "Tell me about it."

She stepped closer. "I'm Jade."

I'm not "Matty" tonight. "Matt."

"What you do, Matt?" Jade asked.

"I'm a lawyer."

Jade narrowed her eyes. "What kind of lawyer are you?"

"I have my own practice."

"Yeah?" Her eyes relaxed. "What you practice?"

"You name it, I do it."

"You got a card? I may need your services before the night is through."

Matthew patted his jacket. "Fresh out, I'm afraid."

She pulled a pack of Newports from her pocket. "You smoke?"

"No."

She returned the pack to her pocket. "Nasty-ass habit. You got any bad habits, Matt?"

"I hook up with the wrong people."

Jade nodded. "Don't we all? If you don't mind hanging with me, I think we can have some adventure together."

"I will enjoy hanging with you, Jade." *This woman has adventure written all over her. Are those prison tats? They might just be. "All Eyes on Me" it says on her chest. I'll bet the actual eyes are—*

"You into sisters, Matt?" Jade interrupted.

"Tonight, I'm only into you."

Jade smiled. "Cool. Very cool, Matt from Brooklyn." She jerked her head to the right. "Shit. I knew that ho would be here. I heard she was out."

Matt looked through the crowd. "Which . . ."

Jade pointed toward the stage. "Nasty-looking, snaggle-toothed bitch over there, the one with the blonde extensions. She shouldn't have come here. She probably tryin' to get back with me."

O . . . kay. "She's trying . . ." *Those* have *to be prison tats on Jade's chest. Jade is feminine in all the right places, but that woman over there is kind of butch, at least six-two and outweighing me.* "Oh. She's your . . . ex?"

"Somethin' like that." Jade grabbed his arm, pulling him up the stairs and into the nearest brownstone. "But that's past history, from when I was in jail."

They walked up a narrow set of stairs through a fog of marijuana smoke. "You were . . ."

"In jail?"

Matthew nodded.

"Yeah," Jade said. "You got a problem with it, Brooklyn?"

"No."

Jade nodded at several people in the first crowded, smoky room, many of them piled onto several couches. "Most men don't have a problem with it."

Matthew looked into her eyes. "Are you still . . ."

"I'm holding onto your arm, man," Jade said. "What you think?"

Matthew put his lips close to the gleaming hardware on her right ear. "I'm thinking . . . cool."

Jade smiled and winked. "Come on."

They weaved through dancing couples into the kitchen, where Jade handed him a cup of red liquid. "Drink it slowly, all right? No tellin' what all's in it." She pulled him into a less-crowded room, a card game going on around a table. "You sure like to stare, Brooklyn. I got something on my face?"

I wasn't staring at your face. "No. I was just wondering what . . ." *Just say it!* "You have a lot of tats."

She took his free hand and put it around her waist. "Yeah, and they're all over my body."

"I can imagine." *Whatever is in this drink is going straight to my libido. I should have eaten dinner.*

Jade rubbed her hip on his leg. "You want to know why I got locked up, huh?"

Matthew nodded. "I'm a curious guy."

"I like a curious man." She rubbed her nose on Matthew's neck. "Oh, assault, malicious wounding," she whispered.

Wow. Anything Jade whispers, even "assault" and "malicious wounding," sounds sexy.

"I'm past all that now," Jade said. "You ever been with a sister, Brooklyn?"

"Do women from Honduras or Trinidad count?" Matthew asked.

Jade smiled. "Oh, you like them light-skinned bitches."

"I like color in all its many forms."

Jade moved his hand into her left back pocket. "I got lots of that. All over, too." She finished her drink and dropped the cup onto the floor. "How tall are you, man?"

"Six-two."

"You tall all over?" she whispered.

What a question! "I . . . yeah. I think so."

Jade kissed his chin. "Good. So you been to house parties before, right?"

"Yes." *But nothing quite like this.*

"Then you know the drill," Jade said. "Get your drink on, don't look cross-eyed at no one, dance only if you can or you don't give a shit if people talk bad about you cuz you can't, and don't play cards if you don't know what the hell you're doing." She looked around. "And don't let go of me at any time."

Matthew nodded. "Them's the rules, huh?"

"Them's the rules."

Matthew and Jade floated from room to room sipping from Matthew's cup, watching games of spades, and getting a contact high, occasionally stopping to dance, her hips to his thighs, the bass making the floor jump.

During Fantasia's "When I See U," Jade put her lips on his ear. "I want to be alone with you."

Matthew felt Jade's heat. "I like the sound of that."

"You do, huh?"

Matthew's hands filled her tiny back pockets. "Very much."

"Let's find us some privacy," Jade said.

Here?

Jade dragged him to a door in a dark hallway. After a flushing sound and a man emerged, Jade pushed Matthew into a tiny bathroom, closing and locking the door behind them.

"Here?" Matthew asked.

Jade slipped out of her shoes, dropped her pants, and hopped up onto the sink. "You wanted some adventure, right?"

I'm in a brownstone in Queens, and there's a half-naked brown woman balancing her gorgeous booty on a white sink. Look at those tats snaking in all directions from under those tight red panties.

"Yeah," Matthew said. "I wanted some adventure."

"Then let's get to it." She unbuttoned her shirt, unsnapping her bra, two tattooed breasts spilling out.

Those aren't breasts. They're art. Just look at those eyes! Matthew's interior brakes, slowed by the alcohol, eventually caught. *I should have borrowed some condoms from Monique.* "I don't have a condom."

Jade pulled one out of her shirt pocket and handed it to him. "Let's see what you got."

Matthew looked at the condom and smiled. *XL.* He then felt the floor sway as he began unbuckling his belt. *Whatever was in that drink is kicking my ass.* As he started to unzip, someone pounded on the bathroom door.

"Jade, you ho!" a woman yelled. "What the hell you doin' in there?"

"Shit," Jade whispered. "The ho found me."

Matthew froze in mid-zip.

"I'm gettin' some, bitch!" Jade yelled. "Come on, Matt," she whispered. "We ain't got much time."

Matthew hesitated, then continued to unzip, his pants falling to the floor.

"You ain't bad-looking for a white man," Jade whispered. "Got something goin' on down there, too. I see it peeking out at me."

Jade's ex pounded harder on the door.

Jade held out her arms. "Come on, Matt."

Matt fumbled with the condom.

The pounding continued.

"Come on, man," Jade pleaded. "Let's do this so I can get out there and straighten that."

The door seemed to move briefly off its hinges, dust floating into the air. "Get your ass out here, bitch!"

Matthew dropped the condom and backed away in search of it.

"Where you goin', Brooklyn?" Jade whispered.

"I can't," Matthew said. "The pounding . . ."

"Get!" *Boom.* "The hell!" *Boom.* "Out here!" *Boom, boom, boom!*

There's way too much bass in the music here. Matthew pointed at the door. "That is ruining my concentration."

The top half of the door began to splinter.

"Oh, *hell* nah!" Jade yelled. She put on her pants, shoes, and bra in a flash.

She has to be the fastest dresser on earth.

Jade buttoned up her shirt. "You stay put, Matt. I'll be back in a minute." She stood at the door as a jagged crack formed in front of her. "Step back, bitch! I'm comin' out!" Jade looked back at Matthew. "Don't go nowhere. We ain't done yet." She jerked open the door, slammed it behind her, and the cursing began.

Matthew looked down. *We have major shrinkage.*

He pulled up his pants, zipped, tightened his belt, found the condom, and tossed it into a wastebasket. As he turned, he saw a picture of black Jesus on the wall. *What would You do? I know. You wouldn't have gotten into this situation in the first place. Could You help me get out of here? I'd really appreciate it.*

He checked the window. *Painted shut and two stories up anyway.* He eased open the door and saw two women scrapping in the hallway, a whirlwind of hands and feet and hair, a tremendous amount of skin, pictures falling off the walls, and drunken people cheering them on. When Jade and her ex tumbled down the stairs to the cries of "Oh, shit!" and "Watch out below!" Matthew heard one last "Bitch!" and then . . . silence.

Is it over?

He edged out the door and down the hallway, stopping at the top of the stairs to see flashing red and blue lights. A man talking to another man at the bottom of the stairs laughed and said, "She knocked her ass *out.* That bitch can punch, yo."

Should I go investigate? I have no doubt that my date "lost." Should I use the back door?

He moved slowly down the stairs and into the doorway in time to see an officer handcuffing Jade, the *other* woman laid out on the ground with two women fanning her face, while other police held back a huge crowd. One officer sat on the sidewalk holding both hands over his bloody nose.

Matthew slipped outside to the stoop, the red and blue lights crisscrossing his body.

"That's my lawyer right over there!" Jade yelled.

Oh shit. Now all eyes are on me. *I wanted to be incognito tonight!*

The officer holding Jade's arm summoned Matthew to him.

Matthew nodded at several people in the crowd as he approached, hoping that by nodding he could clear his head enough to sound lawyerly.

"You're her lawyer?" the police officer asked.

This is no way to get a client. "Yes." *I am now.* "Matthew McConnell. What are you charging her with?"

"What *aren't* we charging her with?" the officer said. "Parole violation, disorderly conduct, drunk in public, assault, and assault on a police officer."

Matthew stared at Jade, and Jade turned away. *She's on parole, yet she's out drinking and fighting.* "Where are you taking her?"

"Criminal court," the officer said. "We might be able to get her there in time."

Night court in Queens. "That's on Queens Boulevard, right?"

The officer nodded and pulled Jade toward the car.

"You *better* come, Matt," Jade said.

Matt looked again at the knocked-out woman and the officer

with the broken nose. "I'll be there, Jade. Don't say anything, okay?"

Jade smiled. "I told you I'd need your services before the night was through, didn't I? Bye."

Matthew debated cutting his losses and running while he took a bus to Queens Boulevard, but he found himself waiting for Jade's arraignment on the benches on the first floor of the Annex just the same.

I just have to see how this "date" ends.

Night court was crowded, but the judge was brutally efficient, dealing with two dozen cases in less than ninety minutes until only Matthew sat alone in the courtroom.

When the bailiff called for Jade Jones, Matthew rose and stood beside her.

"Hey, Matt," she said softly. "Thanks for coming."

I have no idea what to say. I've never practiced this kind of law. "Matthew McConnell for the accused, your honor."

The judge eyed him. "Matt McConnell. I've heard of you. You're Miss Jones's attorney?"

That's twice someone has asked me that tonight. "Yes, your honor."

The judge turned to his left. "What are the charges?"

The prosecuting attorney was a short man with sprouting red hair and rimless glasses. "Parole violation," he said, "disorderly conduct, assault in the first degree, and assault on a police officer."

"How do you plead, Miss Jones?" the judge asked.

"May I confer with my client?" Matthew asked.

"Go ahead," the judge said.

Matthew whispered, "Jade, they might go easier on you if you plead guilty."

Jade sighed. "The ho had it comin' to her," she whispered, "and I only punched that officer cuz he grabbed my ass."

"*I* grabbed your ass," Matt whispered.

Jade shrugged and whispered, "You grabbed my ass nicely."

"There were plenty of witnesses to everything that happened, Jade," Matthew whispered.

"Matt," Jade whispered, "I'm looking at two class-B felonies, man. I can't plead guilty. I'll be forty before I get out."

And every inch of your skin would be covered in tats. Matthew looked up at the judge. "My client pleads not guilty, your honor."

The judge turned to the prosecutor. "Bail, Mr. Zelinski?"

"None, your honor," Zelinski said. "The people request remand. She violated her parole."

I am way *out of my depth here. No bail? Should I let it go? Should I shrug and run? Jade is obviously in a world of trouble.* "How exactly did my client violate her parole? I was only retained by Miss Jones a few hours ago. I am not familiar with her original charges." *That almost sounded professional. The alcohol and marijuana must be wearing off.*

"For one, she's been on house arrest at a halfway house since her release last month, and she cut off the ankle monitor," Zelinski said. "We found it in Long Island City."

Matthew whispered, "How'd it get there, Jade?"

Jade rolled her eyes. "Why are you whispering? That's the man who can cut me a deal."

"We're doing no fact-finding here, Miss Jones," the judge said. "This is only an arraignment."

"I know, your honor," Jade said sweetly. "I have been to a few, okay? I just think it's a waste of time, you know? Ain't like you got any more cases tonight. It's just the four of us up in here." She turned to Zelinski. "I cut off the monitor and put it on the first dog with a collar I could find. I *knew* that dog wasn't from my neighborhood."

Matthew cleared his throat. "What are her other parole violations?"

"She missed two of her four weekly meetings with her PO," Zelinski said.

"He smells funny," Jade whispered. "Like sour milk."

"There's a bench warrant for that," Zelinski continued. "And tonight she failed a sobriety test and a drug test, and—"

"I drank, but I didn't do no drugs," Jade interrupted.

"You tested positive for marijuana, Miss Jones," Zelinski said.

I'd probably fail a drug test now, too, after spending four hours walking in a cloud of marijuana smoke.

"Other people were smokin' it, not me!" Jade shouted. "It was in the air. I have to breathe, don't I?"

"You should never have been there, Miss Jones," Zelinski said.

"I know that, man," Jade said. "I was bored as shit at that halfway house. All they do is watch stupid Lifetime movies on the TV."

Which is what I *should have been doing tonight.* "What is my client facing?"

"For the parole violation, she has to finish the last three years of her original sentence," Zelinski said. "Up to five more for everything else."

Holy shit! She'd get out in eight years. "What if my client were to change her plea?"

"I ain't changing my plea, Matt," Jade said.

Matthew sighed. "May I confer again with my client?"

The judge sighed. "Go ahead. We've got nothing better to do at this time of night."

Matthew stood in front of Jade, whispering, "I don't do criminal law."

Jade smiled. "There you go whispering again. It's kind of sexy."

"Jade," Matthew whispered, "I do wills and probate and simple divorces and look over contracts now. I used to sue people for a living. This isn't like any of that. I am out of my depth here."

"You doin' all right, Brooklyn," Jade said. "You sure sound like a lawyer." She stepped closer. "But I hope you're not saying you can't help me. I'm looking at eight years, man."

"If you plead guilty to something," Matthew said, "maybe it won't be so bad."

Jade shook her head. "That ho came at *me,* and that police officer grabbed my ass!"

So much for a quiet conference. Here goes nothing. Matthew turned to the judge. "Your honor, I was at the party where the alleged assault took place, and I can assure you that my client acted in self-defense."

"This is an arraignment, not a trial, counselor," the judge said.

"I know that, your honor, and I understand why she's not getting bail." He turned to Zelinski. "Can't we work something out?"

Zelinski shook his head. "She knocked out the victim with one punch."

Matthew looked at Jade. "Only one punch?"

Jade smiled. "Yeah. Right cross. Got her on the jaw."

Impressive. "The woman she knocked out started the altercation inside the house. I witnessed the other woman trying to break down a door to get at my client." *While I had my pants down around my ankles and my fingers fumbled with a condom.* "I can also attest to the fact that a *great* deal of marijuana was being smoked in the house at the time. At no time did I see my client smoking marijuana, and we were in close vicinity for the entire evening." *With at least one of my hands in her back pockets.* "As for the alleged assault on a police officer, my client only struck the officer when the officer grabbed her forcefully, as she said, by the buttocks. I'm sure several hundred people saw the officer do that, many of whom may have filmed the assault with their cell phones." He turned to Jade. "Plead guilty to disorderly conduct. It's only a misdemeanor, right?"

"This ain't right," Jade said.

"Jade," Matthew said. "Give a little to get a little."

"All right," Jade said with a sigh. "Yeah, I violated my parole, and I was disorderly along with about two hundred other people who I *don't* see in this courtroom."

Zelinski narrowed his eyes. "You'll plead guilty to disorderly conduct."

"Yeah," Jade said.

The judge stood and stretched. "This is not the time to make deals, Mr. Zelinski. We should be talking about bail or no bail and that's it."

"I know, I know," Zelinski said, "but I'm going to the Bahamas with my wife, and I have to clear as much of my calendar as I can." He nodded at Jade. "Miss Jones, you broke the officer's nose. I can't drop that charge. That's got to go to trial."

"What if I can find a hundred people who saw the officer grab her buttocks?" Matthew asked. "I wouldn't be surprised if the entire incident wasn't running on YouTube right now."

"I'm sure I have bruises on my ass," Jade said. "We could take a look."

Zelinski waved his hands. "That won't be necessary."

The judge unzipped his robe. "Do you need me anymore?"

"No," Zelinski said. "Sorry."

"Have a good time in the Bahamas." The judge left the courtroom.

Zelinski wiggled his lips. "All right, three years for the parole violation, two hundred fifty dollar fine for the disorderly conduct."

Matthew smiled at Jade. "That's a deal, Jade."

"Man . . ." Jade shook her head.

"It sounds like the best deal you're going to get," Matthew said. "Take it."

"Okay, okay," Jade said. "I'll take the deal."

An officer came to collect Jade.

"Thanks for saving me five years of my life, man," Jade said. "You gonna come visit me?"

That would be a no. "I have no real reason to, Jade."

"Well, shit," Jade said, "at least write to me or accept the charges when I call, all right?"

Matthew looked into her fierce brown eyes. "I might."

Jade kissed his cheek. "Sorry we didn't get to finish," she whispered.

"Yeah."

Jade laughed. "You got your adventure, though, right? See you around, Brooklyn."

"See you around, Jade," Matthew said. *In around three years.*

As Matthew rode the J train to Marcy Avenue, he did some soul-searching. *I'm sure there are some wonderful women in Queens, and I'm sure Jade has some redeeming qualities under all those tattoos, but I am staying away from Queens from now on. I should have faded away from her as soon as she said the word "assault." I'm too curious sometimes. I also need to stop drinking whatever anyone hands to me.*

Unless it's coffee, and the server is Angela.

He smiled.

What time is it? A little after two. She won't be open for another four hours. I can't show up smelling like this. He shook his head. *I'm going home from a date from hell to get spiffy for coffee and some pastries.*

My life is so backward.

He closed his eyes.

He could almost smell the coffee.

And he could definitely see Angela's smile.

Chapter 5

Showered, shaved, and wearing clean jeans and his bomber jacket over an NYU sweatshirt, Matthew stood outside Smith's Sweet Treats and Coffee waiting for it to open. He could already smell coffee brewing and pastries baking. As Angela rounded the counter and came to the door, Matthew waved.

Angela smiled.

That's why I came. I came for that smile.

Angela undid a series of locks and opened the door. "This is getting to be a habit, Matthew."

Matthew stepped inside. "I was just passing by."

Angela closed the door behind her. "At six on a Sunday morning."

Matthew followed her to the counter. "I'm a morning person."

"Or you were out all night again." She poured him a tall cup of coffee. "I already have the house blend ready. No cream or sugar, right?"

Matt nodded, took the cup, and sipped. "Yes. Thank you. I am alive again."

"Right." She sniffed the air. "You smell ganja?"

Damn. Why'd I wear this *jacket?* "Yeah, it must be my jacket. It was a crazy night."

"I'll bet." She sighed. "So did you or your jacket get high?"

A little of both, actually. "I was at a house party," Matthew said, removing the jacket and throwing it into the middle booth. "I did not partake, but my clothes got wasted."

"That wild, huh?"

"You wouldn't believe how wild."

Angela shrugged. "Try me. You got ten minutes until your breakfast is ready. Peach and strawberry pastries today. I'll bring you one of each."

"Sounds good." He took a long swig of coffee. "I am already addicted to this coffee."

"Good." She disappeared into the back.

Matthew sat in the middle booth, pushing his jacket against the wall and watching the sunlight intensify. *Peaceful. This place is peaceful. It doesn't make sense. I'm sucking down caffeine and feeling peaceful. I wonder if Angela has Wi-Fi. I could come here every morning, "borrow" her Internet—*

"So about last night . . ." Angela stood beside him, holding out a plate of peach and strawberry pastries.

She moves stealthily in those black walking shoes, and there are at least six pastries on that plate. "Will you join me?"

"For a few minutes I can," she said, sliding onto the bench seat opposite him. "The church crowd won't be here for at least half an hour." She folded her hands in front of her. "So tell me why your jacket got high last night."

"I went to a protest that turned into a block party that turned into a house party in Queens."

Angela blinked and shook her head. "Why'd you go to a house party all the way over in Queens?"

"I needed an adventure."

"I didn't mean it that way," Angela said. "I meant, why'd you go out to *Queens* for adventure? What's wrong with finding adventure in Williamsburg?"

"Nothing. I just wanted to get away, you know?"

"No, I don't know," Angela said. "I'm kind of glued to this place. I'm open seven days a week."

"Oh, right." *No days off? That's a raunchy deal.* "Don't you ever get sick of where you are sometimes and have to go somewhere *else* to realize that where you're from isn't all that bad?"

"I know what you're saying." She pointed at the pastries. "They're getting cold."

"Oh." He sampled one of the peach pastries. "Delicious."

"Thank you."

Her hands never stay still. Is she nervous? "Trust me, Angela, I like Williamsburg a whole lot better than I will ever like Queens. I don't think I'll be going back anytime soon."

"What happened?" she asked.

She seems genuinely interested. Something about her eyes. Great eye contact. They're hard to look away from. "Well, I met a woman who later fought with another woman who was her ex from prison, and I spent the night in Queens criminal court trying to get the first woman's charges reduced."

Angela's eyes popped. "You're a lawyer?"

Why doesn't anyone believe I'm a lawyer? "Sometimes."

"You don't look like one."

"I'll take that as a compliment," Matthew said.

She looked around the back of the booth at the front door. "Not that I know what a lawyer is supposed to look like." She faced him again. "Go on with your story. Did you get her charges reduced?"

"Miraculously, I did," Matthew said. "She still has to go back to prison for three years for violating her parole, but I got the assault charge dropped because of self-defense and the assault on a police officer dropped completely."

"Your date assaulted a cop?" Angela asked.

"Well, she wasn't exactly my date," he said. "We met *at* the party."

"Oh." Angela narrowed her eyes. "So you hooked up with her at this party."

Well, we almost did. Too much bass in the bathroom. "We hung out."

"Uh huh." She sipped her coffee. "And this hookup assaulted a cop."

Angela certainly gets to the point. "We didn't hook up. She broke the cop's nose when he grabbed her, um, her buttocks."

Angela shook her head slightly. "He grabbed her *ass,* and she broke his nose, and because of that, you didn't hook up."

When you put it that way . . . "Yes."

"How big was this woman who was not exactly your date or your hookup?" Angela asked.

Matthew let his eyes move around Angela's upper body. "About your size. She didn't have your smile, though."

Angela looked away.

Matthew heard the soft tapping of shoes on linoleum.

I must make her nervous. When's the last time I made any woman nervous?

"Was she pretty?" Angela asked, her eyes on her hands.

"In a way," Matthew said. "Good smile, nice eyes. She had lots of tattoos, most of them prison tats. She knocked out the other woman, too. Great right cross."

Angela looked up briefly. "You met this *fighter* at a party and you later represented her in court."

"Right."

"Are all your clients like her?" Angela asked.

"She became my client *after* she was arrested, and I rarely meet any of my clients face-to-face. I'm a strictly an Internet-based lawyer now. Simple wills, divorces, estate planning, contracts, that sort of thing."

"No wonder you have such odd hours," Angela said.

"True, but every hour is my own."

"Same here." She pulled her hands from the table. "So you met this woman at a protest-slash-house party in Queens."

Matthew nodded.

"Were you . . . *with* her?" Angela asked.

Strange question. "What do you mean by with?"

"I mean . . ." She sighed. "You just met her, right? You had never seen her before, right?"

Matthew nodded.

"Were you . . . holding hands, talking, dancing, what? That's what I meant by *with*."

"Oh." *Why is this so important to her?* "We danced some, yes." *I'll skip the bathroom scene.* "Until she got in a fight and the cops took her away. Jade rejoined me in the courtroom."

Angela's feet stopped running. "Jade? Was she Asian?"

"No, she was black," Matthew said. "More of a brown actually. I wouldn't call her caramel." He smiled. "She wasn't that sweet."

Angela blinked. "Really. She was . . . African American."

"Yes."

"You don't seem like the type," Angela said.

She's running again. "The type?"

"I don't know, you just don't seem like the type to date black women."

Matthew sat back. "And what is the type of man who dates black women?"

Angela shrugged and said nothing for a few moments. "I mean, you're . . ." Her eyes flitted to his. "You're a . . . you're a nice-looking white man."

"Thank you," Matthew said. *She thinks I'm nice-looking. Cool.* "Angela, is it a good thing or a bad thing that I find women of color attractive?"

Angela shrugged. "It's just an observation." She pressed her lips together and squinted. "So have you always been interested in black women?"

"I'm attracted to color in all shades," Matthew said. "My latest girlfriend, Joy, was Honduran, the other night I went out with a woman from Trinidad, and last night, I went to a party with a black woman from Queens."

"You lead a colorful life, Matthew," Angela said.

"I guess I do."

She looked around the booth again. "You see that mess across the street?"

"Yes."

"Can I sue a business for trying to put me out of business?" She slid out of the booth and stood.

"You want to sue La Estrella," Matthew said.

"I know I don't have a case," she said, pulling at her fingers. "Free enterprise and capitalism and all that, right?"

"Those coffee shops are sprouting up everywhere, aren't they?" Matthew asked.

"They're not shops," Angela said, "they're vultures."

"Like lawyers?" Matthew smiled.

"Like most lawyers," Angela said.

Matthew picked up another peach pastry. "Am I in the vulture category?"

"I'll let you know." She looked from the door to the counter. "I should be getting ready for the church rush. They gotta have their caffeine before the sermon, right?"

Matthew followed her out of the booth and took his cup to the counter. "I'll join *you* this time, then."

Angela nodded. "Okay."

"Are you really worried about La Estrella?" Matthew asked.

"Yes," Angela said. "I have to be."

"Angela, I've lived in Billyburg all my life," Matthew said, "and I've never seen a chain store of any kind *really* make it. The closest surviving Starbucks is in North Greenpoint, and you have to walk more than a mile to Broadway to get to the nearest Burger King. You're in the middle of a city where chains move in and die swift deaths. I think you'll be fine. I hear La Estrella charges too much for everything anyway."

Angela rearranged several pastries on a tray under the glass. "That's what I'm counting on. The only thing they do differently is put a little napkin on the cup." She smiled. "I tried to do that here once with the napkins I use. I never could get the hang of it. The napkin kept falling off the cup." She leaned forward on the counter. "I don't like wasting napkins."

"Are you a Williamsburg native?" Matthew asked.

"Yes."

"I thought so," Matthew said. "Where'd you go to school?"

"Van Arsdale," she groaned. "What about you?"

"Most Holy Trinity."

Angela sighed. "You look like a Catholic school boy."

Should I take that as a compliment? "Most Moldy had its moments," Matthew said.

Angela took a towel and wiped the already shiny counter. "But you're a lawyer and you're still here in Williamsburg? Why aren't you over in Manhattan where the money is?"

Been there, done that, hated it. "I love this place." He took a sip. "I love your place, too. It's always open when I need it to be."

"How long were you waiting outside?" Angela asked.

"Oh, not long," Matthew said. "Maybe ten minutes."

Angela smiled. "I'll try to open earlier on Sundays."

"I can wait until six."

He returned to the booth, ate the last peach pastry in two bites, and carried his plate of three strawberry pastries to the counter. "These are fantastic, Angela. And the coffee is delicious, as usual."

"You've only been here twice," she said.

"And everything was twice as good," Matthew said. "Thanks for the conversation, too."

Angela untied and tied her apron. "Don't your 'not exactly dates' talk to you?"

"Not really," Matthew said. *Not out loud, anyway. Not like this. This conversation is peaceful, too.*

The door swung open, and a dozen chattering women in long coats, dresses, and hats came in. *Angela is about to be very busy serving church ladies.*

"What do I owe you?" Matthew asked.

Angela's eyes darted to the booth and back.

"I'm taking the strawberry pastries to go," Matthew said.

"Oh." She sighed. "You're a very busy man with all that time on your hands."

He pulled a ten from his pocket. "Will this cover it?"

"I'll get your change," she said.

"Keep it," he whispered.

Angela nodded. "Thank you."

"See you."

"Don't be a stranger, okay?" Angela asked.

Matt nodded as he collected his jacket. "I won't. Good-bye, Angela."

"Good-bye, Matthew."

Chapter 6

Matthew went back to his apartment and slept most of the day, ignoring all urges to watch the Super Bowl pre-game shows, the commercials, or the game itself.

With no New York teams in the game, what is the point of watching?

His apartment phone woke him at nine PM. He rolled out of bed and picked it up in the kitchen on the sixth ring.

"What's going on, Matthew?"

Michael. Right on time. "What time is it?"

"That wild, huh? How's Joy? I didn't interrupt anything, did I?"

Matthew sat up in bed rubbing his eyes. "Joy has left me for Carlo di Ponti, an exchange teacher from the Dominican Republic."

After a pause, Michael said, "No shit."

"Go ahead and say it." *I know you want to.*

"Say what?"

"Say I told you so." Matthew pulled on some jeans and a T-shirt.

"Okay," Michael said with a laugh, "I told you so. I'm sorry to hear it, though."

"Right." Matthew opened a bag of microwave popcorn and put it into the microwave.

"Joy was hot, Matt."

Matthew pressed a few buttons and poured himself a tall glass of milk. "And now she's sweating with Carlo in the DR."

"So you're a free man again," Michael said.

"Yep." *And poorer for the privilege.*

"I might be able to help you in that department," Michael said. "There's someone I think you'd like very much. In fact, I think she'd be perfect for you. She is some serious arm candy, and with a little luck, she could help you return to greatness."

"Not likely," Matthew said, retrieving the bag of popcorn. *Only slightly burned.* He tasted a few pieces. *Not bad.* He sat in his easy chair and munched a few less crispy pieces, the glass of milk on the floor beside him.

"You're wasting your talents, Matt," Michael said.

"Oh, I don't know. I'm learning all sorts of new skills." *I've even "won" a criminal court case in Queens.*

"You're wasting your life," Michael said. "You need the right woman to get your old life back, and I have just the woman for you."

I'm going to regret asking this. "Who is this woman?"

"Victoria Inez Preston."

VIP? Who gives their child those initials? "Okay. And?"

"You've never heard of her?" Michael asked.

"Nope."

"Oh, that's right," Michael said. "You don't move in those kinds of circles anymore."

"I move in plenty of circles, Mikey." *Many of them resembling Dante's nine circles of hell.* "Tell me about her."

"Victoria is high end with a very nice, high end," Michael said. "You ever see that Rodin sculpture *Eternal Springtime*? That's her."

Hmm. That's one sexy sculpture. "Where does one take someone whose high end looks like sculpture?"

"Oh, Victoria is strictly Broadway, caviar, and Cristal," Matthew said.

Victoria is strictly ka-CHING. "I'm so excited."

"She's as well-built as she is well-connected, Matt," Michael said. "You won't be disappointed. You want her number, don't you?"

Maybe. "Why would this goddess go out with a man who is wasting his talents?" Matthew asked.

"Just call her." Michael gave Matthew the number. "And call her now."

"Okay." *I have nothing better to do.* "Say hello to Denise for me."

"Denise?" Michael laughed. "She is so last month. I'm seeing a Latvian model named Natalija now. Natalija Naudina. Her last name means 'money' in Latvian, and she has an incredible money-maker."

"And she's found the right man to *invest* in," Matthew said. "Now leave me alone so I can get turned down by the Broadway and caviar woman with the nice end."

"She won't turn you down," Michael said. "Have fun."

Matthew punched in the number. *If something is too good to be true, it usually isn't. Michael sounded so desperate. I'm probably getting one of his leftovers. Here goes nothing.*

"Hello?"

Cultured voice. Definitely not Brooklyn. "May I speak to Victoria Inez Preston, please?"

"This is she."

And formal, too. "My name is Matthew McConnell, and Michael Adamcyk suggested I call on you."

"How is Michael?" Victoria asked.

Why not? "He's busy with a Latvian model named Natalie something."

Victoria laughed. "I can never keep up with him or his women, can you?"

"No." *I don't even try.*

"Wait a minute," Victoria said. "Are you the Matthew who finished *above* Michael in your law school class at NYU?"

A lifetime ago. "Yes, and I was wondering if you're free this weekend to take in a show." *Don't ask me which one. I have no idea what's playing.*

"Oh, I've been dying to see *The New Yorkers* at the Sondheim," Victoria said.

Ka-CHING! And who is "dying" to see an old Cole Porter musical? "And I would love to take you."

"That's wonderful, Matthew," Victoria said. "Where will we eat beforehand?"

At this rate, I will never be able to retire. "What do you suggest?"

"Oh, Le Bernardin, of course," Victoria said.

Of course. Four stars from the Times. *Famous TV chef, too.*

"It's my favorite," Victoria said. "Oh, but it's *so* hard to get a reservation on such short notice."

I'm sure Michael can arrange that for me. "I'll figure something out. I'll let you know our reservation time as soon as I do."

"I look forward to meeting you, Matthew," Victoria said.

"Likewise, Victoria. Bye."

Well, she sounded *normal.* He called Michael. "Can you get me tickets to *The New Yorkers* at the Sondheim and a pretheater dinner reservation at Le Bernardin?"

"No problem," Michael said.

"Just like that?"

"Just like that," Michael said. "I'll have your tickets waiting for you at the box office, and I'll text you your reservation time."

"Okay." *No problem, he says. I used to have that kind of pull.* "What did you tell her about me?"

"Just that you are the smartest man I know and one of the best lawyers I will probably ever know," Michael said. "I didn't mention your meltdown, your slumming at Brooklyn Legal, or your current groveling for chump change on the Internet."

"Thanks for that." He set his popcorn bag aside and downed the rest of his milk.

"They'd still find a position for you at SYG, Matt," Michael said. "Enough water has gone under the bridge. You know your record still stands."

Some record. I have the dubious distinction of having the most billable and paid hours for one month, hours that exceeded the number of hours possible in two *months.* "Does it now?"

"SYG would take you back in a heartbeat and you know it," Michael said. "You'd make partner in no time."

"Unless I have another attack of conscience," Matthew said.

"Yeah, no more of those," Michael said.

"Look, Michael, I've changed. I'm fine." *I'm meeting clients everywhere I go these days, even at block parties in Queens.* "Is there anything specific I should know about Victoria?"

"She's gorgeous, smart, and witty, and she's very, very tan," Michael said. "I know how you like dark ladies."

"Not dark ladies," Matthew said. "Women of color. I take it she's black?"

"As midnight."

There's often plenty of light at midnight, especially in Manhattan.

"I'm sure she's not that dark, Michael. And you know I'm not as interested in a woman's appearance as you are. What can you tell me about her personality?"

"She's smart and witty," Michael said.

That's no help.

"Trust me," Michael said, "she is everything a man like you wants and needs. Victoria is a knockout."

Please don't use that word. "Well, what's she look like? I don't want to look like a fool trying to find her if we have to meet at Le Bernardin."

"Google her," Matthew said. "You won't be disappointed."

Matthew stood, collected his glass and popcorn bag, and went into the kitchen, booting up his laptop. "I will."

"And the show tickets are on me," Michael said. "You'll have to spring for the meal."

The more expensive of the two.

"I know you'll have fun, Matt," Michael said.

"Good-bye, Michael."

"No 'thank you, Michael'?" Michael asked.

"I'll let you know after the date, okay? Good-bye."

Matthew moved his laptop to the window to search for WiggyWoo, a strong wireless connection somewhere nearby. *Good ol' Wiggy-Woo,* he thought. *I'm glad he (or she) hasn't password-protected the connection yet.*

He Googled Victoria Inez Preston and found that she was, indeed, fine to the point of perfection, with a sculpted body, face, and silhouette, a model or beauty queen with money. She was the daughter of Mr. Clayton Williams Preston and Mrs. Sheila Preston-Powers, co-partners in Powers Preston, real estate brokers to the mighty rich and uppity in Manhattan. *Which means our Victoria has most likely never worked a day in her life.*

His cell phone buzzed, and he went into his bedroom to read the text: "6 Friday at Le Bernardin . . . Enjoy!"

Michael has some serious pull.

While looking at a glossy, full-body picture of Victoria in a Guy Caroche dress, he called her on the apartment phone. "Victoria, we have reservations at Le Bernardin for six this Friday, and our theater tickets will be waiting for us at the box office."

"Oh, that is so amazing!" Victoria gushed. "I can't *wait.* Cole Porter musicals are so iconic, aren't they?"

Iconic? Not really. "Yes, yes they are. I look forward to seeing you."

"Oh, likewise, Matthew," Victoria said.

"Victoria, would it be all right if we met at the restaurant?" Matthew asked.

"Oh, is your car in the shop?" Victoria asked.

It might be. I don't own it anymore. "Something like that. I hope that's not too much trouble for you."

"Oh, it isn't," Victoria said. "I will see you Friday at six. Bye."

Matthew immediately researched Le Bernardin to see if he could eat for the rest of the week.

He found that he couldn't.

I can eat crackers and cheese, and I will not be able to get a cup of Angela's coffee or any pastries for the rest of the month.

Prix Fixe at Le Bernardin was $120 a person, and its farm-raised golden Osetra caviar weighed in at $135 an ounce. With a wine pairing on the chef's tasting menu, Michael would be out $330—a *person.* He called the toll-free number on his Visa and found that it might carry him through the night if Victoria didn't opt for the tasting menu.

He looked again at Victoria's picture.

She'll want the full treatment. My Visa is going to get quite a workout.

For the rest of the week, Matthew stayed in and spent no money, moving around his apartment in search of an open wireless connection. In one corner of his closet, he was able to connect to abbaby8675309 and checked his Web site for leads—nothing. He played Internet spades thanks to doobiebro68 and lost more times than he won. With WiggyWoo's help, he tuned in to NBC.com and watched a preview of the opening ceremonies of the Winter Olympics in Sochi City, Russian Federation.

How'd they choose that place? It's right by the Black Sea, known for its caviar and pollution. That snow looks like confetti. I wonder if sturgeons eat paper.

He wasted the rest of his evening watching movie trailers, a series of sequels and remakes for the X-Men, the Green Lantern, SpongeBob SquarePants, Spider-Man, the Transformers series, and

James Bond (the twenty-fourth). *They're remaking* Dirty Dancing *and* Ninja Turtles? *Why? How could you possibly improve on those? Viewers will only say, "The original was better." And Spielberg's* Robopocalypse *sounds suspiciously like* Terminator 4! *There is truly nothing new under this or any other sun. What happened to original thought?*

He fell asleep in his easy chair, and he dreamed, strangely, of Joy, Carlo, and Boston Celtic great and NBA legend Larry Bird. In his dream, he walked into the bedroom and saw Larry Bird resting against his headboard eating Bachman's pretzels and drinking Krug Grande Cuvee while Carlo and Joy were getting busy on top of a stack of pillows rising nearly to the ceiling. "Joy!" his dream self yelled. "What are you doing up there?" Joy peered over the edge of a leopard print pillow. "You cheated on me *first,*" she said. "In a *dream,* Joy," Matt said. "Well, so is this," she replied. "Leave her alone, Matt," Larry Bird said. "You miss every shot you never take." Matt stared at Bird. "Didn't Wayne Gretzky say that first?" Bird shrugged. "Probably. Hey man, it's your dream . . ."

Early Friday morning, Matthew realized he had nothing to wear. He had given away all his Bottega Veneta and Canali suits after he left SYG, and all he had were several blazers at least one size too big. He found a decent off-the-rack navy blue pinstripe suit at Brooklyn Tailors on Grand Street, and with the shirt and tie, he parted with a thousand bucks.

This date is already too expensive. Thanks, Michael. He means well. He benefited most from my leaving SYG because now he's their golden boy.

Maybe this will end happily. And if it doesn't, I'll at least have a nice suit not *to wear again.*

On Friday night, Matthew pushed through the gold revolving door at Le Bernardin on West 51st in Manhattan a little before six.

"Reservation for McConnell," he said to the maître d'.

The maître d' looked on either side of him. "Your guests are not with you?"

"No. I'm early." *Wait a minute.* "Did you say guests?"

"I have a reservation for three," he said. "Is this correct?"

No. "Sure." *Who's the third wheel? Michael? I wouldn't put it past him.*

Seated in a leather chair the color of butternut squash, a glaring lamp behind him, Matthew stared up at paintings of fishermen covering the wall to his left; the nearest fisherman spilled his catch from a wicker basket. Waiters in all-black button-ups, dusty bottles of wine and champagne cradled in their arms, moved under the brightly lit wooden ceiling stealthily pouring and serving a packed house.

After reading through the menu twice, Matthew thought about calling Michael. *But that's what he* wants *me to do. He* wants *me to worry, and I will not give him the satisfaction.*

At six-fifteen, after assuring his waiter that his "party" was on the way, he called Victoria. When his call went straight to voice mail, he hung up.

He repeated these calls until six forty-five.

At 6:49 PM, Victoria and *another* woman who could have been Victoria's shorter, thicker twin swept into the room wearing matching satin blue dresses and high heels, pearls and diamonds swinging wildly as they walked.

They're acting like models. They're walking into a crowded restaurant like runway models. At least they're not anorexic. I'm surprised they're not bumping into chairs or each other and spilling wine.

Matthew stood, his bladder nearly full from two glasses of ice water, and smiled. Victoria was, indeed, flawless in every way, not a hair out of place, with satiny black skin, legs for days, a full bottom lip, at least fifty teeth, and slender arms.

Matthew held Victoria's chair for her as she sat.

"Matthew, so nice to meet you," Victoria said. "This is my oldest and dearest friend, Debbie Lewis-Johnson."

Debbie stared at her chair.

Matthew held Debbie's chair, too.

He also swore he heard the hovering waiter snicker.

So Michael made reservations for three because he knew Victoria never *travels without her best friend, Debbie. No wonder he's not springing for dinner. I'm paying for three!*

"Hello, Victoria, Debbie," Matthew said as he sat.

"Have you been waiting long?" Victoria asked.

Yes. "No, not too long."

Is she going to give me an explanation for (A) being late or (B) bringing her wing woman? Is this normal behavior for rich, unmarried women of privilege?

"Isn't this place amazing, Debbie?" Victoria asked.

"Yes," Debbie said in a husky voice. "It is *certainly* amazing."

"So iconic," Victoria said.

"Oh yes," Debbie said. "This is the *most* iconic restaurant in New York. It's the Temple of Seafood. Chef Ripert is so *amazingly* iconic."

Matthew learned three things from this brief exchange. One, he would get no explanations about anything from these two women, probably ever. Two, these women had the vocabulary of a four-year-old who discovers a new word and says it repeatedly to the detriment of all within hearing distance. And three, he was likely to spend over a thousand dollars on dinner.

"Have you already ordered for us, Matthew?" Victoria asked. "I hear the chef's tasting menu is amazing."

There goes the grand. "Then that is what we'll have."

"Oh, and at least one order of caviar," Debbie said.

Victoria smiled and touched his hand. "Could you make it two?"

"And two orders of caviar." *There goes another three hundred. So* this *is how the Russians are paying for the Winter Olympics.*

"That's so thoughtful of you, Matthew," Victoria said. "Isn't that thoughtful of him, Debbie?"

"It is *truly* thoughtful of you, Matthew," Debbie said. "Thank you for being so thoughtful."

Debbie is Victoria's echo.

During dinner, Matthew blinked and squinted at his food because he wasn't quite sure what was on his plate. *I haven't eaten food displayed like modern art in a long time. Wagyu beef, Osetra caviar, and some kind of wine to wash it down. Not bad. Yellow fin tuna and spicy chutney with a glass of Chablis. Lobster tail in Earl Grey-citrus sauce with some more expensive alcohol. Codfish with another glass of something mind-numbingly strong and mind-altering.*

Matthew was losing feeling in his hands as squash, bass, cucumbers, yogurt, peanuts, and more wine landed and disappeared from the table.

Debbie is about to burst out of her dress. I hope I get some warning. I just bought this suit.

"You look *amazing,* Matthew," Victoria said. "Do you work out?"

I walk the streets before sunrise mostly. "I stay in shape."

Victoria's phone buzzed. "*Hello,* Freddie. How *are* you? I'm at Le Bernardin, and it is *so* amazing . . ."

For the next half hour, Victoria and Debbie talked, texted, and surfed the Internet on their iPhones, pausing only to call the wine "amazing" or the yogurt "amazing" or the silverware "amazing" or the wait staff "amazing" or the weather "amazing" or the ice water "amazing" or the minimalist heels strangling Debbie's feet "amazing."

Birth is amazing, Matthew thought. *Heroism is amazing. A city reborn after 9/11 is amazing. The bill I'm about to get is going to be "amazing." Water? Silverware? The weather? Your shoes? No way.*

"This is such an iconic place, isn't it, Matthew?" Victoria asked once Freddie let her go the *second* time.

"Yes," Matthew said. "Quite."

"Oh, and so is your *ginormous* necklace, Victoria," Debbie said. "It's *so* iconic."

Victoria pulled the necklace from between her ginormous breasts. "Yes, it is ginormously iconic. Isn't it, Matthew?"

Two grown people have used forms of the word "ginormous" within seconds of each other. Don't the rich have to learn vocabulary words like the rest of us?

"Matthew, isn't my necklace iconic?" Victoria asked again.

Matthew nodded. *Not really. Joe DiMaggio was iconic. Robert De Niro is iconic.* Saturday Night Live *is iconic. Your necklace is not iconic!*

Debbie pouted. "I miss Boops."

Victoria pouted. "I miss Boopsie."

These two have the attention spans of gnats. Boops? Boopsie? Please tell me these are animals and not other rich people.

Victoria touched Matthew's hand for a split second before again gripping her wine glass. "We have matching miniature Pomeranians. Boops and Boopsie have been together since birth. I think they're twins."

"They were in a litter of three, Victoria," Debbie said. "They'd be triplets, wouldn't they, Matthew?"

"Yes. I think." *Does this means these two women live together? They share dogs. They couldn't possibly share each other's clothing.*

"We should have brought them along," Debbie said.

"We could have put them in our B Bags," Victoria said. "They would have fit."

What are they talking about? "Your . . . B Bags?"

Victoria held up a clutch purse. "Our Fendi B Bags. Don't you think Boops and Boopsie would look *amazing* in our B Bags?"

Matthew nodded. *I have died and gone to a part of hell Dante never envisioned, where ridiculously named dogs inhabit overpriced clutch purses.*

"Debbie, did you hear about Millicent?" Victoria asked.

"No," Debbie said. "What did Millicent do *now?*"

No. Gnats have longer attention spans than these two.

"She went to Bergdorf's the other day and bought a Chado Ralph Rucci." Victoria's mouth dropped open. "At *Bergdorf's.*"

"She *didn't,*" Debbie said.

"She *did,*" Victoria said.

"Was it?" Debbie giggled. "No, *don't* say it."

"It *was,*" Victoria said.

"She *didn't,*" Debbie said.

"She *did,*" Victoria said.

I am now in an existentialist, absurd play, Matthew thought. *Where's the dumb waiter?*

"She bought it," Victoria said, nodding up and down like a horse neighing, "*off . . . the . . . rack!*"

You like my suit? Matthew thought. *I bought it off . . . the . . . rack.*

"No," Debbie said. "She *didn't.*"

"She *did,*" Victoria said. "Can you *believe* it?"

Debbie fanned her face. "Amazing."

I will probably regret wading into this absurdity. "Forgive me, but I'm lost. What's a Chado Ralph Rucci?"

Victoria smiled at Debbie. "He doesn't know."

"No, he *doesn't,*" Debbie said, smiling back.

"Matthew," Victoria said, "a Chado Ralph Rucci is a dress."

That's a long name for a dress. "Is it expensive?"

"Is it expensive?" Victoria said. "Not really. Millicent said she paid six, but that sounds far too high for Bergdorf's."

"Oh, I agree, Victoria," Debbie said. "She probably paid less than four. Off the rack." Debbie giggled.

Matthew blinked. *Millicent bought one dress for six thousand dollars, and these two think she's lying. Who lies about dropping six grand on a dress with a first, middle, and last name? For six grand, it had better have a social security number and give you a tax break for living in your closet.*

The waiter materialized beside Matthew. "Would you like some dessert, perhaps?"

Would you like to stop coming around and asking them if they're still hungry, perhaps? Perhaps you think I can afford to feed these two all night.

"May we, Matthew?" Victoria asked.

"Sure, why not," Matthew said.

"We'll each have the *gianduja,*" Victoria said.

Matthew looked up at the waiter. "What's that?" *It sounds like a disease.*

"Milk chocolate-hazelnut mousse with caramelized banana and burnt honey-pistachio ice cream," the waiter said.

Whatever happened to a simple piece of apple pie with some ice cream on top? Matthew thought. *Or a simple slice of chocolate cake?*

"And you, sir?" the waiter asked.

"I'm fine."

"Some cheese, perhaps?" the waiter asked.

"No, thank you." *Cheese on top of all this? Is he kidding? I have to go out in public!*

"Perhaps another glass of wine?" the waiter asked.

I'd blow a .15 on the breathalyzer right now, chief. "No, thank you."

"Some coffee, perhaps?" the waiter asked.

Perhaps you can leave me the hell alone! "No, thank you."

And naturally, the women pronounced the caramelized bananas "amazing" and the pistachio ice cream "iconic."

At meal's end, Victoria and Debbie flirted with men around them, waving and naming names, while Matthew paid the bill.

It was only $1,600.

Plus tip.

Outside Le Bernardin on the most perfect sidewalk Matthew had ever seen, he decided they needed to walk to the theater. "The Sondheim Theatre isn't that far from here," he said. "It's not too cold, is it?"

Victoria's jaw dropped between her ginormous breasts. "You aren't *actually* suggesting what I think you're *actually* suggesting, Matthew."

Um, actually, yes. "I was just going to say since we all ate so much, that we could walk," Matthew said. "It's only a few . . ."

Victoria and Debbie gave Matthew the most evil looks he had ever seen, demons possessing only their eyebrows, noses, and lips. It was as if he had just deposited half a ton of steaming diarrhea right there on the perfect sidewalk and expected them to wade through it in their irrational, impractical heels.

"No, you're right," Matthew said. "Ten blocks is *much* too far to walk. We'll take a cab then?" *Even though you two need to walk off those caramelized bananas so your dresses won't explode during the show.*

They took a cab to West 43rd where Matthew used most of his cash and had only a two-dollar tip for the driver. "I am so sorry," he whispered to the driver.

"I understand completely," the driver said. "That right there is a real dame. I'd save my money for her, too. But why's the other one along for the ride?"

"I wish I knew," Matthew whispered.

At the box office, Matthew received *four* tickets. *I'll bet Debbie was supposed to have a date. I can see why she didn't, but Michael had to know about this "arrangement."*

Matthew allowed Debbie to enter their row first, followed closely by Victoria. Before Matthew could sit next to his alleged "date," Victoria set both of their Fendi B Bags on the second seat, leaving Matthew alone on the aisle.

I am having a date with two clutch purses.

At least they're not holding Pomeranians.

And I'm watching an all-white musical first performed for all-white audiences in 1930. And what's the musical about? A wealthy

New York socialite hooking up with a bootlegger. Maybe the fourth ticket was for their purses.

Can this date get any better?

Please?

By the fourth song ("Say It with Gin"), Matthew focused on Victoria's legs and didn't see a single hair on them. *Not one. That can't be possible. Does she wax? I can't see her physically doing anything. She probably has her leg hairs removed individually at $100 an amazing and iconic pluck.*

"Love for Sale," the show's only truly "iconic" song, sent Matthew into a deep depression. *You said it, sister. That's all this date is.* He looked at Victoria and Debbie singing along with the prostitute on stage.

During the intermission, Victoria and Debbie three-way-called Freddie to tell Freddie how "amazing" and "iconic" and "wonderful" the show was. While Matthew wanted to tell Freddie the truth and was glad the women had discovered a new word ("wonderful"), he kept his silence, unhappy that his buzz was quickly wearing off.

During the second act, the utterly forgettable "Sing Sing for Sing Sing" made Victoria's toes tap along all the way to the last song: "Take Me Back to Manhattan."

Please, take me back to Brooklyn.

After the show, they took a cab to Azure, Victoria and Debbie's building on East 91st^{t} Street and First Avenue, a tower held together by thousands of windows. Victoria introduced Matthew to the doorman, who looked like a lost airline pilot, and the concierge, who looked like a lost Charlie Chaplin. When Debbie drifted to the elevator without so much as a "thanks," Matthew wanted to scream.

But he didn't. He was in Azure, home of million-dollar one-bedroom apartments, in a well-lit lobby with a still well-lit date.

Victoria seemed to be looking toward the elevator, too, as if she missed her friend already.

"Quite a lobby," Matthew said absently.

"Isn't it?" Victoria said. "Weil Studio did all the glass artwork on the walls. Isn't it amazing?"

No. "It's nice."

"And we're standing on tundra gray marble." Victoria pointed at the floor for good measure.

I didn't need you to point. I know where the floor is.

Victoria pointed at the wall. "That's American walnut wood paneling."

I still didn't need you to point.

"Where do *you* live, Matthew?" Victoria asked.

Hey, she's trying to engage me in conversation. I feel so privileged. "Williamsburg."

"Virginia? Oh, I love the South."

I can't believe I wanted to touch this out-of-touch woman. "Williamsburg, Brooklyn. On Havemeyer Street."

"Oh," Victoria said.

I've heard that kind of "oh" before. Joy used to say "oh" like that when her stomach was giving her fits.

"I hear Williamsburg is becoming more and more iconic," Victoria said.

If I had a dollar for every time she said—

"What are your common charges?" Victoria asked.

Ah, common charges, those uncommon monthly "charges" for the "right" to live in opulence, charges like insurance for common grounds, the pool, the clubhouse, landscaping, garbage removal, snow removal, the doorman's jacket and white gloves, the concierge's sneer . . .

"I don't have any common charges," Matthew said. *I only have something called "rent."*

"*Our* common charges are over two *thousand* dollars a month," Victoria said, smiling broadly.

And she said it with pride, and those common charges don't include her lease payment, utilities, hair-plucking, dog walking . . .

"Wow, that's . . . something," Matthew said. "What floor do you live on, Victoria?"

Victoria widened her eyes. "We're on the *thirtieth* floor."

That must mean something mind-boggling and expensive. "Great views?"

"They are *amazing,*" Victoria said.

My fault. I set her up to fail with that question. "Are you going to ask me up to see these amazing views?" *I spent on mint on you, so I deserve to see a million-dollar view, okay?*

"Oh, Matthew," Victoria said, smiling. "This is *only* our first date."

And our last. "Of course. You're right."

"I have enjoyed our time together," Victoria said.

If I were to add it all up, we spent no more than, well, the length of this conversation actually together. "I had a nice time, too."

Victoria smiled. "I am so glad Michael gave you my number. I don't have many men interested in going out with me."

And your friend and your iPhone, and your Fendi B Bag, and Freddie, and . . .

Victoria blinked at him.

Oh. I think I'm supposed to compliment her now. "I don't see why, Victoria. You are truly amazing. I'm glad Michael gave me your number, too."

Victoria looked at the tundra gray marble. "Well . . ."

Do I go in for a kiss? I have spent a rent payment on one date. She owes me some kind of affection, not that I will ever call on her again. The view on the thirtieth floor can't be that amazing, and if I ever want to see the view, I can Google it and save another two grand by not taking you, Debbie, Boops, and Boopsie out to eat.

"Quite an iconic building," Matthew said.

"Oh, it is," Victoria said. "Completely iconic."

She either ignores or cannot hear sarcasm. "I had an *amazing* time, Victoria." *She had to hear the sarcasm that time.* That *was sarcasm basted in sarcasm and drowned with sarcastic Chablis and caramelized, sarcastic bananas.*

"Oh, so did I, Matthew," Victoria said. "I had a truly amazing evening."

Not . . . a . . . clue.

Matthew took a brisk step forward and kissed her cheek. *Ow. What kind of armor does she have on her face? I thought her cheeks were soft. I nearly bounced off. My lips are bruised.*

Victoria immediately checked herself in a compact mirror snatched out of her B Bag.

Oh for God's sake! You're just going upstairs!

Victoria snapped the compact shut. "I have to go help Debbie with Boops and Boopsie. They are *so* much like children. They are *such* a handful. I am *sure* they missed me."

"Oh, most definitely," Matthew said. "Pomeranians are iconic."

"Yes." Victoria smiled, all fifty of her teeth visible. "Yes, they *are.* I am *so* glad I have finally met a man who realizes that." She stepped close and kissed Matthew on the lips.

Ow. She has seriously hard lips, too. What did she fill them with? Cement?

"You really are an amazing man, Matthew," Victoria said.

I need to get out of this amazing, iconic place right now before I start looking for Pomeranians to stomp. My lips need an icepack. "Enjoy the rest of your evening, Victoria."

"Oh, I will," Victoria said. "Bye, Matthew. Give my regards to Michael, and feel free to call on me *anytime.*"

Free? There isn't anything free about you, woman. Even kissing you has a price. "Sure."

As Matthew walked slowly down First Avenue toward the Williamsburg Bridge, he loosened his tie and his thoughts. *Do I want to call* on *her again? A phone call to her I can afford. Would I ever want to take her out again?* No. *That would be a ginormous mistake. Victoria asked me only two questions all night: one about my appearance, not my substance, and one about where I lived. I'm glad she didn't ask me what kind of lawyer I was or grill me any more about my "space" on Havemeyer.*

Victoria looked at everything and everyone but me. She talked more to Debbie and Freddie than she did to me. I was a means to an end. I wasn't even arm candy. I sat next to two Fendi B Bags at a Broadway show. The kiss I gave her she immediately wiped off. The kiss she gave me hurt.

Maybe she really is a bronze sculpture, nice to look at but a pain to move.

I was broke before the date, and now I'm broken. I can't even afford coffee and pastries with Angela this morning. I can't afford bus fare, subway fare, or cab fare. I'm free but broken.

He sighed.

It's kind of liberating, in a way. I have nowhere to go but up.

Unless I get mugged.

I hope I don't get mugged. I don't want my mugger to laugh at me. I don't want to say, "Sorry, dude, but I'm flat broke. You can have the suit, even though I did buy it off . . . the . . . rack."

He eventually turned off First Avenue onto Delancey Street and crossed the pedestrian walkway of the Williamsburg Bridge, twenty minutes later settling into his easy chair and burping Chablis.

My body doesn't like the finer things of life anymore. I'd like to meet the discoverer of caviar, because whoever it was watched a fish squirt out some eggs and decided they'd be good to eat on a cracker.

He watched a few snow flurries fly by his window at three AM.

Man, I wish I had some coffee.

He felt under his cushion and found an old pen, a remote to a TV he no longer owned, a cell phone with no battery, and a quarter. He dug under every cushion, rifled through every drawer, checked every pocket, and moved his bed to the side, eventually amassing a small fortune in change.

He even took the pennies from penny loafers he hadn't worn in years

He also found Joy's matching leopard-striped bra.

After counting out the change on the kitchen table, he decided he had enough for one large cup of Angela's house blend with a nickel tip to spare.

After a short nap, he showered, shaved, and put on jeans, Nikes, and a hoody.

Angela was right.

This is getting to be a habit.

Chapter 7

The sun shielded by bulbous dark clouds, Matthew walked to Angela's place.

It's not Smith's Sweet Treats and Coffee to me anymore. It's Angela's place. I am going to Angela's place because that's where she and her smile hang out.

He noticed that the sidewalk across the street from Angela's place had gotten a face-lift, several potholes had been filled in the street near the curb, and brand-new parking meters stood in front of La Estrella. Angela's sidewalk, however, was still hilly, splitting, and treacherous.

When he entered, he saw Angela behind the counter and smiled. "Good morning, Angela."

"Good morning, Matthew," she said. "Happy Kite Flying Day."

Matthew squinted. "But it's winter."

"Hey," Angela said with a shrug. "I don't make the holidays. I only announce them." She smiled. "I haven't seen you in a week."

"Yeah. It's been a long week, too."

"The adventurous life you lead." She wiped her hands on a towel. "What can I get you?"

Matthew emptied his pockets and made a stack of change on the counter. "What can I get with this?"

Angela laughed.

Her laugh has music in it. I like it. "What do I get? I get a laugh and a smile. It was worth the search of my apartment. I think some of these coins are valuable. Look at all the wheat cents and Liberty dimes. That quarter might be pure silver."

Angela scooped them up, separating them into the register. "He pays me with change."

"Sorry," Matthew said. "I had the most expensive date of my life last night."

Angela sighed. "How expensive?"

"If I were frugal, which I'm learning to be too slowly for my own good," Matthew said, "I could use what I spent on one meal last night to buy groceries for the next six months."

"That's expensive." She plucked a large cup from a stack of cups. "Were the police involved?"

"Not this time," Matthew said. "That might have made the evening more amazing and iconic."

Angela blinked. "Amazing and iconic."

"Her favorite two words."

Angela poured him a cup of house blend and handed it to him. "She sounds young."

Matthew took a sip. *Yes. This is so good.* "I actually think she was older than me. I counted at least three layers of makeup on her face." *Like rings on a tree.*

"Does this mean you won't be going out with her again?" Angela asked.

Now there's a direct question. "Let's just say I won't be paying for her *not* to talk to me again."

She pointed at the middle booth. "Your booth is free."

My booth? I like the sound of that. "Will you join me?" Matthew asked.

"I'm not too busy at the moment."

Matthew slid into one side of the booth, Angela into the other.

"Where was she from?" Angela asked.

"Manhattan," Matthew said. "Upper East Side. She lives in Azure. Her building has a name of its very own."

Angela shook her head slightly. "But you chose her, right?"

"Michael, a friend of mine, who really isn't much of a friend of mine anymore, set us up," Matthew said. "He set *me* up. He told me she'd be perfect for me."

"Nobody and nothing are perfect," Angela said.

"I agree." He looked through the front window. "That side of the street almost looks perfect, though. The city is really sucking up to La Estrella."

Angela frowned and sighed. "I know. I've been complaining for years about the sidewalks and the street in front of this place. For a nice multiyear tax break, they get everything pretty. Such a waste of a nice space. It could be a great place for a club or a theater or even a bookstore."

"Anything but a coffee shop, huh?" Matthew said.

Angela nodded. "Right. My luck." A buzzer sounded. "Care for some raspberry pastries?"

"I barely had enough for the coffee," Matthew said.

Angela stood. "On the house. I'm trying a new recipe, and you can tell me if they're any good."

"Okay."

He watched Angela sweep gracefully into the back, returning with a large metal tray. After sliding most of the pastries on the tray onto another tray in the display case, she put several pastries on a plate and brought it to Matthew's booth, setting the plate in front of him.

"It'll cost you a story," she said.

"A story is all I can afford to give you." He took a bite. "This is good."

"How good?" Angela asked.

Matthew savored the flavors. "On a scale of one to ten . . . a nine-point-nine."

"Not a ten?" Angela asked.

"I'd feel better if I were paying you for it," Matthew said.

"Don't worry about it." She slid into the booth. "Tell me about your date with the woman who wouldn't speak to you."

"You can't really be interested in my dysfunctional love life," Matthew said.

"Tell me."

She must be interested. "Her name is Victoria Inez Preston."

"V-I-P," Angela said. "So far so bad."

"And it gets worse. I sat at Le Bernardin for forty-five minutes awaiting her arrival." He took another bite. *Delicious.*

"How trifling," Angela said. "She had to make a grand entrance, huh?"

"And that, dear Angela, is what it was," Matthew said. "Lots of men got whiplash watching her and her *friend* come in."

Angela blinked rapidly. "She brought a friend."

"Her oldest and dearest friend, Debbie, her shorter, stockier twin."

Angela closed her mouth tightly. She sighed. "She brought an ugly friend with her on her date."

"Well, she wasn't *that* ugly." *She had pretty . . . knuckles.*

"Compared to your date?" Angela asked.

"Okay, she was . . . large." Matthew smiled. "She wore shoes far too small for her feet."

Angela shook her head. "Victoria brought her along to make *herself* feel prettier."

"I don't know why," Matthew said. "Victoria is well-made."

"Well-made?" Angela rolled her eyes. "You mean she's a babe, a hottie, a real honey."

Matthew stared at his pastry. "She was fine. Yes."

Angela sighed. "Then what happened?"

"I ate food I couldn't identify and that didn't like me later while they ate me into bankruptcy," Matthew said. "They talked on the phone with Freddie. He sounded gay, but I can never tell. They flirted with any man who would look at them, and they texted each other while they were sitting inches apart."

"How old were these women?" Angela asked.

"Maybe mid- to late-thirties." He squinted. "I don't think the rich ever grow up, mainly because they don't have to."

"How did your evening end?" Angela asked.

Matthew tapped the table with fingers. "*This* is the end of my evening. I walked down First Avenue and across the bridge . . . to see you."

"Uh huh."

"Okay, I went home to shave and shower first," Matthew said. "And to find some change."

"Right."

"Really. I can always count on you, and you don't break my

bank account." He finished the first pastry. "And you make me addictive sweets to eat. These are bangin'."

Angela laughed. "Bangin'?"

"Angela's Bangin' Pastries," Matthew said. "It has a nice ring to it."

Angela shook her head and slipped out of the booth as the door opened and a customer headed straight for the counter. "I think your luck with women is about to change."

"How do you know?" Matthew asked.

"Your luck can only get better, right?"

Matthew tore the next pastry in two, the steam rising in front of him. "I will pay you back for these."

Angela stared at him. "Oh, Matthew, *darling,* that would be so *amazing.*"

"And iconic?"

Angela shook her head. "Just amazing."

Later at his apartment, Matthew checked his Web site. *A client? No way. And on a Saturday? My luck might be changing after all.*

The Haitian Free Pentecostal Church in the Bronx wanted his help getting nonprofit status as quickly as possible. The process, though tedious, was easy to do and involved a stack of 501c forms. He called the number in the e-mail query.

"Haitian Free, this is Mary. How may I help you this blessed day?"

Soft, sexy voice. "Hi, Mary, This is Matthew McConnell. Your church contacted me through my Web site—"

"The Cheap Brooklyn Lawyer site, right?"

I never should have chosen that name. "I wasn't sure if anyone would be there on a Saturday."

"There's always something going on here," Mary said.

"Well, I find that I have a free afternoon today," Matthew said, "and I could come up to walk Pastor Jean through the forms."

"Oh, he'll be tired from service," Mary said, "but you can explain the forms to me. I'm the church secretary and treasurer."

"Splendid. Mary, what's the best route to get there from Williamsburg? It's been a while since I've been to the Bronx. I assume I take the J train then the 4 and then . . ."

"The 2," she said. "We're a block north of the station."

"See you in about an hour then."

"I'll be waiting."

Matthew arrived ninety minutes later at the church, a low-slung storefront that covered half a city block, just as a Saturday service was ending. He walked through a throng into the reception area.

A short, buxom woman stepped up to him. "Are you Matthew?"

Matthew looked down at the woman, her clothes colorful and concealing very little of her dark skin. "Are you Mary?"

Mary nodded. "I'm Mary Primm."

Mary was not what Matthew expected a church secretary to look like. Mary had wavy hair streaked with pink and yellow to match the dress she was almost wearing, a smooth face, dark red lips, and a booty that cried, "Stare at me!"

"Let's go to the office," she said.

Matthew followed Mary's swaying form to a tiny office barely big enough for a desk and two chairs. He took her through the stack of incorporation forms slowly, explaining each one while trying not to stare at her cleavage.

After two hours, he collected one hundred dollars.

"Why so little?" Mary asked.

"I always pray for repeat business," Matthew said.

"We will definitely keep you in mind," Mary said.

And I will keep your compact, sexy body in mind, too. "Have Pastor Jean sign, well, everywhere, and mail everything where it needs to go along with the appropriate fees."

"So many hoops to jump through," Mary said.

Matthew stood. "You're keeping money from the government. They want to make it as hard as possible for you to do so."

Mary put the stack of forms into a file folder. "Matthew, what church do you attend?"

"I occasionally go to Our Lady of Consolation." *Let's see, twice a year at most.*

"You're Catholic then?"

"Yes," Matthew said. "I went to Most Holy Trinity in Williamsburg."

Mary nodded. "I went to Archbishop Molloy. I used to be Catholic."

"Once a Catholic, always a Catholic" isn't true anymore? "Oh?"

"Now I'm a Christian," Mary said. "The Lord has been very good to me."

I will agree to that. Mary has to have the most clearly defined breasts I have ever seen.

"What are you doing tomorrow?" Mary asked.

Sleeping. "It depends."

"You could come to service," Mary said.

Look how her eyes light up. Such dark eyes. "I've had an exhausting few days, Mary." *None of it work-related, of course.*

"What about Wednesday night?" she asked.

I'm being asked out in *a church. This is new.* "I don't think I have anything planned."

"Meet me here at four-thirty," Mary said, "and we'll go get something to eat."

The money she just paid me will pay for the date. Angela was right. My luck is changing. "Okay. And then?"

Mary smiled. "And then . . . we'll see what happens."

As Matthew rode the trains back to Williamsburg, he pondered a Wednesday date. *Why two days* before *Valentine's Day? Why not Valentine's Day itself? Maybe she's testing me out first.*

He closed his eyes and saw Mary wearing a Catholic school uniform, her shapely legs literally smoking out of a tight skirt, her shirt buttons straining. *I wonder if Mary was a typical Catholic school girl. The ones I remember were some wild things. As soon as they left school, out came the smokes, the makeup, the cursing, and the strut. They may have been cowering as they went into confession, but they were grinning when they came out.*

Chapter 8

Mary and Matthew met in front of the church on Wednesday, Mary wearing a long, form-fitting dress in every color Crayola ever created, Matthew in jeans, a white sweater, and a blue windbreaker.

I have dressed all wrong.

She led him to the nearby Gold Star Jerk Center two doors down from Arkansas Fried Chicken and mere steps from the number 2 subway station. She ordered for both of them: gungo peas soup, jerk chicken, and a pie plate full of rice and peas drowning in coconut milk and spicy sauces.

"You *want* some strong coffee to go," the counter girl told Matthew.

That was more an order than a question. "This water is enough," Matthew said. "I'm sure I'll need it."

The counter girl eyed Mary before staring at Matthew. "I *strongly* recommend you get *lots* of strong coffee. At least *two* large cups."

"I'm okay, thanks," Matthew said holding up his cup.

He turned to Mary as they walked away. "What was that about?"

"She knows me," Mary said.

"Am I going to need coffee to keep up with you?" Matthew asked.

Mary smiled. "Something like that."

Since a February picnic on the banks of the Bronx River was out of the question, they walked back to the church, where Mary's office seemed smaller and more intimate. They ate mostly in silence, Matthew occasionally smacking his lips and fanning the air in front of his face.

"I used to be a very bad girl, Matthew," Mary said, dabbing at her lips with a napkin. "You name it, and I did it."

This isn't exactly the place to be naming bad things. I can think them, though. What a way to start a conversation! "We all have our wild sides."

"All I *had* was a wild side," Mary said. "I went to Catholic school, but I didn't learn anything spiritual. I ran the streets the second school ended. I'm not like that anymore. I'm a born-again Christian now, so I don't drink, smoke, curse, or fornicate."

Fornicate?

"Not before marriage," Mary added.

It's strange to hear such an ancient word coming out of such a sexy, young mouth.

"Are you saved, Matthew?" Mary asked.

Oh boy. I ran into this in college with a cute Puerto Rican girl from Paterson, New Jersey. It didn't end well. "I'm not saved as you and your church probably mean. I was baptized."

"Oh, Matthew, Matthew," Mary said. "You know you're going to hell, right?"

And we've just met. "Well, I don't know what to say to that." *Other than it's extremely rude to tell someone you barely know that he's going to hell over some jerk chicken and gungo peas soup.*

" 'The wages of sin is death,' " Mary said, " 'but the gift of God is eternal life in Jesus Christ our Lord.' "

The wages of sin are *death since "wages" is plural, but I won't quibble.* "I know that, Mary. I did study the Bible."

"I was living a life of death when I was Catholic," Mary said. "I was pure evil. I pierced nearly every part of my body."

What parts do you leave out? Inquiring minds want to know.

"I also tattooed places I shouldn't have," Mary said.

Such as?

"The tattoos are fading and most of my piercings have closed up," Mary said, "but they're still a constant reminder of my sin. I slept around, I drank, I smoked, and I did drugs. I did the most sinful things, and I have trouble remembering to this day all the evil I did. You know you've been bad when you can't remember all the bad you've done. But I don't want to talk about my past. I've put my sin far behind me. I want to talk about yours."

"My past or my sin?" Matthew asked.

"They're one and the same, aren't they?" Mary asked.

"Some of it." *And I'm suddenly not hungry.*

Mary smiled, widening her eyes. "You don't think you're sinful, do you, Matthew?"

"I know I am, Mary," Matthew said, "but I don't dwell on it."

"You should," Mary said. "Your sin is keeping you from heaven."

And this conversation is keeping you from a Valentine's Day date with me, Mary. "I still think I'll make it to heaven eventually."

"You don't still believe in purgatory, do you?" Mary asked.

"I've never been very sure about purgatory." *This conversation is kind of like purgatory, though, because a heavenly woman is talking about hell, and I'm in between.* "It seems too much like a cosmic time out."

"Purgatory doesn't exist at all, Matthew," Mary said. "There's no description of it in the Bible. There's only heaven or hell. Jesus said, 'I am the Way, the Truth, and the Life. No man can get to the Father but by me.' Unless you have Jesus in your heart, you are going to hell."

I want to ask her to lighten up, to preach to someone else. Isn't this a date? She asked me out to try to convert me? "I talk to God all the time." *Sometimes in small bathrooms at house parties.* "I often wonder what Jesus would do in some of the situations I've been in."

"That's a start, Matthew," Mary said, "but have you had sinful thoughts this week?"

"Well . . ." *This is beginning to feel like confession. I wish all priests were this sexy.* "I had the opportunity to do some sinning the last couple of weeks, but I didn't."

"But you were in sinful situations," Mary said.

Some more than others. "Yes."

"With women?" Mary asked.

"Yes."

"Matthew, putting yourself in those sinful situations is sin, too," Mary said. "You have to flee lust or it will catch you."

"I did flee." *I put on the brakes with Monique, didn't I? My brakes were slipping with Jade. Luckily, Jade's ex cracked that door.* "But didn't Jesus hang out with sinners?"

"Well, yes, He did," Mary said, "but He was perfect and without sin, and He came to save sinners, so He had to be around them to save them, right?"

I have to change the direction of this conversation. "Is that why you asked me out, Mary? To hang out with a sinner?"

Mary looked away. "No."

Time to press her buttons. "I've had some sinful thoughts about you since Sunday," Matthew said.

Mary looked up. "You have?"

"You are *very* beautiful, Mary." He smiled. "In fact, you are *very* sexy."

Mary pushed her chair back from the desk. "And we are in the house of God, Matthew."

"God made you," Matthew said. "I'm just admiring His creation. Is it wrong to admire God's beautiful creation?"

Mary seemed to catch her breath. "Well, no, of course not, but—"

"You have a beautiful body," Matthew interrupted, "no matter how tattooed or pierced or how much of you is leaking out of that dress for me to look at right now."

"I, I'm not . . ." She pulled her dress around her legs, folding her arms over her chest. "I'm not interested in that kind of thing anymore."

"Why not?" Matthew asked.

"I am a changed woman," Mary said.

"That doesn't change how sexy or beautiful you are," Matthew said. "You are gorgeous."

Mary's lower lip quivered. "Thank you, but the old me is gone, Matthew. I don't even think about sex anymore."

"Really?" Matthew asked.

"Really," Mary said.

Is that even possible? "You don't have any urges or needs?"

"I fight those urges," Mary said. "Sex is wrong unless it happens during the holy bonds of marriage."

Matthew blinked. "You believe sex is wrong."

"Sex before marriage is wrong, yes," Mary said. "Look at all the children born out of wedlock. Look at all the problems of single-parent homes. Look at all the diseases out there."

She has some valid points, but . . . "Wasn't Mary pregnant *before* she and Joseph were officially married?"

"What?" Mary gasped.

I have just stepped on her holy toes. "I know the Bible doesn't use the word 'sex,' but doesn't the Bible say the Holy Spirit came unto Mary and she conceived?"

Mary's mouth opened and closed several times. "Mary had . . . *relations* with the Holy Spirit one night. It was part of God's perfect plan. It was a miracle."

"As one-night stands go, that one was a doozy," Matthew said. "Miracle or not, it changed world history."

"Are you calling the Immaculate Conception a one-night stand?" Mary asked.

Did I do that? I didn't mean to. "I thought you weren't Catholic anymore."

"I'm not." She turned away. "Really. A one-night stand."

"It is one way of looking at it, isn't it?" Matthew said. "Young girl, no husband, suddenly pregnant."

"I will . . . I will pray for you, Matthew," Mary said softly.

She gave up too easily. I was just getting interested. "Why?"

She turned to face him. "So that you will see the errors of your ways and get saved."

"Does this mean that a second date with you is out of the question?" Matthew asked.

Mary frowned. "This wasn't a date."

"Didn't you ask me out to eat?" Matthew asked.

"Well, yes," Mary said, "but we were going to go to prayer meeting for the rest of the evening."

Hence the need for coffee. From this moment on, I will listen to counter girls urging me to get two cups of strong coffee to go. "We *were?* We're not going anymore?"

"I don't think your mind is in the right place to attend an all-night prayer meeting, Matthew." She folded her hands in front of her. "My ultimate goal was to ask you to attend church here regularly."

"By sneakily asking me to a dinner that I paid for," Matthew said.

Mary nodded. "But my motives are pure. I saw you, and I knew your soul was in trouble, so I had to act."

"How'd you know my soul was in trouble?" Matthew asked. "We went over some legal forms for a couple hours."

Mary sighed. "It was the way you were *looking* at me, Matthew." She glanced up. "Like you are now." She looked down. "With lust in your heart."

"I'm giving you all my attention, Mary," Matthew said. "I'm trying to be courteous. It's not lust, Mary." *Now, anyway.* "But if it were, I'd want you to take it as a compliment. You're a feast for the eyes. You can't hide the beauty God gave you." *Did I just say "beauty" or "booty"?*

Mary blinked and looked at her hands. "Matthew, please."

Oops. I said "booty."

"Lust is wrong, Matthew," Mary said. "It leads to a multitude of other sins."

And expenses. "I will try to tone down my lust, but it's going to be difficult."

"You have to fight it, Matthew," Mary said.

And I'm losing. This room is far too small. "You know, Mary, right now there's confusion in my heart. Why, if you're not interested in sex anymore, do you dress so provocatively?"

"I don't dress—"

"I can see every curve and bump on your body," Matthew interrupted. *If she had freckles, I'd be able to count them.* "You have very nice curves. And the colors you wear scream, 'Look at me! I'm hot! I sizzle the pavement when I walk!' "

Mary started to breathe deeply. "I don't . . . sizzle the pavement."

"You do," Matthew said. "I can't help staring at you."

"Staring is rude," Mary said softly.

Most of the time. Not when you're on a date. "Didn't you dress that way so that I *would* stare?"

"No."

She has to be lying. "You give people a great deal to stare at. God made you for me and other men to stare at. You have beauty that bursts. In that dress, you are a sunburst."

"As I said, I'm not that way anymore, so let's not—"

"You're not beautiful?" Matthew interrupted.

Mary swallowed. "I'm not . . . worldly."

"Even in your dreams?" Matthew asked.

"I don't remember my dreams," Mary said.

So sad. "Come on, Mary. You're what, twenty-eight, twenty-nine?"

"I'm thirty-seven." She nodded. "I'll be thirty-eight next month."

Wow. She looks much younger than thirty-seven. "Really. I never would have guessed it."

"Thank you." She looked up.

She looks so vulnerable, sitting there fidgeting and fighting her hands. "Mary, I like you. While I don't agree with you all the time, I like spending time with you. I'm even enjoying this conversation. If I asked you out to, say, a movie sometime, would you go? Or would you be afraid I'd be lusting after you the entire time?"

"I don't go to movies anymore, and I wouldn't go anywhere with you until I'm convinced you're saved," Mary said. "I cannot be unequally yoked with an unbeliever."

Yoked? That's a little severe, isn't it? "I'm not talking about yoking with you." *Is yoking legal in New York?* "I'm talking about another date, just you and me, out somewhere and away from here, where we can talk and get to know each other better."

"I . . . I can't, Matthew," she said, turning away. "I will . . . I will pray for you."

She's weakening. "But Mary, how will you convert me if I'm not around for you to convert?"

"You can come to services," she said to the wall.

"I'd rather have one-on-one conversations with you, Mary," Matthew said. "Just the two of us. Even if only on the phone. What nights *don't* you go to church?"

"Mondays," Mary said. "Pastor needs a day to rest."

"Okay, how about we go somewhere next Monday?" Matthew asked.

Mary sighed heavily, turning to face him. "You haven't been listening to me. We can't go anywhere together until you're saved."

Matthew cleared the pie plates to the side and leaned on the desk. "I hear what you're saying, Mary, but your body keeps contradicting what you're saying. You say 'no,' but your body is saying 'yes.' And your body is definitely talking louder than your voice is. Even now."

"Please go," Mary whispered.

Not yet. Matthew moved around the desk and took her left hand in his right. "I'm happy you're a changed woman, Mary, I really am. I used to be an asshole."

Mary didn't remove her hand from his. "Matthew, we're in a church," she whispered.

"Sorry, God." He squeezed her hand. "Mary, I used to sue people into bankruptcy for a living, and I was good at it. Ruining other people's lives made me happy. One day, I hated what I had become, so I gave all that up to work for people who really needed my help. I did that for three rewarding years at Brooklyn Legal until I burned out from all the misery and went out on my own. I changed the way I did things and the way I lived, but I really didn't change the real me." He lifted her chin with his left hand. "I like you, Mary. I'd like to get to know you better. You are so beautiful it hurts me."

"It . . . does?"

"Yes."

Mary pulled her hand away and leaned back in her chair. "You shouldn't have said that."

"Held your hand or told you what's been going through my head?"

"Both." She folded her hands together.

Matthew stood behind his chair. "So I shouldn't show you affection or tell you the truth?"

Mary pushed her chair into the desk, resting her arms in front of her. "I'm, I'm already spoken for, Matthew."

The Paterson girl said that Jesus was her boyfriend until she was married. I had countered that then she'd be cheating on her boyfriend with her husband. It didn't go too well after that.

"I know, I know," Matthew said. "You have Jesus in your heart."

"No, I mean, yes, that's true," Mary said. "But Matthew, I'm spoken for by someone else."

And yet she asked me out? What's going on? "You have a boyfriend?"

Mary looked at her hands. "Well, no, not exactly." She looked up briefly. "It's hard to explain. I am interested, *very* interested, in someone else."

"Why'd you ask me to dinner then?" Matthew asked.

"To save your soul," Mary said.

"You asked me out to eat so you could tell me I'm going to hell," Matthew said. "How is that supposed to save me?"

"By telling you where you'll end up if you don't change your ways," Mary said. "But that was only part of the reason I asked you to dinner. I also needed . . . to speed things up."

I am so lost. "To speed what up?"

"To make him jealous." She looked toward the door.

No . . . way. "To make who jealous?"

Mary shook her head. "Pastor Jean."

This . . . this is really happening. Mary has a crush on her pastor. "You . . . and Pastor."

"It's not like that," Mary whispered.

"How is it like?" Matthew asked.

"Pastor is a wonderful man," Mary said. "I owe him. He saved me from a life of sin."

"I thought Jesus did."

"Well, yes, of course Jesus did," Mary said, "but Pastor made it clear to me so that I'd repent."

"So you and he are . . . seeing each other."

"Not yet." She smiled. "Soon, I hope."

Not yet? "Does Pastor Jean even know how you feel about him?"

"I think so," Mary said. "I hope so."

How pitiful! "So you don't know how he feels."

"He doesn't seem to love his wife at all," Mary said.

His . . . wife. "Pastor Jean . . . is married. You don't see a problem with that?"

"No," Mary said. "His wife is all about money. She grew up in New Rochelle. She grew up with money. Pastor says this church needs more money. I'm the treasurer, so I ought to know, right? There's never enough money. Pastor wants to expand his ministry, and he has so many great ideas for the community, but her greed is getting in the way of his work."

"You mean *God's* work, right?" Matthew asked.

"Which are one and the same," Mary said.

Are they in every case? I doubt it. "Pastor Jean sounds like an amazing guy. Quite iconic." *Now, where is the exit? Oh, it's right behind me.*

"Oh, he is, but his wife is slowing us down," Mary said. "She's taking nearly *half* of our offerings to use on their house in Beechmont Woods."

And? "I'm sure the good pastor has a say in that, too. And anyway, isn't she entitled?"

"This *church* needs that money, *not* her," Mary said. "I know I'd be a better holy helpmate to Pastor than she will ever be."

This is beyond twisted. "But you're not even sure how he feels about you."

Mary sighed. "I'm not sure he even notices me."

The man would have to be blind. "I'm sure he does, Mary, but I'm also sure his wife has noticed you. You kind of stick out."

"I have been trying to . . . attract him," Mary said. "But he hardly even looks at me."

If his wife is around, Pastor Jean can't risk even looking sideways at you. "Did you ever think that maybe he values his marriage and that he truly loves his wife?"

"She's too worldly for him to love her," Mary said. "You should see what *she* wears. She's shameless. Her dresses are cut all the way up to her hips. Pastor couldn't love his wife. He's only staying with her for appearances."

Or Pastor knows that Mary has a crush on him and will never *mess up the church's finances as a result. It's actually kind of shrewd of him.* "So you thought you could use *me* to make Pastor Jean jealous."

"Right," Mary said. "When you showed up last Sunday, I said to myself, 'He's a lawyer, he's got money, the church needs money, money will make Pastor happy, get him to come back.' "

Mary is extremely devious, too. Her past isn't that far behind her. "You thought all that?"

Mary nodded. "And I also said to myself, 'He's kind of cute, he likes to stare at me, he's probably a heathen going to hell, so maybe I can get him saved and contributing *lots* of money.' "

I'm not that kind of lawyer anymore. "You say . . . amazing things to yourself."

"Matthew, I'm thirty-seven," Mary said. "If I don't get a man soon, I'll be like the other old, unmarried fossils in this church sitting in the back praising God and lusting after Pastor."

"That would be a tragedy, Mary." *It would be. She is exquisite.*

Organ music wafted into the room.

"Does this mean prayer meeting is starting?" Matthew asked.

"Yes." She stood. "Are you going to stay? Please say you will."

No. "Let me get this straight. You want me to stay at an all-night prayer meeting so my mere presence will make a married pastor so jealous that he'll divorce his allegedly greedy wife and marry you, knowing that it will do nothing but serious damage to his ministry."

"God has been known to work in mysterious ways, Matthew," Mary said.

Wow. And I thought I was lost. "Mary, even God does not work in *adulterous* ways. I will pray for *you,* Mary Primm."

Matthew raced to the 2 train platform as the sky darkened.

Angela says she's open until eight.

Matthew checked the time on his phone and smiled.

I'm going to make it.

I have another story to tell her.

Maybe I'll get a few more pastries as payment.

Chapter 9

Angela's place was nearly empty by the time Matthew arrived forty-five minutes before closing. A sexy, light-skinned woman sat in the first booth facing the window, two large, frothy mugs of coffee in front of her. She had long straight hair to her chest, high cheekbones, and blue-gray eyes. *That woman could be a model.*

"It's not a weekend, Matthew," Angela called out. "You're spoiling me."

Matthew strode up to the counter. "I needed a break." He handed her a twenty. "This is for a tall cup of your house blend, two raspberry pastries if you have them, half a dozen of those chocolate chip cookies, and whatever I didn't pay for on Saturday."

"Those pastries were my gift to you," Angela said.

"Then put my change in the tip jar," Matthew said.

"Gladly." Angela made change and stuffed a few bills into the jar. "Will this generous tip cost *me* anything?"

Ah. A little quid pro quo. "You must give me one good tip, one good piece of advice about women before the night is through."

"I'm closing soon," Angela said.

"Okay. Make it a good, quick tip then." Matthew drummed his fingers on the counter.

She handed him his coffee. "What makes you think I'll give you a good tip about women?"

"You're a woman, and I have faith in you." He took a sip. "Delectable as always." He looked at the front booth. "Another regular?"

"An irregular regular," Angela said. She bagged the cookies and the pastries.

"Meaning?"

"There's something wrong with her," Angela said. "I can't put my finger on it, but she always seems to be on the verge of tears. She has sad puppy eyes, you know? She's been here just about every night for the last few weeks at this time, and she just sits there, alone, with two mugs of coffee. I'm not sure, but I get the impression she gets stood up a lot. She's always watching out the window. I never see her with anybody."

That's not a woman you stand up or leave alone for any length of time. "Why would such a pretty girl have any reason to cry?"

Angela stared and blinked. "You don't need to be pretty to have a reason to cry."

"I know that, Angela. I was just saying—"

"Why don't you go find out if you want to know so badly?" Angela interrupted.

That sounded like a challenge. "I just might."

Angela sighed and shook her head. "You want that tip now?"

"Sure."

"Stay away from her," she said.

That was pretty clear. "I think I'm staying away from women for a while anyway."

"Why?" Angela asked.

"I just had another date from hell." *The third circle of hell, I think. Isn't that where Dante put the lusty?*

"You had a date on a Wednesday night?" Angela asked.

Matthew nodded. "It was kind of a church date, actually. A Haitian woman in the Bronx was trying to use me to make her married pastor jealous so he'd commit adultery with her, and she had the nerve to tell me that *I* was going to hell."

Angela squinted. "You have to be making this stuff up."

Matthew held up his right hand. "God's honest truth."

Angela smiled. "Where on earth do you meet these women?"

"Everywhere I go, it seems," Matthew said.

"Everywhere except here," Angela said.

That's true. Angela is so perceptive. "You know, you're right. I've never had any trouble with a Williamsburg woman."

"I meant . . . never mind." Angela wiped the counter.

Matthew looked at the woman in the first booth. "Do you think Gray Eyes is from Williamsburg?"

"How do you know she has gray eyes?" Angela asked.

"I notice these things." He turned to Angela. "Think she's a Billyburger?"

"I doubt it," Angela said. "She sounds like she's from Long Island somewhere. I'm betting Hempstead or Massapequa."

"But she evidently lives here now," Matthew said softly.

"How would I know?" Angela said. "I don't card people."

Ouch. Angela is in a bad mood. "Doesn't her current address count?"

"Well, if she does live here, she's a transplant, a transient, an outsider," Angela whispered. "She's not *from* Williamsburg, right?"

Like Joy. "She could learn." *Hmm. Joy never learned.*

"And you're going to teach her," Angela said.

Matthew smiled at Angela. "I might." He finished his coffee and picked up his bag. "No. I *will.*"

"Now?" Angela asked. "You're going to teach her *now?*"

"Why not?" *The night is young.*

"Wait, Matthew," Angela said. "You want me to repeat my tip?"

"I will take it under advisement, counselor," Matthew said.

"Stay away from her," Angela said. "Don't say I didn't warn you, and you only have a few minutes to make your mistake. I close at eight."

Matthew took his empty coffee cup and bag to the first booth. He had to walk in front of the woman to break her gaze out the window. "Hi."

The woman's sad face lit up. "Hello."

Yep. She's definitely from the suburbs. If I close my eyes, I'll hear the typical Long Island white girl. "Isn't it kind of lonely drinking alone?"

The woman smiled. "I'm not alone now, am I?"

That was an open invitation to sit. "And neither am I. May I join you?"

The woman slid to her right. "Please."

And she wants me to sit next to her. Matthew sat dangerously close to the woman's left leg. "I'm Matthew."

"Allison."

Why doesn't her name surprise me?

"Ten minutes!" Angela yelled.

Matthew turned to see Angela rapidly wiping tables and moving closer to the front of the shop. "We may be kicked out soon. It's almost closing time. Angela runs a tight ship."

Allison cradled the fuller of the two mugs. "Yeah. And she makes the best coffee on earth." She sipped her coffee, her sad, puppy eyes looking at Matthew.

"You want to . . . go somewhere, Allison?" Matthew asked.

Allison reached into a baggy black leather purse and pulled out two tickets. "You like hockey?"

A black woman who likes hockey. In Williamsburg. Allison is definitely a Long Island girl. "Sure." He looked closely at the tickets. "Hey, those are for tonight. The game's about to start."

"I, um . . . I was supposed to meet someone . . ." Tears filled her eyes. "Sorry."

Someone extremely evil stood up this woman. What an idiot! These tickets are in the first row! And it's against the Boston Bruins? What a schmuck! "The jerk."

"Yeah," Allison said. "We were supposed to go out to eat first, too. This coffee is going straight to my brain."

"Tell you what," Matthew said. "We'll get a quick bite on the way to the game, and we'll be in our seats maybe by the beginning of the second period. What do you say?"

"I'd like that a lot, Matthew," Allison said.

This woman has some delightful doe eyes. Matthew looked up and saw Angela waiting by the door. "It must be eight o'clock. Ready?"

Allison gathered her purse and held out her hand. Matthew pulled her across the seat and to her feet.

She only weighs about ninety pounds. I nearly yanked her completely off her feet.

Allison whipped a cell phone out of her purse. "I'll call us a cab. We can eat at TGIFriday's at the Garden. My treat."

I like this girl already. Free food and front-row seats to a Rangers game. Where has this girl been all my life?

Matthew held the door, and Allison went outside to make her call.

"Remember what I told you," Angela said.

"I hope you're wrong," Matthew whispered.

Angela stepped closer. "I don't think I'm wrong about her. You see how eager she is?"

Yeah. Hmm. Monique and Jade were eager, too. "Yeah, but I think you're wrong about her."

"What if I'm right?" Angela asked.

"If you're right," Matthew said, "I'll tell you all about it early tomorrow morning over breakfast."

Angela laughed and took out a scrap of paper and a pen. "How do you like your eggs?"

"You're taking my order now?" Matthew asked.

"I will see you bright and early tomorrow morning," Angela said. "How do you like your eggs?"

"Over easy."

"Bacon or sausage?" Angela asked.

"Surprise me."

"Both then," she said.

"It *might* work out," Matthew said.

Angela shook her head. "You'll be waiting outside for me."

She seems so sure. "Wanna bet?"

"All right," Angela said. "When I win this bet, and I *will,* you have to help me clean up the place for the next three days."

"And when I win?" Matthew asked.

"You won't." Angela smiled.

"And when I win," Matthew continued, "you will provide me with free breakfast for three days."

Angela shook his hand. "You gotta bet." She turned his hand over. "You'll have to use some gloves. I wouldn't want your soft lawyer's hands getting calluses while you scrub my toilets."

Allison returned to the doorway. "The taxi's here! Wasn't that quick?"

Matthew walked out and opened the taxi door, Allison scrambling inside.

"Be careful," Angela mouthed from the doorway.

"Good night, Angela," Matthew said.

"Promise," Angela whispered.

"I promise," Matthew mouthed.

I am sitting next to a gorgeous woman about to go to a hockey game.

What could possibly go wrong?

Chapter 10

On the ride to Madison Square Garden, Allison clasped Matthew's hands in hers. "You are so sweet."

"I can't stand to see a woman cry," Matthew said. *Such soft, small hands.*

"You're a saint," Allison said. "You're Saint Matthew."

"Trust me, I'm not." *I'm having lusty thoughts, even now. Very nice legs, slender fingers, and those eyes! She is lean and sexy.* "I'm no saint, Allison."

"You are to me, Boo," Allison cooed.

A pet name already? Hmm. This is sudden. "Really, Allison, I'm not. I'm a lawyer."

"You are? Wow! That's so cool!" She clutched his hands more tightly. "That is so cool. A lawyer, and only two days until Valentine's Day. My luck is changing for the better!"

And so is mine.

I hope.

At the TGIFriday's at Madison Square Garden, while Matthew picked at the Cajun shrimp, chicken strips, and baby back ribs on the Jack Daniels sampler, Allison ate only half of her chicken *piccata* pasta and sucked down two Heinekens before Matthew could finish half of his Sam Adams.

I've never seen a woman do that. Let's see if she can hold a conversation as well as she holds her beer. "What do you do, Allison?"

"I'm a buyer," Allison said, "well, a junior buyer for Bloomingdale's."

Okay. She's educated, driven, has a job. "Sounds exciting."

"It's okay," Allison said. "I can only afford to live in Williamsburg, though. I have to take the *bus* to work."

She said that with disgust. What's wrong with riding the bus?

"I flat out *refuse* to take the subway," Allison said. "There are far too many criminals on those trains, especially on the L train."

Hmm. She's also slightly bigoted. I blame her upbringing. "I ride the trains all the time, and nearly all of the people on them are just like you and me."

"Sure they are," Allison said.

Okay. She's more than slightly bigoted.

When their server walked by, Allison said, "Two more Heinies." She smiled. "I'm thirsty."

Matthew tore into his last rib, pausing only to wipe his face. He looked up to see Allison staring at him.

"You should chew your food thirty times," she said.

"I thought we were in a hurry." He looked up at the TV. "The Rangers are already losing three to one. The first period's nearly over."

"That's no reason to choke to death," Allison said, finishing beer number three. She planted her bottle in the middle of the table. "How do I look? And be honest."

She certainly flits around in her conversations. "You look . . . cute."

"Thank you."

"What's your heritage?" *Which is safer than asking, "Are you mixed?"*

She tossed back her hair. "I get that question a lot. My father is black, and my mother is white. I am a blended human."

"You're very pretty," Matthew said.

"Oh, thank you, Boo." She picked up and drank half of her fourth Heineken, waving her bottle at a passing server. "My last boyfriend, Tommy, the guy who stood me up tonight, he said I was too fat. Do you think I'm fat?"

"Not at all," Matthew said. "Tommy needs glasses."

"I told him to get an eye exam, but he never did." She pulled up her shirt. "Do you like my stomach?"

That is the flattest stomach on earth. "What's not to like?" *Now kindly cover yourself, Allison. You're getting lewd stares from the men at the bar.*

Allison finished her fourth beer, leaving her stomach exposed. "It's hot in here, isn't it?"

It might have something to do with the amount of beer you've been drinking.

"Have you had your prostate checked?" Allison asked.

And now we're talking about my prostrate.

"What are you, forty?" Allison said.

"I'm thirty-five," Matthew said.

"You should *really* get it checked," Allison said. "My Uncle Jimmy had prostate cancer when *he* was forty. You kind of remind me of him. He's my mother's brother, not my *dad's* brother, of *course.*" She laughed loudly. "You don't look *anything* like my dad's brother!"

The men at the bar still stared.

"Oh, yeah," Matthew said. "I kind of figured that."

"Do you like children?" Allison asked.

From my prostate to children. I'm sure it's a logical sequence in her mind. "Sure."

"I want four little girls named Amaryllis Anne, Bethany Barbara, Carrie Clarissa, and Daphne Danielle," Allison said. "You see what I just did with their names?"

"Not really," Matthew said.

"I'm going to name my children *alphabetically,*" Allison said.

Oh yeah. Neat.

She drew the letter A in the air. "Amaryllis Anne. Two As in a row. Isn't that the most organized thing to do?"

Organized? Well . . . "I guess."

Allison gulped most of her fifth beer the moment the server brought it to her. "Oh, and they'll just *have* to go to school out on Long Island. They can't go to the *wretched* schools in Brooklyn."

"They aren't that wretched," Matthew said. "Some are quite excellent, especially the Catholic—"

"No, they aren't!" Allison interrupted. "Not compared to the ones in Manhasset. The *dumbest* kids in *my* school could be *valedictorians* in Brooklyn schools."

Angela has a good ear for accents—and unhinged women.

"I don't know how *anyone* in Brooklyn can get a good job going to those schools," Allison said.

The server brought her another beer.

That would be number six. I hope it stays full.

"No wonder Pfizer left," Allison said. "They couldn't get any intelligent help."

They actually weren't making enough money, but I won't argue with her. "The Pfizer plant is coming back to life. Brooklyn Soda Works, McClure's Pickles, and Steve's Ice Cream have moved in. Have you ever had Kombucha? They make it there, too. It's really good." *And better for you than* your *beer.*

"Kom-what?"

"Kombucha is kind of like carbonated tea. It detoxes you and makes your intestines happy." *And gives you a healthy buzz.*

"Oh, and I want a big house," Allison interrupted.

That was totally random. From kombucha to a big house.

"You like doing yard work, don't you, Boo?" Allison whined.

I could do without that whine, and please pull down your shirt! The man on the end of the bar has taken at least four pictures of your stomach with his cell phone. "I've really never had a yard to tend."

"You'll have to learn then, huh?" She finished beer number five and sipped from beer number six. "I can see you out there cutting our grass while I flower the weed garden."

I will not correct her. That might be what she actually does *in her garden.*

Allison drained her sixth beer. "This is so exciting. Oh, we need to *go.*" She threw three twenties onto the table, her shirt finally covering her stomach. "Come on! We're missing the game!"

They weren't good seats. They were *great* seats, in VIP Rinkside section 4 a sneeze from the scratched and scuffed Plexiglas.

These seats cost at least nine hundred bucks apiece! Bloomingdale's must pay very well.

"These are great seats, Allison," Matthew said, watching the action.

"Kick some Bruin *ass,* Rangers!" Allison yelled. "Did you say something, Boo?"

"No."

"Take his stupid head off!" Allison yelled while pounding on the Plexiglas.

I'm sure Allison also likes WWF and MMA.

She stood and blocked the view of the couple directly behind them. "I dated . . . that one. Number ninety-eight."

"Down in front!" someone yelled behind them.

Allison sat. "He's Canadian. He was very nice, but he's not as nice as you are, Boo. Oh, but he drank too much Molson. He said Heineken tasted like pee. You don't drink Molson, do you, Boo?"

"No, I—"

"I need another one." She flagged down a vendor and sucked one down while paying for three more. "For me and my friend," she told the vendor.

Matthew had to show his ID.

Matthew would never get a sip of those beers.

Allison set her cups down and pounded on the glass. "C'mon, Rangers! Kick some Bruin *ass!*"

Whenever players zipped by the boards, Allison went off, slamming her fists into the Plexiglas and cursing. When a fight broke out in front of her, she nearly climbed over the glass to join them.

Matthew calmly held her hips and brought her back to her seat.

A few men behind him groaned. Allison had given them all an outstanding view of her booty.

She's rabid, drunk, bigoted, and looking for a husband who does yard work. Her fists have become bruises. If I had let her finish her climb, she would have gotten on SportsCenter. Yeah, I know how to pick 'em. I should have listened to Angela.

When the Rangers fell behind 6–2 late in the third period, Allison started booing loudly and tried to get the fans around her to join her.

They wouldn't.

How do I get out of this? Do I put her in a cab and hope she gets home okay? I can't do that.

The game ended.

Allison tried to get number 98's attention, but he quickly skated away.

I know what you mean, man.

Matthew guided Allison out of the Garden to a cab.

"Allison, where do you live?" Matthew whispered once he had gotten her to sit up in the cab.

Allison looked at him through bleary eyes. "Aren't we going to your place?" She pawed at his leg and missed.

Several times.

"I'd much rather see yours," Matthew said.

Allison licked her lips in what she might have thought was a suggestive manner.

It wasn't.

She looks like I *look after getting a cavity filled at the dentist.*

"I'd like to show you yours," Allison said, giggling, "as long as you show me mine."

Fortunately for Matthew and perhaps unfortunately for the driver, Allison passed out with her next breath.

"Where to?" the driver asked.

"One sec." Matthew dug into Allison's purse and found her ID. "Two-forty-one Wythe Avenue in Williamsburg. And please take the L-I-E to 278."

"I hear you," the driver said.

Twenty minutes later, Matthew hauled Allison up the stairs of an anonymous apartment building, found her keys in her purse, tried twelve keys before finding the right one, and opened her apartment door. He hoisted her onto an all-white couch and found a light.

Ho . . . lee . . . shit!

"Isn't this an apartment to die for?" Allison said.

Maybe to die in. *This is Martha Stewart's apartment. Everything is white, even the floors.* He stared at several white bookcases crammed with hundreds of white photo albums. He looked at the white carpet under his feet. *Who would put down white carpet everywhere, even in the kitchen?*

Allison lurched to her feet. "I'm just going to something into slip more comfortable, Boo." She giggled. "I said something into slip! Ha! I meant, I'm going to slip into something more comfortable. You sit there and wait on Mommy."

I need to leave, I need to leave, I need to leave . . .

Matthew heard her fall heavily twice.

itan, turning south on Driggs past Angela's place. *That's where I'll be working late the next three nights. It's where I belong after these last few weeks. Somewhere safe. Somewhere peaceful. Angela has always been good company.*

Once inside his own apartment, he settled into his easy chair and watched SportsCenter.

He didn't see Allison climbing the glass.

The phone rang. "Hello?"

"Where *are* you, Boo?" Allison cried.

The date that never ends. "I'm at home, Allison. Are you okay?"

"Why?" she whined.

"Why am I asking or why am I at home?" Matthew asked.

"Why aren't you *here?*" Allison moaned.

Because you're a crazy drunk woman. "You needed your rest."

"Please come back, Boo," Allison said with a burp. "I don't feel so good. The bed is tilting. I've already puked twice on my bedspread. It's *ruined.*"

I feel your pain, but only a little. You're the alcoholic who bought an impractical, bright white bedspread. "Allison, I'm really tired, too. Just . . . go sleep on your couch." *Where you might make a matching stain.*

"*You* let me drink all that beer, so it's *your* fault I'm sick," Allison said. "You should have *stopped* me."

"I hardly know you, Allison," Matthew said. "And you're a grown woman who should know when she's had enough to drink."

"I know, I know," Allison said, and she began to cry.

For five minutes.

"I'm so sorry, Boo," she cried. "I didn't mean to yell at you. Do you forgive me?"

Forgiveness is the first step to reconciliation. I do not wish to reconcile with this woman. "Get some rest, Allison."

"I just expected you to be beside me when I woke up," Allison whispered.

And puked the rest of your chicken picatta *and ten Heinekens on me.* "Please get some rest, Allison. You'll feel better in the morning."

"Did you like my drapes?" Allison asked brightly.

She's deaf when she's drunk, too. "Yeah. They're nice. So . . . white." *Why am I still talking to her?*

"I *love* the color white," Allison said.

Technically, white isn't a color.

"Is your place as big as mine?" Allison said.

"Get some rest, Allison," Matthew said.

"Where do you live?" Allison asked.

Do not ever *tell this woman where you live!* "Oh, wow, my cell's battery is dying. I always forget to charge it."

"Plug it in, then," Allison said. "Oh, Boo, the next time you come over, you have to stay, and you won't need a toothbrush. I have plenty of those in every color of the rainbow. Only a few of them have ever been used. Oh, do you like meatloaf? I make the *best* meatloaf."

"Allison, I gotta go. Good night."

"What size do you wear?" Allison asked.

What size?

"I have a closet full of men's clothes from some of my exes who never came back to get them for some reason," Allison said.

They were very wise.

"Oh, I have to write down our date in my diary," Allison said. "Did you see my diaries on the shelves?"

Those weren't photo albums. They were diaries. There must have been four or five hundred *of them.* "Allison, it's very late, and I'm very tired."

"Oh, is my boo tired?" Allison cooed. "I better let my boo go then. Sweet dreams with me on top."

Matthew suddenly had a vision of Allison dry heaving on top of him. He winced. "Bye, Allison." He ended the call.

A minute later, his phone buzzed.

Allison again.

He let it go to voice mail.

He had to shut off his phone five messages later.

In the morning after a few hours of sleep, he listened to Allison's messages as he shaved:

"Why won't you answer? Oh. You're probably dreaming sweet dreams of me on top of you. I need you, Boo. Call me anytime you want. You are my clouds on a sunny day. You are the wings beneath my wind. Did I get that right? Happy Valentine's Day!"

He deleted the message and listened to the next:

"I'm making a heart-shaped meatloaf tonight, Boo. And afterward, we can go to Ikea, okay? It'll be a *fun* Valentine's date. I *love* Ikea. It is such a *fun* place to shop. Then we can go to my place and read *all* my diaries. I want you to get to know me *so* much! I know you'll like what you read. I sometimes even draw pictures. I am the best doodler. You'll see! See you soon!"

Ikea. A fun date. Wow. He deleted the message and listened to the next:

"I wrote a *lot* in my diary just now about you, Boo. Want to read what I wrote? You'll have to come over to do that, silly. Call me soon, okay, or I might write bad things about you in my diary tonight. I'm just kidding. I know I won't be able to concentrate at work today because I can't get you out of my head! You can send the flowers and candy to the Bloomingdale's on Broadway. Isn't it amazing that I know you're sending me flowers later today? Bye!"

It's not amazing, Allison. It's not even iconic.

It's only sad.

He deleted the next *fifteen* messages without listening to more than a few words of each, with "Boo" the most popular greeting.

Very scary.

His phone buzzed again.

Very scary, indeed.

Chapter 11

Matthew's phone buzzed all day Thursday and continued to buzz on Valentine's Day as he stood rubbing his arms and stamping his feet outside Angela's place a little before six AM.

Angela didn't say a word as she undid the many locks and opened the door, ushering him to the middle booth, his eggs, bacon, and sausage already steaming on a large china plate, a large cup of coffee and a small plate of assorted of pastries completing the feast.

Matthew didn't say a word as he sat.

His phone buzzed again.

Matthew turned it off and spun it on the table.

He nodded once to Angela, and he dug in.

Angela slid into the booth beside him. "The Rangers are decent this year, but whenever they play the Bruins, they fall apart."

Matthew grunted.

Angela nudged his knee with hers. "How bad was it?"

Matthew swallowed. "The eggs are good. Nice and cheesy. Just the right touch of pepper, too."

"I know," she said. "I made them." She put her elbows up on her half of the table. "Tell me how bad it was. I want to gloat."

Matthew took a long swig of coffee and swallowed. "Angela, I can never turn on my phone again. I may have to change my number. I will most likely have to go around Williamsburg in disguise." He stared out the window.

"Happy Valentine's Day," Angela said. "Did you bring me flowers, Matthew?"

"No, but Allison is expecting flowers and candy today."

Angela rested her head on her hands. "So soon? I *never* would have guessed she'd be a stalker." She batted her eyes. "You never guessed it either, did you?"

Matthew sighed. "How often did Allison come here?"

"Oh, half a dozen times. She always got two mugs, and I always cleared away a full mug after she left crying." Angela smiled. "From the way you're watching that window, you're expecting her to come walking through that door any second."

"I am."

"You're not afraid of *that* skinny thing, are you?" Angela asked.

Matthew wiped his lips and picked up a pastry. "Don't let her size fool you. She's insane, and even skinny insane people can do a lot of damage."

Angela smiled.

Matthew sighed. "I know why you're smiling."

"No, you don't."

"You're smiling because you were right, and I was wrong." He sighed. "And now I have to clean this place for the next three nights."

"That's part of it." She leaned back in the booth and put her hands in her lap.

"What's the other part?" Matthew asked.

She raised her eyebrows. "I'll let you know later."

Matthew squinted at the front door. "I count . . . seven locks. Are they good locks?"

Angela looked down. "Yes. They're the best."

"The front glass looks thick enough." Matthew bit into a pastry. "Unless Allison has a car. Do you have an alarm system with a screeching alarm?"

"I have a little sticker on my window that says I do," Angela said. "The ADT alarm system I had died one year into a three-year contract, and despite calling them for months, no one ever came out to fix the problem because they said it was working fine at their end. I had four motion detectors, and none of them ever worked. I kept calling and calling, and then they concluded that lightning had hit my shop, and the maintenance contract didn't cover lightning, so if I paid twenty-five bucks for a service call, and oh, I'm sure you need an upgrade. That'll be another three hundred, ma'am." She sighed. "It was pure foolishness."

"*Was* this shop hit by lightning?" Matthew asked.

"No." She smiled. "You look like you've been hit by lightning, though."

Matthew shook his head. "Lightning just keeps striking in the same place for me."

"Uh-huh. Do you really think Allison is insane?" Angela asked.

"Yes." He shook his head. "She's insane when she's drunk and psychotic when she's sober."

"That's some combination." Angela crossed her arms and elbowed Matthew in the side. "When did you know for sure that she was crazy?"

"I think it was when she started naming her future daughters alphabetically," Matthew said.

Angela shrugged. "That's a little strange, but it isn't necessarily crazy."

"Amaryllis Anne?" Matthew said. "Bethany Barbara?"

"She'll have her children stuttering their own names," Angela said. "What else makes you think she's crazy?"

"I am already her boo."

"*No,*" Angela said.

"Yes," Matthew said, nodding. "She's expecting her *boo* to show up for heart-shaped meatloaf and a *fun* shopping trip to Ikea tonight, and she has two entire bookcases full of diaries. Floor-to-ceiling bookcases. There must be five hundred of them. We're supposed to read them *all* tonight so I can get to know her better. She said if I don't call her, she'll write something bad about me in her diary tonight."

"That isn't crazy," Angela said. "I used to keep a diary."

"Were you in your thirties?" Matthew asked.

"I was twelve." She shook her head. "She's still not crazy."

"How's this: her entire apartment is white. The kitchen counters, the appliances, the carpeting, the furniture, the cabinets, the lamps, the drapes, the bookcases, the—"

"I get the picture," Angela interrupted. "Okay. That's a little . . . odd, but it's still not crazy."

Matthew glanced out the window. "I just know she's going to stalk me."

Angela picked up Matthew's phone and turned it on.

It buzzed immediately.

"You see?" Matthew said. "Turn it off."

"Wait a second," she said. "I want to give her time to leave a message." The phone beeped two minutes later. "I'll bet it's a juicy message." She waved the phone in front of Matthew. "Does this have a speaker?"

"You want to listen to it?" Matthew asked.

Angela smiled. "I'm still gloating. Work with me, Matthew."

Matthew dialed his voice mail, turned on the speaker, and set the phone on the table.

"Boo, can you hear me?" Allison asked. "I'm in the shower!"

Angela howled with laughter.

"I only use Roberto Cavalli shower gel and coconut frosting shampoo!" Allison yelled.

Angela continued to howl.

Matthew had to admit it was pretty hilarious.

They heard the water shut off.

"I'm getting out of the shower now, Boo," Allison said. "Don't you wish you could see me? I *bet* you do. I'm all wet and naked."

Angela stopped laughing.

Matthew listened a little closer.

"I'm putting on my Roberto Cavalli body lotion now. Don't you wish you could see me—"

Angela shut off the phone. "Are all her messages like that one?"

Matthew shook his head. *I shouldn't have deleted the other fifteen!*

Angela frowned. "You enjoyed that, didn't you?"

"*I* didn't turn on the phone." He nudged her knee with his. "So, is she stalking me?"

"She's stalking you," Angela said.

"What do I do?" Matthew asked.

Angela looked Matthew in the eye. "This has never happened to you before?"

"Never."

Angela turned her head slightly. "I doubt that."

Matthew smiled. "That was almost a compliment."

"Almost." Angela nodded. "I guess you can hide out here until I close. After that, you're on your own."

"Where does your back door lead to?" Matthew asked.

"Grand Street eventually," Angela said softly.

"I may have to use that exit." He looked at the grand opening sign now up across the street. "When'd that sign go up?"

Angela sighed. "Sometime last night."

"You think they would have opened it a day earlier to coincide with Valentine's Day," Matthew said. "I guess pink clashes with red and yellow."

Angela nodded.

And now she seems sad. Maybe this will cheer her up. "Do you have any Valentine's Day plans, Angela?"

Angela looked at her hands. "No."

And she has a shy streak. "Neither do I."

"I hear the sewage treatment plant on Newtown Creek is offering tours today," Angela said.

"No way," Matthew said. *Greenpoint has all the fun places to visit.*

"I know, nasty, right?" Angela said. "And after looking at how they dispose of poop, they give everyone a Hershey's Kiss."

"That would not be a fun Valentine's date," Matthew said.

She stuck her hands in her apron pockets. "I guess we're stuck with each other, huh?"

"You will get to spend part of your evening watching me clean," Matthew said. "I promise to be entertaining."

Angela sighed. "I may not be here to clean much longer. If La Estrella gets popular, I may have to close up shop permanently."

"You can't, Angela," Matthew said. "I won't have anywhere to hide from psychotic Bloomingdale's buyers."

"She works at Bloomingdale's? They probably hired on her looks alone." Angela put her arms on the table, resting her cheek on one hand.

She's really feeling low. "And I won't have anywhere to go to get good advice."

"And not take it," Angela whispered.

"I will take whatever advice you give me from now on," Matthew said, "and you will have a very clean place, I promise."

"It doesn't matter."

"Yes it does," Matthew said. He touched her arm. "Angela, you're not really serious about closing this place, are you?"

Angela rose up, hiding her hands in her apron pockets again. "I may have no choice. If what goes into that register doesn't cover my bills, I'll have to either relocate or . . . something."

"Would you consider raising your prices?" Matthew asked.

"No way," Angela said. "I have the business I have *because* my prices are low. If I raised them, I'd be cutting my own throat. Imagine what you'd hear in line. 'Oh, Angela's getting all uppity on us because of La Estrella. I never thought *she'd* change. I *knew* she was a closet hipster trying to be trendy.' "

Matthew smiled. "We wouldn't want that. But I don't think you have anything to worry about."

"Says the expert."

Matthew picked up his coffee. "Listen. You make my coffee a little different every day. I'm not sure how, but it's never quite the same, and it's always better than good. But over at La Estrella, it will be the same old thing every day, and it will be much more expensive there than here. They are going to price and bore themselves out of the neighborhood. You'll see."

Angela rolled her shoulders. "Until I see it, I have to worry."

"This place is unique, Angela, it's never boring, and unique and never boring last the test of time in Williamsburg," Matthew said.

"Well, my landlord thinks this unique and never boring place needs a rent increase when my lease is up in June," Angela said. "He says property values are going up because of La Estrella. So come June, I won't be able to afford this place, and I also won't be able to afford moving anywhere else and starting over. I have every reason to worry." She rubbed her right shoulder with her left hand.

Her shoulders are in knots over this. Should I offer to rub them for her? I barely know the woman. "Well, if you absolutely had to close, what would you do?"

"I don't know." She sighed. "I really don't know. It's not something I want to think about, but now you're making me think about it."

"I'm sorry, I didn't mean to—"

"No, no, I should be thinking about it," Angela interrupted. "I know everything there is to know about coffee and almost everything I need to know about baking. Coffee originally grew wild in Ethiopia before they started growing it in Brazil and Indonesia. Did you know that?"

"No."

"That makes coffee originally African, and I'm one of the few Africans selling it around here," Angela said. "I can't leave. Did you know that Americans drink four hundred *million* cups of coffee every day? We drink one-fifth of the world's coffee. This is a *good* business. I don't want to leave it or be forced out of it."

I don't know why I'm pressing this. "But what if you had to? What would you do?"

"I guess . . . I'd have to go work for someone." She sighed deeply.

"I can't see you doing that." *I can't. She's part of the cool décor of this place.*

She nodded and smiled. "Neither can I. I can't be a cook in another cook's kitchen, and I damn sure won't be a barista at one of those places. I brew by feel, not by some diagram on a wall." She craned her neck toward Matthew. "I'm getting too old for a career change, you know?"

"You're not old, Angela," Matthew said.

She stretched her neck. "I'm thirty-five, and I'm not getting any younger."

She can't be my age, can she? "No, really? You look young for your age."

Angela laughed. "Was that supposed to be a compliment?"

"That didn't come out the way I wanted it to," Matthew said.

"You should have stopped at 'you look young.' "

And this moment, she does look young. She has such a smooth face with only a few tiny crow's feet around her eyes. "Honestly, Angela, you look like you're fresh out of college."

"Don't I wish," Angela said. "I didn't get the opportunity to go to college."

"You still can."

"That requires money I do not have." She flattened her hands on the table. "And may never have."

"Maybe going back to school and a career change are what you need," Matthew said. "You're young enough to learn new skills and not too old to hate the learning process. Believe it or not, I used to work for Schwartz, Yevgeny, and Ginsberg."

Angela blinked and shook her head. "You used to work for those idiots?"

She has definitely heard of SYG. "I was one of their biggest idiots."

"Did they fire you, or did you quit?" Angela asked.

"A little of both, and in a blaze of glory. I blew a case on purpose." He closed his eyes. "I had a meltdown during a summation." He opened his eyes. "They frown on that sort of thing at SYG."

Two customers came in.

"Hold that thought," Angela said. "I'll bring you some more coffee, too."

"Okay."

After she waited on the two customers and they left, Angela returned with a fresh pot, filling Matthew's cup to the top. "Tell me about your meltdown."

I haven't told anyone but Joy, yet here I am spilling it to Angela. "Not many people know the full story. SYG kept a pretty tight lid on it. They wouldn't like the world to know that one of their lawyers had a sudden streak of integrity."

"That would ruin them for sure," Angela said. "What happened?"

"We were suing an upscale, state-of-the-art retirement apartment house in New Jersey on behalf of its former tenants," Matthew said. "One of the residents left a pan on the stove too long, and the place burned down. No one was killed, thank God, but we put together a class-action lawsuit that would have destroyed two of the nicest people I had ever met. Bill and Emma Turman. They really took a deep interest in the people in their care."

"But you sued them anyway," Angela said.

"Yeah." *We were leeches.* "And the whole time I *knew* it wasn't their fault. They had everything up to code—the best sprinkler system, every safety device possible, emergency exits clearly marked. All the smoke alarms were blaring, and their outstanding, dedicated staff did an expert job clearing the building. I told the jury all of that in my summation. I even said, 'Ladies and gentlemen of the jury, I'm sorry for wasting your time this past week. Please don't give these money-grubbing people what they *don't* deserve.' And they didn't." He smiled. "After that, I took what SYG affectionately calls 'an early retirement.' " *It was really a ridiculously lucrative severance package designed to keep me quiet. SYG didn't want the world to know how badly they screwed up by making me lead counsel on such a high-profile case.*

"I can see you saying all that," Angela said.

"You can?"

Angela nodded. "Have you ever regretted doing it?"

"No." *Well, only when I look at my bank statements.* "My only regret in life is that I didn't have a meltdown sooner. Okay, I regret quitting Brooklyn Legal, too. I was doing good things all the time there, but there was so much to be done. I couldn't keep up with the misery. There's so much need and misery around here."

"I know." She smiled. "And now you're on your own."

"And living off the money I earned with Schwartz, Yevgeny, and Ginsberg." He sighed. "They paid me an ungodly amount of money for hurting people. And now I don't have many clients, and most of the clients I do work for I never see again. I'm kind of a one-night-stand lawyer. See me once and you'll never have to see me again."

"Who was your last client?" Angela asked.

"The Haitian wannabe adulteress," Matthew said.

Angela blinked slowly. "No way."

"Well, actually her church was my client," Matthew said. "I made a hundred bucks in two hours."

Angela shook her head.

"What?" Matthew said.

"Nothing." Angela wrinkled up her lips. "Nothing at all."

Oh, I think I know what that "nothing" means. "You think I only represent the women I date these days."

Angela shrugged. "It seems that way."

"You know, it does." He shivered. "I hope Allison doesn't need me for anything."

Angela stood, pressing her hands into the small of her back. "You could represent me against my landlord and the ridiculous rent increase he's asking."

She must not sleep well. But who am I to talk? I sleep in an easy chair. "Is it a standard lease agreement?"

"Yes."

"I read thousands of those at Brooklyn Legal," Matthew said. "If you signed it, your landlord has every right to raise the rent when the lease is up as long as he gives you adequate notice of the increase."

"Could you at least talk to him for me? I want to scare the man a little." She picked up his phone and turned it on.

The phone buzzed again.

"Did you two . . . did you . . . get intimate?" Angela asked.

"No," Matthew said, his face reddening. "She passed out. Chicken *piccata* chased by ten beers ended up on her white bedspread. Twice."

"Ouch." She punched in a number. "I'm sure he's awake. Evil never sleeps." She handed Matthew the phone. "His name is Mr. Jacobs."

"Capable Management Company, this is Hal Jacobs."

Capable Management. Man, Angela couldn't have a worse landlord. We received hundreds of complaints against them at Brooklyn Legal. "Mr. Jacobs, this is Matthew McConnell, and I represent Angela Smith. I understand you're raising Miss Smith's rent in June."

"I have the right," Mr. Jacobs said, "and if she can afford a lawyer, she can afford an increase in rent."

Should I tell him I'm being paid only in food so far? "Why are you raising the rent, Mr. Jacobs?"

"La Estrella is opening across the street from her," Mr. Jacobs said.

"We both know La Estrella might not last through the spring," Matthew said. "You saw what happened to Starbucks a few years ago. They put too many stores out there and lost a ton of money."

"I believe La Estrella is different," Mr. Jacobs said. "It fits the neighborhood."

He has a point. The neighborhood is much more Hispanic than when I was young. "Mr. Jacobs, there are at least two dozen coffee shops in Williamsburg that I know of. One more won't make much of a difference. Williamsburgers are a loyal breed. They stick to their favorite coffee shop."

"Until they close," Mr. Jacobs said.

Nice guy. "Aren't you worried that the rent increase will put Miss Smith out of business?"

"So it puts her out of business," Mr. Jacobs said. "That's the way things go sometimes."

Jerk. "And then you'll have to lease out this space to someone new."

"I already have much interest in her property," he said. "*Much.*"

In your dreams, Hal. "Has Miss Smith ever been late on her payments?"

Silence.

"Mr. Jacobs?"

"No," he said. "No, she hasn't."

Matthew covered the phone. "Angela, how many years have you been here?"

"My family has been in this space for forty years," Angela said.

Wow. This is a family business, and I know nothing about her family. He uncovered the phone. "Has Miss Smith or her family ever been late on a payment in forty years?"

"No."

"Mr. Jacobs, that's almost five hundred on-time payments," Matthew said. "Isn't that rare?"

"Well . . . yes."

"Isn't it nice to get a guarantee in life like that?" Matthew asked. "You can always count on Angela Smith, can't you?"

"Yes, and I will count on her to either pay the increased rent or vacate the premises in June," Mr. Jacobs said. "Good-bye, Mr. McConnell."

Matthew closed his phone.

It buzzed again.

He turned it off.

"He's a tough sell," Matthew said sadly. "How much is the increase?"

"Five hundred a month."

"Ouch." *That man is high in every sense of that word.*

Angela drifted toward the counter. "At least you tried. And thanks for saying what you said about me."

"What'd I say?" Matthew asked.

"That he could always count on me."

"Hey, so can I."

Angela smiled. "Finish your breakfast. It has to be cold."

I think I've made a friend. I like to see her smile. Okay, I like to make *her smile.*

Matthew watched Angela interacting with a steady stream of customers from eight until ten. She greeted each customer by name. She knew everyone's "favorite" before anyone even asked. She cracked jokes, and she smiled the entire time. *She does the soft sell so well, but it's her smile that makes the sale.*

This is her place, this is her life, this is her family.

That smile is genuine.

She doesn't put it on. It radiates. The baristas across the street will be in it only for a paycheck and an occasional tip. They'll smile only because it's in the employee handbook. Angela's smile is her livelihood.

Her family has invested forty years here on Driggs through the good times and the bad. She's open seven days a week in all kinds of weather. Would La Estrella be open during a hurricane or a blizzard? No. If this place closed, Williamsburg would miss her. Her customers would miss her.

I'd miss her.

Around 10:30, during a lull, Matthew approached the counter with his plates.

"I would have gotten to them," Angela said.

"But I work here," Matthew said.

"Temporarily." She wiped the counter. "Why are you still here?"

"I have to clean up later."

"So come back later." She polished the already sparkling surface.

He held up his phone. "I feel safer here."

"Go home," Angela said. "Come back later. I'll still be here."

He snatched the towel from her hand. "I need your undivided attention."

Angela blinked at him. "Okay. You got it."

This feels right. "Angela, what if someone covered the increase in your rent?"

"Who would do something like that?" she asked. "And why?"

I would, because I don't want you to go. You belong here. There would be an incredible void on this street without you. "Well, let's say a once high-flying lawyer needs clients because he's rapidly going broke."

And now she's rapidly blinking. And silent? I think I have stunned her. Very cool.

"And let's further agree that potential clients come into this truly iconic coffee shop every day, a small percentage of whom desperately need a lawyer's help," Matthew said. "If said lawyer can help even one person who comes in to drink your coffee and eat your pastries, word-of-mouth advertising will do the rest, and the lawyer will thrive again."

Angela continued to blink.

Is she breathing? "Angela, I can be a coffeehouse lawyer. You'll be the barista, and I'll be the barrister. What do you think?"

Angela pointed to her sign. "I'm *not* a barista."

"I know," Matthew said. "I was making a play on words. So, Angela, what do you think?"

"I think . . . you're as crazy as Allison is, and I think you're even crazier because I know you're sober." She snatched back the towel.

It's my turn to blink rapidly. "It's a completely logical proposition."

"I've never heard of such a thing." She resumed polishing the counter. "A coffeehouse lawyer?"

"Come on, Angela," Matthew said. "The Italians have had something like this for centuries. You need to see the *guy,* you go in to see the *guy,* you ask to see the *guy,* you see the *guy,* the guy hooks you up, you *owe* the guy . . ."

"The *guy* is crazy," Angela said.

She seriously doesn't like my idea. "But I love this place."

She waved the towel at the middle booth. "You love that booth. It already has your butt prints on the seat."

"Well, it's comfortable," Matthew said, "but you'd need to make some changes if I am going to become your partner."

"My what?" Angela asked.

"Do you have Wi-Fi?" Matthew asked.

Angela shook her head slowly. "Are you kidding? I don't want people loitering in here all day and running up my electric bill. No way."

"But we'd have to get Wi-Fi so I can monitor my Web site and get notifications for any updated legal forms," Matthew said. "Legal forms change pretty often, especially when the Republicans are in office. Oh, and I'd need Wi-Fi to listen to music while I work. I work best to music. We could pipe in an Internet station . . ." *She's frowning.* "You're frowning at me." *And it's especially scary when her eyebrows bunch up like that.*

"I don't need a partner," Angela said.

"Call me an investor then," Matthew said.

"I don't need an investor." She pointed toward the front. "I need *that* eyesore across the street to go out of business so I can keep mine."

"And it will, Angela," Matthew said. "You'll see. And in the meantime, you won't have to worry about the rent. Angela, this is a win-win situation for you."

"And now you *sound* like a lawyer." She shook her head. "I'm not interested."

"Okay, okay." *How do I convince her? I'll have to be honest.* "Look. I need this arrangement more than you know, and I need you the most."

"What do you need me for?" Angela asked.

"I need your advice, your calm in the eye of the storm, your sanity, your . . ." *Don't say "your eyes and your smile," though her eyes are suddenly soft and her smile is creeping upward.* "I need your knowledge of the customers. You know them by name. They like you. They trust you. And if you vouch for me . . ." He shrugged. "See what I'm getting at?"

"Yes, I do," Angela said. "But you didn't really answer my question. What do you need me for?"

I thought I just did answer her question. Hmm. I must not have. "I need you for your coffee. It keeps me awake, and your food keeps my brain working. My brain needs sugar to function. And I can always count on you. I need you more than you need me."

Angela turned away and polished an already gleaming coffee mug. "I doubt that. Thank you for the offer, but . . . no thank you."

My argumentative skills have turned to dung. I'd hate to have Angela on a jury. "Will you at least think about it?"

"I've made my decision." She set down the mug and picked up an equally shiny one.

"Think it over for a few days first," Matthew said. "At least do that, okay?"

"It won't change my decision," Angela said.

"Yes, but it will give me a glimmer of hope."

Angela kept polishing.

She's tough. "And hey, if I'm your partner, I'll be here to help you clean up every night."

Angela spun around. "You'll cover the extra rent *and* help me close?"

"Yes." *I knew I could find the button. She's weakening, I can feel it.*

"Will you put a big neon sign in my window?" Angela asked.

"No," Matthew said. "I won't even need a sign."

"No sign? What kind of advertising is that?"

"I won't need that kind of advertising," Matthew said. "I think the soft sell will work best here." He pointed at the middle booth. "And that booth can be my office."

"Where you can better harass my customers while they stand in line," Angela said.

Angela should be a lawyer, too. He moved close to the counter. "I won't say a word to your customers. I'll be the quietest lawyer you *never* heard."

"How is that going to attract clients?" Angela asked.

"Well, you know everyone who comes in here, and they share things with you," Matthew said. "Let's say they say something like, 'My landlord is ripping me off' or 'They owe me back pay' or 'Where can I get a cheap divorce?' Then *you* say, 'I believe that handsome man in the third booth is a lawyer. Why don't you ask him?' "

Angela smiled broadly. "Oh, I see. You want me to be your pimp."

I didn't see that coming. "No! You wouldn't be my pimp, Angela. You'd be like . . . like a talent scout pushing clients my way. I'd even give you a finder's fee, say, ten percent."

"I get a higher percentage than that on tips, and I'd still feel like a pimp," she said.

Matthew turned away and scratched his head. "You *really* don't want my help."

"I didn't say that, Matthew," Angela said. "I just don't think it's a good idea, okay? This is a coffee shop, not a law office. It's been a coffee shop for forty years, and I'd like to keep it that way."

Matthew looked over his shoulder. "You wouldn't be my pimp."

"I *couldn't* be your pimp, Matthew," Angela said. "I couldn't possibly keep up with all your women."

Matthew went to his booth, sipped the rest of his coffee, and turned. "I'll just get my passport and be off then."

"Your passport?" Angela said.

"It's an old lawyer thing." *That line did not work in this situation.* "When do you want me to come back, Miss Smith?"

Angela's smile faded. "Any time before eight."

"I'll be here before eight then." Matthew stood. "Good-bye, Miss Smith."

Angela looked away. "Good-bye."

On the way home, Matthew walked rapidly and felt a frustration he had never known. *I thought it was the perfect idea! What's her deal? Five hundred a month for a suggestion here or there to a customer. How hard could that be? Sure, it will disrupt her normal routine—at first. Once word of mouth gets around, she won't have to say a thing. I'll be "the guy."*

He slowed down.

Maybe that's it. Maybe she doesn't want me to be "the guy." She's been "the girl" for so long at that shop. Or maybe she wants normal, order, routine, the way things have been, the way things should be. I don't blame her for wanting that. That's what most people want.

He looked into the cloud-filled sky. *And what do I want? I want . . .*

He smiled.

I want to be closer to her.

Imagine that.

I want to be closer to a woman who's a challenge.

Maybe she's right.

Maybe I am insane.

Chapter 12

Matthew arrived at Angela's shop at six, acting as if nothing had happened, as if he hadn't offered Angela the opportunity of a lifetime, as if nothing in the world was wrong. Her rejection of his idea still stung, but he wasn't going to let it show.

He put on his game face as he walked through the door.

"You're really early, Matthew," Angela said.

Matthew stood at attention in front of the counter. "You said before eight o'clock, and it is before eight o'clock."

"You listened to me." She smiled.

Angela will not engage me in conversation, Matthew thought. *I will not be affected by her smile. I am "the Help" with a capital H. The Help does not do any playful repartee with the boss at any time. The Help is only here to work.* "May I get started, Miss Smith?"

Angela seemed to hesitate for a moment, her eyes narrowing. "There are aprons hanging up in the kitchen, and all the cleaning supplies are on a metal shelving unit next to the back door. I doubt any of the aprons will fit you, though."

She wants me to comment about my size. I will not fall for that trap. The Help is wary to her schemes. "I will manage, Miss Smith. May I go behind your counter?"

"Sure."

"Thank you," Matthew said, and he swung smartly around the counter and into the kitchen.

This is a very nice kitchen, Matthew thought. *Two stoves, a grill, a triple sink, a refrigerator that would swallow my entire kitchen, a walk-in freezer, and more cabinets than four houses have. And naturally, it is spotless. And not one but two steel doors, both with at least seven heavy-duty deadbolts. Angela is a smart woman.*

He washed his hands in the middle sink, found an apron, and tied it on. It barely reached his beltline.

I will look ridiculous.

He smiled.

And if I have to look ridiculous, I will go all out in my ridiculousness. The Help is allowed to be ridiculous. It's one of the unwritten truths of the universe.

He found some long, yellow rubber gloves and put them on. He tucked every squirt bottle he could find into his belt. He held a bottle of Windex in one hand and a can of Comet in the other. He was ready.

He marched out of the kitchen and around the counter to face Angela. "Where do I begin?"

Angela laughed. "You look . . ."

Ridiculous, I know. It's my new look. I intend to look ridiculous when people shoot down my ideas from now on. "Where do I begin, Miss Smith?"

Angela straightened and pointed. "Start with the bathrooms."

"Fine."

The two small bathrooms were immaculate. *Does anyone ever use these? I've never seen anyone go into either one. Strange. Coffee should have people running to them.* Nevertheless, Matthew shined what was already shiny, cleaned what was already clean, and sanitized what was already sanitary.

He left the bathroom and planted himself in front of Angela, who was staring to her right. "Miss Smith, you now have the cleanest . . ." *What is she looking at?* Matthew turned to look at the middle booth.

Oh . . . shit.

"Hello, Allison," he said rapidly.

Allison rose immediately and caught her thighs under the booth's table. "Ow." She dropped to the seat and scooted out, rising and trying to hug Matthew, but Matthew stepped back.

"There you are, Boo," she said, hugging the air. "Is your phone broken?" Allison was already drunk, her Heineken breath preceding her in putrid waves.

"No," Matthew said. "My phone works fine. I've had it turned off for most of the day."

"Why, Boo?" Allison moaned. "It's supposed to be our first Valentine's Day together!"

"I had it turned off because I didn't want to talk to you," Matthew said.

"You . . . didn't?" Allison's eyes filled with tears. "Why? I made meatloaf *just* for you. It looks like a heart. Kind of. The right side is bigger than the other. Couldn't be helped. I'm right-handed. You *said* it was your favorite, William."

William? Who's William? "I never said that, Allison."

"But you *did,*" Allison said. "After that romantic night at Coney Island last summer, you said, 'Your meatloaf is my *favorite.*' Remember? You won me a big stuffed bear. It was flink and puffy." She swayed to the side. "Pink and fluffy."

Matthew guided Allison to the booth where she sat and swayed some more. "We've never been to Coney Island, Allison, and you are very drunk."

"I've only been drinking since I got home, but I'm okay." Allison tried to flip her hair off her shoulders and missed several times. "Joey, *baby,* I went home sick after a certain *someone* didn't send me flowers or candy today. Oh, and I got sick last night. I woke up in a *big* puddle of vomit, and you weren't *there!*"

Angela appeared at Matthew's side. "I'll call her a cab," she whispered.

Matthew handed his phone to her.

"But I have a limo waiting for us, Ricky," Allison whined. "We're going to the Yankees–Red Sox game, remember?"

"It's February, Allison," Matthew said. "You and I went to a Rangers hockey game last night."

"The Yankees are playing the Red Sox, Ricky," Allison said. "They're your favorite team!"

"Maybe later, Allison." He looked outside and saw a waiting cab. *Geez, that was quick!* "After you get some sleep." He gently took Allison's arm and helped her out of the booth. "Let's get you safely home, okay?"

Allison looked into Matthew's eyes. "You're taking me home?"

Matthew squeezed Allison between Angela and the front door. "The cab is taking you home."

Allison tried to slump to the floor. "I don't want to go home."

Matthew swept his arm under her legs and picked her up.

"If she pukes," Angela whispered from the doorway, "you're cleaning it up."

Matthew nodded. *Oh boy. I hope Allison didn't eat anything red today.*

"Where are we going?" Allison asked.

Matthew leaned Allison against the front door of the cab and opened the back door. "To your place."

Allison smiled. "And we're going to have such a *good* time."

Matthew wrestled Allison into the backseat, pressed the lock, and closed the door. He handed a twenty to the driver. "Take her to two-forty-one Wythe. And could you make sure she gets inside her apartment?"

"All right, all right," the driver said.

That wasn't very convincing. Matthew stared him down. "I am this woman's lawyer, and I had better not hear of anything bad happening to her."

The driver looked at Matthew's apron and yellow gloves. "You're a lawyer?"

"Yes," Matthew said. "One who has successfully sued cab drivers into oblivion."

"All right, all right," the driver said. "I'll make sure she gets into her apartment."

"Number four, second floor," Matthew said. "The keys are probably in her purse. It's the gold key with the pink streak on it."

"All right, all right."

Matthew looked past the driver into the back. "Allison?"

"Johnny, you really should use more lotion on your hands," Allison said. "They felt all rubbery. And you could really use some sun." She rolled down the window to wave at Angela. "Oh, I didn't mean *you,* sweetie. Bye."

The cab rolled away.

Matthew reentered the shop and closed the door behind him. "Sorry about that."

Angela stood a few feet back from the door. "What did she say to me?"

"It's not important." He sighed. "What do you need me to clean next, Miss Smith?" *The Help is back.*

Angela stepped in front of him. "What did she say?"

Matthew shook his head. "She said I needed more sun . . . but not *you,* sweetie."

"Bitch," Angela said. "I'm not *that* dark."

"She was blind drunk, Angela," Matthew said. "You're a wonderful shade of brown." *Oops. The Help is not supposed to compliment the boss.* He sighed. *I'm not very good at being the Help.* "I'm sorry I'm the cause of that little show, Angela. If I had listened to you, she wouldn't have been here tonight."

"You handled it pretty well," Angela said. "What's she weigh, fifty pounds?"

Matthew sighed. "She's heavier than she looks. What's next?"

Angela smiled. "I don't know, Mr. McConnell. Your life is filled with so much drama. I couldn't even dream of what's next."

Matthew slumped into the nearest booth, removing his gloves and shooting them against the wall. "Five in a row. Five dates from hell in a *row,* and this last one keeps coming out of the alcoholic depths of hell to haunt me. How can I be so unlucky?"

Angela stood near the edge of the table. "Five? I must have lost count. There was Jade the ex-con with the great right cross from Queens, Victoria the debutante from Manhattan who has a rat-dog and an ugly friend, Mary the not-so-Christian Christian from the Bronx, and Allison the drunk from Long Island who doesn't even know your name and thinks I'm black when I'm obviously dark brown. Who'd I miss?"

Angela has an outstanding memory. "The first one. Monique Freitas, the party girl from Bushwick."

Angela slid into the booth. "And how did she give you hell?"

Why not? "Monique has a sizable condom collection and likes to dry-hump everyone but her date while dancing at The Cove."

Angela blinked and squinted. "How big of a collection does she have?"

"I think she buys in bulk," Matthew said. "She must use coupons. Some even glow in the dark."

Angela bit her lower lip. “You sure know how to pick ’em.”

“And it all began because Joy left me for a Dominican exchange teacher two weeks ago.” He loosened the string at the back of his apron.

“And Joy was . . .”

“My girlfriend from Staten Island by way of Honduras.”

Angela laughed again. “You get around, don’t you?”

“I’m outwardly mobile.”

“Aren’t you exhausted?” Angela asked.

Matthew nodded. “I am tired. I’m tired of choosing the wrong women.”

“At least you know what you don’t want, right?” Angela said. “That’s a blessing, isn’t it? A lot of people go through life without knowing what they want. You now have some idea.”

“Process of elimination, huh?” Matthew said.

Angela shrugged. “I guess.”

“What if I eliminate myself from the equation?” Matthew asked.

Angela smiled. “You’ll certainly get more sleep.”

“True.” He slid on the gloves and flexed his fingers. “I had better get back to work.” He slid out of the booth and headed to the back tables. “Do these tables need cleaning?”

“Yes.” Angela returned to the counter and began to count down the register. “What were you saying when you came out of the bathroom?”

Matthew paused from wiping yet another clean surface. “That your bathrooms are pristine.”

“Because I already cleaned them an hour before you arrived,” Angela said.

Matthew straightened up. “You did?”

“I did.”

“Why?” Matthew asked.

“Mainly so I can get off my feet quicker,” Angela said. “I don’t want you holding me up.”

Matthew moved to another clean table. “How would I hold you up? Aren’t I cutting your cleaning time in half?”

“You took twenty minutes to clean two already clean bathrooms,” Angela said.

Matthew squirted the table. "I was being thorough."

"You were being slow," Angela said. "I was testing you, and you should have noticed that they were already clean."

Matthew smiled. "So now they're twice as clean."

"I knocked both of them out in five minutes," Angela said. "I've already cleaned most of the kitchen, too."

"I noticed." He looked at the rest of the tables. "They're already clean, too, huh?"

Angela nodded.

"What's left?" Matthew asked.

"The showcase and the counter, but I don't do them until eight," Angela said. "After that, I sweep and mop the entire place."

Matthew refolded his towel. "So I just sit here until eight?"

"You could sweep and mop the kitchen," Angela said. "I'm done for the night back there."

He walked slowly around the counter. "How long *should* it take me?"

"Five minutes."

"Yes, Miss Smith."

He stood in the kitchen and didn't see a single speck of dirt, dust, flour, or debris on the floor.

"And put a new mop head on before you mop," Angela said. "The one on there is nasty."

"Yes, Miss Smith." *I would say, "Aye, aye, Captain Angela," but that would make me a lowly sailor on the Good Ship Sweet Treats.*

It took Matthew eight minutes to sweep and mop the tiny kitchen but only because he had trouble centering the new mop head and tightening it down.

He saw Angela standing in the doorway. "Well?" he asked.

"You used too much bleach," Angela said. "It'll take longer to dry, and it'll be slippery in the morning. Rinse out your mop thoroughly and go over it again only with water."

Matthew mopped the kitchen again.

It wasn't as slippery.

At eight o'clock, Angela turned all the locks on the front door and polished the showcase while Matthew mopped the dining area. She looked up at the clock once she was done. "Eight oh five. Not bad. For a lawyer."

Matthew took off his apron, laying it over his arm. "A lawyer who did this at NYU to help pay his bills."

Angela recounted her bills at the counter. "Yeah?"

"All four years," Matthew said. "I wore a hairnet and everything."

She wrote something down. "I can't see you in a hairnet."

"My hair was longer then." He held up the apron. "I'll take this home and wash it."

"I'll wash it," Angela said.

"I'll do it," Matthew said. "I make the mess, I clean it up. See you tomorrow."

Angela looked past him and out the window. "We might not have much to clean up tomorrow."

I have nothing to say to that. "I'll try to be messier tomorrow then. Good night, Miss Smith."

Angela nodded, her eyes still staring across the street.

She looks so sad. "You might see me for breakfast, and I think I want something different tomorrow. Sausage and waffles, lots of butter and syrup. Okay?"

Angela sighed. "Okay."

"Lots of butter."

"And syrup," Angela said. "I heard you."

"Good night, Angela."

Angela sighed loudly and left the counter. "Good night, man, now get out of here so I can get off my feet."

But you haven't smiled yet. "You know, I could carry you wherever you need to go to give relief to your sore, tired feet. What do you weigh, about fifty pounds?"

"Just . . ." Angela smiled. "Just get on, man."

Angela flicked open the locks, opened the door, and stood back.

"Good night, Angela."

Angela nodded. "Good night, Matthew."

He stood at the door watching Angela locking him out, hoping for another smile.

He didn't get one.

At least I made her smile a few times tonight. I like that smile. I wish I could help her, though. But how do you help a woman who doesn't want to be helped? How do you cheer up a woman who doesn't want to be cheered up? What's most important—how do I wash this apron without any bleach?

Answer: I can't.

Matthew bought some bleach at Melo's and washed the apron in his bathtub. He wrung it out, ironed it on the pockmarked kitchen table until it was almost dry, and hung it in the closet.

I don't do my own laundry for days, but I wash an apron the second I get it home.

I'm sure that means something.

Thanks to WiggyWoo, he sat in his chair and checked his Web site for traffic and his e-mail for clients.

Nothing, as usual.

He checked another e-mail account and found spam for Cialis and Viagra.

Not yet.

He set his laptop aside.

How can I make Angela see that she needs me?

Answer: I can't. That woman doesn't need anyone.

Okay. Think. How can I get her to change her mind?

Answer: I can't. That woman doesn't change her mind.

There has to be a way.

He looked at his reflection in the window.

Some Valentine's Day this has been.

Chapter 13

His apron carefully folded in the pocket of his windbreaker, Matthew jogged down Havemeyer to the Dime Savings Bank ATM across from La Guardia Playground, withdrew forty dollars, and then doubled back, taking South 3rd to Driggs and Angela's, arriving a little after six AM.

He was glad he had hurried.

On the table at the middle booth, a stack of waffles bathed in butter and soaked in syrup, four links of sausage, and a large house blend sat steaming next to a small bowl of assorted gumdrops.

"Good morning," he said. *Gumdrops, too? I wonder why.*

Angela smiled. "Good morning."

Matthew sat. "This looks great. What's with the gumdrops?"

"It's National Gumdrop Day." She picked up a plate of pastries. "Didn't you know?"

"No, but thanks."

She came over to the table and set down the plate. "It's also Singles Awareness Day, but I didn't think you'd want a reminder of that."

Singles Awareness Day, and the day after Valentine's Day. How cruel! Great timing, though. He popped a cherry gumdrop into his mouth. "How do you know all these holidays?"

"I have a notebook full of them," Angela said. "It gives me something different to say every morning besides, 'Good morning.' "

Matthew pulled the apron out of his pocket. "It's a bit wrinkled.

I did try to iron it. My kitchen table isn't a very good ironing board."

Angela took the apron and smelled it. "You tried. It smells like bleach and vanilla."

At least she didn't say oranges. "Yes. Vanilla. Joy's scent permeates everything in my apartment."

"Brew coffee," Angela said. "That'll knock it out."

He picked up his cup. "I'd rather drink yours."

"I didn't say to *drink* it," Angela said. "Just brew it."

"I will." He slid to his right. "Care to join me?"

"I'm really busy," she said.

"I understand."

Customers poured in steadily for the next two hours, most of them getting their coffee and leaving immediately. The last two in line, Mr. and Mrs. Thomas, an older black couple in their seventies, took some time to talk to Angela.

"When's the ribbon cutting?" Mrs. Thomas asked.

"Nine o'clock," Angela said.

"Nine?" Mr. Thomas said. "That's foolish. Most people are already at work *with* their coffee by nine o' clock." He dropped his change into the tip jar. "I will always come here, Angela."

"You got that right," Mrs. Thomas said. "Best cup of coffee in New York and at the lowest price, too."

I should be writing this stuff down. Maybe all Angela needs is a Web site, not that I'm an expert on Web sites. I wonder if Smith's Sweet Treats and Coffee ever had a newspaper review. How do you go about getting one of those? A review or a story in the Brooklyn Daily Eagle *might do the trick. I'll bet there are some reporters over there at La Estrella right now hyping up the grand opening.*

During a lull, Matthew brought his plates to the counter, dumping the rest of the gumdrops into his hand. "I can take these back to the kitchen if you want."

Angela collected the plates. "No problem."

Matthew handed her a twenty. "I'm going for a little walk."

"You want your change?" she asked.

"No." He smiled. "Breakfast was delicious."

"Will I see you later?" she asked.

"Sure," Matthew said, backing away. "I'll be back in a few minutes. I just want to do a little reconnaissance across the street."

"I already know what's on their menu," Angela said.

Matthew drifted back to the counter. "You've seen their menu?"

Angela nodded. "Everything they sell is pre-packaged: the coffee, the pastries, and their so-called 'fresh-baked cookies.' All they're doing is throwing them in a microwave. There's nothing homemade over there, but the word 'homemade' is in all their advertising."

"Do you know what they're charging?" Matthew asked.

Angela shook her head. "Their prices vary by location."

He tapped the counter. "Then I will see how much their prices vary at *that* location."

Matthew crossed the street and watched a speedy ribbon-cutting ceremony filmed by Channel 11. *What was that? Thirty seconds?* He then waded through a mostly younger crowd and went inside.

I have just entered a Burger King. Who decided red and yellow were somehow Hispanic?

Matthew saw plenty of places to sit, including easy chairs, sofas, loveseats, and red and yellow plastic chairs arranged around red and yellow checkerboard tables. Several high tables without seats faced the window. *How considerate of them. Hey, get off the subway or bus where you just stood for half an hour and take a load off standing here with your overpriced coffee.*

Matthew marveled at the prices. *Five bucks a cup to* start. *If you bought only one cup daily, you'd be out more than eighteen hundred bucks a year!*

He watched the young and pretty baristas at work, each checking "how-to-make" signs and adding lots of foam. *The service is slow. I know they'll become more efficient, but the line is threatening to go out the door into the cold.* He watched the totals on the register for a few minutes. *The average price for each order is about seven bucks. Angela has nothing to worry about.*

He didn't see anyone interviewing a manager, customer, or worker inside. *Maybe I'll post a scathing review online for La Estrella and a glowing one for Angela at zagat.com or citysearch.com.*

He returned to Angela's, purposefully looking pitiful.

Angela's eyes widened. "Well?"

Matthew smiled. "You could *double* the cost of your largest cup and it will *still* cost less than what they're charging. Five bucks for a large, two or more bucks for the additives, flavorings, and foam."

Angela placed her hands on the counter. "That's insane. Seven bucks? How many varieties of coffee do they serve?"

"Too many," Matthew said. "That's the problem with those places. They offer too many choices, and they have all these cutesy names like Guadalajara Gold and Tijuana Tango."

"Sounds like they're selling marijuana," Angela whispered.

It does. "And the average time from order to payment is three minutes," Matthew said. "The lines will be long, Angela, and the kids working in there are too precise. It will be like McDonald's—the same taste in every cup. They were charging a buck for whipped cream. I'd bring my own can."

"What about food?" she asked.

"I couldn't smell a thing but the coffee and the paint," Matthew said. "I didn't see anyone getting food."

"What's the seating like?" Angela asked.

"Very plush, and they're going to regret it," Matthew said. "Yellow and red sofas and easy chairs. If they haven't been Scotchguarded, one spill and they'll be ruined. Small tables, a few stand-ups, a half dozen booths. Standard ceiling tiles. Nothing like the classy ceiling like you have here, and the glare from the morning sun is blinding. Everything is red and yellow, right down to the napkins. I've been in nicer Burger Kings. That place definitely has no soul."

He expected Angela to be happy. He expected Angela to jump for joy. He expected her to relax.

She didn't.

"The line looked long," she said.

"Have you ever seen any of those people in here?" Matthew asked.

"I wasn't looking," Angela said quickly.

Yes, she was. "They are definitely a younger crowd who wants to pay way too much for the *experience* of paying way too much for a cup of coffee. They want the *privilege* of telling their friends they spent seven bucks for a cup of coffee. You can relax."

Angela sighed. "Until they wise up and lower their prices. How many people were working behind the counter?"

"Four."

Angela shook her head. "Four. How can they afford that many? What are their hours?"

Oops. "I didn't check. Be right back."

He borrowed a pen and a napkin and crossed the street. He found La Estrella's hours stenciled along the bottom of the front window and wrote them down.

"Who are *you* with?"

Matthew turned to face the speaker. "With?"

The woman waved a notepad. "Which paper? Oh, that's a napkin. Sorry."

Matthew smiled at the woman, who had an olive tone to her brownish skin, furry eyebrows, medium frizzy hair, and dark brown eyes. Nicely proportioned, she had smiling eyes and thin lips like Angela's. "I'm just writing down their hours," Matthew said. "Who are you with?"

"The *Daily Eagle.*" She offered her hand. "Felisa Vecchi."

Matthew shook it crisply. "Matthew."

Felisa looked around him. "There's nothing going on here. This is the third one I've done this month. They've opened so many around the city there's really no story left to tell."

Matthew looked across the street. "There *is* a story to tell over there."

"Smith's Sweet Treats," Felisa said. "I haven't been there in years. They're still in business?"

"Yes, so you see the inherent conflict." He raised his eyebrows.

"I do," she said.

Matthew stuffed the napkin into his pocket. "It might make a good story. Williamsburg landmark takes on a big, mean chain. Will Goliath kill David, or will David rise up and slay the newcomer?"

"Are you in advertising?" Felisa asked.

"Law," Matthew said. "Matthew McConnell at your service."

Felisa cocked her head. "Your name sounds familiar."

I was in all the papers and eventually got a mention in Newsweek *for my meltdown as "the lawyer who said no to frivolous lawsuits" and "the man who may be the last honest lawyer left on earth." SYG's attempt to limit its exposure wasn't very effective.* "I used to work for Schwartz, Yevgeny—"

"And Ginsberg," Felisa interrupted. "You're the honest lawyer."

Guilty as charged.

"What are you doing now?" Felisa asked, flipping to a clean page on her notepad.

"I have my own practice," Matthew said, "but the real story is across the street. I'll even buy you your first cup of coffee."

Felisa smiled. "Deal." She started across the street, and Matthew followed.

Matthew opened the door for Felisa, she entered, and he moved quickly to the counter. "Angela, a large cup of your house blend for my friend Felisa from the *Daily Eagle.*" He whispered, "Is my tab still good?"

Angela nodded and filled a large cup.

"This shop hasn't changed much since I was a kid," Felisa said. "I used to press my nose on the glass to look at all the cookies. Were you here twenty years ago?"

"Yes," Angela said.

Felisa readied her notepad. "What do you think about La Estrella opening just across the street from you?"

Angela handed Felisa the cup. "I need to consult with my lawyer first. Do you mind?"

"Not at all," Felisa said.

Angela walked back to the kitchen entrance, and Matthew followed. "Why did you bring her over here?" she whispered tersely.

"To give you some free advertising," he whispered. "I think she wants to write a David and Goliath piece. Go throw some stones."

"I'd rather not," Angela said. "She should be interviewing customers, not me, because it doesn't matter what *I* think. Of course I think I have the best coffee, pastries, and cookies in Williamsburg. But if *I* say it . . ."

"I see your point." *Her eyes get so fiery sometimes. Fierce. I like that.*

"And she can't interview you, either," Angela said. "I've already told her you're my lawyer. Anything coming out your mouth would be a lie."

"She thinks I'm an honest lawyer," Matthew said.

"There's no such thing," Angela said.

Should I? I think I should. "Perhaps. But I am a lawyer without an office. Tragic, really. I am a lawyer who wants to contribute to the general good of the coffee shop and its beautiful owner as well, but someone with fierce eyes won't let me. This isn't tragic. It's a travesty. No justice, no peace. Fight the power."

"I already told you no," Angela whispered.

Matthew puffed out his chest. "I feel like talking a great deal today for some reason. It must have been the gumdrops. All those little shots of sugar."

"Matthew, please don't." She put her hand on his arm.

We have contact. "Angela, all I need is a comfortable booth and someone to point needy people my way," Matthew said. "That's all."

Angela removed her hand. "No."

"But I have so many good quotes to give her today," Matthew said. "When I have a sugar rush, words just rush out of my mouth."

"You *can't* be quoted," Angela said. "Get her to talk to some customers while they're still here."

I can't win. "*After* you answer her question. I'm kind of curious, too."

"You already know what I think," Angela said.

"No, I don't think I do." *You're hard to read, Miss Angela Smith.*

Angela shook her head. "All right. I'll give her one quote and that's it."

And I won't stop talking until the sun sets. He walked around the counter, smiled at Felisa, and sat in "his" booth.

Angela returned to the counter and stared at Felisa. "What do I think of them? I don't. I have looked out that window since I was a child, and I have seen a number of businesses move into that space only to leave and have another take its place."

"So you're saying La Estrella won't be here long," Felisa said.

"I didn't say that, and don't you write that I did," Angela said, cutting her eyes to Matthew. "All I know is that this place has been here forty years. La Estrella as a *company* has only been around for ten years. This place has stood the test of time, and I defy anyone in New York to find a better large cup of coffee and a better homemade pastry and all for less than five bucks." She took a deep breath. "Would you like to try a pastry? I have apple and blackberry today."

"Apple sounds good." Felisa turned and saw Matthew. "May I join you?"

Matthew looked at Angela. "No comment."

Angela smiled.

Felisa walked over to him. "You're no fun."

"And I intend to stay that way," Matthew said. "I have been instructed by my client not to talk to you. Why not interview some real customers?"

"You're not a real customer, Mr. McConnell?" Felisa asked.

Matthew smiled at Angela. *You haven't defeated me yet.* "You know, Felisa, I *am* becoming a regular fixture here."

Felisa wrote it down.

"Oh no, Angela," Matthew said. "She wrote down what I just said. What will she write down next?"

Angela's mouth parted slightly.

I have her attention. Good. "Felisa, I love this place. It has atmosphere. It has soul. It's open from six until eight, while those knuckleheads across the street are open seven to seven and are closed all day on Sundays."

Angela mouthed, "Really?"

Matthew nodded.

Felisa finished writing. "And how long have you been a fixture here?"

"I can't get the man to leave," Angela said.

Now Angela jumps in, Matthew thought. *This is going to be some story.*

Felisa laughs. "This is good."

"Angela," Matthew said, "tell her why I *can't* leave."

Angela's eyes blazed briefly before softening. "Because . . . because that booth you're sitting in is his office."

Victory is within my grasp!

Felisa looked up from her notepad. "This booth is your office."

Matthew shrugged.

Angela shook her head.

Matthew smiled.

Angela sighed, closed her eyes, and nodded.

I won! Victory is mine!

"Yes, indeed it is," Matthew said. "I am a coffeeshop lawyer, a barrister for the sweetest barista who ever lived. Oh, but don't write that Angela is a barista. She's not a barista. She *brews* and *pours* coffee."

"So how's business in this booth?" Felisa asked.

Well, my business is so new I haven't actually had any. "The first consultation is always free, provided, of course, that you buy a cup of coffee."

Felisa turned to Angela. "So you two are business partners."

Angela approached the booth. "Unofficially. I have yet to see a written contract."

One of these napkins will have to do. "Soon, Miss Smith, soon."

"I want to see that contract today, Mr. McConnell," Angela said. "Before the close of business."

"Yes, ma'am." Matthew smiled.

Angela scowled.

While Felisa interviewed other customers, Matthew wrote a simple contract on a napkin:

> I, Matthew Mark McConnell agree to pay Angela Smith $500 a month starting today for the right to conduct business as a lawyer in the third booth of Smith's Sweet Treats and Coffee on Driggs Avenue, Williamsburg, Brooklyn, New York, USA.

He took it up to her. "Here's the contract."

Angela read it quickly. "I don't need payment now, remember? I need it in June when my rent goes up."

"Take it while you can get it, Angela," Matthew said. "I may not have all of it in June. And this will provide the money for our upgrades."

"What upgrades?" she asked.

"Wi-Fi for starters," Matthew said. "And music. And more seating for open-mike night."

"What open-mike night?" Angela asked.

"You want some of that trendy, hipster money, don't you?" Matthew asked. "Trendy hipsters like to spend money on poetry readings, book talks, and solo musicians. They also like groups like Floetry to serenade them with words. We'll need to get a decent sound system, too."

Angela blinked. "Absolutely *no* karaoke."

"I heartily agree," Matthew said. "That would lower property values from here to Bushwick."

"Do we really have to do all that?" Angela asked.

"Yes," Matthew said. "You said something about the lack of an arts venue in this neighborhood. *This* could be that venue."

"But that would mean later hours," Angela said.

"But only one night a week, say, Friday or Saturday, and maybe only once or twice a month," Matthew said. "This place could fill a void in this neighborhood."

"Cameo is six short blocks away," Angela said.

"You ever been to Cameo?" Matthew asked.

Angela shook her head.

"It's small," Matthew said. "You know how many people you could get in here on a Friday night?"

"We'll talk more about this later," Angela said.

"I like talking to you, *partner,*" Matthew said.

"Oh please." Angela looked at Felisa. "Is *she* your type?"

In another life, yes. Today . . . "No."

"She's Cuban or Italian or both or something," Angela said. "I thought you liked that nice, creamy, tan skin."

I do. "She's too perky."

"Perky?" Angela said.

"She's too perky, energetic, and outgoing," Matthew said. "I'm beginning to prefer nervous, brooding, and worried." He looked into her eyes. "And brown. Most definitely brown."

Angela looked down, a small smile creeping across her lips. "You know anyone like that?"

"I work for her," Matthew said. "She makes me mop the kitchen twice because I use too much bleach."

"She sounds evil." Angela quickly signed the napkin.

"She's not so bad, once you get to know her," Matthew said, "and she has a brilliant smile."

Angela handed the napkin to Matthew. "You still owe her two nights' work."

"Only two? I promised to help you clean up every night."

"Yes, you did, didn't you?" Angela said. "It's not on this contract. All I get is money, Matthew Mark. Do you have a brother named Luke John?"

"Luckily, I'm an only child," Matthew said. "I would have hated to have a sister named The Acts Romans. We will add an addendum to our contract. Miss Smith, what is your middle name?"

Angela closed her eyes. "Simone." She opened them. "And don't give me any lip over my initials."

"I wasn't going to say a thing." He flipped over the contract, writing as he said, "I also promise Angela Simone Smith, who has an extremely *nice, firm* set of initials, to help her close the shop nightly."

Angela looked at the napkin. "You didn't write that."

Matthew turned the napkin around.

"You wrote that." She picked up the napkin. "You really wrote that."

"Because it's true," Matthew whispered.

Angela slipped the napkin into her apron pocket. "You don't write all your legal contracts this way, do you?"

Is she blushing? I can't tell. I hope she is. "Only this one."

Angela turned away to the register and wiped some dust from the screen. "Good."

After Felisa left with the promise to run the story in the next edition, the Friday rush became a trickle. Matthew sipped another cup of coffee while Angela moved back and forth from the kitchen to the display case restocking her sweet treats.

Ah. This is peace. This is a quiet place to think. A great cup of coffee, one more pastry, and—

A thunderous pounding sounded from the kitchen.

Angela literally jumped, and she seemed to frown. "It's my weekly delivery."

"You don't go shopping for all your exotic ingredients?" Matthew asked.

Angela wiped her hands with a towel. "I don't have the time. Everything is closed by the time I'm closed. I'll be in the back putting things away."

Matthew left the booth. "I could do it for you."

"Yes, but I know where everything goes," Angela said.

The pounding continued.

"I could watch and learn," Matthew said.

"Just . . . come get me if anyone comes in." She pointed to the counter.

Matthew went behind the counter. "I could serve them."

Angela shook her head. "Just come get me, and I'll do the serving. Agreed?"

"Okay."

An older black woman breezed in a few minutes later, squinting up at Matthew. "Where's Angela?"

"In the back," Matthew said. "She has a delivery." *Do I get Angela? No. I can do this.* "How may I help you?"

The woman pointed at the tray of turnovers. "A half dozen of those, what are they, raspberry?"

"Blackberry," Matthew said.

"A half dozen of those, a half dozen apple turnovers—are they fresh?"

"Just baked half an hour ago." *I know how to do the soft sell, too.*

"A half dozen of those and . . . two dozen chocolate chip cookies," the woman said. "You work here long?"

"This is my first day."

Matthew expertly collected, wrapped, and bagged her order. "That will be . . ." He checked the price list taped to the counter. "Twenty-six dollars even."

"Twenty . . . *six?*" The woman's eyes popped.

"Yes, ma'am."

The woman handed him a twenty and a ten.

"Would you like some coffee to go?" Matthew asked, ringing up her order and pulling out four ones. "The house blend is especially delicious today." He handed her the money.

"No, thank you." The woman looked around him.

"Is something wrong?" he asked.

The woman shrugged. "No. I've just never seen anyone but Angela or her parents working here, that's all."

Matthew smiled. "I'm Matthew."

"Hello." The woman took her bag. "Tell Angela that Bet was here."

"I will," Matthew said. "You have a great day."

Bet nodded. "You, too."

Piece of cake. I could do this all day and all night.

Angela returned to the counter ten minutes later. She stared into the showcase. "Have you been eating on the job?"

"Bet was here," Matthew said. "She likes your pastries, too."

"How much did you charge her?" Angela asked.

He pointed at the price list. "What it says here."

"Oh no!" Angela cried. "Did she just leave?"

Uh-oh. "About ten minutes ago. Why?"

Angela bumped her hip into his thigh. "I told you to come get me."

"Did I do something wrong?" Matthew asked.

Angela sighed. "Bet is one of my mama's oldest friends. I have *never* charged her full price."

Oops. "I'm sorry."

"What she must think . . ." She shook her head. "It's not your fault. You didn't know." She looked into his eyes. "And she didn't fuss about paying?"

"Not at all."

Angela smiled. "I've been undercharging that woman for ten years at least. You done good, McConnell."

"Thank you, Angela Simone."

"Hush."

Later that evening, after he swept and mopped the kitchen in four minutes, he leaned on his mop and watched Angela polishing the glass in front of the display case.

Angela is a good woman. She's . . . good. Kind, down-to-earth, real. She takes care of family friends. She doesn't give up easily. She works so hard.

And she does have an excellent set of initials. I like the way it wiggles from side to side while she polishes—

"You lose something?" Angela asked.

Just my train of thought. "No."

"Wipe some tables, man."

"Wiping."

While Matthew turned the tables into virtual mirrors of dark wood, Angela counted down her register.

"Did you have a good day?" Matthew asked.

"This doesn't make sense," Angela said. "I made about the same for a normal Friday. Maybe a little more."

Matthew polished away. "And on the day La Estrella had its grand opening. What do you know about that?"

He glanced at Angela and found her smiling.

"It's only because you overcharged Bet," Angela said.

"Oh," Matthew said. "I'm sure *that's* the reason." He leaned on the counter. *I want to ask her out so badly, but she looks so tired.* "Same time tomorrow?"

"Same time tomorrow."

Matthew stuck out his hand. "Thanks, partner."

Angela shook his hand once and dropped it. "I'm still not exactly sure how you did that to me. I'm not normally manipulated that easily."

"Do you regret taking me on?" He untied his apron and took it off.

"No, and don't you ever give me a reason to regret it," she said.

"I won't." *I have the overwhelming need to hug her, but there's a counter between us.* "Good night, Angela Simone Smith."

"I never should have told you my middle name," she said softly. "Good night, Matthew Mark McConnell."

"Will you walk me to the door?" Matthew asked.

Angela came around the counter and went straight to the door. Matthew had to hustle to catch up. She opened the door, Matthew stepped out, and she shut and locked it rapidly behind him.

"Good night," he said.

Angela nodded.

Matthew watched her walk back to the counter, bag her money and receipts, and turn off the lights before disappearing into the kitchen. A few moments later, the kitchen light winked out.

Matthew's heart sank as he looked into the darkened shop. *Why am I feeling this? I know I'll be back tomorrow, but there's something . . . sad about a dark coffee shop.*

No. That's not why my heart hurts.

I'm already missing Angela's smile. Is this what lonely feels like? I haven't felt it for so long.

"Good night, Angela," he whispered.

I didn't really know how lonely I was until I saw your smile.

Chapter 14

Matthew had barely sat down in his booth and was about to devour a stack of pancakes and crispy bacon early Saturday morning when a middle-aged black woman wearing an oversized overcoat and carrying a huge purse burst through the door, yelling, "You the lawyer I read about in the *Daily Eagle* this morning?"

The story is out. But how? The Daily Eagle *only comes out Monday through Friday.* "You read it in the *Eagle?*"

"Yeah, the online one," the woman said. "It was the first story on the page. So are you the lawyer or aren't you?"

Thank you, Felisa. Matthew put down his fork. "Yes, ma'am. I am Matthew McConnell, attorney-at-law. Please sit. Would you like some coffee?"

"I'm good." She sat across from him. "You don't look like a lawyer."

I knew I shouldn't have worn plain gray sweats and my Chucks today. "It's Saturday."

Mrs. James blinked.

"How may I help you?" Matthew asked.

"The police have my son," she said.

I should be taking notes. Why didn't I bring my briefcase or any legal pads? I should have had more faith. "One sec." He went to the counter. "Angela, do you have a pen and some paper I can borrow?"

Angela handed him an order pad and a pen. "And you call yourself a lawyer," she whispered.

"Thanks."

He picked up the order pad and pen, and as he slid into the booth, he snatched and ate a slice of bacon. "Forgive me. I'm hungry. What is your name, ma'am?"

"Toni James, with an I."

Matthew wrote it down. "And your son's name?"

"Xavier."

Matthew wrote it down. "What is he being charged with?"

Mrs. James looked side to side and whispered, "Assaulting a policeman."

He wrote it down. "How exactly did he assault the policeman?"

"They *said* Xavier spit in his face," Mrs. James said, "but the only thing my boy does is spit rhymes. He goes by XS. Everybody around here knows him by that name. He's only eighteen."

Angela brought over a mug of coffee.

"Thank you, Angela," Mrs. James said.

"You're welcome, Mrs. James," Angela said. "It's been a while, huh?"

Mrs. James sipped her coffee. "Mmm. Your coffee is still as good as gold. How's your mama doin'?"

"She's fine," Angela said. "How's Mr. James?"

"Same ol' badass as always," Mrs. James said.

Matthew blinked at Angela, and Angela rolled her eyes and returned to the counter.

"Mrs. James, you say Xavier spit in an officer's face," Matthew said.

"That's what they *said* he did," Mrs. James said. "He was over at Artist and Fleas on North Seventh with his boys free-styling, you know, rapping, two nights ago. They get a big crowd most nights. Sometimes people even give them money. Tourists, mostly. Two nights ago, two cops got too close to my son. Xavier ain't a bad kid. He would never do such a thing on purpose."

"Do they have any evidence?" Matthew asked.

"They *say* they got Xavier's DNA and two eyewitnesses, one of them the cop's partner," Mrs. James said. "I couldn't afford the bail, and his court-appointed lawyer wants him to plead guilty and get eighteen months. Can you believe that shit?"

Matthew circled Xavier's age. "Has he ever been in trouble before?"

"No."

"Before we go any further, Mrs. James, you have to know that I don't have a lot of experience with criminal cases," Matthew said.

Mrs. James sat back. "You got some serious charges dropped over in Queens, didn't you? And that girl broke a cop's nose."

News travels fast. Thanks, Jade. "I was really lucky with that case." *The cop luckily grabbed Jade's ass.*

"Well, I need some more of your luck," Mrs. James said. "And besides, anyone is better than the lawyer he's got. The man didn't even read Xavier's file, just told Xavier to take the deal."

"What's his attorney's name?" Matthew asked.

"Marty Kowalski."

Farty Marty "Take the Deal" Kowalski is still at it. Xavier doesn't have a prayer if Marty's "working" the case. "Mrs. James, you enjoy your coffee while I consult with my business partner."

Mrs. James squinted. "Okay."

Matthew rose and went to the counter. "What do you think? I know you were listening."

"You're the lawyer, not me," Angela said.

"I know that, but you know them," Matthew said. "I just want some family background."

"They're good people," Angela said. "I know Xavier, too. Not a bad rapper either. He calls himself a street poet. He can really flow."

"Good kid?"

"He never gave me any trouble," Angela said. "I let him sweep up one summer when he was maybe ten. He was saving up for a turntable."

Matthew turned toward Mrs. James. "Mrs. James, did Xavier graduate high school?"

"A semester late, but he did it," Mrs. James said. "But what you talking to Angela for? *You're* the lawyer, right?"

Matthew returned to the booth. "I needed Angela to vouch for your son. He worked here once, didn't he?"

Mrs. James nodded.

"We may need Angela as a character witness," Matthew said. "Is Xavier gainfully employed now?"

"He was," Mrs. James said. "As soon as he was arrested, Metropolitan Rec Center let him go. He was a lifeguard."

Her son has never been in trouble, didn't drop out, and has a job. Eighteen months is no deal at all. "Where are they holding him?"

"The jail over on Union," Mrs. James said.

The Ninetieth Precinct, the precinct that rarely answers the phone. That brings back bad memories from Brooklyn Legal. He gulped the rest of his coffee and inhaled another strip of bacon. "I need to go meet my client."

"Now?" Mrs. James said. "It's Saturday."

"They won't keep a lawyer from his client, Mrs. James," Matthew said.

"But you aren't his lawyer yet," Mrs. James said.

"I will be." He carried his plate to the counter. "I can finish this later, can't I?"

"I'll put it in the fridge," Angela said. "Where are you going?"

"To meet Xavier," he said with a wink. He returned to the booth. "Ready?"

"I can't," Mrs. James said, "um . . . afford . . ."

"Don't worry about it," Matthew said. "I think Xavier can work it off here, maybe even tonight." *I'd really like to hear him spit some rhymes at . . . Angela's Arts Adventures. That has a nice ring to it.*

Angela looked up, shaking her head. "You're just trying to get out of cleaning up tonight. A bet's a bet, man."

"I am an opportunist." He smiled at Mrs. James. "Mrs. James, let's go get your son."

Mrs. James struggled out of the booth. "You really think you can get him out today?"

"Yes." *I don't know exactly how yet, but it will come to me.*

Matthew held the door for Mrs. James, who stepped onto the sidewalk and stopped, pointing at an old Buick LeSabre.

"Is that your car?" she asked.

"We're going to walk," Matthew said. "It's a nice day."

"It's over a mile to the police station," Mrs. James said. "Where is your car?"

"I don't have one," Matthew said.

Mrs. James blinked. "You don't . . ." She sighed. "What kind of a lawyer are you?"

"One with *very* low overhead," Matthew said.

Matthew and Mrs. James made relatively good time in getting to 211 Union and the 90th Precinct, arguably the grayest building ever built. Once inside, Matthew recognized the desk sergeant, a tiny black woman with a huge voice. *Babs is still here. Some things never change.*

"Barbara, right?" he asked.

Barbara, all 4-11 and ninety pounds of her, leaned back in her chair, her uniform still too big for her. "Well, if it isn't old three-M."

"I don't use that nickname anymore, *Babs,*" Matthew said.

"You know I hate to be called that," Barbara scowled. "Why are you here?"

"I'm here to meet with a client," Matthew said. "Xavier James."

Barbara narrowed her eyes. "You back at Brooklyn Legal?"

I almost wish I was. "Don't you read the online version of the *Daily Eagle*? I'm on my own now."

"Thank God," Barbara said. She nodded at Mrs. James. "He used to wear me out with his whining. I put up with him for three long years."

Matthew smiled. "This is Mrs. James, Xavier's mother."

"I figured it wasn't *your* mama, McConnell," Barbara said. She clicked some keys on a keyboard. "This says Xavier already has counsel, and it isn't you."

"It will be," Matthew said. "You have Farty Marty Kowalski's home number handy? Please say you do."

Barbara sighed. "You're wise to convince Xavier to change counsel, Mrs. James." She clicked some more keys and recited the number.

Matthew dialed Marty. "Marty? Matthew McConnell."

"You're still alive?" Marty asked.

You still have gas problems? "Yes, Marty, and I'd like to make your life easier. I'd like to represent Xavier James."

"Why?" Marty asked.

"I'm a friend of the family." He smiled at Mrs. James, who winced more than smiled back. *We'll take a cab back to Angela's, I promise.* "I'm at the Ninetieth now. May I confer with your client until we can get the Consent to Change an Attorney form signed?"

"You can *have* the kid, McConnell," Marty said. "Anything to lighten my load. Just fax it to my office once you get Xavier's signature."

"Sure, Marty," Matthew said. "Who's lead prosecutor?"

"O'Day."

My luck is holding out. Patrick "Paddy" O'Day and I go way back. "Is he still the PO'ed one?"

"Yep," Marty said. "He makes a beet look pink."

Paddy is still a heart attack waiting to happen. Everything about Paddy's face is red except his lips, which are unusually gray. "You have his cell phone number handy?"

"It's on this phone," Marty said.

"Could you text it to me, Marty?" Matthew asked.

"Um, sure," Marty said.

"Thanks. I'll have that fax to your office within the hour. Thanks for everything, Marty." He closed his phone. "Barbara, would you happen to have a consent form handy?"

Barbara groaned. "Ain't a damn thing changed, McConnell." She smiled. "I figured you wouldn't have anything handy, so I already printed one out." She slid off her chair and went to a copier, returning with the form. "You need a pen, too?" She handed the form to Matthew.

Matthew patted his empty hoody pocket. "Well, what do you know? I am in need of a pen."

Mrs. James groaned. "He was using an order pad to take notes earlier at Smith's Sweet Treats."

Barbara flipped Matthew a pen. "Don't let his clueless act get to you, Mrs. James. Though he acts stupid, this man is really very sharp." She looked him up and down. "Sweatpants and Chucks? Seriously?" She picked up a phone. "I'll let them know you two are coming."

"I'd like to use an interview room, Barbara," Matthew said. His phone buzzed. *O'Day's cell phone number has arrived. My ducks are lining up.*

"Why you got to be so pushy, McConnell?" Barbara asked. "You haven't changed a bit. I'll see if an *interrogation* room is available, okay?"

"Come on, Barbara," Matthew said. "At least get us a room with chairs from this century. Comfortable chairs. A room with some windows would be nice, too."

"Regulations, McConnell," Barbara said.

"Thank you for trying so hard, Barbara," Matthew said.

"Whatever," Barbara scowled.

Matthew turned to Mrs. James. "Ready to see your son?"

"I can't go back there," she whispered.

"It'll be okay, Mrs. James," Matthew said. "I have a good feeling about this. I'm sure your son will be glad to see you."

"No, I *really* can't go back there," she whispered. "The judge said I couldn't visit Xavier because of a little possession charge three years ago. One measly ounce of weed." She shrugged. "I don't mind waiting," she said, taking a seat.

While he waited for a guard to take him see to Xavier, he stared at Barbara.

"What?" she asked.

"Have you gotten taller?" he asked.

"Shut the hell up," Barbara said.

"The place seems spiffier than the last time I was here," Matthew said. "Smells lemony fresh."

"You know we keep this place clean," Barbara said.

"You just don't answer your phones," Matthew said.

"I *do,*" Barbara said. "Just not all the time."

A guard appeared, and Matthew followed him. *Going "behind the lines" for the first time since my work at Brooklyn Legal. It's still a scary maze. Buzz this, click that, lock this down. I'm glad I'm only visiting.*

The officer opened an antiseptic, windowless, gray interrogation room that contained only a single long gray table and two gray metal folding chairs. *How cheerfully gray and dark.*

"XS will be here in a minute or so," the officer said.

"He already has a following?" Matthew asked.

"He's really good," the officer said, closing the door behind him.

A moment later, another officer brought Xavier James inside and undid his handcuffs. "No trouble now, XS. I'll be right outside." He nodded at Matthew. "How long will you need?"

"Ten, fifteen minutes, maybe more," Matthew said.

The guard left, shutting the door behind him.

"Please have a seat, Xavier, or should I call you XS?"

Xavier, who may have weighed one hundred and thirty pounds and looked swallowed up by his hunter green prison uniform, didn't look like a rapper. *XS has no tattoos. How can he be a rapper in today's music world without tattoos?*

Xavier sat, resting his elbows on his knees. "Who are you?"

Matthew slid the consent form across the table and set the pen on top of it. "If you sign this, I will be your lawyer."

Xavier scanned the sheet. "You don't look like one."

"I'm hearing that a lot lately," Matthew said. "Your mother wants me to represent you instead of Farty Marty Kowalski. She's waiting out front."

Xavier looked up. "She's here?"

"Yes."

"And you're a real lawyer," Xavier said.

"Don't let my appearance fool you, Xavier," Matthew said. "It's Saturday, and this is what I wear on Saturdays. Sign the form, and we can talk."

Xavier picked up the pen. "But neither me nor my mama has any money to pay you."

"You'll be working it off at Angela's, I mean, Smith's Sweet Treats," Matthew said.

Xavier sat back. "Sweeping?"

"Performing," Matthew said. "Hopefully tonight."

Xavier rolled the pen in his hand. "Tonight? Did my mama tell you what they say I did?"

"Yep," Matthew said. "They have your DNA and two witnesses, yada yada yada."

Xavier shook his head. "I'm cooked, man."

"Xavier, I have a good feeling you'll be out of here in time for your first set." *Sign the form, please.*

"Miss Angela's putting on shows now?" Xavier asked.

I like how he respects Angela. "You'll be her first headliner." He nodded at the form. "Sign it, please."

Xavier shrugged. "All right." He signed the form and handed back the paper and pen.

"Now we can talk." Matthew stood and sat on the edge of the

table. "I need to know *precisely* what were you rapping when the alleged spitting incident took place."

"It was a rhyme I made up on the spot," Xavier said.

Shoot. "So it's not written down?"

"No. It's in my head." Xavier tapped his temple. "Most of my stuff's in my head."

Hmm. "Did you dis the police in your rap?"

Xavier smiled. "No, I didn't *dis* the police, not when they're a few feet from me. I ain't crazy."

"So there wasn't anything inflammatory, content-wise, in your freestyle that might have set these officers off," Matthew said.

"No."

"Well, let me hear it," Matthew said.

Xavier squinted. "You want me to perform it right now?"

"Yes."

"You sure you're a lawyer, man?" Xavier asked.

"What? I can't like rap?" *I need to school XS on what I know about the early days.* "I listened to Camp Lo, O. C., Twista, and Company Flow when I was your age."

Xavier laughed. "Damn."

"Do I pass inspection?" Matthew asked.

"All right," Xavier said with a smile. "I'll flow for you. I think I can remember most of it . . .

> *P*eter *P*i*p*er *p*e*pp*er *p*oke,
> *B*illy*b*urg *b*e goin' *b*roke,
> *P*eter *P*i*p*er *p*e*pp*er *p*o*p*,
> they *b*uildin' condos, make 'em sto*p* . . ."

Xavier continued for several minutes skewering Williamsburg hipster culture, landlords who raise already ridiculous rents, and Hasidic merchants exhorting customers to wear sleeves, spittle flying with every B- and P-word.

If I wore glasses, Matthew thought, *I'd need windshield wipers.*

"How was that?" Xavier asked.

"*Perfect,*" Matthew said. *It wasn't spit. It was spittle.* "I'm going to try to get Paddy O'Day, the man who's prosecuting your case, down here to listen to you."

"Today?" Xavier said.

Matthew nodded.

"You know it's Saturday, right?" Xavier asked.

"All day, as a matter of fact," Matthew said. "Saturday has a habit of lasting all day."

"You're strange, man," Xavier said. "Why would he come visit me on a Saturday?"

"So he can hear you reenact the alleged crime," Matthew said. "I'll get you some water. We wouldn't want your mouth to get dry."

Matthew called O'Day, the fierce and freckled one. *I'll bet his red hair is silver by now. He was pushing three hundred pounds the last time I saw him. I used to find and harass him at Reben's Luncheonette on Saturdays. I'll bet that's where he is right now.*

"Who is this?" Paddy asked.

"Hey, Paddy. It's Matthew McConnell."

Paddy cursed. "McConnell, you have no manners."

"Hope I didn't catch you eating at Reben's."

Paddy cursed again. "You did. This had better be good. What do you want?"

Paddy might be pushing three-fifty by now. "Could you come over to the Ninetieth? I need us to sit down with my client, Xavier James."

"He's Kowalski's client," O'Day said.

"Not anymore," Matthew said. *I just haven't sent the fax yet.*

"Come on, McConnell," Paddy snarled. "It's Saturday."

"I know. But it's a slow news day. Channel Eleven and I go way back. They love breaking stories on slow news days." *Lure the big fish in. Dangle the bait.*

"What breaking story?" Paddy asked.

"About how New York's finest is committing a crime by wrongfully arresting an aspiring word artist," Matthew said.

Xavier smiled and nodded.

"Xavier James is no word artist," Paddy said. "He's a spitter. That kid is no saint."

"He doesn't have a record, Paddy," Matthew said.

Xavier shook his head.

"Which only means we haven't caught him breaking the law until now," Paddy said. "Is he ready to take the deal I gave him?"

Matthew covered the phone. "Did anyone make you a deal?"

Xavier shook his head. "All I heard was eighteen months."

"Same here." Matthew uncovered the phone. "What deal? Marty didn't tell me there was a deal."

"He pleads to menacing a police officer, six months," O'Day said.

Is he serious? He can't be serious. Six months in prison because Xavier enunciated his P's and B's? "No deal."

"He spit on a cop, McConnell," Paddy said. "He could get three and a half to fifteen years. You know that. I'm cutting him a huge break."

"Xavier was performing," Matthew said. "He was rapping. He enunciates. It's the way he flows. You want to hear him?"

"*Now?*" O'Day said.

"Well," Matthew said, "as soon as you can get here. We can wait. We have nowhere else to be. You have to hear him in person, Paddy. It won't have the same effect if he performs into the phone, which he *will* do for Channel Eleven if you don't come over right away."

"You want me to leave my brunch and listen to a kid rap?" Paddy scowled. "On my day off?"

"Yes," Matthew said. "And I have Channel Eleven on standby."

"Yeah?" Xavier whispered.

Matthew shook his head. "I'm bluffing," he mouthed.

Xavier rolled his eyes.

Matthew knew it was a safe bluff. Channel 11 always seemed to have trucks crisscrossing Williamsburg and trolling for the odd gunshot and machete victim.

"I'll be there in . . . twenty minutes," Paddy said.

Matthew closed his phone. "He's on his way." He knocked on the door, and the guard opened it. "Could we get XS some water, please? And make sure ADA O'Day gets to us as soon as he gets here in about twenty minutes."

The guard didn't comment, closing the door.

"You bluffed his ass," Xavier said.

"Paddy doesn't look good on TV," Matthew said. "They never light him right or something. Plus, you'd need a wide-screen TV to see all of him. Make sure you scoot your chair closer to him when he gets here."

Half an hour later, Paddy O'Day, sweating and wearing an old white New York Jets jersey, the green numbers straining to flake off, stepped sideways into the interrogation room. "This had better be good, McConnell." He eased up onto the table, and the table complained.

"Go ahead, Xavier," Matthew said.

"All right," Xavier said. "*P*eter *P*i*p*er *pepp*er *p*oke . . ."

Paddy wiped his face four times during the performance.

When Xavier finished, he said, "Sorry about that. It's how I get my sound."

Paddy sighed. "So you *were* only rapping when the officers walked by."

"Yeah," Xavier said. "I was up against a wall, better acoustics that way, kind of like a natural amplifier. Anyway, these two officers walked by, they stopped, and I kept rapping."

Paddy shook his head. "How close did they get to you?"

"A little closer than you are now," Xavier said. "They were laughing along with the crowd at the beginning. And then . . . they hooked me up."

"Why didn't you tell Kowalski this?" Paddy asked.

"He never gave me the chance," Xavier said. "He opened my file, closed my file, and told me to plead guilty before he even introduced himself to me."

"What do you think, Paddy?" Matthew asked.

"I could fine him for spitting in public," Paddy said.

"Are you serious?" Matthew asked. "Oh, the public will love that. Name a Yankee who doesn't spit during a game."

"I can't just drop the charges, McConnell," Paddy said. "I may have to work with those officers in the future."

Paddy hasn't learned his lessons yet. "Hello, this is Channel Eleven reporter Matt McConnell with a breaking news story from the Ninetieth Precinct. Xavier Jones, a lifeguard and high school graduate who has a squeaky clean record, was exercising his right to speak in a public place and causing no disturbance of any kind when two of New York's finest got too close to the performance and arrested XS, as he is known on the street, for assault on a police officer. What? A fine, upstanding black man exercising his freedom of speech is being arrested for assault? He was rapping? What was he rapping? It was a funny rap about his hometown? And it contained no cursing? Why on *earth* did they arrest that *wholesome*, *clean-cut* young man? Let's ask ADA Paddy O'Day. Mr. O'Day, why on earth would—"

"I gotta do *something,* McConnell," Paddy interrupted.

"Let him go," Matthew said. "That's what you can do."

"I can't," Paddy said.

"The officers moved into his field of fire, Paddy," Matthew said. "Xavier didn't ask them to move to the front row. And won't another performance of his rapping play well on TV? Can you see the camera lens, Paddy? Can you? I can."

Paddy ran his fat fingers through his hair. "I can see the lens, McConnell." He slid off the table.

I think I have just heard a table give an audible sigh of relief. "You'll start the paperwork then?"

"I'll start the paperwork. You two sit tight." Paddy left the room.

"Xavier, you're about to be famous," Matthew said.

Xavier stood and stretched. "No offense, Mr. McConnell, but I already am, at least around here. I was kind of hoping for community service."

"Why?" Matthew asked.

"For my rep, man," Xavier said. "Though I *was* arrested for assault on a police officer. That might be enough to get my name farther out there."

What a strange world we live in. "You will be doing a service to your community tonight," Matthew said, "and this is what I want you to do . . ."

After Matthew explained his plan, Xavier asked, "Can I borrow some paper and a pen? I want to get started on that right now."

Matthew dug the order book from his front pocket. "What are you going to rhyme with Angela?"

Xavier looked up. "*Bella?*"

"Angela isn't Italian," Matthew said.

"But she's still fine, right?" Xavier said.

"Very," Matthew said.

"I had a hard crush on that woman when I was ten," Xavier said.

Is that what I have? A crush? Hmm. I have a crush on Angela. And tonight, I hope to be the lucky fella who sees Angela smile that bella *smile of hers at the inaugural Angela's Arts Adventures.*

Hmm. Now when exactly should I tell her she's hosting XS after she closes for the night?

I could just let it happen, you know, as if it happened kind of spontaneously. What do you know? A whole bunch of people just happened *to show up to hear XS. What do you know about that?*

Angela would never fall for that.

I'll have to tell her, even though I have a feeling she won't like it.

No. She won't like it.

Or me.

I hope my soft sell skills have improved.

Chapter 15

"What took so long?" Angela asked as Matthew swept in. "Where's Mrs. James?"

"It was actually quick," Matthew said. "Mrs. James is at home." *She actually enjoyed the ride in the cab.* He pointed at a chocolate chip cookie. "Please?"

Angela wrapped one in a napkin and handed it to him. "Well?"

"Xavier is out, and he's not out on bail," Matthew said. "He's out, free and clear."

"Really?"

Matthew nodded as he tore into the cookie. "Sugar. I've missed you."

"How'd you do it?" Angela asked.

"I got lucky again," Matthew said. "Xavier uses lots of B's and P's when he raps."

Angela peered up at him. "Huh?"

"When XS spits rhymes, he *really* spits," Matthew said. "The cops got too close." He wiped his lips. "You have any coffee for me?"

Angela poured him a small cup.

Only a small? She is so hard to impress. "I'll tell you all about it," Matthew said, "if I can take you out for ice cream or something after closing."

"It's the middle of February." Angela turned away.

Matthew drifted down the counter to catch her eyes. "So the ice cream won't melt. It may even taste warm in comparison to the air. We can go out after the show."

Angela snapped her head toward him. "What show?"

"XS is going to perform here tonight at eight o'clock," Matthew said.

Angela faced him completely. "But I *close* at eight."

Matthew smiled. "Oh, that's right. You do. That's perfect timing, isn't it? You close at eight, and we're having a show at eight. Wow. It must be fate. Got any of those big coffee dispensers?"

Angela rushed around the counter. "No. Matthew, I'm *not* staying open past—"

"*We* are staying open," Matthew interrupted. *So much for the soft sell.*

"No, *we're* not," Angela said, cocking her head. "*I've* had a busy day. *I've* been earning money. *I* need to get off my feet."

Matthew looked at her feet. *I'd like to sweep you off your feet if you'll let me, Angela.* "It's too late. The word is already out on Facebook, and it's spreading like wildfire. I believe there will be a nice crowd in here well before eight o'clock."

"Not if I lock the door," Angela said.

"You won't." He looked into her eyes.

"Why won't I?" Angela asked.

"You're curious about what would happen." He nodded. "You're the curious type, all right."

Angela looked away. "It would have been nice if you had *asked* me before making this decision which affects *me* the most."

He stepped into her field of vision. "You'll be able to sit the entire time, I promise, and I'll do the entire cleanup afterward."

"Just this *one* time," she said, zipping behind the counter again.

I won again? Wait a minute. That was too easy. Either I'm wearing her down or something else is going on.

Matthew leaned on the counter. "So, Angela, if we get one of those big coffee dispensers, it will make it easier for people to serve themselves during the performance. You know, the honor system. We'll put the tip jar next to the dispenser."

Angela groaned. "That's *not* the way I do business. Customers aren't always honorable."

"Don't you pour out what doesn't sell at the end of the night?" Matthew asked.

"Yes, but—"

"So you'll make money you wouldn't normally make," Matthew interrupted. "You can say, 'Last call' or something like that at seven forty-five, and you can put any coffee you have left in the dispenser. You could even mix it all together and call it Jamaican Mountain Blue Breakfast House Blend." *It makes perfectly logical sense.*

"Dispensers aren't cheap." Angela squared her shoulders. "A dispenser is not in my budget this month."

"I'm buying." *She can't out-argue me.*

Angela wrinkled her lips. "Okay."

Matthew smiled. *I won again! I won again! But why am I winning so easily now?*

"But new, not used, Matthew," Angela said. "I don't want anyone else's coffee contaminating mine."

"I got this, Angela," Matthew said. "I'll even throw in some Styrofoam cups."

Angela shook her head rapidly. "No Styrofoam. Drinking cups. Dixie. The ones especially for hot liquids, like the ones I already use."

"Okay." He sighed. "Relax. It'll be fun."

"It better be," Angela said.

"It *will* be."

Matthew spent most of the afternoon getting the "show" on the road. He bought a white ceramic coffee dispenser from Class Hostess on Flushing Avenue and a heavy box of white twelve-ounce Dixie cups from Ring & Bring on Lynch Street. He also made a deal with Soundhouse NYC on Broadway to bring a simple sound system to Angela's at 7:30 by offering them free advertising.

After running home to shower, shave, and change into jeans and a clean hoody, he carried the dispenser and the cups into Angela's shop at 6:30, and there were already people sitting and waiting.

Very cool.

Angela watched him remove the dispenser from its box. "White? Why'd you get white, Matthew? It's going to stain."

"I bought white to match the Dixie cups," Matthew said, patting the top of the box of cups. "I got two thousand of these bad boys."

"But white for a coffee dispenser? Really?" Angela shook her head.

Maintain your calm so she can calm down. "I didn't think you'd like the green one. It was an eyesore and reminded me of my great-grandma Fiona. She was from Ireland, and everything in her house was green. It would have definitely clashed with your old-school decor. And doesn't baking soda and vinegar get coffee stains out?"

"Yes, but . . ."

"You're surprised I knew that, aren't you?" Matthew asked.

Angela almost smiled. "Kind of, but . . ."

Matthew opened the top of the dispenser. "It holds forty-two cups and has a metal spigot with a rubber gasket up top. It's built to last. I think the wrought-iron stand is kind of classy, too."

"What'd you pay?" Angela asked, looking inside the dispenser.

"A hundred for the dispenser, seventy-five for the cups," Mathew said.

"I'll reimburse you."

Wow. She has to have the upper hand at all times. "Angela, I still owe you more than three hundred more this month, right? It's in the contract."

"I don't need your money, Matthew," she said.

So serious. "I wish you had told me that earlier . . ."

Angela widened her eyes.

"I'm kidding." He put his face in front of hers until she looked at him. "It's no problem."

Angela leaned back. "Okay, Mr. McConnell, where exactly will this show take place? He's not dancing on my counter or walking around on top of my display case."

He faced the front of the store. "I see him in the left corner near the window. He can stand on a table or two. That way the overflow crowd and people walking by can see him through the window."

"He's going to stand on my tables?" Angela asked.

"They're sturdy, and he's skinny," Matthew said. "He's been eating prison food for a few days, right? You might want to make a special batch of cookies just for him."

She waved at the display case. "I have plenty. Now if this place fills up, how are they all going to hear him?"

"I have a sound system on the way." He touched his head with a finger. "I thought of everything."

She crossed her arms. "We'll see about that. And don't be running up my electric bill."

He nodded toward the back. "Go . . . make some cookies."

"I told you that I have plenty."

No, you don't. "A younger crowd has a sweeter sweet tooth."

Angela blinked. "You're right."

"Every once in a while."

"This . . ." She backed away toward the kitchen. "This *better* work."

"It will. I promise."

While Angela made more cookies in between constantly serving customers, many of them brand-new to her, Matthew watched a decidedly younger crowd gathering outside, many getting coffee and sweets and returning to the sidewalk.

It smells like heaven, Matthew thought. *At least I hope this is what heaven smells like.*

The sound system parted the crowd and rolled in at 7:20, and the Soundhouse NYC crew set up a large amplified speaker, a mixer board, and a wireless microphone near the front window in a matter of minutes. After a quick sound check, Matthew took and kept the microphone.

By 7:30, a mostly laid-back group of young people of every race, creed, and socioeconomic status filled every chair and booth except the middle booth, where Matthew had Mr. and Mrs. James sit with him to watch the show.

"That boy told me he wouldn't be late," Mr. James said.

"He's out trying to get his job back," Mrs. James said.

"I doubt it," Mr. James said. "He's just trying to make a grand entrance. He gets that from your people."

"Drink your coffee, old man," Mrs. James said.

"Did Xavier tell either of you anything about tonight's performance?" Matthew asked.

"No," Mr. James said. "Or he might have. I can't understand the boy half the time."

"He told me he was doing his community service tonight," Mrs. James said.

Matthew looked out to the sidewalk. *I hope the police are kind to us tonight. They look at least six deep out there.*

"Last call for coffee!" Angela yelled.

I didn't know she could yell like that! He checked the time on his phone. *And it's exactly seven forty-five. She listened to me. I am having a great day.*

As a line formed quickly at the counter, Xavier sneaked in and slid into the booth. He wore black jeans, black boots, a plain black hoody, a solid black baseball hat, and not a glint of bling.

"Ready?" Matthew asked.

"There's a lot of people here, man," Xavier said.

"Where you been?" Mr. James asked.

"Did you get your job back?" Mrs. James asked.

Xavier smiled. "They were trying to call me all afternoon. Word got around fast. I even get my old shift back. Where do I set up?"

"Your stage," Matthew said, "is on those corner tables near the window. I have your mike. Do you mind if I introduce you?"

"No offense, Mr. McConnell," Xavier said, adjusting the bill of his cap, "but I don't need an introduction."

"Let him introduce you," Mr. James said. "He's the reason you're even here."

"Work with me, Xavier," Matthew said. "This may be my only brush with *your* greatness. I have to do a little advertising first to help pay the bills. Then the next hour is yours."

Xavier nodded. "All right. That'll work."

At 7:55, Matthew waded through the crowd to the tables in the corner, climbing up in time to see Angela filling the dispenser and getting the tip jar ready. He turned on the mike. "Good evening, ladies and gentlemen, and welcome to Angela's Arts Adventures, the first of what we hope will be *many* live shows at Smith's Sweet Treats and Coffee." He smiled at Angela, who sat on a high wooden stool to the right of the counter. *She's rolling her eyes at me.*

"Let's give a hand to the woman who is the most beautiful coffee brewer and server in Williamsburg," Matthew said, "and *please* don't *ever* call her a barista. Give it up for Miss Angela Smith!"

Angela shook her head throughout the ovation.

But she looked at me the entire time. I like keeping her attention. I like that she pays attention to me. Sometimes.

Matthew also detected a small smile on her beautiful red lips.

"Tonight's show is brought to you by Soundhouse N-Y-C, which is providing this incredible sound system. You want to be heard—Soundhouse N-Y-C is the word." *Okay, that's one word and an abbreviation.* "Tonight's show is also brought to you by the law firm of Matthew McConnell, and that would be me, and the state of New York and the Ninetieth Precinct for realizing the error of their many, *many* ways by releasing tonight's performer about five hours ago."

Matthew heard some laughter.

Matthew detected a larger smile on Angela's beautiful red lips.

"Here to share some wisdom with you this evening," Matthew said, "please give a warm welcome back to freedom to Williamburg's own street poet . . . *X-S*!"

Xavier bounced through the crowd as the applause rose, getting dap and hugs from dozens of adoring fans.

After jumping down and handing Xavier the microphone, Matthew weaved through tables to stand next to Angela.

"I knew you were a ham," she said.

"I know how to bring home the bacon," Matthew said. "I thought it went very well for my debut, don't you?"

"Shh."

Once Xavier was up on the tables, the crowd seemed to lean in. "What up, Billyburg?" he asked.

Now that *is a cheer. It's definitely not a Bronx cheer. Brooklyn people know how to make windows rattle.*

"Hey y'all, I used to work here," Xavier said. "Really. Miss Angela gave me my first job, and trust me, she worked me to *death*. Y'all clean up after yourselves, okay? I don't want her naggin'." He opened a sheet of paper. "Y'all know I don't normally write anything down, but I *had* to write this one down. This one's for my favorite boss, Miss Angela. I call it 'Dignity' . . .

Flour on her face, her arms, her palms,
At Smith's Sweet Treats, she is da bomb,
She made me work with bleach, degreaser,
I wish I'd had her for a teacher.

Tight starched apron, lookin' *bella,*
The best boss I ever had, Miss Angela . . ."

Matthew glanced at Angela's face. *Look at that shy face glow! It's about time she got some recognition.*

> "Up before sun, up after moon,
> In coldest winter or hottest June,
> She pours coffee with integrity
> And she taught me that work is dignity.
>
> Tight starched apron, lookin' *bella,*
> The best boss I ever had, Miss Angela . . ."

Angela turned to Matthew. "Did you put him up to that?"

She didn't like it? "I might have."

"It was good," Angela said.

She liked it!

Xavier tucked the paper in his pocket. "Now we gonna do some free flow, all right? This is the one that got me arrested." He smiled broadly and laughed. "Y'all in the front row might want to lean *way* back . . ."

An hour later, after chair dances, after two hundred hands waved in the air, after kids danced on the sidewalk, after the sound system rolled out, and after the crowd did an admirable job of cleaning up after itself, the shop was empty.

Matthew pointed at Angela's tip jar. "Would you look at that." *There are mostly ones in there, but it's almost filled to the top.* "There has to be at least two hundred bucks in there."

Angela lifted the lid off the coffee dispenser. "It's empty." She narrowed her eyes. "And it's more like a hundred bucks in here. Forty-two cups for a hundred bucks. They made out like bandits. I may have to put a little sign that says, 'Two dollars per cup suggested.' " She walked to the front and locked the door.

"So?" Matthew said.

Angela walked past him to the tip jar. "So what?" She began pulling out bills and stacking them on the counter.

"The *show,*" Matthew said. "Angela's Arts Adventures. Success or failure?"

"The name . . . failure," Angela said. "It wasn't *my* arts."

"I was going for a triple-A," Matthew said. "How about Angela's *Artistic* Adventures?"

Angela dug out more bills. "Does my name have to be in it?"

This is no time to be humble. "No. We could call it 'Sweet Arts.' "

Angela laughed slightly. "Boo."

"Other than the name, was it a success?" Matthew asked.

"It worked out." She turned the tip jar over slightly, coins cascading to the counter.

"Which means what exactly?" Matthew asked.

She scooped coins into a zipper pack. "Just what I said. It worked out."

"Will you do it again?"

"I *may* do it again," she said.

She'll do it again. "Tight starched apron, lookin' *bella,* the best boss I ever had, Miss Angela."

"My apron isn't that tight," Angela said.

"It ain't the apron that's tight, yo," Matthew said.

Angela smiled and shut her eyes. "Shut up and start mopping the kitchen."

Matthew stepped closer. "Are we still on for ice cream?"

Angela put the empty tip jar onto the counter. "What is it with you and eating ice cream during the winter?"

"I need my sugar year round," Matthew said.

Angela pushed the stool behind the counter. "I will need this stool tomorrow, I'm sure."

"Well?" Matthew asked. *I'm wearing her down. I can feel it.*

"I don't want ice cream," Angela said.

But she wants something. Yes!

"I'd rather have . . . some pizza . . . from . . . Mezza Luna," Angela said. "You buying?"

Yes! "Does this make it . . . a date?"

Angela opened the cash register. "Date, nothing, man. It's my *dinner*. I eat at eight-thirty every night, and you kept me from eating. Now get to work so I can go eat."

Chapter 16

Angela took a long time to get ready.

Matthew ate five more chocolate chip cookies while he waited.

When she finally moved gradually out of the kitchen, she zipped and rezipped her coat twice. She checked her shoelaces. She went back to check the locks on the back door in the kitchen. She felt in her pocket for her keys.

"Will I be warm enough?" she asked. "I should get a heavier coat."

"You'll be fine," Matthew said. "It's not too cold tonight."

She took a step toward the front door and winced. "My feet are killing me."

"I could go get it and bring it back," Matthew said.

She shook her head. "I don't eat cold pizza."

"You could put it in the oven," Matthew said.

"I don't want garlic in any of my ovens," Angela said. "Imagine biting into a raspberry pastry and tasting even a hint of garlic."

Not good. "We could take a cab down and back."

"No, that's a waste of money." She seemed to pace in front of the door. "They deliver, don't they? No, no. The pizza will be even colder, and they add a mint to the total for delivery. Besides, what would it look like if a coffee shop got a pizza delivery?"

"That the owner likes pizza?" Matthew suggested.

"Did I lock the back door?" Angela asked.

Matthew nodded.

"Okay." She took a deep breath, held it, and exhaled. "Okay. Call it in first so it's ready when we get there."

"What do you like?" Matthew asked.

"It doesn't matter, but no meats or anchovies," Angela said. "Not this late at night."

Matthew called Mezza Luna and ordered a mushroom, black olive, and fresh garlic pizza while Angela sat in the first booth, her shoes drumming the floor.

She certainly seems nervous. Or is it excitement? I hope it's excitement. "Our pizza ought to be ready by the time we get there, so if we start walking . . ."

Angela exhaled slowly. "Okay." She left the booth, and Matthew opened the door. Angela stood unmoving in the doorway.

Wow, she looks really tired. "I'll walk down and take a cab back with the pizza if you're too tired. I know you've had a longer day because of me."

Angela shook her head, stepping out onto the sidewalk. Matthew stepped outside, and Angela locked the door. "It's about ten blocks, right?" she asked.

"Closer to eight."

"Okay." She pulled on the door. "All locked up. Okay. Let's . . . let's go."

Angela took off like a shot down Driggs Avenue, Matthew trying to stay close.

We are rolling! "What's the rush?"

Angela looked back. "I'm just trying to stay warm."

"Don't blink or we'll pass my apartment on Havemeyer," Matthew said, finally beside her. "I'll wave at it as we pass by. I'm sure it misses me. Where do you live?"

Angela looked straight ahead. "I don't give out that kind of information."

"Oh. Sorry."

"You haven't figured it out?" Angela asked.

"You live . . . above the shop," Matthew said. "The other door in the kitchen leads up to your apartment."

"Correct." They came to South 3rd Street. "Left?"

"Yes," Matthew said, and he had to speed up again. "I'm glad you invested in steel doors."

"Yeah," Angela said. "So am I."

"You have a short commute," Matthew said. "And I bet your

apartment smells like heaven. You can smell the air and wake up instantly, huh?"

"I only drink decaf," Angela said. "Otherwise I'd never sleep."

They came to Havemeyer.

"We go right here, don't we?" Angela asked.

"Yeah," Matthew said. "You're not lost, are you?"

"No," Angela said. "I haven't been down this way in a while."

Matthew pointed toward Mittman's Pharmacy. "That's where I live. Above the pharmacy. I wake to the glorious aroma of antiseptic and rubbing alcohol."

"And vanilla," Angela said.

"Yeah." *This is no fun at all! I can't see her eyes, and I'm starting to get winded. I guess Angela isn't into romantic walks.* "Have you lived above your shop all your life?"

Angela nodded, said, "We're here," and with a burst of speed ripped open the door to Mezza Luna and went inside, sitting at a black and white table in the back.

I would have held that door for you.

Matthew paid for and brought the pizza and two ice waters to the table. "Hope ice water is okay."

"It's fine." She opened the box a pulled out a slice. "Looks good."

Matthew pulled two slices out and slammed them together. "I have worked up an appetite after our workout."

"Sorry." Angela nibbled at her pizza.

"It's okay," Matthew said. "I needed the exercise."

Angela hardly looked up from her pizza or away from her water for the next five minutes, seeming to keep her eyes glued to the table, her shoulders hunched, her body stiff.

"You okay?" Matthew asked.

She looked up. "Yes. Why?"

"You don't look very relaxed," Matthew said.

"I had a stressful day," she said. She sipped her water. "And you caused most of the stress."

"Guilty as charged," Matthew said. "How can I unstress you?"

Angela shrugged slightly. "I don't know. Tell me more about your date with Monique 'the Freak' Freitas."

And this will unstress you? "Do you know Monique?"

"I've heard some stories," Angela said softly.

"Well, it was a strange date," Matthew said.

"Aren't all your dates strange?" Angela asked.

"Recently, I'd have to agree with you," Matthew said. "This isn't strange, is it?"

"No, it's not strange," Angela said, "because it's not a date. It's a long walk to eat dinner."

Eight blocks is not a long walk, it's not even half a mile, and it feels like a date to me, Matthew thought. *Except for the race-walking.*

Angela wiped her lips with a napkin. "Now tell me more about your date with Monique. I'm all ears."

She's all ears. She has cute ears. "You don't want the play-by-play, do you?"

"Was there any play-by-play?" Angela asked. "All *you* said was that she had a large condom collection."

Matthew grabbed another slice. "I think Monique is a collector, a connoisseur of condoms." He took a healthy bite, chewing rapidly.

"She sounds more like a dispenser," Angela said.

Matthew nodded.

Angela frowned.

Oops. "Oh, but I didn't . . . we didn't." He swallowed. "I wouldn't."

"You . . . wouldn't." She stared at him.

"No." He sipped some water. "Not that she didn't try."

Angela sat up straighter. "And how hard did she try?"

Why did I say that? "You really want the play-by-play."

"No, I don't," Angela said, "but I think I can guess." She narrowed her eyes. "You went back . . . to her place."

"Why not mine?" Matthew asked.

"You live over a pharmacy that smells like antiseptic, which isn't exactly romantic." She stared at his hands. "Then somehow she lured you into . . . her bedroom."

"Yes," Matthew said, "and I had to duck under a ceiling fan."

"Low ceiling?" Angela asked.

"Low fan," Matthew said. "Definitely not up to code. You're going to eat another slice, aren't you?"

"No, and don't try to change the subject," Angela said. "How exactly did Monique lure you into her bedroom?"

By getting naked. I can't say it that way. I'm on a date, even if Angela says otherwise. I know the rules. "By disrobing. I blinked, and she was in the buff."

"And that's all it took?" Angela asked.

Matthew nodded.

"So if a woman gets naked for you, you'll follow her anywhere," Angela said.

"Well, almost anywhere," Matthew said. "I wouldn't follow a naked woman off a cliff or to a Knicks game. Or to another Cole Porter musical. Maybe to a Brooklyn Nets game. They're playing a lot better now." He smiled at Angela. "Go Brooklyn, you know?"

Angela blinked. "And did you . . . you know?"

"Did we?" Matthew said. "Did we—oh. Oh, no. I kept my clothes on the entire time."

"Oh." She fiddled with the straw wrapper. "Do you regret not having . . . no, I have no right to ask you that."

"I have no regrets, none," Matthew said. "I made the right decision."

"Good to know," Angela said.

"Glad to let you know." *Changing the subject.* "So . . . you've lived above that shop your entire life."

"What if I'm not done asking about your date with Monique?" Angela asked, smiling.

"There's nothing more to tell," Matthew said. "I went home." He smiled. "Speaking of home, where are your parents now?"

Angela rolled her eyes. "You really don't want to tell me any more, huh?"

"Because there's nothing more to tell," Matthew said. "Now tell me about your parents."

"My parents are in Monte Cristi in the Dominican Republic," Angela said.

"The . . . Dominican Republic." *Why does that place keep haunting me?*

"My mama's half Dominican, half Haitian," Angela said. "She liked Williamsburg, but she missed Monte Cristi, where she grew up. It's on the border with Haiti, right on the coast. My grandfather was Haitian, and my grandmother was Dominican. You do the math. My daddy went down there with Mama about ten years ago. I'm sure they're enjoying warm weather now."

"Have you ever been to visit?" Matthew asked.

"No."

"Do you plan to?" Matthew asked.

Angela looked away. "Maybe someday."

"How often do you call home?" Matthew asked.

"Not often."

"They left you all alone," Matthew said.

She fiddled again with the wrapper. "Well, not completely. Anymore, anyway. I now have a partner, right? What about your parents?"

"They ran McConnell's Supermarket and Deli on Bedford Avenue for forty-five years," Matthew said. "I'm not sure, but I think that's a record for Williamsburg."

"Yeah? I used to go in there to get Blow Pops and Laffy Taffy," Angela said.

"We lived right above the store," Matthew said. "You probably saw me a couple times."

She squinted. "Nope. Don't remember you."

Ouch. "Anyway," Matthew said, "they've both retired to Charleston, South Carolina."

"Not Florida?" Angela asked.

"They were on their way to look at condos in Tampa, stopped for the night in Charleston, and they never left," Matthew said. "That's the story, anyway. I think my mother got carsick and they had to stop."

"Do you see them often?" She stood and closed the box, sliding it across the table to him.

Does this mean it's time to go? We were only here fifteen minutes! "My last visit was five years ago." He picked up the box.

Angela zipped up her coat and picked up her cup. "Ready?"

"Sure."

He followed Angela first to the trash can, where she dropped her cup, and then to the door, where he saw her take a deep breath before pushing through it and heading up Havemeyer at a fast clip.

He caught up with her, but the pizza box slowed him down. "You really have some Dominican in you?"

"One-quarter," she said, her eyes dead ahead. "The rest of me is black."

"Do you speak any Spanish?" Matthew asked.

"If I have to." She glanced sideways at him. "Do you mind if we walk a little faster? I have to get up at four."

"Sure."

They covered the eight blocks in five minutes, Matthew at least a step behind her the entire way. *While the view of her initials is nice, I think I've just walked off my dinner.*

Angela unlocked the door to her shop, heaved open the door, and stepped inside.

Matthew stood at the door catching his breath.

Her forehead beaded with sweat, Angela turned and smiled. "Thank you for dinner, Mr. McConnell."

"Such a formal ending to a date," Matthew said. *Should I ask if I could come inside? I'll wait for her to invite me.*

"This wasn't a date, Matthew," Angela said.

"If you say so," Matthew said. "When's the last time you had a real date, Angela?"

"No comment." She dabbed at her forehead with the back of her hand.

"So you expect me to spill my past while you hold onto yours," Matthew said.

"Yeah."

"Isn't that unfair?" Matthew asked.

"Yes, it's completely unfair," Angela said. "But only to you." She reached for the door and almost shut it. "I'm sorry, Matthew. That was . . . that was harsh."

I'm talking to my date who says it wasn't a date through a crack in the door. "No, it's fair. You really don't know me yet."

"It's not that," Angela said. "I trust you and believe *most* of what you say. I'm not sure I trust me."

Huh? "You don't trust yourself . . . to do what?"

"Good night, Matthew," Angela said. "See you soon."

"Of course."

Angela eased the door shut.

Matthew pushed gently on the door. "You know, you can't drop something like that at the end of a date."

"It *wasn't* a date," Angela whispered.

"Okay, okay, it wasn't a date," Matthew said. "We race-walked together and ate half a pizza." He shook the box. "You want the rest of it?"

Angela shook her head.

She didn't like it. No black olives next time. "Angela, what did you mean by 'I'm not sure I trust me'?"

"Can I plead the fifth?" she asked.

"A-ha! So you'd incriminate yourself if you gave an explanation."

"Not necessarily," Angela said.

Matthew sighed. "Angela, I am an open book. Ask me anything you want to know, and I will tell you."

"Will you give me an honest answer?" she asked.

"I will."

"Any question?" Angela asked.

"Anything you can think to ask me," Matthew said.

Angela nodded. "Okay. Matthew Mark McConnell, have you ever truly been in love?"

Wow. I didn't expect that question. "I thought I was. With Joy. But . . . no. I don't think so. I don't think I've ever truly been in love."

"Neither have I." She looked down. "Good night, Matthew." She closed and locked the door.

"Wait," Matthew said.

Angela turned to face the door.

"Thank you for allowing me to use the best booth in the shop for my office," Matthew said.

Angela put her palms on the door. "It's not the best booth. You can't see the street from that booth."

"Maybe I don't want to see the street." *And I don't.*

Angela turned away smiling.

"See you in the morning." He waved his free hand, but Angela had already walked through the shop and around the counter, turning out lights as she went.

What a "not-a-date" that was.

As he walked back to his apartment, Matthew gave himself a grade of C–. *I should have at least tried to hold her hand as we walked. We would have looked ridiculous, though, with her dragging me along and the pizza box flapping in the wind. Hmm. Maybe I'm pacing myself for the first time in my life. Yes. I'm pacing myself. Maybe I deserve a C+ instead.*

And now I'm pacing home . . . thinking only of Angela.

And her smile.

And how fast she can walk.

Alone in his apartment, relaxing in his easy chair, he thought about everything Angela had said during the "not-a-date." *She said, "I don't trust myself." What does she mean by that? Is she worried how she would act around me if we were on a real date? We've been alone quite a bit in her shop. She never seems worried then. And what's up with "Have you ever been in love? Neither have I." What does that mean? Does that mean she's as scared as I am about relationships? Or is she trying to see if any of those other women meant anything to me?*

Maybe both?

He opened his phone.

I could call her.

I should *call her.*

I need to place my breakfast order, right? No. She'll see right through that. How many calls does she get? I never hear the shop phone ringing. A phone call might be what she needs.

No, she's tired. She has to get up at four to get things going, and it's nearly midnight. I'd hate to wake her . . .

He closed his phone and turned it off.

I wonder what her hands feel like. I've shaken her hand twice, but I haven't held it yet. I'd expect her hands to be rough with all the hand washing she does all day. She always follows it with a squirt of lotion, though.

He closed his eyes and saw her smile. He saw her eyes.

The way she looks and talks and what she says aren't extraordinary at all, yet the combination stops my heart. Is her apron starched, or does her body starch the apron? I think her body . . . whoo. She has a magnificent body.

So what attracts me so much to her? She isn't bouncy and bubbly like Joy, flighty and fast like Monique, dangerous like Jade, buxom like Mary, chiseled like Victoria, or svelte like Allison. They are all the things Angela isn't. That sounds like a song. I like her for all the things she isn't. What rhymes with "isn't"?

Caricatures. I've been dating caricatures, exaggerations and misrepresentations of real women. I used to be a caricature, too. I was the wayward, irresponsible playboy, an overgrown boy at play in a city that erroneously values irresponsibility, rudeness, and wealth.

I can't be that way anymore if I want to be with Angela. I have to be what I've always been—a kid from Williamsburg who made good. For the most part.

Well, who is Angela Simone Smith? She's wonderful, the calm in the eye of the storm, a study in quiet passion, a race-walker extraordinaire, a master cook and coffee brewer.

Angela is . . . amazing.

Matthew laughed.

I may have finally found an appropriate use for that word.

Angela Simone Smith is amazing.

And I have just decided that this easy chair is iconic.

I think I'll end my evening with that assertion.

But Matthew couldn't sleep because of the stream of unanswered questions in his head, each blended into one overwhelming question:

How do I win the heart of this amazing woman?

Chapter 17

A crowd greeted Matthew at Smith's Sweet Treats and Coffee at 6:30 AM on Sunday morning.

I'm glad I wore khakis, a white Oxford shirt, and the a. testoni Oxfords today. At least I look like a lawyer for a change.

Black, brown, and white people filled all but his booth "office," and only a scattering of chairs around the tables was empty. Most people were sipping coffee and eating pastries and turnovers, and Angela never looked busier serving coffee and bagging sweets.

To avoid the dozens of eyes looking at him, Matthew looked at the beat-up briefcase he carried and hoped he had brought enough legal pads and pens. He waited in line behind several customers before standing in front of Angela. "What day is it?"

"Sunday," she said.

"I know that," he said. "What holiday is it?"

Angela consulted her little notebook. "Random Acts of Kindness Day."

Matthew widened his eyes. "Appropriate."

She slid a large cup of coffee toward him. "I'll bet they've never known a lawyer who had Sunday morning hours. Why'd you dress up?"

"I had a hunch." *I was really trying to impress only Angela.* Matthew took a sip. "Mmm. You added a touch of chocolate today."

"Thought you might need a little extra sugar," she whispered.

"Thanks." He glanced again at the crowd. "I'm sure they're here because of the free consultation," he whispered.

"And what you did for XS."

He sniffed the air. "Cherry?"

Angela nodded. "I'll bring you two. You better get to work. Some of these people need to get to church."

Matthew tried to smile, turned, and addressed the crowd. "Good morning."

A few people returned the greeting. The shop filled with silence.

"I'm glad you're all here," Matthew said. "To expedite our consultations today, I'm going to take everyone first arrived, first served." *And if this keeps up, I'll have to get a "take-a-number" dispenser.* "I will leave that up to you. Some consultations take minutes, and others may take longer. Thank you in advance for your patience. Make sure you drink lots of Angela's world-famous coffee, and always remember to tip her generously." He pointed at the tip jar. "Who's first?"

From that moment until eleven, Matthew helped dozens people with questions about the making and executing of wills and estates, and problems with past-due bills, collection agency notices, and eviction notices. Because of the season, however, he mainly looked over tax forms.

"The candles you bought for your church, yes," Matthew said, "you can deduct those, Mr. Cabrera, but I don't think you can deduct the goat."

"Why not?" Mr. Cabrera asked.

"It's a goat," Matthew said. "It's considered livestock. You're not a farmer, are you?"

"No," Mr. Cabrera said. "I drive taxi. I drive upstate to get goat. One *hundred* dollars."

"What did the church use the goat for?" *Please say a potluck dinner.*

"*Ceremonia* for priests," Mr. Cabrera said.

For a Santeria sacrifice. "Was the goat, um, consumed afterward?"

"Oh, *sí.*" Mr. Cabrera smiled. "Delicious."

Sounds like a potluck dinner to me. "Well, in that case, I think the IRS might let the goat fly . . ."

"Mr. Quarles," Matthew said, "you can't deduct the cost of your daughter's wedding just because you handed out your business card at the reception."

"Isn't there something you can do?" Mr. Quarles asked. "It cost me fifty grand."

"Ouch."

"You're telling me," Mr. Quarles said. "She had to have it at the Eden Palace. Sixty-five bucks a plate at the reception, and two hundred people showed up."

Geez. "I wish I could help you, but a wedding is not a business expense."

Mr. Quarles sighed. "What if I list it as a charitable expense?"

"How did the wedding benefit a charity?" Matthew asked.

"The groom," Mr. Quarles said. "My daughter is blind. He is an ugly man. *He* is the charity case . . ."

"I can't see the IRS approving your dog as a security expense, Mrs. Bernstein," Matthew said, "especially if it doesn't patrol or guard your family business."

Mrs. Bernstein exhaled abruptly. "That dachshund cost me five hundred bucks!"

"That doesn't matter to the IRS," Matthew said, "and I don't think dachshunds are considered a protective breed."

"Ducks keeps my husband away from me just fine," Mrs. Bernstein said.

Your cigarette breath could keep anyone away from you. "You can't deduct the cost of Ducks."

Mrs. Bernstein slid to the end of the seat. "What if Ducks barks so much that he scares off burglars?"

"You'd have to be able to prove that," Matthew said. "Can you?"

"Sure I can," Mrs. Bernstein said. "*No* one has robbed me since I've owned that dog . . ."

"Can I deduct the cost of Knicks tickets?" Mr. Perrone asked.

"Do you conduct business during the games?" Matthew asked.

"I network a little," Mr. Perrone said.

Translation: Not really because I'm there to see the game and get drunk. "Mr. Perrone, I had this problem once before. I tried to deduct the cost of Yankee season tickets because I often did a little business during the game, but the IRS only lets you deduct the national *average* ticket price for a baseball game, which is only around sixty bucks a ticket."

"What did *you* do?" Mr. Perrone asked.

"I became a Mets fan," Matthew said. "*Their* season tickets were cheaper . . ."

"I'm sure your cat is an integral part of the family, Mrs. Lotowski," Matthew said, "but she doesn't have a social security number. You can't list Mrs. Fluffy Tail as a dependent."

"What if I can get Mrs. Fluffy Tail a social security number?" Mrs. Lotowski asked.

"Good luck with that," Matthew said. "If you are successful, however, I wouldn't tell *anyone* how you did it . . ."

"You can't deduct the care and cultivation of your marijuana plants as business expenses," Matthew whispered to a man who wouldn't give him his name.

"Why not?" the man asked.

"You'll be arrested and the government will seize everything you own," Matthew said.

The man thought a moment, and then asked, "Why else?"

He's been using too much of his product.

A woman who called herself Tee showed Matthew an elaborate and intricate tattoo of two angels' wings framing the letter T on her lower back.

Now that *is a random act of kinkiness.* "It's a beautiful tattoo," Matthew said.

Tee turned and sat. "It didn't hurt too bad. I've gotten lots of attention because of it, but it cost so much. Can I deduct it on my taxes?"

Short answer: no. Judicious answer: "I don't think so."

"A friend told me you could deduct tattoos as a medical expense," Tee said. "It *is* a medical procedure, you know. They puncture the skin, right? And it's like medicine, you know? I feel so much better about myself, you know?"

It isn't gonna happen, you know? "Tee, you can't deduct the cost of a tattoo as a medical expense no matter how much self-esteem it gives you . . ."

When the shop was nearly empty, Matthew used the bathroom and got a refill. "Angela," he whispered, "did you tell them I was a tax lawyer?"

"I didn't tell anyone anything," Angela said. "The article did all this, not me. Why?"

"I'm feeling like one today," Matthew said, "and I only took two classes in tax law."

Angela stared at him. "What was that Puerto Rican girl showing you?"

She was Puerto Rican? She could have been from Trinidad. "Her self-esteem," Matthew said. "She wanted to know if she could deduct her tattoo on her taxes."

"That wasn't all she was showing you," Angela said.

"Are you making cracks about her crack?" Matthew asked softly.

"So you *did* see her crack," Angela said.

"The life of a lawyer is occasionally fraught with peril," Matthew said.

"*Right.*" Angela winced. "Do you think tattoos back there are sexy?"

"Some are nice," Matthew said.

"Right above the crack like that?" Angela whispered.

Don't answer. Don't say something stupid like, "Well, sometimes it's nice to have some art to look at when you're back there." "Do you have a tattoo?"

"No," Angela said. "It's just me back there."

Matthew smiled. "I know."

Angela smiled and put two toasted bagels on a plate, slathering them with butter and strawberry jam.

"How did you know I needed more sugar?" Matthew asked.

"These are for me," Angela said. "I need a snack."

"Oh."

She shook her head and handed him the plate. "I'm kidding. How are you doing?"

"I may have some potential future business," Matthew said, taking a healthy bite of a bagel.

"And you may not," Angela said.

Matthew chewed and swallowed. "True. What's ten percent of nothing?"

Angela rolled her eyes. "So you've already 'paid' me my finder's fee."

"How are you doing?" Matthew asked, glancing at the cash register.

Angela hit a few numbers on the cash register, and a small receipt printed out. "I've already set a Sunday record." She shook her head. "I can't believe it."

"I guess I'm *your* pimp now, huh?" Matthew asked. "I'm a coffee pimp."

"That's not true, Matthew," Angela said.

"I am what I am." Matthew carried his plate to his booth, motioning to a tall black woman sitting on the edge of her seat two tables away. "Thank you for your patience."

"It's okay," she said. "I'll wait until you finish eating." She was probably in her mid-fifties, her hair gray, her dark black dress and heels simple and elegant.

"No, please come into my office," Matthew said. "I'm keeping you from church, aren't I?"

"I've been late before," she said. "It's quite all right."

"Please," Matthew said.

The woman stood and walked quietly to the booth and sat. "I didn't see you charge a single person."

"I give free consultations," Matthew said, wiping his lips with a napkin.

"That's unusual, isn't it?" she asked.

"I'm an unusual guy," Matthew said.

"That's the truth," Angela said.

The woman smiled at Angela. "Are you two . . ."

Matthew grinned at Angela. "Yes, Angela, are we two . . ."

Angela sighed and went back into the kitchen.

"She's a little shy," Matthew said. "What can I help you with today, Mrs. . . ."

"Simmons, Gloria Simmons."

Matthew wrote her name on the top of a new sheet.

Gloria's eyes welled with tears. "I need . . ."

"Take your time," Matthew said.

"I need your help to get my husband some help," she said, tears sliding down her cheek. "He's not the same man I married thirty years ago, and I can't bear to see him like this anymore. He needs more help than I can give him."

"What's wrong?" Matthew asked.

"Timothy has all the symptoms of post-traumatic stress disorder," Gloria said, "but the U.S. Army doesn't think so because Timothy wasn't actually in combat."

Finally. A real case. He opened a compartment in his briefcase and pulled out a microcassette recorder. "Do you mind if I tape this?"

"No."

He turned on the recorder as Angela returned from the kitchen to the counter. "I'm talking to Gloria Simmons about her husband, Timothy. Mrs. Simmons thinks Timothy has PTSD, but the U.S. Army doesn't think so. Go on, Mrs. Simmons."

"Timothy was an anesthetist at Landstuhl Regional Medical Center in Germany, you know, where they send the wounded soldiers from Iraq and Afghanistan," Gloria said. "He saw all those boys coming back without arms and legs, such horrific injuries, and a few years after he left the army and came home for good, it eventually got to him. Our marriage has been for worse and for worser ever since."

Matthew slid a napkin across to her.

"Thank you." She dabbed at her eyes. "I didn't think I had any tears left."

"It's okay," Matthew said.

"We have tried every kind of therapy we can afford, which means not very many kinds," Gloria said. "Counseling sessions with our pastor seemed to be helping until Timothy told our pastor that . . . that God *couldn't* exist after all he had seen. He had a decent job at Woodhull Medical, but he, um, had an incident in the OR two years ago."

Matthew wrote "OR incident?" on the legal pad.

"We've been living off my paycheck and help from our church," Gloria said. "Our kids help out when they can, but they're just getting started in the world and don't have much to give us. If I can get Timothy on disability and get him some real help, I know we can survive this."

"What exactly did the army say about your husband's condition?" Matthew asked.

"The army says there's nothing wrong with him," Gloria said. "Not a thing. And the state of New York won't give him disability until the army says something is wrong with him. My friends, even my friends from the church, have told me to cut my losses and divorce Timothy so the state will *have* to take care of him." Gloria looked at the ceiling. "I love him too much to do that. I want him back, and I'm afraid the only way to do that is to get a lawyer involved, and I, um, I can't pay you much."

"Today is free, of course, and on your case, I would work . . . for whatever you feel is right to pay me." *That's the first time I've ever said that, and it felt good to say it.* "If I am successful at getting your husband the help he needs, he might be due some back pay and disability payments." *I have no idea if that's possible, but I can't charge this woman a cent. While so many want to be* rid *of their spouses, this woman wants her spouse* back.

"You have to make a living, don't you?" Gloria asked.

"We'll discuss payment, but only if I'm able to get some people to listen," Matthew said. "Okay, first I'll need a copy of his service record."

"I have a copy at home," Gloria said.

"How was he discharged?" Matthew asked.

"He received an honorable discharge," she said.

"When did he stop working at Woodhull Medical?" Matthew asked.

"Two years ago . . ." She nodded. "Two years ago tomorrow."

Matthew wrote it down. "When can I meet him?"

"Timothy hasn't left our apartment since the incident," Gloria said. "He, um, he looks out the window most days."

Two years. "I'll go to him then. When is a good time?"

"He won't speak to you," Gloria said. "He doesn't speak to anyone."

I'll have to ask him the right questions, then. "I'd still like to meet him, say, sometime tonight?"

"So soon?" Gloria asked.

"He needs help soon, right?" Matthew asked.

"Right." Gloria smiled. "Any time after six is fine." She gave Matthew an address on Berry and South 2nd Street. "It's only a few blocks away."

Matthew looked at Angela. "I have to help Angela close up shop. Is after nine okay?"

"Yes," Gloria said. "We live near Milly's. You can't miss it." She slipped out of the booth. "Thank you for caring. So many people I've talked to simply don't care at all."

"I can't promise you anything, Mrs. Simmons," Matthew said.

"I know," Gloria said, "but for the first time in a long time, I feel hope."

After Gloria left, Angela brought over a grilled cheese sandwich on a plate. She sat across from him. "What *can* you do for them?"

"Is this for me?" Matthew asked.

"Yes," Angela said. "Now, can you help them or not?"

Look at all that cheese! "If her husband is as impaired as she says he is, all I need to do is get him reexamined and put him in front of the powers that be. I may not need to go to court at all."

"You don't have to help me clean up tonight," Angela said.

"I want to," Matthew said, taking a huge bite of his sandwich.

"You're going to have a longer day than I had for a change," Angela said.

"Would you like to go along?" Matthew asked.

"To see her husband?" Angela asked.

"Yes," Matthew said. "I was planning *not* to take you out to dinner again tonight since we're *not* going on dates."

Angela slid around the table and sat next to him. "Scoot over."

Matthew scooted. *I like her initiative.*

"You want to take me to dinner again?" Angela asked.

Matthew nodded.

Angela put her hand on his arm. "Where would you take me?"

"We could grab a quick bite at DuMont Burger on our way." *Please leave your hand there. I like you to touch me.*

Angela squeezed his forearm and dropped her hand. "I don't know."

"I'm dying for a bowl of corn chowder and some of their onion rings," Matthew said.

"No burger?" Angela asked.

"Not for fifteen bucks," Matthew said.

Angela blinked. "They're getting fifteen bucks for a burger now?"

"Yeah," Matthew said, moving his leg to brush hers. "And if they don't cook it all the way through, it makes a mooing sound every time you chew."

Angela laughed.

Take her hand, take her hand . . . No. She's gripping her other hand too tightly. "And I don't want to break the bank on our second not-a-date."

"Our what?" Angela asked.

"Our not-a-date," Matthew said. "It's just two people going out for dinner."

"Hmm." Her knee brushed his. "Chowder and onion rings. An interesting combination."

"I have interesting tastes," Matthew said. He slid a full inch to his left and pressed his leg into hers. "Will you go with me? It's only a few blocks."

"But it will be late," Angela said, "and Monday is always my busiest day."

"I promise to have you home by ten," Matthew said.

"That's not it, Matthew, I just . . ." She sighed. "I mean, I love a good bowl of corn chowder. The onion rings? Not so much."

"Order something else then," Matthew said. "What's really stopping you?"

Angela pulled her right hand from her left and placed it on Matthew's leg.

There's a hot hand on my leg. I like a hot hand on my leg.

"Nothing, I guess," Angela said. "We'll have to do some precleaning from seven o'clock on so we can leave right at eight."

"I told Mrs. Simmons I'd be there after nine," Matthew said.

Angela shrugged. "It doesn't sound as if her husband's going anywhere, and we are eating first, right?"

"Right." He put his hand lightly on top of hers. "So . . . it'll be a not-a-date."

Angela turned her palm up, and squeezed Matthew's hand gently before sliding out of the booth. "Okay."

"Okay."

Why can't I breathe properly? Yes, she touched me, and I touched her. Her shyness is intoxicating! That gentle squeeze has to be the most intimate thing I've ever felt in my life.

We are going to clean this place in record time tonight, oh yes.

And they did, leaving the shop at eight and walking briskly a few blocks to DuMont to eat corn chowder and share an order of onion rings.

"How exactly do you pay your bills?" Angela asked.

"Unlike how you walk," Matthew said. "I pay them slowly."

"Sorry," Angela said. "I like to walk fast."

"After being on your feet all day," Matthew said.

Angela shrugged. "I use different muscles when I'm working."

This is a golden opportunity to flirt. "I like your muscles. Especially the ones in back."

Angela's mouth dropped open for a moment. "I don't see how you can keep up with your bills. You don't charge anyone."

"You have so *many* nice muscles, too, Angela," Matthew whispered. "Nice and smooth. Excellent definition, too."

Angela looked away. "What am I supposed to say to that?"

"I'm jealous of your aprons," Matthew said. *Her aprons get to hold her.*

"Matthew, a woman isn't supposed to be too muscular," Angela said. "A woman is supposed to be toned."

"You are seriously toned then," Matthew said. "Especially in the back."

Angela drank some of her Coke. "Have you been staring at me, Matthew?"

"I can't help it," Matthew said, pushing his bowl aside. "You walk faster than I do. I can't help but look at what you let me see." *Ah, now her lips are smiling. No teeth yet.* "And I also watch you from the booth, too. I have the *best* view."

Angela toyed with an onion ring, removing bits of the breading, a half-smile on her face. "So how are you paying your bills?"

She's hard to flirt with! "I'm dipping into my retirement funds," he said. "Here and there, nothing major." He looked at her fingers. "Are you going to eat that onion ring or strip it naked?"

Angela looked at her plate. "Maybe I like to eat my onions naked."

"Now there's an image." *A* very *sexy image.*

"I meant..." Angela smiled broadly. "You know what I meant."

Matthew's shoe found hers. "I like the other meaning better."

"Has your rent gone up, too?" Angela asked.

She's always trying to change the subject. "Not as much as yours is, only two hundred more for an apartment that is falling apart while they build all those factory condos on the shore."

"You mean those 'people storage facilities,' right?" Angela said. "I've seen pictures of them in the paper. They look like maximum security prisons."

"They do." He smiled. "I'll never live in one of those. But... I'll have to find another place in Williamsburg when my lease is up at the end of March."

"Have you already started looking?" Angela asked, disrobing another defenseless onion ring.

"Not at apartments," Matthew said.

She looked up. "Oh? So you're looking for a house?"

"No." *How long can I hold you in my eyes?*

Angela looked away.

Not long enough. I will try again. "Where do you think I should look, Angela?"

"I don't know." She looked at Matthew again. "Maybe... on South Ninth."

That's ten blocks in the wrong direction! "I'm thinking somewhere closer to your shop."

"You are?" she asked.

"Not that I'd actually use it for more than sleeping, shaving, and showering," Matthew said. "I mean, I practically live at your place as it is."

Angela nodded as her fingers tapped the table. "I never thought Williamsburg would ever be truly trendy, did you?"

The subject changes again. "Billyburg is trending itself out of a population."

"What time is it?" Angela asked.

Matthew checked his phone. "Almost nine. We better go see Mr. Simmons." He stood and put on his coat.

Angela didn't move. "We? I can wait here, can't I?"

"I want to be with you, Angela." *Did I say that right?* "I mean, I want you with me. I want you in there with me." *Oh, look at her eyes! They are sparkling. I have to say more things "wrong" to her.*

"Why do you need me in there?" Angela asked.

I do believe she's catching on. "I need another pair of beautiful eyes and another pair of cute ears. I want to know your honest assessment of the man."

"Does this mean that you doubt his wife's story?" Angela asked.

"Not at all," Matthew said. "I trust your judgment and value your opinions."

Angela put on her coat. "Are you trying to sweet-talk me?"

"Yes," Matthew said. "Is it working?"

Angela stood and nodded toward the door. "I'll let you know."

As they rapidly approached the entrance to the Simmons' apartment building, Angela took Matthew's arm. When he opened the entrance door to a dark stairway, she gripped his elbow.

"It's dark," she whispered. "Is there a light switch?"

"I don't see one," Matthew said. He felt along the wall near the railing.

"I don't want to fall," Angela whispered.

"I got you," Matthew said. "We'll go slow."

On the way up the stairs, Matthew felt his arm go numb from Angela's firm grip. Angela didn't relax her grasp until they were standing outside the Simmons' third-floor apartment.

"Well, knock already," Angela said, hovering inches from the door.

Matthew knocked. "You okay?"

"I'm fine," Angela said. "I just . . . I'm fine."

I hope she is. I know my elbow has to be bruised.

Chapter 18

Timothy Simmons, former soldier and anesthetist, was as gray as the blanket covering him as he sat inert and catatonic in an easy chair facing the window looking out onto South 2nd Street. His close-cropped hair and beard had flecks of gray, and his lips were a chalky white.

"Timothy," Gloria said, "this is the lawyer I told you about."

While Angela hugged the arm of a simple blue couch and Gloria sat in an armchair near Timothy, Matthew pulled a kitchen chair close to Timothy. He turned on the microcassette recorder.

"Mr. Simmons, I'm Matthew McConnell."

Timothy's eyes remained glazed.

"Your wife has retained me to help you get the help you need," Matthew said.

Timothy blinked but otherwise remained motionless.

"May I call you Timothy?" Matthew asked.

No response.

"Or would you prefer I call you Lieutenant Simmons?" Matthew asked.

Timothy's lips twitched.

Hmm. It might be too soon to bring up the military. "I'll call you Timothy. Timothy, I'd like to ask you some questions, if I may, and I'm going to record them and take some notes, too, all right?" He wrote Timothy's name on a legal pad. "Okay, when did you first notice that things weren't right in your life?"

Timothy blinked.

"When did you realize you weren't feeling right?" Matthew asked.

Timothy sighed.

This isn't working. I need specific answers, so I have to ask specific questions. "Timothy, how many operations did you witness over in Germany?"

Timothy turned his head slightly.

We have movement. "How many operations did you witness over in Germany? A dozen, fifty, a hundred, a thousand?"

Timothy's lips parted slightly. "Too many," he whispered.

Gloria gasped.

Matthew felt goose bumps on his arm. *He's in there.* "How many?"

Timothy blinked rapidly. "I lost count," he whispered. "Hundreds."

Matthew wrote "find out # of operations." He moved his chair to the side of Timothy's easy chair. "What kinds of surgeries were they?"

"All kinds," Timothy whispered.

"Were they mainly amputations, reconstructions, what?" Matthew asked.

"All kinds," Timothy said, his voice hoarse and dry.

Okay, he's talking. Time to gently shock him. "What made you break down in the OR over at Woodhull Medical?"

"What?" Timothy said. He dropped his right hand off the armrest and pulled the lever, his legs dropping, and he turned the chair to face Matthew.

I have his attention now. "What triggered the incident in the OR over at Woodhull?"

"What incident?" he asked, the dark wrinkles around his eyes tightening.

He has to remember. "Timothy, you had a meltdown in the OR at Woodhull and lost your job," Matthew said, staring into his eyes. "I've had one of those myself. They're no fun to relive, but I need you to do that now. Please describe your meltdown for me."

Timothy blinked and squinted. "It was a . . . a motorcycle accident. A man's . . . his legs were . . . threads."

"And seeing the motorcyclist's leg reminded you of what you

witnessed at Landstuhl in Germany." Matthew gripped his pen. *This is the moment. This is where it has to spill out.*

Timothy nodded, his ashen hands rising and covering his face. "It brought it all back."

"What did you *really* see in the OR, Timothy?" Matthew asked.

"What did I . . . really see?" Timothy's hands shook.

"Yes," Matthew said. "Tell me what you really saw that day."

"I saw . . ." Timothy parted his hands and glanced up at Matthew. "I saw an eighteen-year-old kid with fuzz on his chin, fuzz like a kiwi fruit, you know?"

"Peach fuzz," Matthew said.

"Yeah," Timothy said. "I don't think the boy had ever shaved in his life."

"Do remember the soldier's name?" Matthew asked.

Timothy seemed to search the room, his eyes darting. "I can't remember."

Matthew wrote, "find soldier's name, 18, leg injury." He smiled at Timothy. "It's okay. I have trouble remembering names, too. What did the soldier say or do?"

Timothy's chin quivered. "He came in screaming. They had to restrain him. He kept trying to reach down to his legs, but they weren't there. And then the captain yelled, 'Knock his ass out, Simmons, that's an order!' "

Gloria and Angela jumped on the couch.

"And did you?" Matthew asked.

"I tried," Timothy said, his voice straining, "but he was a big kid, and he kept moving his arms, and he was screaming, 'Don't let them take my legs! Don't let them take my legs!' "

I don't want to ask this. "Did you see his legs?"

Timothy nodded. "What was left of them."

I don't want to ask this either. "What did his legs look like, Timothy?"

"His right leg was gone below the *tibialis* anterior," Timothy said, "and the left leg was gone below the *vastus lateralis.* Both of his *rectus femoris* were in shreds. They were . . ." He blinked away a tear. "They were already gone, man. They were already gone."

Matthew jotted down a few notes. *I'll have to look up those terms later. The man really knows his stuff.* "And then what happened?"

"I put him under, and they removed . . . *everything* up to his hips." He wiped tears off his nose. "I thought about putting him to sleep permanently, you know? He was eighteen. No legs. In a chair for the rest of his life . . ." He shook his head. "Like me."

"What exactly did you do in the OR at Woodhull Medical that day to lose your job?" Matthew asked.

"This," Timothy said. "I cried. I cried my guts out, right there in front of everybody."

Their basis for firing Timothy was him weeping? An anesthetist felt for his patient, and they fired him. That doesn't sound right.

"I have never felt so alone in all my life." Timothy looked at Gloria. "Until you came to get me."

Gloria's eyes shone. "Of course I did."

Matthew noticed Angela wiping away a few tears.

This is getting to me, too. I have to remain objective. "Did Woodhull pay you that month?"

Timothy looked at Gloria. "Did they?"

Gloria nodded. "They even gave us money for his unused sick and vacation days and kept him on their health plan through the rest of that year and most of the next. They did right by us."

No compensation there. "From that day on, did you leave this apartment?"

"No," Timothy said.

I can't even imagine that. "Do you have nightmares?"

"Yes, but I'd rather not tell you about them," Timothy said.

"It might help your case," Matthew said. "It can *only* help your case."

"I doubt it," Timothy said. "I was never in battle."

"Try me," Matthew said.

"I already told the army, and they said—"

"I need to hear your nightmares, Timothy," Matthew interrupted.

Timothy looked at Gloria. "I don't want her to hear them. I don't want to give her nightmares."

"I think she can handle it," Matthew said. *That is one tough woman.*

Timothy leaned forward and looked only at his wife. "I should have told you already, huh? So you'd know why I couldn't sleep."

"It's okay, Tim," Gloria said. "You're telling me now."

Timothy took a deep breath and exhaled. "In the dream, I'm in a field of bloody arms and legs and there's a boy with peach fuzz on his chin screaming at me to find his legs. Only I can't find any that match and this one's too long and that one's too short and this one's too wide and that one doesn't have a foot and this one's missing toes and the boy . . . keeps . . . *screaming,* 'Don't let them take my legs!' "

That would drive me insane. "How often do you have this dream?"

Timothy turned to Matthew. "Just about every time I close my eyes."

"Have you tried sleeping pills?" Matthew asked.

"I won't let her get me any," Timothy whispered. "I might take them all. I've already put her through this hell. I don't want to put her through more. I've been asking her to divorce me and go on with her life, but she won't do it."

Gloria left the couch and knelt in front of Timothy, taking his hand in hers. "And I never will."

Timothy's eyes welled with tears. "You're too good for me, you know? God broke the mold when He made you."

Matthew saw Angela wipe away another tear.

"Do you really think you can help me?" Timothy asked.

Matthew nodded. "I will do my best." He turned off the recorder and put it in his pocket. Then he stood and shook Timothy's hand. "I'm proud to know you, Timothy. Thank you for serving my country with distinction and courage."

Timothy shook his head. "You shouldn't thank me. I've still got my legs."

"You helped save a lot of lives," Matthew said. "And I know you'll be using your legs again soon."

Gloria rose and handed him a large envelope. "Here are Timothy's service records."

"Thank you," Matthew said. "I have your number. I will be in touch." He held out his hand to Angela, and she took it long enough to stand.

Angela nodded at Gloria, smiled at Timothy, and led Matthew to the door. In the hallway, she grabbed Matthew's elbow, and they descended the stairs. Once outside, she released her grip and immediately headed toward Driggs Avenue.

"You okay?" Matthew asked.

"That was . . . pretty intense," Angela said softly, glancing back.

"Yeah," Matthew said, quickening his pace to keep up. "What do you think?"

"I think he's due everything this country owes him," Angela said.

"So do I," Matthew said. "What do you think about their relationship?"

"It's true," Angela said. "It's real."

"There's true love there, huh?" Matthew asked.

Angela nodded.

"For worse and for worser." He offered his elbow again.

Angela took it.

She must have a thing for elbows. And speed. I need to wear my running shoes on our next not-a-date.

At the door to Angela's shop, she rapidly unlocked the door and held it open. "You could come in for some coffee."

An invitation. He stepped inside. "I should have some of your decaf. I'm having trouble sleeping."

"I'll put some on." She locked the door behind them.

"You're a master locksmith, Miss Smith," Matthew said.

"Funny," she said.

Matthew sat in his booth, Angela brought two cups, and they sat beside each other in silence, sipping and sighing.

"That hit the spot," Matthew said. "I didn't know decaf could taste so good."

Angela stretched out her arms. "I'm magic."

"Yes, you are," Matthew said. *And I mean it.*

Angela yawned. "It's getting so late. I am going to have trouble getting up tomorrow morning."

I know what that means. "I guess I better be going then."

He followed Angela out of the booth and to the door. "Thank you for another not-a-date."

Angela opened two of the deadbolts. "It might have been a date." She looked up at him. "It was mostly a date."

"What is your definition of a date?" Matthew asked.

"Time spent with someone . . . you like," Angela said.

She likes me. Well, she mostly likes me. "But you said it was only *mostly* a date."

She unlocked four more locks and the main deadbolt. "You didn't spend the entire time only with me, did you?"

"Ah," Matthew said. "No work next time."

Angela looked down. "If there is a next time."

Hmm? "I hope there is. Don't you?"

"Maybe," she said.

She is so cute when she's trying to be shy. Matthew stretched his arms, his hands dangerously close to Angela's shoulders. "I will see you bright and early in the morning, Angela."

"You look so tired," Angela said. "Why don't you sleep in? I can call you if anyone needs legal help. You do free consultations over the phone, too, right?"

That's no fun. "And miss breakfast? I have nothing to eat in my apartment except last night's pizza."

Angela reached out her hand and touched his forearm. "You look worn out. The circles under your eyes have circles. Why don't you get some extra sleep? I'll call you if anyone needs to talk to you."

Matthew rubbed her arm. "What if you need me, Angela?"

"I'll . . . I'll call you." She slid her arm out from under his hand.

"I'll keep my phone charged," Matthew said.

"Good." She opened the door. "Good night, Matthew."

He turned in the doorway. *I want to kiss her cheek so badly, and it's only inches away. If this was only mostly a date, should I* almost *kiss her?*

He stepped onto the sidewalk instead. "Good night, Angela. See you tomorrow night, right?"

Angela nodded and closed the door.

He watched her finish her routine of shutting off lights, and then he turned and headed home.

If she needs me, she'll call. I hope she needs me. And even if she doesn't, I hope she calls.

He flexed his elbow and winced. *She has to have the strongest hands of any woman on earth. I may have "Angela elbow." I may need to wear elbow pads from now on.*

Chapter 19

Matthew slept in until noon, and when he woke, he called Angela.

The phone rang twelve times before going to voice mail.

She must really be busy. He left a message: "Thank you for suggesting that I sleep in, partner. I really needed the sleep. I'll call you later, and I will be there to help you close. Bye."

He spent the afternoon surfing the Internet and collecting information on PTSD, most of it from the Mayo Clinic Web site. What he learned reinforced his belief that Timothy had a classic case of PTSD:

- PTSD triggers: war and its effects, rape, child abuse, physical attack, being threatened by a weapon, fire, natural disasters, a mugging, robbery, assault, civil conflict, car accident, plane crash, torture, kidnapping, life-threatening medical diagnosis, terrorist attack . . .

We should all have some form of PTSD from simply waking up in the morning and turning on the TV.

- Flashbacks, fear, nightmares, and overpowering thoughts are symptoms, and memories of the event refuse to go away. Early treatment is imperative. PTSD can show up anywhere from three months to years after the event.

Timothy didn't get much treatment. I hope it isn't too late to help him.

• PTSD sufferers ignore and reject other people, feel numb, and avoid doing things they once enjoyed. They feel hopeless. They have difficulty remembering things. They have trouble concentrating and difficulty maintaining close relationships. They are irritable, feel guilty, often drink too much, sleep little, are easily frightened, and hear or see things that aren't there.

That last sentence could apply to the current Congress.

• Symptoms of PTSD come and go, particularly during times of great stress, and many who endure PTSD attempt or commit suicide. Doctors believe PTSD is caused by inherited risks of fear and depression, childhood trauma, and the way the sufferer's brain works.

In other words, doctors don't have many clues. It must be hard to gauge how a single event, such as 9/11, might not *affect one person too badly while reducing another person to PTSD.*

• Females, the depressed, people who live alone, and those who were abused as children seem prone to PTSD. Untreated PTSD can lead to heart disease, chronic pain, arthritis, thyroid disease, bone problems . . .

Okay, what specifically caused Timothy's PTSD? Prolonged exposure to surgeries on wounded soldiers. Is it a chronic condition? Yes. He hasn't left his apartment in two years. Does he have flashbacks? Yes. One flashback cost him a good job. Does he have nightmares? Every time he closes his eyes. Is he avoiding life in general? Yes. Does he seem numb? Yes. Does he have trouble sleeping? Yes. Is the relationship with his wife in danger? Yes and no. Is he suicidal? Not sure, but he said he didn't want sleeping pills. I'm sure he has thought about suicide.

I think we have a case.

Criteria from the DSM—the *Diagnostic and Statistical Manual of Mental Disorders*—cinched it. Timothy had witnessed events that involved death and serious injury. He felt fear and helplessness. He relived those horrific events daily. He avoided talking about any of it—until now. *Two years of silence! Does he seem "on his guard"? Not sure. He didn't seem too paranoid. Is PTSD destroying his life? Yes.*

Okay, he has it, despite what the U. S. Army says. How do we treat it?

Matthew read down the list of treatment plans. Timothy would need antipsychotics, antidepressants, something to help him sleep, and psychotherapy—both group and individual—to help him cope. Even acupuncture might help. *All of these combined might help Timothy break the cycle of his fears.*

Matthew thought about Mrs. Simmons. *She obviously has "compassion fatigue." She may need some therapy, too.*

Matthew looked back at his copious notes, focusing on the symptoms.

I may have mild PTSD from all these dates from hell. How am I coping? With Angela's help. She's making me talk about it. Talking is the best kind of therapy.

And I need to talk to her some more.

He checked the time. *Three-fifteen. I hope she isn't too busy.*

Angela answered on the second ring. "Smith's Sweet Treats and Coffee."

"I missed you this morning." *I really missed her all day.* "You busy?"

"It's quiet now," she said softly.

"I hope you didn't fix me anything for breakfast or lunch," Matthew said.

"I didn't," Angela said. "I knew you'd listen to me for a change. How much sleep did you get?"

"Twice as much as usual." *Too much. I still feel groggy. I need some coffee.*

"What are you doing now?" Angela asked.

"I'm researching PTSD," Matthew said. "I think Timothy has a strong case. He has many of the symptoms."

"What are they?" Angela asked.

"Flashbacks, nightmares, emotional numbness, avoiding the world, hopelessness, difficulty in his marriage, guilt, trouble sleeping, concentrating."

"And what kinds of treatment will you recommend that the army pay for?" Angela asked.

He leafed through his notes. "Antipsychotics for starters."

"Like Abilify?" Angela asked.

He looked down the list of antipsychotics and found Abilify. "Right. Or antidepressants such as Zoloft or Paxil, and something called Prazosin to help him sleep. None of those are cheap."

"Should he be seeing a psychiatrist?" Angela asked.

"He'll need lots of individual and group therapy," Matthew said. "I'm sure there are others out there who are in the same boat."

"Are there any other treatments?" Angela asked.

"One study suggested that acupuncture might help," Matthew said.

"Have you ever tried that?" Angela asked.

"No, but if all else fails—"

"I have a customer," Angela interrupted.

Don't go yet! "Did you get my message?"

"Yes," Angela said. "When are you coming to help clean up?"

Is that eagerness in her voice? I hope so. "I'll try to be there by seven-thirty, okay? I have some laundry to do."

"Okay. Bye."

Click.

"Okay," he said to the static. "See you soon."

Matthew did two loads of laundry, showered, and shaved, arriving at Angela's a little before 7:30. He immediately put on his apron and got to work, mopping the kitchen floor, sweeping the dining area, and polishing tables. At 8:00, Angela locked the front door, and Matthew mopped the dining area. At 8:04, she finished counting down the register and looked at Matthew, who had already taken off his apron.

"That was a record," she said. "Four minutes."

"We'll beat it tomorrow," Matthew said.

Angela nodded and walked to the front door.

That's it? No decaf? No conversation? "I'll be here bright and early in the morning."

"Good." She extended her arms, took a step forward, and gave Matthew a fierce hug.

Matthew put his hands lightly on her back.

Angela stepped back and fumbled with her hands, staring at the floor. "I'll have your breakfast ready. What would you like?"

She's shaking. Her whole body is shaking. Why is she shaking? "Surprise me."

"I'll try." She looked up briefly. "Bye."

Matthew stepped outside.

Angela closed the door.

Matthew waved.

Angela nodded, then swept through the dining area, turned off lights, and disappeared into the kitchen.

That was completely *unexpected. It was very nice, and as hugs go, that one . . .* wow. *Her shoulders pressed into my chest, her arms squeezed me like a boa constrictor, her head rested on my shoulder, and her hips locked onto my thighs. It lasted so long I could feel her heartbeat in my stomach. Or was it my own heartbeat? Maybe a little of both. And such heat! She kind of smelled lemony, too. Lemons and coffee and pastries. She smells as sweet—and sour, but in a nice way—as she is.*

She missed me, too.

I should not *see her more often.*

Maybe if I stay away for two *days, I can get a kiss.*

Chapter 20

Matthew beat Angela to Smith's Sweet Treats and Coffee, arriving at 5:55 AM and peering up at swollen, black storm clouds moving through the gloom overhead. *We are going to have a major snowstorm.*

Angela opened the door and cocked her head toward his booth.

"French toast?" Matthew said, entering and ripping off his coat.

"You said you liked variety," she said. "I hope you like blackberry syrup."

Matthew looked at his plate, powdered sugar floating on a lake of syrup. "I like." He sat. "The clouds out there look pretty ominous today. And the temperatures seemed to drop the closer I came to the shop."

"Ha ha." Angela sat across from him.

What did I say? "Oh, I didn't mean it got colder—"

"I know what you meant," Angela interrupted, glancing at the window. "I've already turned up the heat twice. We're supposed to have quite a storm. Maybe even a blizzard. They're predicting up to two feet."

"We'll still be open for business, no matter what, right?" Matthew asked.

"Right." She glided out of the booth. "I have to check on the coffee."

Matthew reached for her arm and missed. "Angela?"

She turned.

"Thank you for the hug last night."

She nodded.

"It kept me warm all the way home," Matthew said.

"Me, too." She sighed. "I'll get your coffee."

Matthew dug into his French toast, and the second Angela tried to join him in the booth with her coffee, a serious rush began.

"This always happens just before a storm," she said. "You have work to do, right?"

Matthew nodded. "Thank you for breakfast, Angela."

"You're welcome," Angela said.

Matthew took out his notes and listened again to Timothy's interview. In the old days with SYG, he would unleash a media firestorm on television and the Internet to force a plaintiff to do the right thing. He knew he couldn't do that with this case. *I have to go in low-key. The U.S. Army probably doesn't like to be blindsided. I know they'll put up a wall of silence, but if I keep pushing gently, I may get somewhere.*

I have to make friends with the enemy this time.

He sifted through Timothy's files and found the name of William Wick, MD, the psychiatrist at the VA hospital in Manhattan who last treated Timothy.

Time to start some noise, but not as a lawyer. That's a surefire way to get nowhere. I'll have to become a potential patient instead.

He dialed the main number for the hospital.

"Good afternoon, how may I direct your call?" a bored female voice asked.

At least it's not a computerized system with all that button-pushing. "Could you transfer me to Dr. William Wick's office? Thank you. It's an emergency."

A few *minutes* later, a woman answered. "This is Dr. Wick's office. How may I help you?"

"I need to talk to Dr. Wick," Matthew said breathlessly. "I'm just back from Afghanistan, and I'm in crisis. A buddy of mine told me Dr. Wick was the man to talk to in case of emergency."

"Are you currently contemplating or in the act of committing suicide?" she asked.

What a question! "No, ma'am, but thanks for asking."

"Would you like to set up an appointment?" she asked.

Ignore the question. "My buddy's name is Second Lieutenant Timothy Simmons. Dr. Wick helped him about two years ago. I *really* need to speak to Dr. Wick."

"One moment."

I hope she's checking the records. She'll see I'm telling the truth—at least about Timothy. The next part is going to be tricky. "You still there? It will only take a few minutes, I swear. Please. I beg you."

The woman sighed. "I'll transfer you."

I like receptionists who have a heart. Many don't, acting as if their bosses are demigods who can't be bothered without an official appointment that only they can approve.

"This is Dr. Wick. To whom am I speaking?"

No more lies now, and it's time to talk fast. "Doctor Wick, I'm Matthew McConnell, and I'm calling in reference to a former patient of yours who I am representing, Second Lieutenant Timothy Simmons. You assessed him two years ago after an incident in the OR at Woodhull Medical. Does any of this ring a bell?"

"*First* of all—"

"I know you can't talk about any of your patients, Doctor," Matthew interrupted. "I just want to know if you remember treating Timothy. He was an anesthetist at Landstuhl who claimed to have PTSD."

"I can't—"

"All of this is completely off the record, I promise," Matthew interrupted. "I only need some hypothetical information for argument's sake."

"What kind of information?" Dr. Wick asked.

Always confuse them with vague phrases. "Or I can talk, and you can feel free not to answer."

"I'm really very busy," Dr. Wick said.

"Yes, I'm sure you are very busy denying PTSD status to suffering soldiers," Matthew said. *We'll let that hang in the air a second to let him feel the* real *reason I'm calling.*

"I'm going to hang up," Dr. Wick said.

"If you really wanted to end this conversation," Matthew said, "you would have already hung up. You remember Timothy, don't you?"

"I can't say whether I remember him or not," Dr. Wick said.

"Let me refresh your memory then, hypothetically speaking, of course," Matthew said. "Let's say an OR anesthetist witnesses hundreds of gruesome operations and amputations, say, at Landstuhl, operations made necessary by combat in Iraq and Afghanistan, and two years after his discharge this anesthetist has severe difficulties. He comes to a VA psychiatrist, someone very much like yourself, for help, only this psychiatrist determines there's nothing wrong with him because he was not in active combat." Matthew took a breath. "This hypothetical anesthetist then becomes numb, never leaving his apartment for two years, unable to hold a job or sleep through the night without terrible nightmares. You still there, Dr. Wick?"

"I am," Dr. Wick said.

This is a good sign. Maybe his conscience is bothering him about Timothy. "What do you think of my hypothetical situation?"

"Is this hypothetical anesthetist still taking the hypothetical antidepressant I might have hypothetically prescribed?" Dr. Wick asked.

Aha! Dr. Wick prescribed an antidepressant. Why do that if Timothy wasn't depressed? "He cannot currently afford to take antidepressants because he cannot hold a job. He and his wife are living on her salary and the help of their church. Why would a psychiatrist prescribe an antidepressant to a soldier who had been out of the service for two years? Hypothetically speaking."

"Perhaps because of separation anxiety," Dr. Wick said. "Soldiers sometimes get depressed when they leave the service. They miss the order of things. They miss their comrades-in-arms. Thus, a psychiatrist might prescribe something like Abilify to ease the transition."

Matthew found and circled "Abilify" in his notes. "In this hypothetical case I'm describing, is the *only* reason this soldier wasn't granted PTSD status because he was never in combat?"

"Hypothetically speaking, yes," Dr. Wick said.

"This hypothetical soldier saw the *results* of combat, Doctor Wick," Matthew said.

"And so did other military medical personnel and thousands of combat soldiers who are currently leading normal lives," Dr. Wick said.

"As far as you know," Matthew said.

"I only see them when they're in crisis, Mr. McConnell," Dr. Wick said.

"So you agree that my hypothetical soldier was in crisis," Matthew said quickly.

"This conversation—"

"What about the nightmares he has every time he closes his eyes?" Matthew interrupted.

"Can you *prove* he has nightmares, Mr. McConnell?" Dr. Wick asked.

"No, but you can't prove he *doesn't* have them, can you?" Matthew asked.

"Good day, Mr. McConnell."

Click.

Matthew frowned and finished his cup of coffee.

If I were still at SYG, at this point I'd have our investigators dig up some dirt on Dr. Wick to use against him. There was always some kind of dirt, and that often gave us the advantage we needed to win the case. I wish we already had Wi-Fi so I could do some Internet searches on the guy. Patients "grade" their doctors more and more online. Maybe he's an incompetent doctor.

No. I didn't get that vibe. The fact that didn't hang up on me speaks volumes. He listened. That's more than I expected him to do. Maybe he feels some regret and will give Timothy another exam.

He also made an outstanding point. How can you prove a person has nightmares? If I can prove that Timothy has debilitating nightmares, I have a case.

How do I do that?

Angela refilled Matthew's cup. "That didn't sound too good." She rolled her eyes. "You were in crisis?"

Angela's cute little ears pick up everything, even when she's swamped with customers! "I had to get my foot in the door somehow."

"You're a pretty convincing liar," Angela said. "I only caught the first part, though. Who were you talking to?"

"Doctor Wick, the psychiatrist who originally examined Timothy after his meltdown," Matthew said, shaking his head. "You know, if Timothy went out and committed a crime, he wouldn't be able to use PTSD as a defense because according to the U.S. Army, he doesn't have it, and if the U.S. Army says it, it must be true."

"Get another psychiatrist to examine him," Angela said.

"I could, but I don't know that many psychiatrists, especially ones who deal with PTSD on a regular basis," Matthew said.

Angela went behind the counter and came back with a business card. "You could call him."

Matthew looked at the card. "Doctor Kenneth Penn." *With an address on North 7th Street, a few blocks from here.* "How do you know him?"

"He's a friend of the family," Angela said. "He's retired now, but he still sees patients."

"How long has he been retired?" Matthew asked.

"Five, maybe six years," Angela said.

Shoot. "I need a practicing psychiatrist."

"Doctor Penn served in Vietnam as a medic," Angela said. "And if a Vietnam medic turned psychiatrist says a current vet has PTSD . . ."

"He was regular army?" Matthew asked.

Angela nodded.

"So he should know all about PTSD," Matthew said.

"Yes," Angela said. "Want me to give him a call?"

"You're not my receptionist. Angela. I'll call him."

"I know the man," Angela said. "I have to vouch for you first. He's retired, remember? He has his own hours, just like you do." Angela placed the business card on the table and picked up Matthew's phone. "May I?"

"Sure."

She punched in the number. "Oh, I have some cookies coming out." She walked around the counter. "Hi, Doctor Penn? Angela Smith . . ."

Matthew stared at the business card. *What makes a person become a psychiatrist? How can anyone listen to other people's misery for a living? Hmm. I kind of do that, too, don't I?*

Angela returned a few minutes later. "The doctor will see you now."

"Just like that," Matthew said.

She handed him the phone. "Don't keep him waiting."

"Where are the cookies?" Matthew asked, putting on his coat.

"Oh, they weren't quite ready." She smiled. "Hurry back, or I'll eat them all."

"Okay."

Matthew walked through snow flurries that turned into a steady rain of snow by the time he reached North 7th and Roebling and Dr. Penn's all-brick house, a classy brass nameplate on the door announcing: "The Doctor Is In."

Matthew rang the bell, and a tall black man wearing jeans and a T-shirt under a brown blazer opened the door.

"Mr. McConnell?" he said.

He was in Vietnam? His hair doesn't have a speck of gray in it. "Yes sir," Matthew said.

"Come in, come in," Dr. Penn said.

Matthew followed Dr. Penn up a shiny wooden staircase to an open area where comfortable-looking brown leather couches and wingback chairs surrounded a coffee table.

Dr. Penn sat in one of the wingback chairs, Matthew in the other.

"Thank you for meeting with me on such short notice, Dr. Penn," Matthew said.

"I'd do anything to help another soldier," Dr. Penn said. "We're all in the same family. Tell me about his case."

Matthew took the microcassette recorder from his briefcase. "I'll let him tell you." He played the tape.

When he finished, Dr. Penn smiled. "You drew him out very well, Matthew."

"It wasn't easy," Matthew said. "Do you think we have a case?"

"It seems clear-cut to me," Dr. Penn said, "but I will need to examine Timothy in person to make a more accurate assessment."

"I can set it up," Matthew said, "but as you heard on the tape, Timothy hasn't left his house in two years."

"I'll gladly make another house call," Dr. Penn said. "I need the exercise."

Matthew took out his phone. "When would be the best time for you to meet with Timothy?"

"Soon," Dr. Penn said. "He needs help now."

"Could you see him today?" Matthew asked.

Dr. Penn looked out the window at a literal wall of snow. "Hmm. Today would be fine, but only if I can see him within the next two hours. Will you look at that? It's been a couple years since our last blizzard. We were due for this one."

"They live over near Milly's at Berry and South Second," Matthew said.

"I know the place," Dr. Penn said. "It still has the old vinyl Coke signs out front."

"So . . . in an hour? Two?"

"Make it two," Dr. Penn said. "I need to find my snowshoes."

Matthew blinked. "Your . . . snowshoes."

"I have a pair," Dr. Penn said. "Got them after the blizzard of 2006, and they came in mighty handy during the blizzard of 2010. Go ahead and call them while I try to find those shoes." He stood and walked downstairs.

Matthew called Gloria's work number. "How's Timothy doing?"

"Better," she said. "He's eating two meals a day now. He even answered the phone when I called him during my lunch break."

That sounds promising. "When will you be home?"

"They're sending us home early because of the snow," Gloria said. "I'll be home in twenty minutes or so. Why?"

"I'm sending a psychiatrist named Dr. Kenneth Penn to talk to Timothy," Matthew said. "Dr. Penn was an army medic in Vietnam, and he'll be there in about two hours. I thought we could use his expert knowledge." Matthew told her about the call to Dr. Wick. "I hope this doesn't put you out."

"No," Gloria said. "I'm simply amazed how fast you work, Mr. McConnell."

Dr. Penn clunked up the stairs holding an enormous pair of snowshoes.

"Expect Dr. Penn to arrive at your place in two hours," Matthew said. "He will be wearing his snowshoes."

"His . . . snowshoes," Gloria said.

"I'll let him explain why he has them," Matthew said. "Give my best to Timothy."

"I will," Gloria said. "Thank you, Mr. McConnell."

He closed his phone. "Those are huge."

"They work," Dr. Penn said.

"About your fee," Matthew said.

Dr. Penn set his snowshoes on the floor. "Don't worry about it. Glad to help."

"Are you sure?" Matthew asked.

"Sure I'm sure," he said. "I'm doing this as a favor to Angela." He placed his feet on the snowshoes.

Matthew stood. "How do you know the Smiths?"

"Oh, only in passing," Dr. Penn said. "Whenever I need real coffee I can afford or the most delicious pastries on this or any other planet, I go to Smith's Sweet Treats. My children always loved their cookies."

Matthew waited to hear more, but Dr. Penn said no more. *How, then, is he a friend of the family?*

Dr. Penn stepped off the snowshoes. "A pleasure meeting you, Matthew. Thank you for being Angela's friend."

"Sure." *Something's not clicking here. A friend of the family should know more about the family.*

"After I meet with Timothy, I'll write up my report," Dr. Penn said. "I assume you'll need me for court."

"I hope it doesn't come to that, but if it does, yes, I will need you," Matthew said.

Dr. Penn extended his hand. "I will be glad to help."

Matthew shook his hand. "Thank you."

While shaking off snow as he returned to Angela's, Matthew couldn't shake off his suspicions. *Dr. Penn is a retired psychiatrist who* still *makes house calls. He said he'd be glad to make* another *house call. He's doing this as a favor to Angela, who says he's a friend of the family but acts as if he doesn't know them well at all.*

And Angela punched in Dr. Penn's phone number without looking at the business card.

"Thank you for being Angela's friend," he says. Is Angela his patient? She might be. She's certainly anxious when she's out with me. She's anxious whenever she's outside at any time. All those locks and the heavy-duty steel doors in the back. She's afraid of something, and maybe she hugged me so fiercely because she was scared.

But she let me leave right after that hug.

What could that woman possibly be afraid of? Love? I hope not.

She takes my elbow, not my hand, hugs the skin off me, and seems hesitant to touch me unless she *initiates the contact. And when I touch her, she . . . recoils.*

What happened to her?

Snow cascaded like a waterfall in front of Angela's, and the sidewalk was covered by at least four inches of snow. He glanced across the street and didn't see La Estrella's garish neon lights.

He stamped his feet just inside the door, and the sound seemed to echo. The dining area was empty, and Angela sat on her stool in front of the counter reading a newspaper.

"When did La Estrella close?" he asked.

Angela folded the paper. "About an hour ago."

"Good for us." He advanced toward the counter.

She looked around the empty dining area. "Really?" Angela poured him a large cup of coffee. "How'd it go with Dr. Penn?"

He reached for the cup.

Angela drew it away and walked around the counter to the booth.

So now *she wants to talk. So do I.*

Matthew sat, Angela sliding in beside him.

"So, how did it go?" she asked.

She certainly seems eager to know. "Dr. Penn is going to make another house call."

Angela exhaled softly. "Oh?"

"I didn't know psychiatrists made house calls, did you?" Matthew asked.

"Dr. Penn evidently does." She gripped her cup. "When will he see Timothy?"

She's about to crush that cup. "In about two hours," Matthew said, taking a sip of his coffee. "This is so good. It's like taking a sip of heaven." He nudged her knee with his. "Dr. Penn says he likes your coffee and pastries. Does he visit you often?"

"Not . . . very often," Angela said. She looked at an older white couple banging through the door and shaking off snow. "It's Mr. and Mrs. Visco." She stood. "They're kind of loud," she whispered. "And they never tip."

"Angie, did you see?" Mrs. Visco yelled, "La Estrella is closed!"

Angela rolled her eyes and went behind the counter, popping

up two large cups. "Some people just can't handle a little storm, Mrs. Visco."

"Why'd they even open for business in the first place?" Mr. Visco asked. "They're open, they're closed."

Angela poured their coffee. "The usual?"

"To go this time, Ange," Mr. Visco said. "We want to get home before it gets too bad out there. The wind's already kicking up."

Angela bagged two of everything in her showcase.

That's a substantial "usual."

"It has all the ingredients of a blizzard, Angie," Mrs. Visco said. "Will you be open tomorrow?"

"I'll be open." She took their money, gave them their change, and handed Mr. Visco the bag.

A buzzer sounded from the kitchen.

"I'll be back," Angela said, and she hurried back to the kitchen.

Yeah, I'd run away from them, too. Oh, here they come to shout at me.

Mr. and Mrs. Visco stopped beside Matthew's booth.

"So you're the coffeehouse lawyer," Mrs. Visco said.

"Yes." *And I'm only a few feet away from you, ma'am. Maybe they can't hear themselves talk unless they shout.*

"I may have you look over our estate plan," Mr. Visco said. "I'm sure it needs some work."

"I'd be glad to," Matthew said.

Mrs. Visco stared at the front window. "It's getting bad out there."

"It'll be fine, Vi," Mr. Visco said. "It's not supposed to be as bad as the blizzard of 2006. Twenty-seven inches we got from that one."

Mrs. Visco shivered. "We didn't get out of our apartment for three days."

"And that one was nothing compared to the blizzard of '78." He smiled at Matthew. "Probably before your time."

"I was only a baby then," Matthew said.

"We had hurricane-force winds during that one," Mr. Visco said. "They had thirty inches of drifting snow out on Long Island."

"That last one we had was pretty bad, too," Mrs. Visco said. "A day or two after Christmas, wasn't it?"

"I believe it was, Vi." He turned to Matthew, setting the bag on the table. "I had invested in a snow blower by then."

Mrs. Visco frowned. "Smoky thing."

"But it made a clear path for us, didn't it, dear?" Mr. Visco asked.

"If you call coughing the entire time walking," Mrs. Visco said.

"Didn't we come here that day?" Mr. Visco squinted. "I think we did. But Angie was closed. Funny, I remember that now. I pushed that blower all the way from our house to that door, but the door was locked, wasn't it, Vi?"

"I think you're right," Mrs. Visco said. "It's the only time I remember Smith's being closed in all the years it's been here." She nodded at the front window. "Unlike *them.* I'll bet they'll be closed for a week."

"Two weeks." Mr. Visco picked up his bag. "We better be going. I need to get some gas for the blower. Nice to meet you."

"Nice to meet you," Matthew said.

After they left, Angela brought out a tray of fresh oatmeal and raisin cookies and placed them in front of Matthew.

"Are they all for me?" Matthew asked.

"Not all of them." She picked up a cookie. "Weren't they a trip?"

"They were nice," Matthew said, folding a warm cookie and popping it into his mouth.

"They're excellent customers, and they've always been loud," Angela said. "My mama tells me I used to hold my ears whenever they were in the shop when I was little."

Matthew swallowed and took a sip of coffee. "They told me they once came here, and you were closed, Angie, during the blizzard of 2010."

"I *hate* that name," Angela said. "Do I look like an Angie? It's almost as bad as Mr. Visco calling me 'Ange' or someone calling me Angel. I'm no angel. And the *way* she says it. I'm Brooklyn, but that woman is from the bottom of the brook."

Hmm. She tried valiantly to deflect my question, but I'm not flinching. "So, were you closed that day?"

Angela's eyes darted to her hands. "Yes. I think I was. The whole neighborhood shut down."

"What was that like?" Matthew asked.

"It was pretty quiet." She picked up another cookie.

"So that's been your only day off ever?" Matthew asked.

She took a bite and nodded.

"What did you do on your day off, *Ange*?" Matthew asked.

"Well, *Matt,* I couldn't go anywhere, could I?" Angela said. "Twenty inches of snow, high winds, snowdrifts everywhere. I lost power a few times. I was upstairs . . . for most of it."

He stretched his arm out behind her, gripping the top of the booth. "How did you stay warm?"

Angela immediately leaned forward. "I have something called blankets."

I put my arm up, and she leans forward. He pulled his arm back.

Angela leaned back into the seat.

That's . . . not normal. "What if this storm turns into a blizzard?"

"As long as I have power, I'll stay open," Angela said.

Let's try this again. He rested his arm on top of the booth behind her.

Angela leaned forward.

Is she doing that on purpose? "But how will you stay warm if you lose power, Angie?"

"I still have blankets, *Matty,*" she said.

He slipped his hand off the top of the booth and rubbed her back.

Angela's shoulders tensed.

Matthew lifted his hand, returning his arm to the top of the booth. "It's getting pretty thick out there. I may not be able to see well enough to get home. I'd hate to start home and end up in the East River."

"Or Manhattan," Angela said. "Or Bushwick, or the Bronx, or Queens, or Staten Island, or Long Island, or Trinidad, Haiti, or Honduras." She glanced up at the window. "You should leave now while it's not too bad."

She really *doesn't like my arm behind her.* He pulled his arm back and folded his hands in his lap. "And not help you clean up? I can't miss my daily workout. You're getting me back into shape."

Angela leaned back in the booth. "I haven't exactly been busy, and I probably won't get many more customers."

Time for one more experiment. He slid his left hand to her right thigh. "I want to stay. I can't think of anyone I'd rather be snowed in with."

Angela scooted to her left, Matthew's hand dropping to the seat. "You don't have to stay. I'll be fine." She slid out of the booth and stared out the front window, her eyes glazing over.

She doesn't like me touching her at all. *Wow.* "Angela, I won't be fine if I leave. I'd need snowshoes to get home now. I can sleep right here in this booth. I could borrow a few blankets from you, couldn't I?"

Angela turned from the window, her eyes on the floor. "Then I'll be cold."

"You could . . . join me," Matthew said.

She looked up.

"And we could watch the snow together." He slipped out of the booth, dragged the table out, and pushed the two seats together. "Instant bed."

Angela smiled briefly. "You make it look *so* tempting."

"With some blankets and a few pillows," Matthew said, "it will be a booth bed fit for a queen. Got any popcorn?"

Angela nodded.

"We'll have the world's largest widescreen TV in front of us, a beautiful snowy scene to watch, a bowl of popcorn, and lots of quiet. What could be more peaceful?" *I should have said "romantic."*

"It sounds . . . it sounds good, Matthew." She smiled.

There's the smile I love to see. "Now, will this be a date or a not-a-date?"

She looked away. "I'll let you know."

And there's the shy girl I love to watch.

"I'll go get us some blankets," she said.

"And two pillows," Matthew said.

Angela returned with two blankets and *one* pillow.

Matthew was about to ask for an explanation when she draped one blanket over him, positioned the pillow between them, wrapped herself tightly in her blanket, and bounced into the booth, leaning lightly against the pillow.

At least it's not a Fendi B Bag this time.

"I bet you we don't see a single snowplow," Matthew said, as nothing and no one traveled by Angela's window but twisting sheets and walls of snow.

"That's an easy bet to win," Angela said.

"Okay, I bet we don't see a single emergency vehicle," Matthew said.

Angela leaned into the pillow, and Matthew felt the pressure. "That's another easy bet to win. Driggs will be covered for days."

"Don't you like snow, Angela?" Matthew asked.

She shook her head. "I don't like anything that cuts down on my profits."

Matthew leaned to his left, trying to catch her eyes.

She looked away.

"I love snow," Matthew said. "I remember so many good times. Sledding at Fort Green Park, snowball fights, building snow forts on opposite sides of Bedford Avenue and having snowball wars. You have any memories like that?"

Angela shook her head. "I was always working here. I went to school, I came here, I worked, I did my homework, I said my prayers, and I went to sleep. Some childhood, huh?"

"I worked in my parents' store, too, but I always found a way to escape into the snow." He watched the snow. "Look at it! I wonder if that snow is good for packing. Let's make a snowman."

"You're kidding," Angela said.

"Okay, a snowwoman." *A snow person?*

She leaned harder into the pillow. "But I just got comfortable."

"We can put a 'Yes, We're Open' sign on her." He slid his feet to the left and met hers.

"You want to go out there now?" Angela asked.

He pulled off his blanket. "Why not?"

"It's cold," Angela said with a shiver.

He folded the blanket and placed it beside him. "It won't take us that long."

Angela sighed. "What if I'm comfortable where I am?"

He crawled over her and put on his coat. "Then I will build *you* a snowwoman." *I wish I had gloves. It will have to be a small snowwoman.* "You make the sign."

"You're serious," Angela said.

"I'm always serious about fun," Matthew said.

Angela swung her legs off the seat but didn't take off her blanket. "Seriously."

While Angela took small steps to the kitchen to find some cardboard, Matthew fashioned a snowwoman about three feet high, complete with an ample bosom and Angela's exquisite booty.

"Come out and see," Matthew said, blowing on his hands.

"I am *not* catching a cold, Matthew," Angela said. "I can see it fine from here." She fed a cardboard "Yes, We're Open!" sign through a crack in the door.

Matthew took the sign and placed it carefully in the snowwoman's "arms," adjusting it so it didn't completely block her chest.

Angela handed him a steaming mug of hot chocolate after he removed his sodden shoes and draped his coat over a chair at the first table.

He took a sip. "Real chocolate."

"Did you expect anything less?" Angela asked.

"No." *It's like drinking a hot Hershey's candy bar.*

Angela looked closely at the snowwoman. "She's a little thin. Except for her front and back."

Matthew stood behind her. "Remind you of anyone?"

Angela stepped to the side. "That's not me."

"Booty is in the eye of the beholder," he said. "I have beheld, and that is an accurate representation of *bella* Angela."

"It's a little too white," Angela said.

"True, but she has a cute little shelf there." Matthew pointed.

Angela turned from the door. "Which will only get bigger."

"You're in exceptional shape, Angela," Matthew said.

"I wasn't talking about me," Angela said. "I was talking about the snowwoman. She'll probably add ten inches back there by morning."

Matthew smiled. "That's a lot of snow booty and snow-ulite."

Angela laughed. "You have the strangest thoughts."

Is she finally loosening up? "You bring out the strange in me. Is it time for popcorn?"

"Sure. It's upstairs." She shuffled toward the counter.

"May I help?" Matthew asked, following closely behind.

Angela turned to face him, backing into the kitchen. "I don't need help microwaving some popcorn."

Matthew stopped at the counter. He heard locks clicking, a door opening, shutting, and several locks clicking again. *I wasn't going to follow you. All those locks for an* inside *door. That borders on paranoia. I'm here. What's she afraid of?*

Unless she's afraid of me *somehow?*

He returned to his half of the booth bed, pressing his feet into the cushion on the other side. *This is almost like sleeping in my easy chair.*

A few minutes later, he heard the locks, a door open and shut, and then a single lock clicking. The kitchen light winked out, and Angela shuffled to the booth carrying a huge silver bowl. She handed the bowl to him, re-wrapped herself in her blanket, and settled in next to the pillow.

"I'm hurt," Matthew said.

"Not enough popcorn?" Angela said.

"No. I'm hurt that you locked your door," Matthew said. "I don't go where I'm not invited."

She grabbed some popcorn. "Habit, I guess."

Or severe paranoia. "Yeah, it's a good habit when you're a beautiful woman living alone." He scooped out some popcorn and stuffed it into his mouth. "Nice. Garlic butter?"

"Yes." She picked out a few pieces.

"Like the popcorn at the Nitehawk," Matthew said. "Ever been?"

Angela sighed. "A long time ago."

"A-ha!" Matthew shouted. "You had a date at the Nitehawk."

"Maybe."

Maybe? The Nitehawk is a couple's theater. "The seats there are arranged in pairs."

Angela rolled her eyes. "I could have gone alone."

"A-ha! You didn't go alone or you would have said so."

She laughed. "A-*ha,* maybe I just like to keep you guessing."

He leaned to his left. "So, who was he?"

Angela tossed a few pieces of popcorn into her mouth. "Someone."

"You have to be more specific than that," Matthew said.

"I could be more specific, but I won't." She slapped his hand out of the way and scooped up some popcorn.

This is so unfair! "Angela, you know just about everything about the women I've dated."

"More than I've wanted to know about them, actually," she said.

"Stop asking about them, then." He nudged her with his left knee.

Angela nudged him back. "You could refuse to answer."

Where's the fun in that? "Come on, Angela. I know nothing about any of your men."

"Man."

Okay, now we're getting somewhere.

"Singular," she added.

"I find that hard to believe," Matthew said.

Angela shrugged.

"But you're so . . ." He shook his head. "You're so beautiful."

Angela only sighed.

"When was this?" Matthew asked.

"When I was in high school," Angela said.

Eighteen years ago. "No way."

"We saw *Jerry Maguire,*" she said.

She can't be serious. "Show me the money, right?"

Angela nodded. "And that's the last movie I've seen in a theater."

That's . . . that's incredible.

"You remember that scene where Tom Cruise says, 'You complete me'?" Angela asked.

"Sure," Matthew said. "It's one of the all-time great movie lines."

"I think it's crap," Angela said.

So opinionated! "You think one of the most romantic lines in movie history is crap? You better explain what you mean by that."

She rested her head on the pillow. "It made them seem so weak, you know? They thought they each needed somebody *else* to give their lives meaning and purpose. They were complete people already, you know? If anything, *love* completed them."

That's deep. I will never say that line to this woman. "I like how you think."

"Tony didn't, and we broke up later that night," Angela said.

I finally have a name. "Tony, huh?"

"Past history," Angela said. "Not worth discussing."

Matthew waited.

Angela kept her silence.

"We should go to the movies sometime," he said.

Angela closed her eyes. "I'd probably fall asleep. I'm kind of sleepy now."

She moved the pillow to Matthew's lap and rested her head on it.

This is unexpected, but it's very nice.

"And movies are a waste of money," she said softly. "If you wait a few weeks after one comes out, you can get the bootleg version from anyone on the street." She yawned. "And the popcorn is so overpriced. I'd rather curl up on the couch and look at a movie on TV, wouldn't you?"

This woman completes me. Even if I'll never say it, I can still think *it.*

Angela opened one eye and looked up. "You got all quiet."

"I'm listening to your wisdom." He smiled. "You're very deep."

"No, I'm not," she whispered.

"Speaking of deep, can you see the snow from down there?" Matthew asked.

Angela sighed. "I've seen plenty of snow through that window."

Matthew put his hand on her shoulder. "Is this okay?"

"No."

Matthew picked up his hand. *I cannot read this woman at all!* "Sorry."

Angela closed her eyes and smiled. "Not there. Lower."

"Oh." He placed his hand in the small of her back, just above the swell of her booty.

"That's *much* better, Matthew . . ."

In minutes, Angela was asleep, her arms gripping the pillow, her breathing soft and steady.

Matthew watched her dream, felt her heat, and smiled.

Now this *is peace.*

He rubbed her back gently, careful not to let his hand stray too low. "Good night, Angela," he whispered as he, too, fell asleep while the world outside filled with snow.

Chapter 21

Matthew woke a few hours later.
Angela was screaming.

"What's . . . what's wrong?" he asked breathlessly.

Angela sat bolt upright and rigid next to him, tears streaming down her face, her breath coming in staccato bursts.

Don't touch her. Just . . . talk. "What's wrong?" He followed her eyes to the window and only saw sheets of snow. *Is someone out there?* "Angela? Is there someone out there?"

She turned her head slowly toward him.

"Is there?" he asked.

She shook her head.

"Bad dream?" Matthew asked.

She nodded.

I want to hold her so badly. He touched her hand. "It's okay. I'm here."

Angela threw off her blanket and leaped out of the booth, wiping her face and stumbling backward toward the counter.

Matthew left the booth, tossing his blanket behind him. "You okay?"

Angela stared outside.

He moved carefully to her side. "Angela?"

Angela folded her arms in front of her, her hands gripping her shoulders tightly, her lower lip and jaw quivering.

"Bad one, huh?" Matthew whispered.

Angela looked away from the window.

"Is it one you've had before?" Matthew whispered.

Angela nodded once, and more tears flowed from her eyes.

I don't want to ask this. "Was it a dream about something that really happened to you?"

Angela looked up at Matthew and nodded.

It wasn't a dream. She's just had a flashback. Matthew wiped a tear from her cheek with the back of his right hand. "Something that made you put all those locks on the doors."

Angela grabbed his hand. "Yes," she whispered.

Oh God! "When did this happen?

Angela's eyes traveled to the window.

"When it snowed before like this?" Matthew whispered.

Angela nodded, her breathing slower, her body still trembling.

During a blizzard, maybe the one four years ago. We haven't had one since. Did this storm trigger the flashback?

Matthew got her blanket, wrapped it around her, and guided her back to the booth where she sat facing him.

"Do you want to talk about it?" Matthew said.

Angela shook her head.

"Can I . . . may I hold you?" Matthew whispered.

Angela nodded.

Matthew pulled on her shoulders gently until she turned and lay stiffly against his chest, her arms tucked under herself.

I wish I could say something, anything to heal her pain. What happened to her?

After a long silence, Angela whispered, "Thank you."

Matthew held her more tightly. "For what?"

Angela burrowed her head into his chest. "Just . . . thank you."

Angela soon fell asleep, her breathing steady, her body relaxing.

Matthew rubbed her shoulders and upper back.

He didn't think he would ever sleep again.

Something happened here.

Someone hurt her during the last snowstorm, maybe attacked her, maybe even—

I don't want to think about that happening to this gentle, sweet woman.

She rarely goes out, but when she does, it's as if she's trying to escape from someone. She's a virtual prisoner in her own shop and her own apartment. She knows a psychiatrist who makes house calls and who's a "friend of the family," only the psychiatrist really doesn't know her family. She's been watching the world go by that window, maybe for years, so worried that La Estrella would put her out of business because she'd have to leave here, knowing it would be difficult if not impossible to walk out that door.

She gripped the skin off my elbow going up and down the dark stairway at the Simmons' apartment.

It could have happened on her back stairway.

Someone broke in and surprised her.

She closed up shop for one day, and it was during that blizzard.

Did she file a police report or go to the hospital? She might have.

Yet she opened the day after that.

He watched her sleeping peacefully now, but he wondered how often she relived her nightmare.

She's so strong and yet so full of fear.

Angela's arms reached around and circled his neck, a sigh escaping.

He stroked her hair. *So beautiful, so tender.*

Why didn't I see this coming? I should have paid more attention. She cried while Timothy was talking because in a way he was talking about her. She asked all sorts of questions about treatment for PTSD. She has flashbacks, nightmares, and occasional emotional numbness. She avoids the world. She feels hopelessness and maybe feels guilty for whatever happened to her. She obviously has trouble sleeping.

And she definitely has trouble with relationships. More specifically, she has trouble letting someone touch her.

Now this snowstorm arrives to trigger this flashback.

God, how can someone so strong be so fragile? Help me help her.

But mainly, give her good dreams for the rest of the night.

She moved up higher on his body, her arms under her, her head on his shoulder. Matthew moved his hands lower and held her close.

No one's going to hurt you, Angela.

I promise.

Chapter 22

"Matthew?"

Matthew looked down at a pair of sexy brown eyes. "Hi."

"Any idea of what time it is?" Angela asked.

She's holding onto me, she isn't shaking, and she doesn't seem to mind my touch. "No."

"I think it's four," she said. "My body usually wakes me at four."

Is this the same woman I heard shrilly screaming a few hours ago? She seems so calm and in control. "You don't need an alarm clock, huh?"

"Not anymore." She pushed off his chest and sat up, looking out the window. "The snow's almost halfway up the door." She wrapped her blanket around her, left the booth, and shuffled to the front window.

Matthew bounced out of the booth and joined her. "Got a shovel?"

Angela smiled up at him. "There's one outside the back door, but it's still coming down. Why don't you wait till it stops? No one's coming out in this mess. I don't expect anyone to show up today." She wiped sleep from her eyes. "No one likes my coffee this much."

I do.

"Think it's a record?" Angela asked.

"Might be." *Do I ask about last night? I have to, don't I?* "You seemed to sleep much better the second time."

She reached out and squeezed his hand. "I did. Thank you."

"Were you warm enough?" Matthew asked, holding her hand.

"You kept me warm enough," Angela said. "Did you get any sleep?"

"I watched you sleep," Matthew said. "I might have given you the world's longest backrub, too."

Angela sighed. "My shoulders have never felt better."

And we're still *holding hands. I want to ask her so many things. I want to ask her about what happened to her. I want to tell her that I can help her, that we can work through this together, that I'm here for her. But I'm holding her hand, and she's holding mine. I don't want to break this contact.*

"I could make *you* breakfast for a change," Matthew said.

Angela took his other hand and rested her head on his chest. "I don't have any Pop-Tarts for you to burn."

This is so ordinary, yet it is so intimate. Holding hands, her head on my chest, snow piling up outside, and we're talking about breakfast. "Is that what you think of my culinary skills?"

"Yes." She looked up, her lips mere inches away from his. "What *can* you cook me for breakfast?"

"Toast," Matthew said. "Plain white toast and jam."

Angela shrugged. "And what else?"

"Crispy bacon and a cheese omelet." *I have made a cheese omelet exactly once, and it was a runny disaster.*

Angela wrinkled up her lips, her eyes still smiling.

I want to kiss those wrinkled up lips so badly. "And some hash browns."

Angela slipped her hands around his waist. "You're going to feed me all that?"

Matthew rubbed her arms. "Aren't you hungry?"

"Not for all that." She tugged at his belt loops. "You could make me oatmeal."

Matthew smiled. "With raisins, brown sugar, cinnamon, and butter."

Angela pulled him closer, her forehead brushing his lips. "Sounds good. Except for the raisins, brown sugar, and butter." She rubbed her nose on his collarbone. "I have something better in mind."

"You do have those little packets, right?" Matthew asked. "The ones you add water to."

She shook her head, her hair brushing his chin. "Nope. We do things from scratch around here."

"Uh-huh." He pulled her closer, letting her hair tickle his nose. "Do you have any recipes back there?"

"Nope," she said. "They're all in my head."

He lightly kissed her hair. "Will you help me?"

She closed her eyes. "You said you were going to make me breakfast."

"I am." *If I ever leave this embrace, and I'd be a fool to leave this intimate moment now.* "I just need some guidance. It's your kitchen, right? I wouldn't want to break anything."

Angela opened her eyes, stepped back, and took off her blanket. She took his hand. "Come on. Let's go cook."

I like the sound of that.

She led him to the middle sink. "We have to wash our hands properly first." She stood behind him, reaching her hands around him to the tap, turning it and waiting for the water to warm up, her head resting on his back. "It takes about a minute to get hot."

I like this position very much.

"Get our hands wet," she whispered.

Matthew checked the water then placed their hands under the stream.

"Now soap us up," she whispered.

He soaped his hands and hers, massaging her fingers.

"That feels good," she whispered.

"The water's not too hot, is it?" Matthew asked.

He felt her head moving on his back. "Just right. You can dry us off now."

He took a towel from a metal hook and dried her hands first, digging his thumbs into her palms.

"You're good at this," she whispered.

"It's my first time," he said. *Stay gentle.*

She spun him around and looked at his hands. "You have big hands."

"Is that a good thing or a bad thing?" Matthew asked.

She placed her small hands in his. "A good thing." She sighed. "Get a saucepan." She pointed at several hanging from a rack above his head.

Matthew stepped over and tapped a large one. "Are you this hungry?"

She shook her head.

He pulled a smaller saucepan from the rack and placed it on the smallest eye on the stove.

Angela opened a drawer and handed him a measuring cup. "Add two and a half cups of water."

As he filled the cup and emptied it into the saucepan, he felt her hot hands on his hips. He set the measuring cup in the left sink. A small saltshaker appeared in front of his belt.

"Add a dash of salt," she whispered.

He shook it once into the saucepan.

"Turn the heat to high," she whispered.

It already is. Angela has busy little hands. He turned the knob as Angela's hands and body disappeared. A moment later, a container of oats and another measuring cup appeared in front of him, her heat returning to his back.

"Measure out one heaping cup," she whispered.

Matthew poured the oats into the measuring cup, Angela's hands clasped together in front of him. "Is this heaping enough?"

Angela ducked her head under his arms. "Yes. Is your water boiling?"

Matthew looked down. "It's bubbling."

"Turn it to low and stir in your oatmeal," she whispered.

A spoon slid into his hand.

Some magic trick. He stirred in the oatmeal. "It's getting thick."

Angela hugged him tightly from behind. "Let it cook a bit."

He covered her hands with his. "How long do we let it cook?"

Angela sighed softly. "A bit."

"Don't you time anything?" Matthew asked.

She rubbed her face back and forth on his back. "I cook by feel."

"I like cooking with you," Matthew whispered.

Angela's hands left his, and he felt her step away.

I'm actually cold. He turned. "What's next?"

She pointed left to a cupboard. "The cinnamon's in there."

Matthew turned and extended his arms to open the cupboard, Angela's hands reaching under his arms to grip his shoulders. He saw vanilla extract, cinnamon, ground allspice, cardamom, cloves, nutmeg, poppy seeds, juniper, whole allspice, cinnamon sticks, coriander, and sage. "This is a very spicy cupboard." He took down a metal container of cinnamon.

"Add a pinch to the pan," Angela whispered.

He poured a tiny amount into his hand and turned his hand over. "Cinnamon in."

Angela's hands slid slowly off his shoulders, drifted down his chest, and stopped on his hips. "In the middle cupboard above your head, there are some chopped walnuts."

Matthew reached up, and this time Angela's hands slid down to his thighs. *This is getting very interesting.* He moved aside packages of shredded coconut, cashews, almonds, peanuts, hazelnuts, and pecans until he found the walnuts. "How much?"

Angela's hands wormed their way into his pockets. "A handful."

I like how Angela's little hands think. He opened the package and filled his hand, shuffling back to the saucepan as Angela held on. He dropped them in. "Should I stir it?"

"*Yes,*" she whispered, hold a long time onto the S.

He stirred the walnuts and cinnamon into the oatmeal.

"Behind us in the top left cupboard are some dried cranberries," she whispered.

Do I turn around? I don't want her hands to leave my pockets. "Is my caboose ready to move?"

Angela dug her hands deeper into his pockets. "Yes."

He turned slowly and faced the cupboard, opening it and finding dried apricots, cherries, and cranberries. "Another handful?"

"Yes," she whispered.

He measured out a handful of dried cranberries, dropped them into the saucepan, and stirred them into the oatmeal.

Angela's hands left his pockets. A moment later, a lid appeared. "Put it on and turn off the heat."

He set the lid on the saucepan and turned off the heat. "How long do we wait?"

Angela's hands returned to his hips. "Until it's done. I need to steer you to the refrigerator."

I like how she drives me.

She spun him a half turn and pushed him toward the refrigerator. "Open it and take out the milk."

He opened the door and took out a carton of milk.

"Close the door," she whispered.

He closed the door.

Angela steered him back to the saucepan. "Put the carton down."

He did.

She turned and positioned him under another cupboard. "Get out the blackstrap molasses."

"No brown sugar?" Matthew whispered.

"Blackstrap molasses is best," she whispered. "Above the spices."

Matthew found the molasses, and she drove him back to the saucepan.

"Take off the lid," she whispered.

He picked it up and set it to the side.

"Add some milk and some molasses." She ducked her head under his arm and picked up the spoon. "I'll stir it in."

Matthew splashed the milk in as Angela stirred, her hips grinding on his leg. He dribbled some molasses into the oatmeal, and Angela continued to stir and grind.

And this is just oatmeal. I can't wait to make pancakes and sausage with this woman. A four-course meal could result in twins.

"Is it ready?" Matthew asked.

"Yes," she said. "Pick up the pan."

He did.

"Get another spoon from that drawer," she said.

He did.

"Let's go back to the booth," she said.

Matthew moved carefully out of the kitchen and around the counter to the booth, Angela's fingers hooked onto two of his back belt loops. He walked on his knees into the booth and extended his legs. Angela slid in beside him and snatched the other spoon.

"No hogging the cranberries," she said.

"I wouldn't think of it," he said.

They alternated spoons full of oatmeal until they were scraping the bottom of the saucepan, finishing their breakfast in less than five minutes.

"Now isn't this better than those little packets?" Angela asked.

"I will eat nothing else for breakfast as long as I live," Matthew said.

"It's not *that* good," Angela said.

It's good when the preparation of the oatmeal is erotic! Her whispers were driving me insane! "It is when you've never had real oatmeal before. It's so rich."

"About three hundred calories per serving," Angela said. "And it's good for you. Eight grams of dietary fiber."

I'll be a regular guy.

Matthew set the empty pot aside and stretched out his left arm.

Angela squirmed closer, placing his hand on her side.

This is more like it. "So, Miss Smith, what are we going to do all day?"

Angela rested her left hand on his chest. "What do you suggest?"

"We could go for a walk once the snow stops, or even if it doesn't," Matthew said. "We could make the world's deepest snow angels."

"I'm not going out there, Matthew," Angela said.

Wrong idea. "I assume you have a television upstairs."

Angela nodded.

"We could do something innovative with it," Matthew said.

"What?" Angela asked.

"We could watch it," Matthew said. "I'm sure we can find an old movie to cuddle to."

Angela turned further into him, sliding her right arm behind him. "I have the most basic cable, and the picture is often as fuzzy as the snow in the window, and you know whatever we watch will be interrupted with weather bulletins."

I hate those. "Ladies and gentlemen, we interrupt something a lot more interesting than what we're about to tell you to tell you what you *already* know if you look outside, and we're going to interrupt what's not *really* your favorite show but it's better than watching an infomercial, and we're going to annoy you for as *long* as we can because we think you're in danger even though we know you're safely in front of your television watching this bit of fluff that justifies our ridiculous jobs."

Angela blinked rapidly. "You're quite entertaining. You're better than cable any day."

"Thank you," Matthew said. "Do you have a DVD player and some movies?"

Angela shook her head. "I never got into that."

"Well, I could run home," Matthew said, "get my DVD player and some movies, we could hook it to your TV, and you could make more garlicky, buttery popcorn. It'll be like a snow day."

"A what?" Angela said.

"A snow day," Matthew said. "You know, no school because of inclement weather."

Angela rubbed her cheek against his chest. "I went to public school. I don't remember having any of those."

"Oh yeah." *She had a raunchy childhood.* "Well, what do you think of my incredible idea?"

Angela sighed. "I think you're crazy to go out in that."

"You could go with me and share in the insanity," Matthew said.

Angela pulled his hand off her hip and tightened it around her stomach. "Matthew, I . . . I have a problem . . . with all that snow."

"I'll be with you, Angela," Matthew said.

"I know that," Angela said. "It's just . . . that night . . . I couldn't find anyone to help me because of . . . because of the blizzard."

"What happened that night, Angela?" he whispered.

Her body shook.

"It's okay, it's okay," Matthew whispered. "You don't have to tell me."

"No," Angela said. "You need to know." She sighed. "And I need to tell it to someone. Lucky you."

He smiled. "Lucky me."

She glanced back to the kitchen. "He . . . he got in . . . somehow . . . through the back door. I always lock it, I always, *always* lock it, you know I do, but that night I forgot. And he was . . . on my stairway . . . waiting for me." She closed her eyes. "And I . . . I ran out into the snow . . . and couldn't find anyone . . . to help me because there was so much snow."

She skipped over the attack completely. Maybe that's just as well, and not only for her. I don't really want to know either.

"No police, no emergency vehicles, not even a snowplow driver," she said. "No one. Just me in all that snow. I . . . I pounded on doors, but no one could hear me because of the wind, no one came to their door to help me. And when I finally came back inside, and after I looked everywhere, I pulled the refrigerator in front of the back door and locked myself in." She opened her eyes and looked up at Matthew. "I spent the next thirty hours locked in my bathroom. I heard customers knocking on my door downstairs, but I couldn't move. And all I had was a hammer."

He stroked her hair. "You're a dangerous woman."

"I only had a hammer to defend myself, Matthew," she said.

"You were hoping to nail him," Matthew said.

She sighed. "It was the only real weapon I could find in the apartment. I forgot about all my knives downstairs in the kitchen. I didn't even have a screwdriver. I fell asleep in the bathroom. My back hurt so bad the next morning. It's not a big bathroom."

I know the type.

"When I woke up at four o'clock the next day," Angela said, "I opened the store and went about my business."

As if nothing ever happened. "Did you ever call the police?"

"I thought about it, but they had their hands full that night and for many days afterward. It was a blizzard, right? This city shuts down during blizzards." She shivered slightly.

Matthew covered her with her blanket. "Did he . . ."

Angela shook her head vigorously. "He tried, but I got him good. I think I might have maimed him for life."

I don't know if it's true. I guess I'll have to accept it.

"I wore long sleeves for a while. I had bruises everywhere. On my arms and on the back of my neck. My heel took longer to get better." She smiled. "He came up behind me . . . and . . . and I kicked back like a mule."

I hope she split one of his testicles in two and turned the other one into a grapefruit.

"And then I ran out." She sat up slowly and held her knees. "When we went down to Mezza Luna, that was the first time I had been outside in over four years, Matthew."

Four years.

My God.

"That's why I was crying when we were at the Simmons'," she said. "I knew *exactly* how Timothy felt to be stuck in front of a window afraid of what might be outside. My heart nearly thuds out of my chest whenever I lock up."

"Is this why you don't like me behind you at any time?" Matthew asked.

Angela nodded. "I know it's stupid, but I feel more in control if I'm facing someone. I'm working on it, though."

"I'm glad you're working on it with me," Matthew said. "Do your parents know about any of this?"

"I didn't tell them, and I'm never going to tell them," Angela said. "When they call, I tell them business is good and that the coffee's still the best in New York. They worry too much about me being here all alone as it is."

"So do I, Angela," Matthew said.

"You shouldn't." She grabbed his hand. "Come see."

Matthew trailed her to the other steel door in the kitchen. She unlocked and opened it, and an extremely bright light illuminated a square landing, stairs rising to the right. She took two steps and reached around the corner, returning with a fully charged and crackling Taser.

"Whoa," Matthew said, stepping back.

"It's charged at all times, and I keep it in a little holster hanging on the wall during the day," Angela said. "I also put it under my pillow at night."

That doesn't sound safe.

Matthew stepped up to the landing and looked to the top of the stairs. "Is that a thousand-watt bulb?"

"Five hundred, and I never turn it off. I have plenty of new ones ready, too." She slipped the Taser into a leather holster attached to the wall near a blank light switch. "I covered up the switch so I don't turn it off by mistake, and I also have a set of knives upstairs now. I still keep the hammer on my nightstand."

"You have a fire escape, don't you?" Matthew asked.

"Yes, but I nailed all my windows shut. In case of fire, I can break a window with my hammer." She backed down the stairs to the kitchen, squeezing and pulling her fingers in front of her. "So now you know everything."

Matthew left the stairway and shut the door behind him. *Not everything.*

Angela rushed by him and locked it. "You're only the second person who knows."

"Dr. Penn knows," Matthew said.

Angela nodded and leaned back against the refrigerator. "He visits every now and then to check up on me. Usually on Mondays."

Matthew leaned against the middle sink. "Which is why you wanted me to sleep in on Monday."

"Yeah, sorry about that," Angela said. "After listening to Timothy tell his story and hearing that a blizzard was in the forecast, I . . . I panicked. I asked him to come over so we could talk."

"He's a good man," Matthew said.

"Yeah," she said. "He reminds me so much of my daddy. My daddy is a strong man. And so are you."

"I'm not that strong, Angela," Matthew said.

"You're still here with crazy me," she said. "I don't care for any of the women you date, but . . ."

Matthew left the sink and stood in front of her, taking her hands. *They're so cold!* "I don't care for the women I dated, either. Good thing we haven't gone on any dates."

Angela smiled. "Not-a-dates."

"Right." *This is the moment. This has to be the moment.* "What would you say to a . . . not-a-kiss?"

Angela inhaled audibly. "I've never had one of those."

Matthew picked up Angela's hands and put them around his neck, his hands sliding around her waist. "Neither have I. I'm not sure how to proceed."

"I'm not sure either," Angela said.

"I suppose I could dip my head down to yours." He slouched until he was staring into Angela's eyes. "Like this."

"That . . . that might work."

Those eyes, those sexy brown eyes. "And then I could move closer until . . ."

Their lips touched.

Angela pulled back bit by bit. "So that's a not-a-kiss."

"I think we've just invented it," Matthew whispered. "May I not-a-kiss you again?"

"No," she said, grasping his face. "I want a real kiss this time."

She pulled his face down, and they kissed, Matthew pulling her hips close to his thighs before moving his lips to her cheek and hugging her tightly.

"I tasted cranberries," he whispered. "I knew you got more than I did." He rested his forehead on hers. "What I said earlier about going out into the snow, I wasn't thinking clearly." He kissed her again. "Mmm. Molasses that time." He took her hands. "I need to warm you up."

"You do," Angela said softly.

"Let's go back to our booth bed," Matthew said.

Angela nodded. "And, I want to . . ." She bit her lip. "I'm going to try to walk and not run in front of you, okay?"

"Okay." He released her hands. "Tell me if I get too close."

She took a step. "I want you close but not too close."

She took a deep breath and took several steps, Matthew keeping pace behind her. As she rounded the counter, she looked back.

"Shoot." She stopped.

"What?" Matthew said.

"I looked back," she said. "I had to make sure where you were."

"That's okay."

"No, it isn't," Angela said, continuing to the booth and climbing in. "If you haven't already noticed, I have major trust issues. It's what Dr. Penn and I talk about most. I want to trust you, Matthew, I do, it's just hard for me to do right now."

"So we'll walk beside each other," Matthew said. He crawled over her legs and slid to the other end of the booth near the wall. "Where's that pillow?"

Angela tossed him the pillow, and he placed it on his lap.

"You seemed to sleep best this way," he said.

Angela crept to him, moved the pillow higher, and lay face down, her arms around his waist. "What if I don't want to sleep?"

Matthew rubbed her lower back.

"If you do that, I'll be asleep in no time," she whispered.

Matthew continued to rub. "You have some catching up to do." *Four years' worth of sleep. I can't even begin to imagine what that must be like.*

She rose and pushed the pillow up to Matthew's chest. "Can I wrap myself around you?"

"Sure."

"Lean forward," she said.

Matthew pushed away from the wall, and Angela sat on his thighs, wrapping her legs around him. She slid the pillow behind him and rested her head on his shoulder, her arms circling him under his arms.

Matthew pulled one of the blankets over them.

"Matthew?" she whispered.

"Yes?"

"What are you thinking right now?" she asked.

"I'm where I should be."

"You're being smothered by a crazy woman in a booth at a coffee shop during a blizzard," she whispered.

"You're not crazy, Angela." He dug his fingers into her lower back. "And you're not smothering me."

"What about all your fine, fancy, hot, dysfunctional women?" Angela asked.

"They are permanently not invited to our snow day." He rubbed her sides. "And you are fine, fancy, hot—"

"And dysfunctional," Angela interrupted.

"You're not."

"I haven't seen the sun in over four years," Angela said. "We went to Mezza Luna at night, remember?"

"You will see the sun soon. Just not today." He worked his fingers down to the top of her pants, pressing gently. "You're hot."

"It's your heat, not mine," Angela said. "I'm still cold."

He pulled the other blanket around them. "Better?"

"It doesn't matter how many blankets I use," she said. "I'll still be cold." She wiggled. "Keep rubbing my back."

"Gladly." He pulled up the edge of her shirt and slid his hands onto her hot skin. "Angela, seriously, your skin is an oven."

"It's your hands," she whispered.

"What if some customers came in right now?" Matthew asked.

"I'd get up and serve them," Angela said.

"There's nothing moving out there but snow in the wind," Matthew said. "Why don't you close for the day?"

"I'd hate it if anyone brave enough to come out in this mess found me closed," she whispered. "And the snowwoman still says we're open, and my light is on."

"You don't even have coffee brewing," he said. "The only thing percolating in here is you. I thought you'd be sleepy."

"I'm wide awake now, and I have a feeling you're not going to let me sleep anyway," she said. "Your hands never stop moving."

"It's not only my hands moving," he said. "You keep moving your body underneath my hands."

"You've noticed." She kissed his neck and sat back. "I have a feeling that you're going to stay another night."

"Is it a good feeling?" Matthew asked.

"Yes."

I couldn't leave now anyway. "Do you have any other feelings?"

Angela kissed him. "I have a feeling you'll be upstairs with me tonight."

"I love your feelings," Matthew said. "Feelings are so underrated, don't you think?"

She tightened her legs around him. "And we'll get lots of sleep."

"Is that all?" Matthew whispered.

"For now," Angela said. "I kept you up for most of the night, didn't I?" She touched his face lightly with her fingertips. "You look exhausted."

He let his hands stray to her thighs. "Actually, I've never felt more alive."

Angela grabbed his hands. "Neither have I, but we have to sleep."

Matthew turned his wrists to escape her grip and massaged the tops of her thighs. "I'll try to sleep, but I can't guarantee anything. I want to keep you warm, and my hands just won't keep still."

Angela grabbed his hands, lifting them and holding them to her stomach. "I only have a full-size bed."

Matthew relaxed his hands, his fingers tracing circles on her shirt. "I really can't guarantee *anything* now. A full is larger than a twin but smaller than a queen, right?"

Angela nodded.

"Will we fit?" Matthew asked.

"I will," she said. "Comfortably."

"Which means . . ."

"You get the couch." She smiled. "It's a very nice couch."

Matthew sighed. "I'm sure it is."

Angela flattened his hands on her stomach. "I may let you tuck me in."

"I hope you do." He caressed her stomach with his thumbs. "And I hope it takes a long time to tuck you in."

She fell forward and hugged him. "It might." She sighed. "Especially if you keep touching me like that."

He grazed her shoulder blades with his fingertips. "How do you make deposits?"

"Where's this question coming from?" Angela asked, leaning back and resting her hands on his shoulders.

"Just wondering," Matthew said. "If you don't go out, how do you do things?"

"All my bills debit out automatically," Angela said. "I don't have to write checks or mail them anymore. I used to ask customers to drop off my bills in the mail. I hated doing that."

"What about making deposits?" Matthew asked.

"I worked something out with HSBC," Angela said. "My family and I have used them for a long time, and for a small fee, they send someone to collect my deposits whenever I call them, usually Mondays, Wednesdays, and Fridays."

"I've never seen that happen," Matthew said.

"I try not to make a big deal out of it," Angela said. "I told you I had a delivery the other day, and sometimes the buzzer that sounds in the back isn't for another batch of cookies."

"You've really managed."

"I've done what I had to do." She put his hands behind her and snuggled into his chest. "I don't have much to deposit this week because of this storm."

"You have to keep it somewhere until they come to collect it, right?" Matthew asked.

"I have a safe place." She sighed.

"Am I asking too many questions?" Matthew asked.

"No. It's nice to talk to someone." She sat up. "No one's coming in today. I've had enough." She hopped out of the booth, ran to the door, locked it, flipped the sign to "closed," and returned to the booth, holding out her hand. "Come on."

Matthew took her hand and walked beside her around the counter and into the kitchen. She checked the locks on the back door, snapped off the kitchen lights, unlocked and opened the stairway door, and dragged Matthew to the landing. She closed and locked the stairway door and snatched the Taser from its holster.

"Will that be necessary?" Matthew asked as they stepped up to the apartment door.

"Maybe." She unlocked several more locks and opened the door. "Welcome to my apartment."

Matthew took the last step and saw a long dark blue couch, a stack of blankets and a pillow at one end.

"You were expecting me," he said.

"Yeah," Angela said, locking the door behind her. "Eventually. And now you're here. Ready for the tour?"

Matthew nodded.

"And you won't have to move." She hopped up onto the back of the couch. "If you look to your left, you will see two doors. The one on the left is my parents' bedroom. I don't have a reason to go in there. The other is for the laundry room. In *this* room is the world's smallest color TV on a stand built by my father when I was little. I can still hear him cursing the directions. That wingback chair was here when they moved in. The rug and the coffee table are older than I am. My parents bricked in the fireplace when I was five. To your right is my kitchen, so you know it's spotless." She smiled. "Through the kitchen are my bedroom and my bathroom." She dropped off the couch. "Follow me."

Angela's bedroom was as Spartan and plain as the living area. A solid blue comforter covered a full bed, several pillows propped against a low wooden headboard, a hammer resting on the night-stand under a simple white lamp.

"It's definitely warmer up here," Matthew said.

"Yeah." She slipped off her shoes, removed her socks, and wiggled out of her jeans, pulled back the covers, and got in bed.

Matthew stood motionless. *Those were some smoking hot legs.*

"You okay?" Angela asked.

"You have excellent legs," he said. "Like sculpture."

"Thank you." She buried her head in a pillow. "Are you going to tuck me in now?"

"I've never tucked anyone in before," Matthew said. "I'm not sure what to do."

"You could pull the comforter up to my neck," she whispered.

"I can do that." He reached across her and grabbed the top edge of the comforter, pulling it snugly up to her chin. "What's next?"

"Make sure the covers are tucked in tightly all around me," she whispered.

He ran his hands between the mattress and box spring from one side to the next. "All tucked in. Anything else?"

"I guess that's it," Angela said. "Good night."

"But it's still morning," Matthew said. He knelt next to the bed and kissed her cheek. "I hope you have sweeter dreams."

She freed her arms from under the covers and pulled his face down to his, kissing him tenderly. "Now I will."

Matthew stood, staring at the outline of Angela's body. *I want to stay.* "I'll be out there if you need me."

"Isn't it obvious that I already do?" Angela asked.

She needs me. I need her, too. Matthew nodded. "I'm glad you do. Get some sleep." He turned to leave.

"Oh," Angela said.

He looked back. "Yes?"

"Keep watch over my money while you're out there," Angela said.

Matthew looked through the kitchen into the living area. "You keep it in the couch?"

"Your pillow has an inner zipper," Angela said.

Smart. "It must be a heavy pillow with all that change."

"I leave the change and about twenty in bills in the cash register, Matthew," Angela said. "I sometimes have to make change for the parking meters. And in case someone desperate breaks in down there, at least they'll have something for their trouble and hopefully won't trash the place."

"You think of everything," Matthew said.

"I try."

"Good night, Angela."

"Good night, Matthew."

Matthew wasn't tired or sleepy, not with Angela asleep and already purring less than twenty feet from him. The couch was also too short for his legs. He settled into the pillow and heard the crunch of paper. *I literally have my mind on her money.*

He looked at the mantle over the fireplace and saw a few pictures of her parents. *Her mother was beautiful, light-skinned and short, her father tall, dark-skinned, and handsome. Angela has her father's eyes and her mother's shape.*

In between cookbooks on a small bookcase, he noticed a few pictures of a young Angela, all knees and legs and smiles. The coffee table to his left contained no magazines, newspapers, not even a *TV Guide.*

I'm resting in a time capsule. I'm back in a simpler time when family was everything that mattered. The Smiths had no time for anything else to matter.

He counted the kisses he had received and remembered three really good ones. *What does it mean if I can rank the kisses I get? Angela obviously believes in quality over quantity. I have to make every kiss count.*

It has been a very *good day.*

Matthew felt himself dozing off and dreaming of Angela's sculptured, toned, brown legs . . .

Chapter 23

Matthew felt a hot, sweaty, sexy weight on his chest when he woke several hours later.

Angela has to be the best kind of blanket ever created. I love how her form fits to mine.

He slid his hand down her back and felt more sweat.

Angela opened her eyes.

"How did you know I needed another blanket?" Matthew whispered.

"I'm surprised I didn't wake you," she said. "I've been here for at least an hour. You sleep so deeply."

I've wasted an hour of my life I can never get back. "Did you miss me or were you cold?"

"I was cold." She crawled higher. "And I missed you." She rubbed her nose on his neck. "And I had another bad dream."

"Want to talk about it?" Matthew asked.

"No." She kissed his ear. "Not now."

"Okay."

"You are so warm," she whispered.

He caressed her back through her thin T-shirt. "I'm hot because I was dreaming about you."

"Were we cutting down a forest in your dream?" Angela asked.

Matthew smiled. "No."

"Sounded like it." Angela kissed his chin. "It's actually comforting to hear." She looked out the window. "Look. It's stopped snowing."

"It has?" He massaged her lower back and found it less sweaty.

Angela crawled even higher.

Matthew found his hands completely covering her booty. "There you go, moving your body under my hands again."

"Is this going to be a problem?" she whispered.

"No." He squeezed. *My hands are in heaven.* "Is *that* going to be a problem?"

"No." She inched even higher. "You're not comfortable."

"No, no," Matthew said, cupping her buttocks. "I'm good."

She sat up. "Let's go see if we fit in my bed." She flung back the blanket and stood. "Come on."

Matthew followed her into the bedroom, where she had already pulled back the covers.

"You first," she said.

Matthew slid under the covers, and Angela crawled on top of him, pulling up the covers behind her.

"Angela, we are going to roast." *I'm so overdressed.* "Unless I take off my jeans."

"Then take them off," she whispered.

Angela didn't move while Matthew removed his pants, dropping them onto the floor.

"Is that better?" she whispered.

"A little." *It's still too hot, and I'm getting bothered by her soft, hot flesh.* "The, um, this position and the way you're, um, *positioned* is putting me in an awkward position."

"Good," she whispered.

"My boxers have an exit, Angela."

She wiggled. "I feel you, man."

And now she's wiggling. "I may escape and do you harm."

"Oh no, not *that,*" she whispered. "Down, boy."

He took several deep breaths. "It seeks warmth, and you are certainly warm."

"Don't think of me as a woman," Angela whispered. "Think of me as a blanket."

There's no way I can do that. "You are the sexiest, silkiest, smoothest blanket ever created. You feel very nice."

"Thank you." She wiggled again.

"Angela?"

"Yes?"

"Please don't wiggle like that," Matthew said. "I was beginning to calm down."

"I'm trying to get comfortable," she whispered.

"By grinding on me," Matthew said.

She looked up, batting her eyelashes. "I'm shaking the present."

"You're doing what?" Matthew asked.

"Didn't you ever pick up a present and shake it a little to see if you could guess what was inside?" Angela asked.

"Yes," Matthew said, moving her hips slightly to the side. "But that's not what you're doing."

"Sure I am," Angela whispered, centering her hips on him again. "I'm checking out the package."

Funny. "And what do you think of the package?"

"I can't wait to open it." She wiggled again.

"You're not nice," he said.

"Come on, Matthew," she said. "Don't you know that it's International Flirting Week?"

"You're not flirting, Angela," Matthew said. "You're hurting."

"I'll stop." She slid her hands under his arms, massaging his shoulders. "I only want you to hold me anyway."

"I can do that," Matthew whispered. *Let's take this slow so it will last.*

"Wait." She slid her hand under the pillow and pulled out the Taser, placing it next to the hammer on the nightstand.

My head was inches from electrocution. "Thank you."

"But if you snore too loudly . . . *zzzt.*"

I hope she's kidding.

"I am so comfortable." She kissed his cheek. "Good night."

"Should my hands stray during the night," Matthew whispered, "I want you to know that they are straying without my permission."

"I'll be sad if they don't," she whispered. "Good night, Matthew."

"Good night, Angela."

Matthew stayed as still as he could, but Angela continued to wiggle and grind. As a result, Matthew's hands started to stray to her booty, her thighs, her sides, and the back of her neck. He slid lower in the bed until his lips found hers, and for a few furtive moments, they were dangerously close to becoming one.

Angela sighed. "That's . . . that's feeling too nice, Matthew."

Too nice? "I was shaking the present."

"Consider me shaken," Angela said. "You know exactly where to touch me."

"And you respond exactly when I want you to," he said.

She slid down and rested her head on his chest. "I'm not sure I'm ready."

"I can wait, Angela," Matthew said. "We don't have to rush anything."

"Thank you." She kissed his hand. "Thank you. I'm . . . I'm just a little scared."

"It's okay." He massaged her shoulders. "Go to sleep."

"Good night."

Matthew again watched Angela sleeping and felt calm and peace fill his body.

He also felt sweaty.

He noticed a great deal of steam on the window.

We did that. We're doing that.

Very cool.

Chapter 24

Matthew woke to the sound of the shower.

He swung out of the bed, went to the window, and looked outside. He saw nothing but a narrow alley and a Dumpster sporting a high hat of snow.

He looked at the bathroom door after the water stopped, wondering how Angela would come out of the bathroom.

A robe would be okay. A towel would be better, especially if it's small. If she comes out dripping wet as only her sculptured self, then that would be best.

Matthew sat on the edge of the bed and waited, hoping for the best.

Angela opened the door and came out fully clothed in a black sweater, black shoes, and blue jeans. The only thing missing from her "uniform" was her apron.

Matthew pouted.

"What's wrong?" she said.

Matthew stood. "You're fully dressed."

Angela blinked once. "It's cold." She threw her hair into a ponytail. "I'd wait at least thirty minutes before you take your shower."

"You're opening?" Matthew asked.

"It's not snowing anymore, and I'm awake and well-rested for a change." She looked at the bed. "Thanks to you."

"What if no one shows up?" Matthew asked.

She pulled up the sheets and comforter, propping up the pillows. "If no one shows up by ten, we'll do something else."

"Nine, and we'll come back up here to take another nap," Matthew said.

Angela smiled. "Nine-thirty."

"Nine-fifteen?" Matthew smiled.

"We'll see." She smoothed out the comforter. "Don't you have a case you could be working on?"

"I'd rather work on you," Matthew said.

Angela walked into the tiny kitchen. "We have to make a living."

Matthew caught up to her at the stairway door and turned her around. "I like the way you said that. *We* have to make a living."

"You're putting *us* behind schedule already, man." She kissed him briskly. "You don't have to get up now, you know."

"I know." He took off his shirt. "But I want to help." He dropped his boxers to the floor. "Is there a towel in the bathroom for me?"

Angela stared at Matthew's chest, her eyes drifting lower.

"Angela, is there an extra towel in the bathroom?" he asked again.

Angela looked up. "The water won't be hot yet."

He kissed her forehead. "It doesn't matter to me, as long as it's *wet.*"

Angela's eyes dropped briefly before flitting up to his chest again. "Please wait until it warms up."

He turned and walked into the kitchen. "I'll be down in a few minutes." *I hope she's watching.* He looked back and saw her watching. *Yes.* "Don't you have a coffee shop to run?"

Angela nodded, smiled, and left the apartment.

Monique taught me well, didn't she?

Matthew entered the bathtub and turned on the hot water.

It wouldn't warm up.

Okay then. We'll have to rough it.

He turned the shower lever, and icy water stung him like a Taser.

He took a two-minute shower.

He wouldn't feel his feet for several hours.

After drying himself and fastening the towel around his waist, Matthew "borrowed" some toothpaste and brushed his teeth with his finger. As the first wave of Angela's coffee rose up around him, he looked at the boxers, jeans, hoody, and T-shirt he had worn for two days.

I can't wear them again.

Angela has a washer and a dryer.

She doesn't expect me down there for a while.

Why don't I do some laundry?

While he did a quick mini load, he leafed through several cookbooks, marveling at the many uses for basil. After putting his clothes into the dryer, he hopped up onto the dryer to warm his feet while enjoying an interesting recipe for oatmeal pancakes that used wheat germ and buttermilk syrup.

Angela burst through the stairway door minutes later and smiled. "I was wondering where you were."

Matthew tried to cross his legs, but the towel wouldn't cooperate. *I'll just be exposed then, shall I?* He lowered the cookbook. "Just catching up on some reading," he said. "Fascinating stuff. Basil has *so* many uses. I'll be down in a few minutes."

She laughed. "From now on, whenever I do my laundry, I will think of you in that little towel."

"I'm so glad I am already giving you memories," Matthew said. "Are you ready to open already?"

"I'm not open yet, and there's nothing moving out there anyway. Driggs hasn't been touched." She approached him gradually, biting her lip. "And the longer I stay up here with you, the more memories I'll have."

He closed the cookbook and placed it on his lap. "My load should be done in a few minutes."

She stood in front of him, placing her hands on his thighs.

"Don't even think about it," Matthew said.

"Think about what?" She moved her hands under the towel.

"You have me at a severe disadvantage, Miss Smith," Matthew said, scooting back. "Please behave like a lady."

Her hands stopped in the middle of his thighs. "I don't know how I'm supposed to behave. I've never had a nearly naked man reading a cookbook on my dryer before." Her hands continued to his hips. "What *should* I do?"

"I am at your mercy," Matthew said. "Be gentle."

She slid her hands down his legs to his knees. "I have so much power."

She does.

"The things I could do," she whispered.

"Yes." *Thank goodness this cookbook is heavy. Her hands were making me rise to the occasion.*

She licked her lips.

That wasn't nice. Well, it was, but her timing wasn't nice.

"I'll be downstairs waiting." She skimmed her hands down his calves and backed away.

"I'll be right down," Matthew said. "To do some shoveling."

Angela went to the stairway door. "The shovel's probably buried by the back door." She turned and squinted. "You look *good* in a towel."

"Thank you," Matthew said. "I'll bet you look good in a towel, too."

"Bye."

As soon as the door closed, Matthew jumped off the dryer and checked his clothes. *Dry enough.* He put them on and hesitated at the stairway door. *Lock or not? I had better lock it and the landing door, just in case.*

He clicked open the series of locks on the back door of the kitchen, opened it, and kicked snow away until he found the shovel. He also noticed footsteps going into and out of the alley. *Someone got seriously lost last night.*

He walked past Angela at the counter and headed to the front door with the shovel, grabbing his coat from the first chair.

She poked out her bottom lip. "I'm sad."

"Why?"

"You're not wearing the towel."

"I'll just have to do more laundry later," he said.

She smiled. "Don't hurt yourself. That looks like heavy snow."

Matthew threw on his coat, pushed hard on the door, and the drift against it collapsed. He closed the door and shoveled out a ten-by-ten-foot section of the sidewalk as the world brightened around him. He made a pile high enough to block any view Angela might have of La Estrella. *Her competition is still closed. Good.* He packed more snow onto the snowwoman, adding some bigger cleavage and subtracting several inches from her rear. He reentered the shop, swatted snow from his shoes, and locked the door.

"Are we open yet?" Matthew asked.

"Not yet."

I can't believe it's not even six yet. He pulled off his hoody and sniffed the air. "What is that heavenly smell?"

"I'm baking some apple turnovers," she said. "I hope you didn't freeze off anything important."

He approached the counter. "I'm all *present* and accounted for. I'm sweaty, though. I need another shower, and I'll need to do more laundry afterward . . ." He raised his eyebrows.

"We might not stay open past nine now." She offered him a cup of coffee.

"Good." He took the cup. "How about eight-thirty?"

"Maybe." She nodded toward the door. "Go open us."

"My pleasure." He went to the door and flipped the sign. "Now what do I do?"

"Work your case," Angela said.

"It's six AM, Angela," Matthew said. "I don't want to wake anyone up."

"Dr. Penn keeps early hours," she said.

"He does, does he?"

Angela nodded.

"I'll give him a call." He returned to the booth, noticed only two battery bars on his cell phone, and dialed Dr. Penn's number.

"Good morning, Matthew," Dr. Penn said. "What's it look like down your way?"

Matthew smiled at Angela. *It actually looks beautiful.* "The streets haven't been touched. How about you?"

"Nothing yet," Dr. Penn said. "The snowshoes came in mighty handy last night. Twenty-six inches. Incredible."

"Were you able to see Timothy?" Matthew asked.

"Yes."

"How'd it go?" Matthew asked.

"In my professional opinion," Dr. Penn said, "Timothy has a strong case, one of the strongest I've seen for a soldier who didn't see combat. As an anesthetist in any other war, he would have been stationed on or near the battlefield to do his job at a MASH or Combat Support Hospital. I believe Timothy has a classic case of PTSD, and I willing to attest to that in court."

Good. "How is Mrs. Simmons?"

"She is a rock," Dr. Penn said. "Given time and the proper therapy, both of them will make it through this. Where should I send my findings?"

"Well, I obviously don't want you to come over to Angela's today," Matthew said.

Angela raised her eyebrows.

"She's open?" Dr. Penn asked.

"Yes, *we're* open," Matthew said. "Regular time. No customers yet, of course, but you never know."

"And you're there now," Dr. Penn said.

"Yes, I'm open for business, too, Doc."

"How is she?" Dr. Penn asked. "I meant to call her yesterday during the storm."

Matthew smiled at Angela. "She's good. She's very good."

Angela bit her lower lip and turned away, heading into the kitchen.

She is the best flirt! "Dr. Penn," Matthew said softly, "Angela told me about what happened to her four years ago."

"I hoped she might," Dr. Penn said. "How do you feel about it?"

"Her telling me or what happened to her?" Matthew asked.

"Both," Dr. Penn said.

Matthew exhaled. "I don't know, privileged she told me and mad as hell that it happened to her. I still don't have all the specifics."

"And we may never know them all because Angela may never tell us," Dr. Penn said. "The assault itself was sudden, unexpected, and unpredictable, and how and if she reveals anything to us may come just as suddenly and unexpectedly."

"Does she have PTSD?" Matthew asked.

"I believe so, yes," Dr. Penn said.

Matthew sighed. "So there's no telling how long this will last."

"You're right," Dr. Penn said. "There's no telling. The mind is as sturdy as it is fragile, Matthew. What we have to do is keep what's sturdy strong and rebuild what's fragile. Her isolation seems to be ending because of you, and it might scare her and thrill her at the same time. She feels strong and fragile at the same time. Do you understand?"

"I've seen it in action, Doc. It's . . ." He shook his head. "Honestly, it's sometimes spooky how she can be sweet then sour from one day to the next, even from one moment to the next. She's consistently inconsistent."

"That's an accurate description of anyone suffering from PTSD," Dr. Penn said. "But take heart, Matthew. Your friendship has obviously already done wonders for her. You are the first person she has allowed into her isolated world in four years."

"You, too, right?" Matthew asked.

"Not nearly as much as you," Dr. Penn said. "She sees me as a means to an end, a potential cure. She truly sees you as a friend."

Matthew smiled. "I'm more than a friend to her, Dr. Penn. I'm not sure exactly what I am, but I know I'm more than a friend."

"Do you love her, Matthew?" Dr. Penn asked.

Why'd he have to ask that? "I honestly don't know."

"*Could* you love her?" Dr. Penn asked.

"Yes. Easily. I've never met anyone like her. I think I have a crush on her. I'm a grown man with a crush. What's that say about me?"

"That you're romantic," Dr. Penn said.

"Maybe."

"Angela is making all sorts of breakthroughs," Dr. Penn said. "Mrs. Simmons said Angela was at her apartment the other night."

"We've been out twice together," Matthew said. "Pizza the first time."

"Pizza!" Dr. Penn shouted. "Oh, I could use some, but no one's open and probably won't be for a few days. All this is remarkable, truly remarkable, Matthew. You know, you could have a career in counseling, counselor."

"I'm not trying to replace you, Doc," Matthew said. "I have a feeling Angela still needs you."

"And I'll be here," Dr. Penn said. "I want to caution you, though, Matthew. It may take Angela a long time to recover, and she may never fully recover. How do you feel about that?"

"I'd do anything for her," Matthew said. "I care about her more than I've ever cared about anyone." *Wow. Why are my eyes tearing up?*

"Love is the best therapy," Dr. Penn said.

"I don't know if it's love, Doc," Matthew said, rubbing his eyes.

"It sounds like love to me," Dr. Penn said.

It can't be love yet, can it? My eyes certainly seem to think so. "In your considered opinion as a psychiatrist."

"No, in my considered opinion as a man," Dr. Penn said. "I knew you were a good man the moment I met you."

Angela returned to the counter with a tray of turnovers.

"Listen, Dr. Penn," Matthew said quickly, wiping his eyes, "why don't you e-mail your findings to me as an attachment, and I'll print it out at my end when I can." He gave Dr. Penn his e-mail address. "I'd also like you to e-mail your findings to Dr. William Wick at the VA."

"You mean *Major* William Wick, don't you?" Dr. Penn said.

"He was a major?" Matthew asked.

"In the U.S. Army, yes sir," Dr. Penn said.

Dr. Wick was or is still a soldier. How, then, can he be so cold to other soldiers?

"I know I have his e-mail address around here somewhere," Dr. Penn said. "I'll send him my findings today. Give my best to Angela."

"I will."

"Stay warm," Dr. Penn said.

"I will." Matthew closed his phone.

Angela brought over a plate of turnovers. "You aren't coming down with a cold, are you?"

"No." *I only did a little crying. I can't remember the last time I cried.* "It might be allergies. I'm okay. Dr. Penn sends his best."

"How's he doing?" She slid in beside him.

Matthew bit into a turnover. *Is it okay to say that food is orgasmic? This turnover is orgasmic.* "He sounds great. He's snowed in like the rest of us. He says Timothy has a strong case."

"That's good," Angela said. "What did you mean when you said I was very good?"

"You're a very good person in every respect," Matthew said, "and you were a very good blanket last night. And you're also a very good flirt. When you bite your lip like that, I get all tingly inside."

She laughed. "Maybe I'm not flirting." She rubbed his thigh. "Maybe I'm on the prowl."

"Are you?" *Please say you are.*

She looked outside. "I'm thinking we can close at seven-thirty now."

Matthew wolfed down the rest of his turnover. "I should probably get in the shower now then, huh?"

Angela squeezed his thigh. "You know, I could close . . . now."

"You just opened," Matthew said.

"I know." She bit her lower lip.

"You're doing that biting of the lip thing," Matthew said.

"I know." She bit her lower lip again.

"There it is again," Matthew said. "My tinglings are turning to stirrings."

"I think I will close." Angela ran to the front door and locked it, flipped the sign, and turned out the dining room lights.

Matthew met her at the counter, and they raced through the kitchen and up the stairs to the apartment.

Angela stopped him at the top of the stairs. "I want you to watch what I do *very* carefully."

"You have my undivided attention."

Angela kicked off her shoes and pulled off her socks, tossing them onto the couch. She took two steps into the kitchen and took off her pants, leaving them in a heap. She pulled off her sweater and threw it behind her. She reached under her T-shirt and removed her bra, letting it drop as she entered her bedroom.

She turned to Matthew at the foot of her bed. "Were you watching?"

Matthew nodded. *That was a show I could get used to seeing every day. I especially liked the bra removal trick.*

"I'd take off more but I'm freaking cold," she said, rubbing her arms.

"I understand completely," Matthew whispered. "I like what I see completely, too."

Angela pulled back the covers and got into bed. "Hurry," she whispered.

Matthew hurried to take his shower, because once again, there was no hot water. He pulled on his boxers and joined her, and as he did, she crept on top of him.

"You smell better," she said, rubbing his chest. "But I need to warm you up."

"I'm definitely warming up, thank you." He kissed her. "Should I hold you again?"

Angela slid beside him, and Matthew turned to face her. "Do you want me, Matthew?"

"Yes," he said. "With all my soul."

"I like you wanting me. I want you, too, but . . . but please understand. I'm . . ." She sighed. "I'm afraid of . . . of being out of control, of losing control. What happened to me damaged me badly. I'm starting to realize how badly because of you. I want you so bad I can taste you in my heart. Please believe that. But the moment I think that, I think about that night and . . ." She blinked away a tear. "I can't get that night out of my head, Matthew. I know you'd never hurt me, I do, and that gives me so much strength. You're so gentle, so . . ." She shook her head. "I'm so messed up, aren't I?"

"No." He caressed her face. "You're a survivor."

"I don't feel like one," she said. "I'm still afraid of him being out there."

"I'm here now, right?"

"Yes, you are, and I thank God you're here," Angela said. "But I'm still messed up. We should be making sweet love to each other on our snow day. Right?"

Well . . . "I like talking to you, too." He rubbed her arm. "We could talk instead."

"What would we talk about that would keep our minds off making love to each other?" Angela asked.

Yes. What would we talk about while lying side by side and barely dressed in a cozy, full-size bed? "Oh, life, the future, you know, everything. Anything." He felt down the contour of her side to her hip. "As long as I can touch you while we talk, we can talk for the next twenty-four hours. You have so many interesting places to touch." He caressed her thigh. "I like this thigh."

"It likes you, too." She smiled. "Turn onto your back."

Matthew lay on his back.

Angela crept up and propped her head up on her hands, her elbows resting on his chest. "Now I can see you better."

He wormed his hand under her shirt and rubbed her back. "And I can give you a one-handed backrub."

"You figured me out," she said. "What do two people talk about for twenty-four hours that doesn't involve sex?"

"We could try a little Q and A," Matthew said. "I'll ask a question, you answer. You ask a question, I'll answer. You go first."

Angela squinted then opened her eyes wide. "Do you like children, Mr. McConnell?"

"Sure," Matthew said. "My turn. How many children do you want?"

"Two," Angela said. "A girl and a boy, in that order. You?"

"That sounds good," Matthew said. "Do you have your children named?"

"No, not yet," Angela said. "Do you?"

"No." *I have to ask more probing questions.* "How soon do you want these unnamed children running around here?"

Angela didn't answer immediately. "Not nine months or even a year—or two—from now, not until I'm sure of *our* financial future. Do you mind if we don't get intimate until we're sure of each other and our futures?"

"I must be honest here," Matthew said. "I do mind, because I can't resist stroking and rubbing and kissing your body, and I have a feeling you like me stroking, rubbing, and kissing you."

"I do," she whispered. "Very much."

He slipped his hand down her back, finding the edge of her underwear and sneaking his hand under it. "You like this."

Angela moved higher. "Very much."

"Isn't this being intimate?" Matthew asked.

Angela nodded.

He squeezed. "And neither of is sure of our futures at this moment."

Angela climbed up on him. "Use both hands."

Matthew kneaded and squeezed her booty. "Like this?"

"Yes." She kissed him. "But we can't go further than this. For now."

Matthew sat up. "I understand." He kissed her neck and pulled her into his lap. "As long as we don't arrive at the natural conclusion."

Angela nodded.

He smiled. "I can think of so many things we could do without going that far."

"So can I." She kissed his chin. "I just don't know if I can trust myself to stop."

"We'll create a contract and seal it with a kiss," Matthew said.

"Okay." She smiled. "You say it, and I'll sign it."

"We agree not to make love to each other until we're financially secure and completely secure with each other," Matthew said. "How's that?"

She kissed him. "It's a contract." She smiled. "I can't believe I'm here in this bed with you."

"Why?" Matthew asked.

"I didn't think I could compete with the women you usually go out with," Angela said.

He ran his hands up her sides, squeezing and feeling her hot flesh. "There's no competition. You've won. I think you're incredibly sexy."

"I'm not sexy at all," Angela said.

He shook his head. "Angela, you have the brightest smile, the softest lips, the nicest initials, the smoothest skin, the firmest muscles, and the sexiest booty."

"Matthew, I'm not exotic or tall or thin or endowed or tattooed or pierced, and I'm so much darker than—"

"Angela, you are perfect," Matthew interrupted. He lifted her shirt and smiled at her breasts. "Sexy."

She pushed down her shirt. "I'm not. I'm a plain Williamsburg woman who only has a high school education."

"There's nothing plain about you. Your ears are perfect." He kissed each one. "Not too big, not too small. I have never seen such symmetry. Your hands are not too soft, not too rough, and so strong." He kissed each palm. "You hold me so fiercely. I like to be held tight. And your skin is warm, smooth, and firm. If you have an ounce of fat on you, I haven't found it yet. And your smile is so sexy, especially when you act shy."

"I don't act shy," Angela said. "I *am* shy."

"Shyness is sexy to me," Matthew said. "Shyness also tells me you're humble. You're not stuck up or vain in any way. You are nothing like the women I've been wasting my time with. And . . ." He kissed her neck. "You taste good all over. But what I like the most is that your eyes *only* see me. I'm not used to that. You're not distracted by anything. You focus on me. You hear me, and you even listen to me some of the time."

"Most of the time," she said.

He locked his fingers with hers. "Angela, I never knew how lonely I was until I saw your smile. I left here every night with an incredible ache in my heart. I missed your smile. I would do anything to see you smile."

Angela smiled. "I'm smiling now."

"Thank you."

"I just worry that when the time comes," Angela said, "I won't be able to please you completely."

Matthew shook his head. "I have *no* doubt that you will be able to send me into paroxysms of ecstasy." He pulled her closer, moving her legs around him. "I have no doubt that you can rock my socks off." He wiggled his toes. "See. You've already knocked off my socks."

"But when we finally become one," Angela said, "I want to be able to be with you in every way possible. I guess you've already noticed that I feel safer on top. I feel safe now." She looked down. "But even when I'm on top of you, I get claustrophobic sometimes. I fight back the covers. I have to have my arms free."

"Did you feel that way last night?" Matthew asked.

"No," she said. "Last night you held me gently. You didn't restrain me. I felt safe. I don't think I've ever felt so safe."

Matthew glanced at the nightstand. "Will I replace the hammer and the Taser?"

"Not yet," Angela said. "I hope you're not mad."

"I'm not." He kissed her. "You are so pretty."

"But I'm not," Angela said. "Don't you wish I had longer legs?"

"No." He stroked both of her thighs.

"But then I'd have more of me to wrap around you," Angela said.

"You have perfectly proportioned legs," Matthew said. "Don't be surprised if you feel my lips on your thighs sometime."

"When?" Angela smiled. "If I'm on top, I'd have to climb all the way up your body to the headboard for that to happen. Your head would have to be between my legs and . . ."

"Yeah." Matthew exhaled. "That would be . . ." *My poor boxers.* "Yeah. Thanks for that image."

Angela looked down. "I feel you. That's all it took?"

"I have an excellent imagination," Matthew said.

Angela tightened her shirt against her breasts. "Don't you wish I had perkier breasts? I'd be curvier."

"They're beautiful," Matthew said. "You are curvy enough for me. Any curvier and I'll get motion sickness. I want to prove it to you, but you can't move."

"I'll try not to," Angela whispered.

Matthew put his hands on Angela's face and moved them leisurely down her neck to her breasts, squeezing lightly before moving down her sides to her booty, hips, and thighs. "That's curvy. My hands are dizzy."

"Can we . . . can you lie back?" Angela asked.

Matthew slid down, and Angela became a blanket again.

"I wish I could get over my fears," Angela said. "I imagine having you on top of me, and I get a little scared thinking about it. I imagine backing up on you to let you hold me from behind, and I'm terrified."

"Angela, I completely understand," Matthew said. "I wouldn't be able to see your eyes or smile that well from behind you anyway. I have to see your eyes at all times."

She moved higher and looked into his eyes. "I have to see yours, too. I only wish I was, I don't know, sexier. I'm lying on you in a plain white T-shirt and some white underwear. How sexy is that?"

"Very," Matthew whispered.

"It's not sexy at all," Angela said.

"Sit up," Matthew said.

Angela rose and placed her hands on his chest as Matthew sat up.

"Raise your arms," Matthew said.

She raised her arms.

"Close your eyes," Matthew whispered.

"I don't know if I can," Angela said.

"Okay," Matthew said, pulling her shirt over her head and tossing it toward the window. "You can watch." He kissed above each breast, lightly sucked on each nipple, and kissed between her breasts. "Very sexy. So is your stomach. Lean back."

Angela leaned back.

Matthew kissed all over her stomach. "If you straighten out your legs and scoot up a bit, I can kiss your thighs. You may need to put your feet on the headboard."

Angela straightened her legs, raising them to the headboard.

Matthew kissed each thigh while he massaged her calves. "You're exceptionally sexy, Angela."

"Matthew," Angela said breathlessly, "can I go higher?"

"Don't move," Matthew whispered. "Let me go lower."

As he slid down, he gripped and lifted her thighs off him. He moved her underwear aside with his teeth and found her sweetness, licking in rapid strokes while massaging her booty until her legs began to quiver.

I am holding Angela in the air.

"Matthew, you're going to make me come," she whispered.

He darted his tongue inside her.

Angela moaned. "Damn . . ."

Matthew eased her onto his chest and pushed himself back to the headboard, maneuvering her onto his lap. "Are you really coming?"

"Yes." She looked away. "I'm so embarrassed."

"Don't be," Matthew whispered. "With your booty pressing against me like this . . ." *Damn* . . . "Oh shit, so am I." *I definitely have to get home to get more boxers.* He tried to smile. "Sorry about the mess. You okay?"

Angela nodded, pulled the cover over them, and lay flat on top of him, her feet rubbing against his calves.

"You sure?" Matthew asked.

"I'm sure." She sighed. "I'm happy."

"So am I." *Geez! What did I last, five seconds? How can I be happy about that?* He hugged her. "I like making you happy."

"Now what do we do?" Angela whispered.

"We could rest," Matthew said.

"Okay," Angela whispered.

Two minutes later, Matthew whispered, "Angela?"

"Yes?"

"That was easily the most erotic thing I have ever done," Matthew said.

"Me, too," Angela whispered. "I wasn't too heavy, was I?"

"No."

"You had me floating in the air," Angela whispered.

Two more minutes later, Angela whispered, "Matthew? Can we do that again in a little while?"

"Yes."

One minute later, Angela whispered, "Matthew? Has a little while passed?"

"You stay put this time," Matthew said, kicking the covers off the bed and sliding lower.

"I doubt I can do that," Angela moaned.

Matthew removed her underwear. "Then don't," he whispered, raising her hips.

"Especially if you do that . . . *yes* . . . and *that* . . . oh, *yes, right there* . . ."

Chapter 25

The next morning after again seeing Angela come out of the bathroom fully dressed, Matthew shoveled away what city snowplows had maliciously returned to the sidewalk, and Williamsburg came back to life under a shining sun. Customers trickled in, previously snowed-in vehicles reappeared and then vanished, and La Estrella opened again.

His cell's battery flashing, Matthew waited until customers filled half the booths and chairs before approaching Angela.

"I've got to go back to my apartment for my charger," he said. "Think you can manage for an hour without me?"

"An hour?" Angela asked. "It shouldn't take that long to get a toothbrush."

He had told her about brushing his teeth with his finger.

She had not been amused.

"I need to pack a few things," he said. *Boxers, mostly.* "I'd like to hang around for a few more days. If it's all right with you."

Angela smiled broadly, leaned across the counter, and kissed him. "Hurry back."

Matthew felt the eyes of customers on him. "You just kissed me in front of all these people," he whispered. "Aren't you worried about the scandal? Did you see that? They're *really* partners."

Angela kissed him again. "Hurry back."

That kiss answered that question.

Matthew slogged through mountains of snow to Havemeyer, climbed the steps above the pharmacy, and entered his apartment for the first time in days. It didn't smell or look any different, but his easy chair now commanded a view of snow-covered garbage bags.

He took a long hot shower, shaved, put on clean clothes, filled a bag with toiletries and two more changes of clothes and every pair of boxers he owned, and ate a slice of cold Mezza Luna pizza. He noticed his answering machine flashing, so he checked his messages. *I have twelve messages. When is the last time I had twelve messages?*

The first message was from Michael:

"Matt, when are you going to change your recording? You can't expect to get a new woman interested in you if your ex is still on the recording."

Oh yeah. I had better change that. I really should disconnect this dinosaur. What do I need an answering machine for when my cell phone has voice mail?

"Listen, Matt, Victoria is simply *dying* to see you again, though I can't for the life of me figure out why. She has called me *seven* times asking for you. I don't know what magic you used on her, but I think she is seriously hungering for you, big dog. What's your secret? I got nowhere with her and Debbie Does What Victoria Does for *six* months! She's already talking about introducing you to Boops and Boopsie. I never got that far. Give me a call and I'll set you two up again. My treat for everything this time. Call me back!"

Why didn't Victoria call me? She had my number. I guess it's the same pattern. She needs a go-between or a buffer for dating. Sorry, Victoria. You were fine, but wealth for wealth's sake isn't sexy, and I'd rather eat cake than try to kiss through the makeup caked to your cheek.

The next message, from a 963 number at eight PM three days ago, was a few seconds of static. *Probably a wrong number.*

The next message dropped him into the easy chair.

"Matthew, please pick up, I'm begging you!"

It's Joy. Why don't I feel any?

"*Please* pick up. *Recoja el teléfono maldito! Please* give me a call at this number in about fifteen minutes. It's a pay phone. It's a matter of life and death! Call me!"

Joy sounds so desperate. She called three days ago. Hmm. There must be trouble in paradise.

He listened to the next message.

"Matty, I'm sorry about the other night. I shouldn't have kicked you out."

Monique?

"You were actually treating me with a great deal of respect. Not many guys have ever done that for me, and I'm not used to it. I didn't know how to react. Maybe we could go, I don't know, to a movie sometime. No dancing at The Cove, I promise. Give me a call. Please. I want to try again."

Sorry, Monique. You were strikingly gorgeous, but a drawer full of exotic condoms is scary, not sexy.

Joy struck again in the next message.

"Matthew, where *are* you?"

Desperation suits her.

"Look, I'm *sorry,* okay. Pick up! I know I hurt you, but I need your help desperately. I know you're listening. I know you're screening your calls. I don't blame you. What I did was so foolish and stupid. I don't expect you to forgive me, but if you could wire me some money to get back home, I would really appreciate it. Call me at this number in the next five minutes, please! I'm running out of change!"

I was so cruel to her three days ago by not calling back, and I wasn't even here to enjoy it.

Joy owned the next message, too.

"I don't understand you!"

Joy has no patience. That wasn't five minutes. It was more like two.

"*Usted es tal ano!* We spent a *year* together, Matthew. Doesn't that mean anything to you? Okay, so it didn't mean that much to me in the end. That's my fault, not yours. You see, I'm flat broke. *No tengo ningún dinero.* Carlo was F-ing married. He lied to me! He has *four* children. He put me up in *un hotel sucio,* some dingy, cheap hotel because, get this, he said he was remodeling his house and we couldn't go there yet. *Soy tan estúpido!* I even loaned him five hundred dollars to get his roof fixed. When my money ran out, the hotel put me out on the street. Help me! Oh, and by the way, that cheap microwave you bought died the *first* time I plugged it in down here. Call this number now! Please!"

Matthew smiled. He knew he shouldn't have, but he did. *I've helped Carlo fix his roof for him, his wife, and his four kids. I have done a good thing for the man who stole my old girlfriend. And it doesn't bother me at all. In the grand scheme of things, if it weren't for Carlo, I wouldn't have met Angela. The smell of oranges will no longer upset me.*

He listened to the next message:

"I've been doing a lot of soul-searching since we talked, Matthew."

Mary! Wow.

"I realize that you're right about me. I really haven't changed. I still have very strong urges, and I felt something burst in me whenever you were around me. I also know that I've been wasting my time with you know who. Perhaps we could go out sometime, or we could just go for a walk, or you could come over to my place, and I'll cook for you. Let me know."

Sorry, Mary. You were stimulating to all my senses and even crept into my daydreams, but hypocrisy isn't sexy.

The next message of static was from the same 963 number that called at eight PM two days ago. He checked the Caller ID on his phone—"NY GOV." *Jade from jail?*

The next message made him check to see if he had locked his door.

"I hope this is the Matt McConnell who took me to the Rangers game."

And now, Allison. This stuff never *happens, not even in the most convoluted movies. But why didn't she call my cell phone? She was blowing it up for two days!*

"If it isn't, please ignore this. If it is, I just want to thank you for making sure I got home safely the other day. I really embarrassed myself, didn't I?"

I'm surprised she remembers anything about that night.

"I would have called you on your cell phone, but I must have erased your number from my memory while I was drunk. I am *so* sorry for everything I did or said to you. But guess what? Surprise

surprise, I'm not drinking anymore. Five whole days. I went to my first AA meeting last night. I'm also giving my diaries a rest. I've been reading them, and they are really awful. They were fun to read when I was drinking, but they're brutal to read when I'm sober. If there is any chance in the world we could, I don't know, meet for coffee sometime, like at the place we met, I'd really appreciate it."

That's not happening.

"You're a special man, Matt. And if you don't call back, it's cool. I just wanted you to know these things and know how sorry I am for the way I acted. Bye."

Good for you about sobriety, Allison, but you might still be crazy, and insanity isn't sexy at all.

More static from the same 963 number followed. *It has to be Jade. I wonder if she has any new tats yet. Or a new girlfriend.*

"*Yo me siento muy cansado de esta mierda!*"

Joy is really *pissed now. She's getting tired of this shit. So am I.*

"Because of you, *pendejo,* I had to get money from my parents, and you *know* how much I hate them. If they call you, you are to tell them I was on vacation in the Dominican Republic when I got robbed. Got that? I was on vacation and got robbed."

Joy doesn't want her parents to know how truly foolish she is. I'm sure they already know. And what does that say about me? I asked Joy to move in. I was foolish, too.

"I should be home by the nineteenth."

Joy may already be here.

No. I'm sure the storm delayed her. Nothing was flying in or out of JFK or LaGuardia during that storm.

The last message, however, proved him wrong.

"*Comer mierda y morir!* Where the *freak* did you put my clothes?"

I guess her plane got through the blizzard. And somehow, she got into the apartment.

He leaped out of his chair.

"I need them, you *hijo de puta!* You're wondering how I got in. I had another key made three months ago, *pendejo!* Don't be surprised if you have a pissed-off visitor *very* soon, and I will *not* be knocking first!"

He erased all the messages, unplugged the answering machine, and searched the apartment for any signs of Joy, relieved he didn't find her or smell any fresh vanilla.

Do I change my locks or go retrieve her clothes? I'm sure the thrift store sold them the first day. She had some really nice stuff. Looking back, I probably shouldn't have gotten rid of her clothes. Or her shoes. However, it was the logical thing to do at a very illogical time. At least I didn't throw them out into the street. I could have done that.

Matthew smiled.

Joy has returned, badly dressed and broke. I think I'll call her parents in Staten Island, just to see how she's doing . . .

Unfortunately, Joy answered. "Matthew, is that you?"

Shoot. I wanted to talk to her parents. Maybe one day. They'll answer first eventually. "Hi, Joy."

"Where are my clothes?" she whispered tersely.

At least now I know her parents are nearby. Joy has never been a whisperer. "How was your trip to the Dominican Republic? I bet they didn't have any snow down there. Did you bring back any neat souvenirs?"

"I want my clothes, Matthew," Joy whispered.

"And I wanted a commitment," Matthew said. "Easy come, easy there you go to the DR with a married man who smelled like oranges. You should have known that vanilla and orange only go together on a Creamsicle."

"I'm not going to ask you again," Joy whispered.

"Good," Matthew said. "I don't like echoes." He heard a door open and shut. *I'll bet she's going outside so she can yell at me.*

"*Where . . . are . . . my . . . clothes?*" Joy screamed.

She's so predictable. She's outside, and she's so dramatic. I can be dramatic, too. "Your . . . clothes . . . are . . . at . . . the . . . Salvation . . . Army . . . Thrift . . . Store . . . on . . . Bedford . . . Avenue."

"*What?*" she screamed.

"I thought you were gone for good with my rent money that eventually repaired Carlo's roof," Matthew said, "so I donated your clothes to the less fortunate."

"That's so f-ed up, Matthew!" Joy shouted. "*I'm* the less fortunate now!"

And like desperation, her misfortune suits her, too. "*And* you owe me eighteen hundred dollars."

"You aren't getting it," Joy said. "You can't *prove* I took your money."

I could take her to court, but I don't want to have anything more to do with her after this conversation. "Were Carlo's kids cute? And he had four? My, he was a potent one. Were you using protection? I hope you were."

"*Bastardo!*"

"Would any child you had with Carlo be considered a Hondurican?" Matthew asked.

"*Le odio!*"

I rather hate you, too. "What was his wife like? I'm thinking she was beautiful. Dominican women are gorgeous, you know. How's that roof look? What's it like hanging around a pay phone? Meet any interesting people?"

"*Beso mi culo!*"

Oh, I know this *phrase.* "No thank you, Joy. I'm done kissing your ass. I am seeing someone with amazing initials. *Adios*. Sorry. Smiley face." He hung up.

That went very *well.*

I think I have gained closure.

He looked at the front door. *Should I change the lock? I'm almost out of this apartment. What's the point? I'm practically living with Angela as it is.*

Matthew felt a flutter in his heart.

And I miss her.

But if Joy has a key, she could return the favor. I can't have that.

He dug in a closet and found two long duffel bags, packing them with his cell phone charger, most of his clothes, all of his shoes, several jackets, another coat, the suit, towels, and even the thin washcloth. He emptied his mostly empty refrigerator into an old laundry bag. He took his "new" sheets and comforter off his bed and put them high up in a closet where he hoped little Joy couldn't reach them.

Anything else, she can have.

He stared at the easy chair.

She'd never take that, would she?

Hmm. She would. She'd probably set it on fire on the Williamsburg Bridge.

I will have to make two trips.

He looped the laundry bag over his neck, slung the two duffel bags over his shoulders, and trekked over chunks of ice and deep snow back to Angela's, wondering how much to tell her.

All these women seem to want a piece of me, but I only want Angela, now and forever. I thought the process of elimination was over. Maybe this is the last step of that process. Do I want to be with any of them again? No. No way. But should I tell Angela? Would I want a woman to tell me that six men have been filling up her answering machine? I don't think so.

Matthew banged through the door, letting the duffel bags clunk to the floor. *That was loud. Now everyone's looking at me, Angela most of all.* He took a deep breath and hoisted them back to his shoulders, walked through the dining area nodding his head at customers, eased around the counter, and headed toward the kitchen.

"What took you so long?" Angela whispered.

"I'll explain once I drop my load," he whispered.

He found the stairway door open and left the bags on the landing. After emptying his refrigerator's contents into Angela's, he returned to the counter.

I can't lie to her. "I had a few messages on my answering machine."

"From potential clients?" she asked.

"No." He sighed. "From a few women."

Angela climbed up on her stool. "How many?"

"Twelve."

"Twelve women?" Angela asked.

"Twelve *messages* from six women and Michael, who used to be my best friend." *She's neither frowning nor smiling. Is this a good or a bad thing?* "Do I need to name them all?"

"Do you?" Angela asked.

She wants me to name them all. "Well, let's see. The first one was from Michael."

"What did he want?" Angela asked.

"To set me up with Victoria again," Matthew said, "but I'm not returning his call."

Angela nodded, pulling at her fingers. "Who else?"

Who's the next safest? "A couple calls from jail. That would probably be Jade."

Angela blinked. "You were barely with her, Matthew."

"I seem to have a lingering effect on women," Matthew said. "Monique, Mary, Allison, and Joy also called."

Angela counted on her fingers. "*All* of them called you?"

Matthew nodded.

"What for?" Angela whispered.

"Except for Joy, they called to, um, to ask me out, but I don't want to have anything to do with any of them," Matthew said quickly. "I've made my choice, and I'm sticking with you." He stepped close and kissed her cheek. "If you'll still have me."

Angela shook her head slightly. "Why did Joy call?"

"Oh, she needed me to wire her some money. She's back from her tryst with Carlo." He put his hands on her knees. "Carlo was married."

Angela smiled. "No way. How stupid was she?"

"Her *baleadas* were smarter," Matthew said. *And that makes* me *look stupid for being with stupid Joy.* "Oh, she also wants her clothes."

"She didn't take them with her?" Angela asked.

"She was in a hurry." *Oh, but she did have time to soil my bed first.*

"Well, give them to her," Angela said.

"I can't." Matthew winced. "They're at the Salvation Army Thrift Store."

Angela laughed. "You gave them away?"

"I know I shouldn't have done that." He rubbed her thighs. "But it sure felt good to do at the time."

"That's cold, Matthew," Angela said, still smiling.

"And so is she. Most of them were winter clothes. I'm sure I'll see some of her outfits walking around Williamsburg once they clear away all this snow." He took her hands. "I'm sorry about all this."

"Don't be," Angela said. "You didn't call them. They called you." She squeezed his hands. "I know why they all wanted to see you again. After what we did last night, they'd be insane not to call you."

"But we never . . . I never did anything with them." *Except for Joy. I hope Angela wasn't listening too—*

"You and Joy didn't . . ."

She was listening. I'll hand it to women. They can hear what you don't say, too. "Yes, but nothing like what happened last night. You're not worried, are you?"

"Should I be?" Angela asked.

Matthew shook his head. "No. I've found the one for me." He kissed her.

Angela looked at the door as several customers came in. "You really know how to pick 'em."

Matthew backed away. "I'm done pickin'."

After carrying his bags upstairs and putting his toothbrush in Angela's medicine cabinet, he went to his office booth and plugged in his charger. He then tried to set up an appointment for Timothy with Dr. Wick.

It was a lost cause.

"Hi, I talked earlier to Dr. Wick about—"

"Dr. Wick is unavailable," the secretary interrupted. "Is there anything I can help you with?"

No. "When will Dr. Wick be available?"

"I'm not at liberty to say," she said.

And you're obviously not at liberty to help me either. What happened to your heart of gold? "If I left my number for him to return my call, would you give him the message?"

"I'm not at liberty to say, *Mr. McConnell,*" she said with attitude. "You lawyers are all alike. Nice trick you pulled the other day. It nearly got me fired. Have a nice day."

Click.

Damn Caller-ID. I try to be a completely honest lawyer and get shut out.

Later that night, after closing, Matthew coaxed Angela out to the sidewalk to help him build a snowman for the snowwoman.

"Hey, I'm outside," Angela said.

"Yeah." Matthew tried to block his latest handiwork.

"Stop that." She knocked off the snowman's penis for the fourth time. "You are a child sometimes."

"Snow brings out the child in me," Matthew said. "When we're done, we could walk to Snacky for some hot dogs."

Angela removed some snow from the snowwoman's cleavage. "Snacky serves hot dogs? Isn't that a Chinese place?"

"Yes," Matthew said.

"I don't know." She stood beside the snowwoman and turned side to side.

"Your booty is nicer," Matthew said.

Angela backed toward the door. "Stop looking at my booty."

"I can't help it," Matthew said. "We *could* walk down to Twenty Sided Store on Grand to look at some old-school games. It's only two blocks away."

"I'm not sure," Angela said.

"It's barely two blocks," Matthew said.

"Maybe another night, okay?"

How do I convince her? "Okay, the winner of whatever game we buy gets to decide what kind of bliss we'll have later tonight."

"How old school are we talking?" Angela asked.

I have her attention. "Oh, something like Trouble, Yahtzee, Operation. I used to like Hungry Hippos."

"I never played that one." She formed and threw a snowball across the street, and it banged off the dark La Estrella sign.

"Nice shot," Matthew said.

She looked at the door to her shop. "I had a Simon."

"I didn't," Matthew said. "I was heartbroken."

"I wasn't very good at it." She blew out a smoky breath. "It's getting cold."

Matthew took her hand. "Then we need to go for a walk to warm us up."

Angela tried to twist her hand away from his.

Matthew gripped her hand more tightly. "Two blocks."

"Okay." She locked the door and took a giant step toward Grand Street.

Matthew tugged her back. "Not yet."

"Why?" she asked.

"Can we try to walk at a reasonable pace this time?" he asked.

"I'll try."

Angela didn't try.

They sped down Driggs and through the first block of Grand past The Lucky Cat bar dodging cars and snowplows spraying snow, graffiti trailing behind them on construction site plywood. They flew past two more bars and a store called Fugedaboutit in the second block.

Angela stopped at the corner of Grand and Havemeyer. "You said *two* blocks. Where is this place?"

"It's at the end of the block on the other side." Matthew pointed to the right.

"That's Marcy Ave. right in front of us, Matthew," Angela said. "We're practically at the Expressway."

"I miscalculated," Matthew said.

"You think?" Angela shouted.

"Sorry," Matthew said. "It's only one more block, Angela."

Angela sighed. "All right. Come on."

Matthew let her drag him across Grand to Twenty Sided Store, where several tables contained people playing board and card games. Games Matthew had never heard of, like Dark Ascension, Dominion, and Defenders of the Realm, stocked the shelves.

Angela called him to a shelf of vintage games.

"We're not playing Parchesi or Monopoly," she said, catching her breath.

"How about . . ." He pulled out an ancient Sorry! game. "This?"

"Whatever," Angela said. "Let's get it and go."

Matthew took it to a counter. "How much?"

"Nine," the guy said.

Matthew turned the box around. "This box is taped up, man. It might fall apart before we get home. Six."

"It's an antique," the guy said. "Eight."

"Come on," Angela whispered.

"Seven," Matthew said.

"Cool," the guy said.

As they hustled out of the shop, Angela turned and said, "You paid too much."

Angela dropped Matthew's hand, throwing out her hands as if clawing the air, glaring into every alley, and leaning around corners to look before proceeding. She tried to avoid, step over, or skim the deeper snow, leaping to rare clearings on the sidewalk whenever she could.

It's as if she's running through a minefield, which is more of a mind*field. She seems to be reliving her escape right in front of me.*

At the Sweet Treats entrance, she shook off her shoes, hastily opened the front door to the shop, and jumped inside.

"I thought this was your hometown," she said flatly.

Matthew stepped inside and took off his shoes. "I was only off by one block."

Angela kept walking toward the counter. "You tricked me."

"I forgot. Really. It's not a store I go into that often." He caught up to her in the kitchen.

Angela opened the stairway door. "How do you know it even exists?"

"I got corralled into going to a Magic tournament there once." *With a very freaky girl who was tattooed from head to toe and thought Carlos Castenada was God. That "date" ended when she decided to play Magic with some Gothic dudes instead of going back to my place.*

"I won't ask what a Magic tournament is." She leaped to the landing and started up the stairs.

"Am I welcome or should I get my bed booth ready?" Matthew asked.

Matthew heard Angela sigh. *She's thinking about it.*

"You can come up," she said.

"You sure?"

"Come on."

Matthew bounded up the stairs, but then he sat on the couch for ten minutes waiting for Angela to come out of the bathroom.

Too soon, too soon. Why am I rushing her? I can't rush her. I did, and now I'm paying for it.

Matthew set up the game on the coffee table and shuffled the Sorry! cards at least fifty times.

When Angela returned, she sat in the wingback chair instead of on the couch next to him.

She has sent a message.

"Okay," Matthew said, setting the deck on the board. "Here are the new rules. Any time you send me back with a Sorry! card, I remove one article of clothing. Any time I send you back—"

Angela flew out of her chair and came back five minutes later wearing shoes, two sweaters, a coat, a hat, and a pair of fuzzy mittens.

"I'm only wearing five pieces of clothing," Matthew said.

"Home field advantage," Angela said. "What do I win when I win?"

I am being manipulated. "Whatever bliss you decide to have later."

Angela smiled. "Let's play."

Angela lost only two shoes and a sock and had Matthew naked and shivering in no time. Once Angela had all four of her pieces "home," she said, "Oh, I'm *so* sorry."

"I used to be good at this game," Matthew said, doing his best to keep his package warm. "What kind of bliss do you want? And, if I might add, could you decide quickly what that bliss might be? Parts of me are apt to turn blue."

Angela stood. "We have laundry to do." She went to the bedroom and came back with a pile of sheets and pillowcases.

Matthew stood, his hands folded carefully below his waist. "You find bliss in doing laundry?"

"I hope to," she said.

Angela removed her only sock, tossing it and the sheets into the washer and adding detergent. Then she removed her hat, mittens, coat, sweaters, and jeans.

"Don't stop," Matthew said.

She pulled her shirt little by little over her head and removed her bra.

"More, more!" Matthew cried.

She peeled her underwear down her legs before flipping them into the washing machine.

"Do it again!" Matthew shouted. "Encore! Encore!"

"Hush."

Angela closed the lid and set the controls. As the water began to fill the tub, she climbed up on the washing machine, dangling her legs. "I want to go for a ride while we do the wash. It should take exactly seventeen minutes to do this load. You have seventeen minutes to give me some bliss."

There's a naked woman on a washing machine, and I have seventeen minutes to turn her on.

This will not be a challenge.

He started with her toes, kissing them lightly while massaging her feet. He ran his hands up to her hips while he kissed her calves, her knees, and her thighs. He lightly touched her clitoris with the tip of his tongue before kissing her stomach and breasts, earning him a single "Oh."

Yep. That's what I was going for. I have plenty of time.

He returned to and kissed her clitoris repeatedly until Angela began to slide closer to him as she tried to wrap her legs around his head.

"Stop teasing me," she whispered.

"I have at least ten more minutes," Matthew whispered.

He held her booty in both hands and went to work, his tongue flitting while Angela panted and raked his back with her nails.

Angela only lasted another thirty seconds.

"Damn, man," she whispered. "You can even make a chore less of a chore."

He squeezed her feet. "How do your feet feel?"

"I don't feel my feet right now," she said. "But you can still massage them."

When the spin cycle stopped, Angela hopped down and put the sheets, clothes, and pillowcases into the dryer. "Your turn."

"You won, Angela," Matthew said. "I should be giving you more bliss."

"Maybe what I plan to do to you gives me bliss."

Matthew hoisted himself onto the dryer. *I won't need that heavy cookbook tonight.* "What should I set the dryer setting for?"

"Energy preferred," Angela said.

He turned the dial and started the dryer. "How long will that be?"

She moved her hands up his legs. "From the looks of *thing* there, not very long."

While Matthew massaged her shoulders, Angela used her hands, lips, and tongue to bring Matthew to the brink of ecstasy.

Then, she stopped.

She looked up. "Is *your* load almost finished?"

Matthew nodded. "Oh yeah, it's ready . . ."

Angela bit her lower lip and gave one, gentle squeeze . . .

As Matthew held Angela close to his chest later that night, he decided that he and Angela would do a *lot* of laundry in the future.

Chapter 26

Streams raced down Driggs Avenue, and customers streamed into Angela's all day on Saturday to get their coffee and sugar fix after three days of going without.

Matthew had no clients, potential or otherwise. *Couples were cooped up for nearly three days inside. You'd think I would have at least one divorce case by now.* He added nine months to the time of the blizzard. *Maternity wards are going to be full this coming Christmas.*

"I need your help," Angela mouthed around noon.

That line hasn't thinned all day, and she needs my help. I feel so privileged. I hope I don't mess things up again.

Matthew left his office booth and came around the counter.

She handed him an apron. "Put this on," she whispered.

It barely fit him, as usual.

"You pour and bag, I'll cook." She pointed at a price list taped to the counter. "Follow this."

"What if Bet shows up again?" Matthew asked.

"Charge her regular price," Angela said.

"Do I get to keep my tips?" Matthew asked.

"You don't have a tip jar yet," she said, fading quickly into the kitchen.

I need to get a tip jar. He smiled at the first customer. "How may I help you?"

"Large Jamaican blend and two apple turnovers." He handed Matthew a ten.

Matthew snatched some plastic gloves from a box under the

counter, wrapped and bagged two turnovers, and poured the man a large cup, snapping on a lid. *Let's see. Three for the coffee, a buck-fifty for each turnover.* He rang the man up and gave him four crisp ones.

The man left without tipping.

Have a nice day.

The next five customers left with coffee, pastries, turnovers, or cookies—and all their change.

How does Angela do it? That jar is usually at least half full by the end of the night.

Angela brought in another tray of pastries. "How are we doing?" she asked.

"Steady," Matthew whispered. "How do you get your tips?"

"I smile."

Oh yeah. I need to smile more.

Matthew smiled and joked with the next four customers.

The tip jar remained unfulfilled.

I must not be smiling correctly.

He checked Angela's holiday notebook. *Hmm. It's Texas Cowboy Poetry Week. That might not work in Williamsburg. Neither will saying, "Happy National Eating Disorders Awareness Week." It might make someone with a sick sense of humor laugh, but . . . Oh, here's one. I will use this.*

"Happy International Sword Swallowers Day," he said to the next customer, a man about his age wearing brown corduroys, black socks and Birkenstocks, a black leather jacket, and a pink knitted scarf.

The man did not tip him.

I guess I have to pick my spots.

He checked the next holiday and smiled at the next customer. "Happy Open That Bottle Night."

"Happy what?" the woman asked. She wore an oversized red down jacket that hung to her shins, her dark brown face round and shiny.

"Happy Open That Bottle Night," Matthew repeated.

"What's that?" she asked.

"I guess it means you open a bottle of something bubbly tonight." He smiled.

"I got four kids," the woman said, "and one of them is only six months old."

Oops. He raised his eyebrows. "Just make sure that *you* drink from the right bottle."

The woman laughed. "I'll try to remember that."

She tipped him a quarter.

So that's *how you do it. I need to rescue that quarter and display it somehow as "Matthew's First Tip."*

Angela returned to the counter an hour later, pressed a few buttons, and read from a slip spitting out of the cash register. "You had a good hour," she said. "Any tips?"

Matthew pointed at the quarter. "That quarter."

"Oh boy." She stood on tiptoes and whispered, "If you weren't so Caucasian, you would have done better. But it's a quarter more than I had this morning." She rubbed his chin. "And you need to shave."

Matthew felt his face. "It's only a little stubble."

"For later, man," she said with a smile. "Go back to your work."

"There isn't any," Matthew said. "We are empty."

She pointed toward the kitchen. "Then get to cleaning."

"It's not even one o'clock," Matthew said.

"I made a mess in there," she said. "I always make a mess when I'm in a rush."

Matthew saw flour on the prep table, the floor, and the top of the stove; some even hung in the air. *I may die of white lung.*

After a profitable day, Angela felt confident enough to take a two-block walk to the Bedford Cheese Shop, where Matthew bought a wicker basket filled with six half-pound wedges of cheese, an aged salami, a jar of MeadowCroft Farm Amaretto Apricot Peach jam, a box of crackers, and a small block of dark chocolate.

As they ate back at the apartment, Angela again trounced Matthew at Sorry!

"You stacked the deck," Matthew said.

"I don't have to," she said. "I never lose."

Matthew cut his eyes to the laundry closet.

"Not tonight," Angela said. "Why don't we go downstairs?"

Matthew looked at his naked body. "Like this?"

"We'll wear some blankets down there," Angela said. "You have to go first to get the booth ready."

Matthew wrapped himself in a blanket and ran to the booth, pulling out the table and sliding the seats together. Angela, wrapped in two blankets, followed with a single candle, setting it on the nearest table. After they snuggled a while, Angela looked over the top of the booth at the window.

Matthew joined her. "Are we people-watching?"

"I wonder if anyone can see us," she whispered.

"There's one way to find out," Matthew said. "I dare you to stick one of your sexy legs out of this booth."

Angela ducked down and wormed her foot out of the blanket, extending it gradually out of the booth.

"That's only a sexy foot," Matthew said. "Where's the rest of your leg?"

"I'm getting there." She slid farther to the left until all of her leg but her hip and booty stuck out into the candlelight. "Is anyone walking by?"

"No," Matthew said. "No one is walking. They've all stopped to stare at a living piece of sculpture."

Angela withdrew her leg. "What?"

"I'm kidding."

She lay with her head facing the window, peeking around the edge of the booth. "I don't know if I can concentrate down here."

Matthew parted her blanket and kissed her stomach, removing her underwear. "You have to concentrate?"

"Sometimes," Angela said.

Matthew removed her T-shirt and kissed lower. "Are you concentrating now?"

Angela shook her head.

"You keep watch," Matthew said, kissing her inner thighs. "And try not to fall out of the booth."

By the time she reached orgasm, Angela's entire upper body was outside the booth. "Pull me back in," she whispered, and Matthew gripped her legs, gently sliding her closer.

"You okay?" Matthew asked.

"Yes," she whispered. "Anyone walking by just now would have seen about half of me."

"And your nipples," Matthew said. "How hard were they?"

She felt up his leg. "About this hard." She shivered. "I'm going upstairs."

"With or without a blanket?" Matthew asked.

"With, of course," Angela said.

That's no fun. "I dare you to run upstairs without a blanket." He smiled.

"Are you kidding?" Angela asked.

"Okay, don't take the dare," Matthew said, gathering the blankets. "I won't think any less of you."

Angela peered around the booth. "No one will see me, will they? They'd have to be standing with their faces pressed to the window."

"So . . . go."

She took a deep breath, scooted to the edge, and took off first to the candle, blowing it out. Then she slipped around the counter and flew into the kitchen.

That is an image I will never forget. She's quite a sprinter.

Matthew wrapped himself in all three blankets and shuffled to the kitchen, where Angela stood shivering at the stairway door.

"You didn't?" she said. She tore off his blankets. "You go back out there."

Matthew shrugged and casually walked all the way to the front door and back as Angela watched. "Nothing to it," he said.

"You're crazy," Angela said.

"And cold," he whispered.

Angela smiled. "Not all of you." She moved up the stairs, dropping blankets as she went through the kitchen. She sat on the edge of the bed and reached out her hands.

Matthew bent down and kissed her.

Angela looked around him. "Stand against the window."

Matthew backed up. "There's a full moon in the window." *And it's freaking cold!*

Angela walked on her knees from the bed to the window. "Then you'll have to be quick, huh?" She put both hands on his penis, stroking gently. "The quicker you are, the warmer you'll be."

"Shh, I'm trying to concentrate," he whispered.

She squeezed gently. "You feel that?"

"Yes."

"You feel this?" she whispered.

He caressed her hair. "*Oh* yeah . . ."

As Matthew drifted off to sleep with Angela as his blanket, he swore he had a slight case of frostbite on his booty.

But it was worth it.

Chapter 27

Sunday was a repeat of Saturday, with Matthew filling in behind the counter while Angela tried to keep her display cases filled with pastries, turnovers, and cookies. Matthew had little to greet customers with since it was National Pistachio Day, For Pete's Sake Day, and Levi Strauss Day, according to Angela's holiday notebook.

If they look nutty, I'll hit 'em with the pistachios. If they look frustrated, we'll use Pete. And if they're wearing Levi's, we'll praise their choice of jeans.

Unfortunately, the mostly churchgoing crowd didn't look nutty or frustrated, and none of them wore jeans.

During his *three* hours behind the counter, Matthew received no tips.

He did, however, receive a series of phone calls that had his cell phone buzzing.

"You going to answer that?" Angela asked as she rushed a tray of cinnamon twists into the case.

"It'll go to voice mail," Matthew said.

"You can answer it." She started counting raspberry turnovers.

I prefer to give whomever it is the silent treatment. "I'm getting slammed over here," he said, smiling at a customer dressed to the nines in a black three-piece suit. *If he isn't the preacher, he should be.*

Angela touched his elbow. "It's all right. It might be a potential client." She whispered, "And if it's one of your exes, you have to let me listen to any message they leave, okay?"

Matthew nodded. "How may I help you, sir?"

"Two large house blends," he grunted.

The churchman is in a bad mood. Matthew smiled. "Coming right up."

The churchman did not tip him.

I need to get a tan.

Late that night, after giving the entire shop a thorough cleaning, Angela curled up with Matthew on the couch and listened to Matthew's voice mails.

The first, a 963 number at eight PM, was only static.

"That would probably be Jade," Matthew said.

"She's certainly persistent," Angela said. "How'd she get your cell number?"

"No idea," Matthew said.

"It's probably written on the wall of some cell at the jail," Angela said. "Which isn't that bad for a lawyer who needs clients. What did you see in her?"

"I was looking for danger that night, so I guess I saw danger," Matthew said.

"I'm pretty dangerous," Angela said.

"Yes, you are," Matthew said. "You have a hammer and a Taser. You're also quite a streaker."

"I can't believe I did that," Angela said.

"I will never forget how the candlelight hit your booty," Matthew said, "until you blew it out, that is."

"I nearly slipped and fell," Angela said. "When's Jade get out?"

"Three years," Matthew said.

Angela kissed the back of Matthew's hand. "She has missed her window of opportunity forever."

Michael's voice then crackled from the cell phone:

"I know you haven't been home because you're not calling me back. I hope you survived the storm in style, big dog. Do I know her? Hey, Victoria is burning up my ears, man. I think she not only wants to go out, she wants to hook up. Do you know how *rare* that is? She says she might actually invite you up to see the *view.* You know what that means? Wall Street was in a bull market the last time she showed anyone the *view.* You have her panting like one of her Pomeranians, man. Give me a call."

"Victoria can't seem to lower herself to call me herself," Matthew said.

"Is she really . . . gorgeous?" Angela asked.

"I'm sure she paid a great deal for her body," Matthew said. "There was something unnatural about her. I like natural."

Angela held his hands to her chest. "You better. That's all I've got."

Mary's message came next: "Matthew, it's Mary, and I can't stop thinking about you. Give me a call."

"Guess she and Pastor are off," Angela said. "You adultery wrecker, you."

I don't think she and Pastor were ever on.

Allison's bouncy voice then filled the room. "I found your cell number! Sort of. I had erased it from my cell phone and my message board, but I was still able to see part of it. I only dialed four wrong numbers before I heard your sexy voice. Guess what, Matt? It's been eight days! Can you believe it? I'm so proud of myself. I boxed up all my diaries and put them in storage. I'm just going to take life one day at a time from now on. Give me a call if you ever get bored. Bye."

"What's been eight days?" Angela asked.

"Since her last drink," Matthew said. "She's going to AA now."

"So she says," Angela said.

"She certainly sounds soberer." *Is that a word?*

"Drunks drink to *sound* sober sometimes," Angela said. "She says you have a sexy voice."

Matthew kissed her ear. "Do I?"

"Sometimes."

The last voice mail was from his father: "Matthew, it's Poppa. Hope you're all right. That was some storm! Let us know how you're doing sometime. Bye."

Matthew picked up his phone. "I better call him." He hit the number 2 on the keypad.

"You have your parents on speed dial?" Angela asked.

"It's the only one I've ever set." He turned on the phone's speaker and placed it on the coffee table.

"Hello? Is that you, Matthew?" his father asked.

"Hey, Pop," Matthew said. "How's the weather down there?"

"You know I can't complain," his father said. "Mid-sixties. How many inches did you get?"

"Officially twenty-six," Matthew said.

"Wow," his father said. "How's business?"

"Good, Pop." He smiled at Angela. "Hey, I've put you on speaker so you could talk to someone."

"Let me do the same here so I don't have to repeat everything to your mother," his father said. "Can you hear me?"

"Yes, Pop," Matthew said. "Mom, you there?"

"I'm here," his mother said. "It's so *nice* of you to *finally* call."

She's angry. I need to call her more often. "I'd like you both to meet Angela Smith. She's sitting here with me." He nodded at Angela.

"Hi, Mr. and Mrs. McConnell," Angela said.

"Hello, Angela," his father said.

"Did he say Angela?" his mother asked. "I thought her name was Joy."

"Mom, Joy left me a few weeks ago, and now I'm seeing Angela," Matthew said quickly.

"Where did Joy go?" his mother asked.

"To the Dominican Republic," Matthew said.

"Wasn't she from Honduras?" his mother asked.

"It's a long story, Mom," Matthew said. *Which she will want to hear now.*

"I *like* to hear long stories from the boy I gave birth to," his mother said. "I don't hear them that often, you know."

I really *need to call her more often.* "Joy ran off with an exchange teacher."

"They have those?" his mother asked.

"Yes, they have those, Mom," Matthew said.

"I never liked her, you know," his mother said.

"I know you didn't," Matthew said. "I've been meeting clients in Angela's coffee shop. You remember Smith's Sweet Treats and Coffee on Driggs Avenue?"

"Oh, sure," his father said. "Great coffee."

"Their apple turnovers were to die for," his mother said.

"They still are, Mom," Matthew said. "Angela runs the place by herself now."

"That's not quite true," Angela said. "Matthew helps me run the register when I'm really busy, and he helps me clean up, too."

"You have him cleaning up?" his father asked.

"Yes sir," Angela said.

"That's one thing I could never get him to do around our store," his father said. "Did he tell you about our store?"

"I went there a few times when I was little," Angela said. "Your prices were always fair."

"Thank you, Angela," his father said. "That's nice to hear."

"So," his mother said loudly, "are you two an item?"

Here it comes. "Yes, Mom. We are in a committed, monogamous relationship."

Angela stared at Matthew.

"Just listen," he mouthed.

"But you only just met each other, right?" his mother asked.

"Yes, Mom."

"How committed could you two be in such a short time?" his mother asked.

"We're very committed, Mom," Matthew said.

"Are you living together?" his mother asked.

Matthew shrugged. "I'm spending more time at her apartment than mine, but I haven't moved in with her nor she with me."

"Oh?" his mother said.

I hate when she does this. "That's where I am now."

"Oh?" his mother said.

I will not go for three oh's in a row. "I'd like to come visit you two this summer." He looked at Angela. "And I'd like to bring Angela with me."

Angela shook her head. "I have a store to run," she whispered.

And a life to run away from.

"We'd love to have you, Angela," his father said. "You know the guest room is always ready for you, Matthew."

"Thanks, Pop," Matthew said. "How's your hip, Mom?"

"She's gone to the kitchen, Matthew," his father whispered. "I'm taking you off speaker."

Matthew heard a *click.*

"She's not doing any worse," his father said. "We're both slowing down."

"You're both taking all your medications, though, right?" Matthew asked.

"Like clockwork." His father sighed. "She's calling me for something. I have to go. Angela?"

"Yes, Mr. McConnell?" Angela asked.

"Take care of our boy, okay?" his father asked.

"I'll try," Angela said.

"Thanks for calling, Matthew," his father said. "I hope to see you both this summer. Good-bye."

Matthew closed his phone. "What do you think of my mother?"

"You take after your daddy for the most part," Angela said. "But why did you include me in your visit? You know I can't leave the store."

"Even for a few days?" Matthew asked.

"No."

Matthew nibbled at her neck. "Not even for one day?"

"Stop." She leaned away from his lips. "Maybe one day." She rubbed her neck. "Don't take this the wrong way, but how mean is your mother?"

"She's not mean," Matthew said. "At least I don't think she means to be mean. She has never approved of unmarried people living together. It's the main reason she hated Joy."

"Ah," Angela said. "So it wasn't because Joy had the brains of a pigeon?"

"I'm sure that played a part," Matthew said.

"So it's best we don't live together, for her sake." She wrinkled up her lips.

What about my sake? Or Angela's sake? "When my lease is up at the end of March, I was hoping I could move in here with you."

Angela blinked. "You were?"

"I am."

"Really?"

"Really. It will help us both financially, right?"

"Right." Angela stretched her arms over her head and ran her fingers through his hair. "But I want your mother to like me. If you move in . . ."

"She'll like you," Matthew said. "And if we talk marriage and children, she'll love you."

Angela smiled. "Marriage and children."

"Joy avoided that subject at all costs," Matthew said. "She once told me she was allergic to marriage." *She also told me she was allergic to babies. Who could be allergic to a baby?* "What do you say to marriage?"

"With whom?" Angela asked, her eyes wide.

"With me," Matthew said.

"Well, I *guess* I like the idea," Angela said.

"You don't sound too enthusiastic, Miss Smith."

Angela pulled his face to hers and kissed him firmly. "Okay, I *love* the idea, Matthew." Her eyes drifted toward the bedroom.

Matthew didn't notice.

"Hey, man, I'm making some bedroom eyes over here," she said.

"Oh." Matthew slid from behind her and stood. "And I will carry you and your bedroom eyes to the bedroom."

Angela stood on the couch with her arms around his neck. "Don't drop me."

"I won't."

He scooped her up and walked deliberately though the kitchen and into the bedroom. He set her on the bed, where she stood bouncing, her hands on the ceiling.

"I want to try something different tonight," she said.

Matthew stripped down to his boxers. "I'm all for something different."

She stripped down to her underwear, pulled back the covers, and lay on her side. "I want you to sleep behind me."

"You sure?" Matthew asked.

"No," she said in a small voice.

Matthew slid in behind her, careful not to put any pressure on her booty.

Angela pulled his left arm over her. "Just like this, okay? I need to get used to the idea slowly."

"So do I," Matthew whispered. "You feel extremely soft, firm, and round."

"*You* don't," Angela said. "You feel extremely hard."

"It's because *you* feel extremely soft, firm, and round."

She sighed and held his arm tightly. "Did you really mean what you said about marriage?"

"Yes."

She wiggled her booty against him. "I am going to have great dreams tonight."

Angela slept through the night without a single nightmare.

But in the morning, she became Matthew's blanket again.

It's a start.

I do believe she's getting better.

Chapter 28

Matthew spent Monday morning wondering how he could help Timothy—and, by extension, Angela.

How can I prove Timothy has flashbacks and nightmares? They have tests to determine when someone is dreaming, but those tests can't testify to the quality *of the dream.*

He had walked up and down Driggs with his laptop until he found animalcrack69, checked his e-mail, and downloaded Dr. Penn's assessment. As he read the assessment in his office booth, however, he couldn't come up with any solutions.

"Happy Polar Bear Day," Angela said, pouring him his first cup of coffee.

"Fitting," Matthew said. "That pile of snow out there seems to be getting larger, not smaller, and until we get Wi-Fi, I'm going to be a polar bear."

She slid in next to him. "We'll get it one day, okay? But just for us."

"Okay."

"It's also No Brainer Day," she said.

"So I should be doing only simple tasks today," Matthew said.

"What's wrong?" Angela asked.

"I'm having lawyer's block," Matthew said.

She pointed at the screen. "Is that Dr. Penn's report?"

"Yes, and it's very thorough," Matthew said. "It should be enough to change anyone's mind, but I need something more."

"Hey, I have an idea," Angela said. "It's a real no-brainer. Call

Dr. Penn, Mr. Polar Bear." She stood and greeted a few seated customers.

Call the doctor. Duh. He dialed the number.

"Hello?"

"Dr. Penn, it's Matthew McConnell. Your assessment is fantastic, but I'm worried about one thing. How can I *prove* that Timothy has flashbacks and nightmares?"

"Put him in a similar situation," Dr. Penn said.

That doesn't seem possible. "Literally?"

"If you can," Dr. Penn said.

"So I should take him to an operating room," Matthew said.

"Or a reasonable facsimile," Dr. Penn said. "Take him as best you can to the place of his original trauma. I've taken a few patients to the Towers site. The Towers may be gone, but they're still there in the minds of many people."

"That must be a rough trip," Matthew said.

"It was, is, and will probably be for many years to come," Dr. Penn said, "but it's worth it for many people."

Hmm. That sounds logical. "Does it work?"

"For some, it worked very well," Dr. Penn said. "They relived that horrifying day at the very spot it happened and got past that day. Oh, not without weeping and a great deal of cursing."

"You said 'for some,' " Matthew said. "So others don't respond."

"Some don't," Dr. Penn said, "and they may never respond."

"How dangerous is recreating the original trauma?" Matthew asked. "That's what we're doing, isn't it?"

"Yes," Dr. Penn said. "Under the right conditions, and with the right questions, it's fairly safe."

I don't know about that. "Could it be done, say, in a doctor's office?"

"It could be done anywhere," Dr. Penn said.

"Well, I can't very well fly Timothy back to Landstuhl." *As if the army would let me do that.* "So I simply present the original trauma as best as I can and watch him fight his way out of it."

"Something like that," Dr. Penn said. "And it *will* be a fight."

"Do I really want to put him through it?" Matthew asked.

"He's tougher than he looks," Dr. Penn said.

"But we don't want him to be tough," Matthew said. "We want him to fall apart, don't we?"

"No," Dr. Penn said. "We want him to get better. It's possible that reliving what happened will help him to live again. The use of virtual reality simulations, though they are early in their development, have helped people get to and get *through* their memories. There's an old school of thought that says the best way *out* is always *through*, the idea that confronting is much better than avoiding. I've read about soldiers returning from Iraq and playing video games like Call of Duty to help them cope with what's holding them back."

"They don't have a simulation for what happened to Angela, do they?" Matthew asked.

Dr. Penn didn't respond immediately. "I think so. I remember reading about one a few months ago."

"That's creepy." Matthew shuddered.

"To you and me, it's absolutely abhorrent," Dr. Penn said. "But you and I did not go through an attack of this magnitude. To people who have survived attacks and cannot lead a normal life and face reality because of them, a trip into *virtual* reality might be exactly what they need."

Matthew sighed. "I wish there were some guarantees."

"The only guarantee I can give you is that Timothy will not get better if nothing is done," Dr. Penn said.

I have to ask this. "Is it the same with Angela?"

"Everyone is different because everyone is wired differently," Dr. Penn said. "Angela has learned to cope in her own way. She has rewired the way her brain processes the world. To you and me, the way she's coping might seem a little crazy. To her psyche, it makes perfect sense. She has put up a great deal of armor to protect herself, and it will take time for her to remove that armor so she can be her old self again."

"I don't know if I want to remove any of her armor, Doc," Matthew said. "It seems to be part of her personality, and I love her personality. She's tough, kind, sweet, sarcastic, organized, suddenly passionate, and frequently shy."

Dr. Penn laughed. "You like the challenges she presents to you."

"Yes." *But every day shouldn't have to be a challenge.*

"Angela has many layers," Dr. Penn said. "Many, many layers."

"I think I find new ones every day," Matthew said. "But I can't begin to fathom Angela reliving her attack or facing her attacker."

"Matthew, Angela has to go through to get out," Dr. Penn said. "She may have to relive her attack *and* face her attacker in order to achieve a greater measure of peace and happiness in her life."

"I like to think I'm providing her a measure of both," Matthew said.

"Oh, you most certainly are," Dr. Penn said. "And if she gets the opportunity to either relive her attack or confront her attacker, it will not be easy, and it may actually be more painful than the original attack. Her mind has used the last four years to build up that one awful moment to the nth degree, to a severity that may be a hundred times worse than the original moment."

I've already seen this in action. "So what do I do?"

"Be patient with her," Dr. Penn said. "Remember that *she* has to break through. It's not up to you to break through her defenses."

"I feel so helpless sometimes." *Like now.*

"Simply love her, Matthew," Dr. Penn said.

"Love is the best therapy, right?" Matthew asked.

"You're learning," Dr. Penn said. "If you need anything else, don't hesitate to call."

"I won't." Matthew closed his phone.

First things first. I need to speak to Dr. Wick. His defenses are pretty stout. I can't call his secretary anymore. She'd never put me through.

I have to be sneaky again. He smiled. *Dr. Wick is about to have a virtual fender bender.*

Matthew called Paul Kiser, an old friend from his high school days at Most Holy Trinity. Paul worked at the DMV over on Atlantic Avenue.

"Haven't heard from you in years, Matt," Paul said. "Do you need to have another accident?"

He still remembers the scam. "Yes. I need to have a minor fender bender this time. I need to hit someone named Dr. William Wick. He might be listed as Major William Wick."

"Hold on a sec," Paul said. "Got any cross references?"

"He works at the VA," Matthew said, "and he may have a Manhattan address."

Paul hummed under his breath. "Computer's slow. Monday, you know. Uh . . . black oh-nine Chrysler Three Hundred, physician's plates. Here's the number."

Matthew wrote it down. "Thanks, Paul."

"You know where to send the tickets," Paul said. "I'll need two."

"Which game?" Matthew asked.

"The next time the Miami Heat are in town, man," Paul said. "Who else?"

This is going to be an expensive favor to pay for. "I'll try. That's a tough ticket, Paulie. What if I can't find any?"

"The Wizards, then," Paul said. "At least I might see the Knicks win that one."

"Gotcha."

"Good luck," Paul said.

Matthew called the VA hospital switchboard.

"How may I direct your call?" the operator asked.

"Hi, I'm trying to locate the owner of a black oh-nine Chrysler Three Hundred," Matthew said. "I had a fender bender this morning in your parking lot, and I was in a hurry so I didn't leave a note. I feel *real* bad about it. It was a really nice car. It might have been a doctor's car." *Lure her in . . .*

"What makes you think that vehicle is still here, sir?" the operator asked. "It may have been a patient's car."

"Oh, I'm sure it was a doctor's car," Matthew said. "It was parked where all the doctors park. It had a VA sticker on it and a physician's license plate. Is there any way you could check who the owner is? I only need a name. Maybe security can give me a name. I can use the phone book to find more information once I have a name." *Call security, please.*

"One moment."

Matthew sipped some coffee.

"Sir?" the operator said.

"Yes?" *It's nice to be called "sir."*

"I've explained the situation to security," she said. "I'm transferring you now."

Time to act scared. "Security? I'm not in any trouble, am I?"

"I don't know, sir," the operator said. "They handle this sort of thing all the time. Hold for security."

Matthew took another sip. *So far, so good.*

"Security Officer Wright."

Gruff male voice. Good. I need a no-nonsense kind of guy who feels the need to boss me around. "Did the operator explain my predicament? I feel *so* bad. I know I should have stopped."

"Yes, you should have," Officer Wright said. "From the description you gave us, you roughed up a doctor's car, mister. A retired major doctor's car."

A retired major doctor's car? Is there such a thing as a major doctor? "Oh no. I do hope you have his name for me. I feel terrible."

"His name is Dr. William Wick," Officer Wright said.

"Let me write that down." Matthew counted to three. "Is he still there by chance? I don't live far from the hospital and can meet him at his car."

"Let me check," Officer Wright said.

While he waited, Matthew marveled at the ease at which he had been able to get information over the years. *People will believe anything, especially if a minor disaster is involved.*

"Yeah, he's still here," Officer Wright said. "Let me transfer you to his office."

No! "Could you transfer me directly to his phone? I assume he has a secretary, and I don't want to get the runaround from his secretary and have to leave a message with her. I want to explain everything directly to Dr. Wick so there's no misunderstanding about how stupid I've been."

"I can try," Officer Wright said.

"Oh, please do," Matthew said. "You've been so helpful, Officer Wright."

"Drive more carefully from now on, okay?" Officer Wright said.

"Oh, I will." *If I had a car, I would.*

"Transferring your call," Officer Wright said.

And now I must talk extremely fast.

"This is Dr. Wick."

Bingo. "Did you read Dr. Penn's findings on Timothy Simmons?" Matthew asked.

"Who is this?" Dr. Wick asked.

"Matthew McConnell. Dr. Penn should have sent them to you in an e-mail a few days ago. Did you read it?"

"How did you get through to my private line?" Dr. Wick asked.

I dented your fender. "Did you read Dr. Penn's assessment?"

"I did," Dr. Wick said.

"And what is your assessment of his assessment?" *That was redundant.*

"It's interesting reading," Dr. Wick said, "and I almost dismissed it until I read the last paragraph."

What was in the last paragraph? Matthew scrolled down the document on his laptop. *Ah. Dr. Penn's bio and service record.* "Did you know Dr. Penn?"

"When we were both in Vietnam, yes," Dr. Wick said.

"So do you think Dr. Penn's findings have merit?" Matthew asked. *This is the moment.*

"They do," Dr. Wick said.

Yes! "Will you reexamine Timothy?"

Dr. Wick sighed. "I am *very* busy."

"Too busy for fifteen minutes?" *Come on, come on . . .*

"Mr. McConnell," Dr. Wick said, "I am so busy I have to come in on weekends to catch up with my work."

Because so many soldiers have come home from overseas recently and need help. "One more assessment, that's all I'm asking, and then I'll leave you alone."

"I doubt that," Dr. Wick said.

He got me. "You're right, Dr. Wick. I won't leave you alone. I believe in this, and I'm not doing this for the money."

"I doubt that, too." Dr. Wick sighed again. "Let me check my schedule."

Yes!

"I can squeeze Mr. Simmons in . . . tomorrow at seven-thirty AM," Dr. Wick said. "After that, I don't have an open date for two months. *Don't* be late."

Yes! "We'll be there. Thank you, Dr. Wick."

"Good-bye, Mr. McConnell."

Matthew turned off his phone. *Yes!*

Angela drifted over from the counter. "I only caught bits and pieces, something about hitting a doctor's car?"

"I used a fender bender scam to get past his secretary." He smiled. "Old habits die hard."

Angela nodded. "I guess."

"But we did it. Timothy has an appointment tomorrow morning with Dr. Wick. Isn't that great?"

"Yeah," Angela said. "But don't you think you should run that by Mr. and Mrs. Simmons first?"

"Oh yeah." Matthew dialed the Simmons. "Gloria, Matthew McConnell. I've got some *outstanding* good news . . ."

Getting Timothy out of the apartment on Monday morning wasn't as difficult as Matthew thought it would be. Timothy marched straight from the apartment into a taxi.

"We've been going on short walks," Gloria told him as taxi moved off.

"And my legs are killing me," Timothy said, taking his wife's hand. "I get winded so easily. I am so out of shape."

"You do all right," Gloria said. "We shouldn't be in a rush at our age anyway."

The taxi crossed the Williamsburg Bridge and headed into Manhattan and up First Avenue, retracing Matthew's walk from Victoria's apartment only three weeks before.

I had the wrong woman—check that. I had the wrong women *on my mind then. I have the right woman on my mind and in my heart now. I wish Angela could have come with us today. She is such an important part of all this, but I couldn't convince her to close her shop even for a few hours. I don't blame her. That blizzard seriously dented her receipts. And mine, sort of. A pair of Knicks-Heat tickets for Paul set me back more than five hundred bucks, and the seats were behind the basket and five rows up. It was worth it, though, because here we are.*

The taxi pulled into the VA hospital parking lot on East 23rd Street a few blocks from Bellevue, the legendary public hospital known for its psychiatric services. Matthew didn't want Timothy to end up at Bellevue if this meeting didn't go well.

They took an elevator to the tenth floor and sat in Dr. Wick's waiting room, where his secretary gave Matthew evil looks.

Matthew smiled at her. *I'm here. We're here. Whatchagonnadoaboutit now?*

"The doctor will see you now," she said precisely at 7:30.

"Have a nice day," Matthew said to her as he walked past her desk.

I couldn't resist. I wish I had a smiley face sticker to give her.

Dr. Wick's office was an anally organized industrial white and gray, with a utilitarian desk, two chairs, and wide gray filing cabinets. Dr. Wick did not rise from his desk but just sat there, shining his glasses on his sleeve, his thick gray hair as unmoving as his lined face. He reminded Matthew of Dale Dye, an actor who plays army generals, captains, and colonels in the movies.

Timothy and Gloria sat in the chairs in front of Dr. Wick's desk. Matthew stood at the window looking out at the East River.

"Well?" Dr. Wick said.

Matthew turned. "Well, what?"

"You're on the clock, McConnell," Dr. Wick said.

Excuse me? Matthew narrowed his eyes. "I thought that you were going to examine Timothy today, Dr. Wick." *Isn't this your office? Isn't that your job? Aren't you supposed to be in charge?*

"Fifteen minutes isn't long enough for *any* psychiatrist to do a thorough examination of *any* patient," Dr. Wick said. "Dr. Penn should have told you that. You wanted this meeting, so it's your show. Get on with it."

If I had thought to bring the tape of our initial meeting, I'd play it now. "You don't want to speak to him?"

Dr. Wick stared at Timothy. "I want to see what you have prepared."

I have nothing prepared.

I sucker-punched the guy into taking this meeting, and he just counterpunched me. I may as well come out swinging.

Matthew left the window and stood in front of Timothy. *Sorry, man. I have to put you back in an operating room somehow.* "Timothy, describe what you witnessed in the OR at Woodhull Medical the day you had your meltdown."

"It was a motorcycle accident," Timothy said. "A man's leg was in shreds."

"What did this incident remind you of?" Matthew asked.

"A soldier with peach fuzz on his chin who didn't have much left of his legs," Timothy said.

"And where and when did you originally see this soldier?" Matthew asked.

"At Landstuhl two years before," Timothy said softly.

"Do you remember the soldier's name, Timothy?" Matthew asked.

Timothy's eyes glazed over.

"What was the soldier's name, Timothy?" Matthew asked.

Timothy looked down.

I'm losing him. Forgive me, Timothy. This is for you own good. "Knock his ass out, Simmons, that's an order!"

Timothy sat bolt upright.

Gloria flinched.

Matthew got in Timothy's face. "Soldier, did you *hear* me? I *told* you to knock his ass out! *That's an order!*"

Timothy looked up at Matthew. "Yes sir. We need to restrain him better, sir. He keeps getting his arms free. He's strong as a horse, sir."

"Restrain his ass now, soldier!" Matthew shouted.

"Yes sir, right away, sir," Timothy said.

Matthew noticed Dr. Wick shift in his seat. *We have his attention, and I intend to keep it.* "Don't let them take my legs!" Matthew shouted in Timothy's ear.

Timothy didn't turn. "They're gonna help you, man. Rest easy."

"Don't let them take my legs!" Matthew shouted again.

"They're gonna try to save them, kid," Timothy said, his voice shaking. "They're doing the best they can."

"Don't let them take my legs!" Matthew shouted again.

"Rest easy, kid. Rest easy, Homer . . ." Timothy blinked his eyes rapidly and looked at Gloria. "I remember his name. Gloria, I remembered. His name was Homer Kuhn. He was a Marine Corps corporal from Ohio, from North Star, Ohio, the smallest town in Ohio. He was the only survivor when his Sea Stallion went down on a humanitarian mission to drop supplies in Afghanistan." He looked up at Matthew. "They had to take both of his legs. I stayed with Homer in post-op. When he woke up . . ." He looked at Dr. Wick. "When he woke up he screamed and had to be sedated. And then he said, 'You let them take my legs. Why did you let them take my legs? I told you not to let them take my legs.' "

"Did the patient at Woodhull Medical lose his legs?" Matthew asked.

"I don't know," Timothy said. "They took me out of the OR before they even started the operation."

I needed to establish that the mere sight of anyone's damaged legs started Timothy's meltdown and that he didn't have to see a missing limb to lose his mind. "Timothy, describe your dream."

Timothy's eyes glazed over again. "I'm in a field filled with bloody arms and legs and there's a boy with peach fuzz on his chin screaming at me to find his legs." He looked at Gloria. "I see Homer Kuhn in my dream plain as day, Gloria."

"We'll write to him," Gloria said, wiping at tears. "Maybe we'll go visit him, too."

"I'd like that." Timothy focused on his hands. "So I'm trying to find Homer's legs in my dream, but I can't find any that match. Homer was about six-five, and none of the legs were long enough. 'Rest easy, rest easy,' I keep saying, but Homer keeps screaming, 'Find me a new set of legs, Lieutenant! Find me a new set of legs!' "

Matthew saw Dr. Wick write something down. *That's a good sign.*

"Thank you, Timothy." *Rest easy, man.* Matthew turned to Gloria. "Gloria, you've known Timothy longer than anyone else in this room. How has he changed since his return from Landstuhl?"

"He's not the same man I danced with at our senior prom, that's for sure," Gloria said. "That man was young and unafraid of anything. He's not the same man I married. That man spent his life outside with his children. I could never get them to come inside when I called the first time. 'Just a little longer,' he'd tell me. 'They're kids. They need to play.' " She looked down. "And he's not the same man I've shared a bed with for thirty years either."

Timothy's eyes filled with tears.

"But he's my man." Gloria stared through teary eyes at Dr. Wick. "And I want him *back,* and *you're* going to give him back to me."

Matthew fought at the lump growing in his throat. "Thank you, Gloria." He inhaled and exhaled several times. "Dr. Wick?"

Dr. Wick pushed back his chair and stood. "Soldier."

Timothy's eyes snapped up. "Yes sir?"

"How often do you have this dream?" Dr. Wick asked.

"Every time I close my eyes, sir," Timothy said. "I don't sleep much, sir."

Dr. Wick sighed and nodded. "You deserve some sleep, soldier. You deserve some rest."

Timothy sat up straighter. "Yes sir. Thank you, sir."

This is the moment. This is the overwhelming silence before the jury's verdict.

"We're going to help you, Lieutenant," Dr. Wick said.

Timothy stood. "Sir, yes sir. Thank you, sir." He held his hands out to Gloria. "I'm going to be your man again."

Gloria stood and hugged him. "You've always been my man."

Dr. Wick came around his desk. "Mrs. Simmons, please tell my secretary to put Timothy on my schedule by the end of this week, and if she gives you any grief, you come right back in here and tell me, and I'll straighten her out."

After Timothy and Gloria left the office, Matthew looked Dr. Wick in the eye. "Thank you, Major."

"I'm only a doctor now," Dr. Wick said.

"You'll always be a soldier, sir," Matthew said.

Dr. Wick nodded. "And that's what you want me to remember from now on, isn't it?"

Matthew nodded. "Yes sir."

"I'll never forget being a soldier." Dr. Wick took off his glasses and rubbed his eyes. "That was quite a performance."

"It wasn't a performance," Matthew said.

"I know it wasn't, Mr. McConnell, and I know you didn't prep him at all," Dr. Wick said. "The look of shock and recognition on Timothy's face was genuine. I've seen it before. On my own face. But that's not what really convinced me. It was his wife. I know someone just like her who stood by her man after he came back badly shaken from Vietnam." He turned a picture on his desk toward Matthew. "They don't make women like her anymore."

Yes, they do, and Angela is one of them.

Dr. Wick extended his hand, and Matthew shook it. "Give my regards to Hospital Corpsman First Class Kenneth Penn. Tell him we have some catching up to do."

"I will." Matthew turned to leave.

"Tell me something, McConnell," Dr. Wick said. "Are you really doing this for free?"

"Yes sir." *For the land of the free, and the home of brave men like Timothy.*

"If you ever need any counseling for that," Dr. Wick said, "you give me a call."

Matthew paused at the door. "No offense, Dr. Wick, but I hope I never have to see you again."

Dr. Wick nodded. "Don't forget to have 'Kenny Penny' give me a call. That was the nickname we gave him in 'Nam because he was always showing up when things were very bad."

A good penny turns up when things are bad.

"Good thing he did back then," Dr. Wick said.

"*And* now," Matthew said. "Thanks again."

While they waited for a taxi, Matthew called Angela with the news. "We did it!"

"Fantastic," Angela said. "But I didn't do anything."

"Sure you did," Matthew said. "You went with me to visit Timothy, and you made sure I stayed in touch with Dr. Penn. I couldn't have done any of this without you."

"I'm glad Timothy's getting help," Angela said.

I hear what she's not *saying: "I wish I were getting help, too."*

"Have you let Dr. Penn know?" Angela asked.

"I had to tell you first, didn't I?" Matthew said. "I'm going to call him to meet us at the shop so we can all celebrate. Could you whip up some fresh apple turnovers?"

"I don't *whip* up anything, Matthew," Angela said.

"Could you *create* some then?" Matthew asked.

"Yes, Matthew," Angela said.

"See you in a few minutes."

Matthew called Dr. Penn and told him the news.

"He told you my old nickname," Dr. Penn said. "I didn't know if he'd remember me. I was only a corpsman."

"Did Wick have a nickname?" Matthew asked.

"Oh, we called him 'Tricky Wicky,' " Dr. Penn said. "That man got us out of so many scrapes. He knew all the tricks."

"Can you celebrate with us at Angela's shop in the next hour or so?" Matthew asked.

"I wouldn't miss it," Dr. Penn said. "Does she still bake those chocolate chip toffee cookies?"

I haven't seen them in the case. "I'll have her make you a fresh batch."

"Wonderful," Dr. Penn said. "See you there."

He called Angela.

"They're in the oven," Angela said before Matthew could speak.

"The turnovers, right?" Matthew asked.

"No, the chocolate chip toffee cookies Dr. Penn likes," Angela said.

I shouldn't ask this, but . . . "How did you know?"

"I know all of my customers, Matthew," Angela said.

I knew that. "Are you busy?"

"Steady."

"Will you be able to join us?" Matthew asked.

"I'll try."

In the old days, Matthew would celebrate a multimillion-dollar judgment in the upstairs party room at Peter Luger's, located on the south side of the Williamsburg Bridge. He'd have several bottles of Krug Grande Cuvee, a porterhouse steak, and warm apple strudel drowned in homemade whipped cream.

Today Angela's coffee and some fresh, hot apple turnovers will taste infinitely better.

Chapter 29

The celebration, though low-key and contained mainly in Matthew's booth, was full of smiles and laughter.

Timothy and Gloria sat on one side holding hands and eating apple turnovers, while Angela refilled cups and covered the table with plates of pastries, turnovers, and cookies. Timothy quietly followed the conversations with wide eyes. Dr. Penn, who sat beside Matthew, ate half a dozen chocolate chip toffee cookies as he regaled the table with the life of a hospital corpsman in Vietnam.

"Believe it or not," Dr. Penn said, "a Bengal tiger once crossed our path while we were on patrol near Khe Sanh. It was a magnificent animal nearly ten feet long. We stared at it, it stared at us, and it slinked off into the jungle. Tricky Wicky turned to me and said, 'That tiger is a long way from Detroit!' And you know what? It was 1968. The Detroit Tigers won the World Series that year. I'll never forget it."

"Matthew," Gloria said during a lull, "we need to discuss payment."

"Buy me breakfast sometime," Matthew said. "That will square us." He held out his cup to Angela, and she filled it to the top. *We may have a long night ahead of us. That's my third cup in the last hour.*

"Oh no," Gloria said. "We have to do more than that."

Matthew looked at Timothy. "Just get better, okay? That will be my payment. A full recovery will be payment in full. You'll have to come here often, okay?"

"I'll try," Timothy said. "Thank you, Mr. McConnell."

Matthew followed Angela to the counter to help carry the next round of sweets.

"What would you have normally charged them?" Angela asked.

"It's not important," Matthew said.

"How much?" Angela whispered.

"I spent maybe ten hours on the case, at four hundred an hour, about four grand," Matthew said.

Angela shook her head slightly. "They have to buy you breakfast for the next three years."

"I feel good about this, Angela." He rubbed her shoulders. "I actually feel great about this."

"I know you do," Angela said. "But couldn't you use that money?"

"They're barely making it on her salary," Matthew whispered. "All that money I made before only meant I made money. Today I made a difference." He looked behind him. "What a nice coincidence. Ace reporter Felisa Vecchi is here."

Felisa walked up to the counter. "Hello."

"Hi," Matthew said.

Felisa looked around the shop. "Business looks good."

"It is," Angela said. "How may I help you?"

Was that an icy edge to Angela's voice? I think it was. I think I shall fade back to my celebration. "Good to see you again," he said to Felisa, and he returned to the booth with a plate of cookies.

Felisa soon glided over to the booth with her coffee. "If I didn't know better, I'd say this was a celebration of some kind."

"Oh, it is," Gloria said. "Mr. McConnell won a case for us today."

"I didn't win a case," Matthew said. "All of us got some justice for Timothy today."

"Oh?" Felisa said. "May I join you?"

It's getting a little crowded in my office. "Sure," Matthew said, and he and Dr. Penn slid over a few inches.

Felisa sat mere millimeters from Matthew. "What was the case?" she asked.

"It wasn't a court case," Matthew said.

Felisa took out her notepad. "What was it then?"

Matthew looked at Timothy. "I'll let Timothy tell it."

Timothy, though hesitant and halting at first, eventually told his tale, Felisa taking copious notes and seldom interrupting.

The man can really talk, Matthew thought. *He's been dying to tell his story for so long, and now all of Brooklyn will read about it.*

As Gloria described their marriage, Matthew excused himself to use the bathroom. On the way back to the booth, he stopped at the counter.

"What is *she* doing here?" Angela whispered.

Brr. Her words are hypothermic. "I think Felisa came in for some great coffee, and she will leave us with a great story. More free advertising for us."

"And you didn't call her," Angela said.

"No," Matthew said. "I don't even have her number."

"Uh huh."

He leaned across the counter and kissed her cheek. "Really, Angela. This is a happy coincidence."

Felisa stood, stretched, and came to the counter with her notepad. "You're getting a fantastic reputation, Mr. McConnell. You're the coffeehouse lawyer who gives hope to the hopeless. Was your fee really the cost of breakfast?"

"Felisa, if you print that," Matthew said, "I will never be able to pay my bills."

"It *was,*" Felisa said, writing it down.

"Please don't put that in the paper," Matthew said.

"It's too good *not* to," Felisa said. "A winning lawyer who isn't after the money."

Oh boy. I'm going to gain so much weight. Bran muffins for me from now on.

Felisa tapped her pen on the counter. "First XS and now Timothy."

Should I mention Jade? No. I feel Angela's icy eyes on me.

"What miracle will you perform next?" Felisa asked.

"It wasn't a miracle," Matthew said. "Timothy had a strong case without me. Dr. Penn's assessment was key. I just pushed the right buttons on a telephone to get everybody together."

"You made it happen, Matthew," Felisa said.

"No, I didn't," Matthew said. "I really didn't. Angela deserves a lot of the credit, too. She pushed me in all the right directions."

Felisa smiled at Angela. "He's so humble. Is it true you two are dating?"

"Yes," Angela said, glaring at Matthew.

Felisa sighed. "I'm always too late. If he weren't taken . . ." She winked at Matthew. "Great coffee as usual, Angela." She pulled out her cell phone. "Do you mind if I take a picture?"

Matthew nodded at the booth. "There's your picture."

"No, no," Felisa said. "I want you in the picture, too."

"Not me," Matthew said. "Timothy and Gloria are the story, not me."

Felisa took several pictures of Gloria and Timothy holding hands in the booth. As Felisa turned, she took a picture of Matthew. "You could have smiled," she said.

"You could have warned me," Matthew said.

"Why don't you want your picture in the paper?" Felisa asked. "Most lawyers would kill for this kind of publicity."

"I'm not that kind of lawyer anymore," Matthew said. "Please don't use it for the story."

Felisa smiled. "I won't use it for the story, I promise."

"When will the story run?" Matthew asked.

"As soon as I can write it," Felisa said. "Gloria, I have your number. I may be calling for more information if they let me expand on this."

"That's wonderful," Gloria said.

Felisa raised her bushy eyebrows. "I may have to hang out here more often. There are so many interesting stories waiting to be told here. Bye."

Dr. Penn slid out of the booth, shaking Timothy's hand. "I should be going. If there's anything you ever need, give me a call."

"I will," Timothy said.

"I have your number, Dr. Penn," Gloria said. "Thank you so much for all you've done."

Matthew walked Dr. Penn to the door. "I have a feeling you have replaced me," Dr. Penn said, looking back at Angela.

"She'll still need you," Matthew said. "*I'll* still need you."

"Don't hesitate to call." He smiled. "Is it love now?"

Is it? "I think so."

"Good," Dr. Penn said. "Good."

Angela was unusually quiet for the rest of the day, and after they cleaned up, she headed quickly to the kitchen.

"Want to go for a walk?" Matthew asked.

"Not tonight." She opened the stairway door.

Matthew followed her up the stairs. "Want to beat me at Sorry! again?"

She opened the apartment door. "No."

He entered the apartment. "Do we have any laundry to do?"

"No."

"Anything on TV?" Matthew asked.

Angela sighed. "It's Tuesday night." She went through the kitchen into the bedroom.

Matthew stood in the bedroom doorway. "Is everything okay?"

She turned and half smiled. "Yes. I'm going to turn in early tonight. I'm really tired." She pulled back the covers and took off her shoes, socks, and pants. "Good night." She slipped under the covers and pulled the comforter to her shoulders.

Matthew sat on the edge of the bed. "Is there something wrong?"

"Nothing's wrong," Angela said. "I'm tired. It's been a long day. Good night."

Something is definitely wrong. He rubbed her back. "Angela."

She turned sharply and said, "What?"

Something tells me I should leave her alone, but I can't. "What's wrong?"

"You really want to know?" she asked.

It's going to be bad, and from the look in her eyes, it's going to be very bad. I'm not so sure I want to know now. "Yes."

She sat up against the headboard and crossed her arms deliberately. "It goes something like this. He's *so* humble. I'm *always* too late. If *he* weren't taken. I may have to hang out here *more* often. There are *so* many interesting stories here."

Angela has a very good memory. "I don't understand."

"She was flirting her ass off," Angela said, her eyes turning into dark brown dots. "Right in front of me."

"She knows we're a couple," Matthew said. "You told her we were."

"She took your picture for no good reason," Angela said.

I'm sure Felisa had a reason. Whether it was good or not, I'll never know. "But without my permission."

"And she practically sat in your lap," Angela said.

There's some truth there. "The booth was crowded. I may need to expand my office."

"I saw how you were looking at her," Angela said.

"How could I not look at her?" Matthew said. "Felisa sat *next* to me. I was looking across the table at Timothy and Gloria."

"I saw you," Angela said. "Whenever you drank your coffee, you sneaked looks at her. You had your eyes all over her."

"I didn't," Matthew said. "I had my eyes on your cookies."

"You drank *three* cups of coffee, Matthew," Angela said. "You kept drinking your coffee so you could look at her."

What does that have to do with anything? "You kept refilling my cup."

"I saw you looking at her tits and her ass," Angela said. "You want her, don't you?"

Wow. Who is this person in this bed with me? "Angela, no, of course not. She's not my type at all. You are."

Angela's right arm shot out, and she pointed at him. "You're lying. You like perky and mixed and light-skinned and tall and thin and green-eyed and obviously open for business."

"No, I—"

"You would have let her *do* you right there in that booth if you could have," Angela interrupted.

"Angela, there is no way—"

"I saw her perky tits hanging out," Angela interrupted, "so I know you saw them, too. I saw her shaking her ass for you. You saw that, didn't you?"

"I didn't notice it, Angela, and I have absolutely *no* desire—"

"Liar!" she shouted. "I know you want to hit that in every position all night long! Don't try to deny it!"

"I have to deny it because it *isn't* true," Matthew said.

She folded her arms again. "So I'm seeing things?"

If I say yes, she'll say she's crazy. If I say no, I'll be lying. "You are misinterpreting things. I can't see what you see, Angela. All I know is that I only have eyes for you, and I have made it very clear that I *only* want to be with you. You have me here right now, don't you?"

Angela looked away. "You'd be crazy not to run away from me and get with that nice piece of educated ass. I'll bet she went to Columbia or some other Ivy League school. I'll bet she has a two hundred IQ. You two can make smart light-skinned babies with long legs."

"Angela," Matthew said softly, "you are easily the smartest woman I've ever met."

"*Bullshit!*" she shouted. "I don't have a college degree."

"You don't need a college degree to be smart," Matthew said. "Bill Gates, Steve Jobs, and Ted Turner all dropped out of college."

"At least they had a *chance* to go to college," Angela said. "I didn't."

She got me there.

"Oh, and you and Felisa can go on really *long* walks together," Angela said. "Her legs are long enough. She could wrap them *twice* around you. You could ride the subway with *her.* You could go to Yankees games with *her*. You could go anywhere in the world with *her* while I can't leave this *fucking* apartment for more than two or three blocks at a time!"

She is definitely heating up. I need to cool her off. "We're working on that, aren't we?" Matthew said softly, rubbing her leg. "You're getting there. One step at a—"

"Don't keep *fucking* saying that!" she shouted. "I can't fucking stand that! One step at a time. It's fucking bullshit!"

Matthew lifted his hand off her leg. *That didn't work.*

"I am going nowhere, Matthew!" she shouted, tears forming in her eyes. "I'm *not* getting better. Speed-walking around Williamsburg is *not* going to cure me. I *hate* going for walks as if I'm some sort of dog. I think the only reason you try to get me out of here is to scare the living *shit* out of me so you can play the hero when we get back."

"That's not it at all, Angela," Matthew said. "What you're saying is—"

"Crazy?" Angela interrupted. "Go ahead and say it. Say, 'Angela, you're fucking crazy.' "

"Angela, I will never say that," Matthew said.

She started rocking back and forth. "I'm as useless as a wooden frying pan, Matthew. Admit it!"

"Angela, that's not true," Matthew said. "I need you."

"No, you *fucking* don't." She took a deep breath. "I want you to go."

I am not moving from this spot.

She pointed to the window. "Go find your mongrel bitch in heat! She's out there running the streets you like so much! She's waiting for you!"

"No," Matthew said softly.

She threw back the covers and jumped out of the bed, pointing into the kitchen. "Leave! Return all those phone calls! You know you want to, and don't try to lie! Victoria will show you the *view!* Monique will let you use her *entire* condom collection! Mary will do you while she's praying! Allison will relapse, and you can do *whatever* you want with her drunk ass!"

"I'm not leaving," Matthew said, trying to stay calm.

"Get the *fuck* out of here!" Angela shouted.

"No," he said softly. "You're stuck with me. I'm not leaving."

Angela's eyes filled with tears. "I've got *nothing* to offer you, Matthew!"

Do I dare touch her? Not yet. She's still on fire. "You have everything I need, and you even have things I didn't know I needed."

"I'm nothing!" Angela shouted. "I'm less than nothing! I can't even walk two blocks without getting scared of every man passing us or every man leaning up against a building or the sound of a strange man's voice. All a man has to do is clear his throat and I want to start running in the opposite direction. I try so hard to swallow my fear until we get back, and sometimes I nearly vomit my guts out."

Matthew took one of her hands in his. "We'll be walking everywhere together soon. You'll see."

Angela wrenched her hand from his and walked to the window. "Don't you wish I was normal?"

"You are by far the most normal woman I've ever met," Matthew said.

She spread out her arms. "*This isn't normal! None of this is fucking normal!*"

"No, it isn't," Matthew whispered. "It's extraordinary, and I love you."

"I am *not* normal, Matthew!" Angela shouted.

She didn't hear me.

"I am out of my mind! I have nothing to offer—" She blinked. "What did you say?"

She did hear me. Even said softly, those are three powerful words. "I said, what we have is extraordinary, and I love you."

Angela's jaw quivered, her eyes blinking.

"I love you, Angela." He smiled. "I really do."

Angela paced beside the bed. "Why? How? *How* can you love me? I'm crazy. I'm damaged. And you still have women blowing up your phone and flirting right in front of me. You could have any woman in the world."

"That's not true," Matthew said. "The only woman in the world I want is you."

Angela stopped pacing. "But why? Why do you love *me?* I am a lost cause!"

He rose and stood beside her, wanting to hold her so badly. "I love you because the air tastes sweeter around you."

She looked briefly into his eyes.

"It does," he said. "The air around you has a taste. The air has weight around you. I can swallow it. It nourishes me. I breathe easier around you. I love you for that."

"But you can't," Angela said.

Matthew ignored her. "I love you because I haven't smiled so much in my entire life. Life, my life, is sweeter because of you. I love *you*. I love you the way you are." He rubbed the backs of her arms. "I even love you right this moment."

"As messed up as I am," Angela said.

He gently turned her around and took her hands. "As *wonderful* and *incredible* as you are. When I look at you or talk to you or simply hold you, I'm happy, truly, unbelievably happy. I've *never* been this content. I love you and want you and need you. I have never said any of this to anyone ever. Please don't ever ask me to leave you again. I am going to be with you for better or worse."

Angela looked at the floor. "As long as I don't get worser, right?" she whispered.

He stepped closer. "I think you're getting better."

Angela stepped back, pulling her hands away from him. "You

think *this* is an improvement? I just screamed my guts out at you. I just told you to go hook up with your dates from hell. I just accused you of wanting to sleep with Felisa." She turned away. "I saw you looking at her, and I . . . I started thinking so many . . . horrible things. I have to be crazy."

"Jealousy is something most sane people feel at one time or other. Jealousy is normal." *I can't see her eyes.* "Please look at me."

Angela turned slowly. "I'm surprised you want me to. I am an emotional wreck."

Matthew smiled and caressed her face with his fingertips. "You're *definitely* not emotionally *detached* now. Numb Angela has left the building, and fiery, passionate Angela is in this room. I like this woman very much."

"You can't like me," Angela said.

"I do. Don't you see what's happening?" He held her face. "Angela, you're coming out of your shell. You're loosening your armor. You're becoming wild and untamed, and it's very sexy." He pushed his fingers through her hair. "Your hair is a mess for the first time probably ever. I like it. I'm always worried I'll mess up your hair, and here it is already messed up, so if I feel like doing this . . ." He ran his fingers through her hair from her forehead to her neck. "I won't feel so bad. You also dropped the F-bomb several times. And the shouting, though quite loud, is filled with fire. It's quite a turn-on."

Angela blinked. "My anger and frustration arouses you?"

"Your *passion* arouses me," Matthew said. "I'm hoping that you will tackle me and make passionate love to my helpless body."

Angela laughed slightly. "You'll never be helpless."

"Nor will you," he said. "Nor *are* you." He slid his hands around her waist. "Nor will you ever be."

Angela buried her head into Matthew's chest and wept.

"I won't let go of you," he whispered. "I'm never letting go of you."

He guided her to the bed, where he sat, settled Angela into his lap, and let her body shake and her tears soak his shirt for several minutes.

"I'm sorry I yelled at you," Angela said, wiping at her eyes. "I'm a little insecure, huh?"

"Just a wee bit," Matthew said. "But you have no reason to be. I'm yours."

"I'm stuck with you," Angela said.

"Yes."

Angela looked at the bed. "Okay." She closed her eyes. "I've made a decision." She opened her eyes. "And I'm scared."

"I'm right here," Matthew said.

"I want to sleep with my back to you again," Angela said, "only this time I'm not going to look back. I was up most of the other night checking to see if you were still there. No, that's not true. I was looking back to make sure it *was* you."

"What exactly do you feel when someone is behind you?" Matthew asked.

"I feel like I'm being hunted, I guess," Angela whispered. "I hunch up my shoulders and drop my head lower as if I'm trying to make myself smaller or something, to make myself harder to see."

Or to find.

"And I can't stop looking around." She rubbed the back of her neck. "It's why my neck and shoulders get so sore. I'm constantly watching my own back."

He laid her down on her side. "Let me watch your back for a while." He slid in behind her.

Angela instantly looked back.

"Hi," he whispered. "Do you come here often? My name is Matthew. What's yours?"

Angela sighed. "This is hard for me."

"It's only me, Angela."

"I know." She turned her head toward the window and backed her booty into him.

"I like this view," Matthew whispered.

"I don't." She began to breathe heavily. "Maybe some other time." She flipped onto her back. "I know, I know. It's stupid." She pounded the bed with her fists. "I'm sorry. I just have to be able to see your eyes so I know it's you."

Matthew rubbed her stomach. "You know, if we had a mirror, we could set it up against that wall, and you would see me any time you opened your eyes."

Angela sat up. "I think there's one on the back of my parents' door. My mama used to get dressed in front of it."

"One mirror coming up," he said. "I'll be back in a sec."

Matthew rushed to the other bedroom door, which complained with a harsh creak as it opened to a room covered in a layer of dust.

Angela hasn't been in here in a long time. A vacuum cleaner would die a dusty death in five minutes in here.

The room had a larger bed, a small couch at its foot, a massive twelve-drawer dresser, and two wingback chairs in front of a broad window facing another part of the alley. After Matthew looked behind the door and found the rectangular mirror, he turned the top two clips to the side and slid the mirror free.

He carried it into Angela's bedroom and propped it up next to the window. "How's that?"

"Get beside me," she whispered.

He jumped into the bed, resting his cheek on hers.

"Move it to the right some," she said.

He adjusted the mirror and returned to her side. "Can you see my eyes?" he whispered.

"Yes." Her breathing slowed substantially. "Hi."

"Hi. You're kinda cute."

She reached her left arm up to caress his face. "I like you behind me."

"May I kiss on you while you watch?" Matthew asked.

Angela smiled. "Yes."

Matthew kissed the top and sides of her head. He kissed her left ear, left cheek, and the left side of her neck.

"You still watching?" Matthew whispered.

"Yes," Angela whispered.

He pulled up her shirt, exposing her breasts and kissed her side, her breast, and her stomach.

"Can you still see me?" Matthew asked as he kissed her hip.

"Yes."

Matthew looked at Angela's eyes in the mirror. "I don't remember your eyes sparkling like that. You look dreamy. Are you relaxed?"

"Yes and no. You missed a spot." She pressed back with her booty.

"Hmm," Matthew said. "You'll have to turn onto your stomach for me."

Angela turned onto her stomach, her head facing the mirror. "Like this?"

So eager. "Yes."

Matthew tugged at the elastic of her underwear. "You still watching?"

Angela nodded.

He smoothly removed her underwear, kissing down her booty and legs as he did.

"You're wearing too many clothes," Angela whispered.

Matthew set a personal record for disrobing. "Is this better?"

"Much better," she said. "You still missed a spot."

He kissed each cheek of her booty. "Did I get it that time?"

"No."

"You want to see me kiss your ass," Matthew said.

Angela nodded.

Matthew started at the top of her booty, gripping her firm flesh, and worked his way down, in between, and under. Angela raised her hips, and he ran his tongue to her clitoris.

"Oh shit," Angela sighed.

Matthew moved up the bed. "Are you okay?"

Angela lowered her hips. "Yes. That was . . ." She seemed to shiver. "Go back."

He rubbed her back. "You want me to finish the job."

"Well, um, stay here for a second." She smiled at him in the mirror. "Is this what you see when you watch me sleep?"

"I don't see myself at all," Matthew said. "I only see you."

"I see *us.* I like this mirror." She turned onto her back. "I want to watch you kissing me other places."

"Only if I can use my tongue, too," Matthew whispered.

She sighed. "You better."

Matthew started at her neck, lingered a while at her nipples and breasts, devoured her stomach, and parted her legs, letting his tongue run wild. He turned so he could see Angela's eyes opening and closing, the arch of her neck and back, and her tongue licking her lips. When she gripped the covers with her hands, Matthew knew she was close. He moved his left hand up her left leg, extended a finger, and slid it inside her.

"Oh yes! Shit! *Oh my God!*"

And now it's my turn. Damn. Why'd she have to shout like that? Matthew tried to stop himself, but he couldn't. "Angela, I can't stop it," he whispered as he found release, mostly on the comforter. "I'm so sorry."

She reached out and stroked him. "Don't be."

What a mess. Gee, I'm up to all of ten seconds.

"We'll just have to do more laundry," Angela whispered. "You came because I did?"

"Yes."

She turned her booty to him. "Let me feel it on me."

He positioned his penis between her cheeks.

"I may never fall asleep again," she whispered. "Did you want to be inside me just then?"

"Yes, and you would have had quintuplets," Matthew said. "Tomorrow."

"Only two, remember?" Angela whispered.

"They would have been twins, each weighing in at twenty pounds," Matthew said.

"Ouch."

Matthew laughed at the woman in the mirror. "Do you realize that we're probably the only two people in the world who use a mirror *not* to have sex?"

"We are so dysfunctional." She turned into him and climbed up on his body.

"Oh, *now* she mounts me," Matthew said.

Angela laughed. "Because it's safe. There's no chance of anything large going into a small space to make twenty-pound babies coming out of a small space." She kissed his lips tenderly and wrapped her arms around his neck, resting her head on his chest.

"I don't know how you can sleep like that," Matthew said.

"I just listen to your heartbeat until I fall asleep," Angela said. "*Th-dum, th-dum, th-dum.*"

"What's my heart saying now?" Matthew asked, stroking her hair.

"I love you," Angela whispered.

My heart can articulate that phrase? Wait. She *said it.*

Angela lifted her head. "I love you, Matthew."

"I love you, too." Matthew pulled her higher, kissing her tenderly. "That was unexpected. I didn't expect you to say that to me for a long time."

She rested her head on the pillow. "Why?"

"After what you've been through, I thought it would take longer," Matthew said. "I even decided that I didn't need to hear you say it as long as I felt it. I have felt your love since the first time you poured me a cup of coffee."

"I'm really not that loving," she said.

He hugged her. "You are. I feel loved. Therefore, you are *full* of love."

"For you," she said with a sigh. "I think I have loved you from the moment you got me out the door to get some pizza."

"There's something ironic about that," Matthew said. "Especially since we walked fourteen blocks round-trip that night. That's our record."

"I guess my love for you made me walk all that way," Angela said.

Matthew did the math. "That means you fell in love with me ten days ago. I've only been in love with you for the last hour or so."

Angela plucked one of Matthew's chest hairs.

Ow.

She grabbed and twisted his left nipple. "This is next. Do you wish to rephrase your answer?"

Rephrasing. "Angela, I have loved you all my life, and I'm sorry it took this long to find you. Please don't hurt my nipple. It's very sensitive."

Angela released his nipple. "When did you *really* know?"

"I knew I was falling in love with you when you asked if I had ever been in love." *And there's something ironic about that, too.*

"So I got you thinking about it," Angela said.

"Not about it—*you,*" Matthew said. "You are love, love is you. If anyone ever asked me to define love, I'll just say your name."

"That's . . . that's so sweet." She sighed. "I wish I didn't have such a long road ahead of me."

"*We* have a long road ahead of us," he said. "I don't know

what's going to happen tomorrow or next week or next month. But you know what? I don't care. I don't care what happens as long as I'm with you."

"I don't care either," Angela whispered. "Mmm."

"What's that 'mmm' for?" Matthew asked.

"I have a feeling I'll have a very erotic dream tonight," she said.

Matthew pouted. "Without me?"

"Oh, you'll be there," Angela said. "And when I really get going, I will start grinding on you in my sleep, and one thing might lead to another . . ."

"Don't tease me, Angela," Matthew said.

"What if I'm not teasing you and *this* is my dream?" Angela asked.

I love how she thinks! "Say it is."

"Do you want to hear what I'm going to dream about?" she whispered.

"Yes."

"I'm lying on top of a good man, a handsome man, a gorgeous man, whom I love very much," Angela said.

"I wish I had popcorn," Matthew said. "This is going to be a great movie."

"Shh. I kiss him tenderly." She kissed him with some serious tongue. "He looks into my eyes and says . . ."

Oh, it's my turn. "I'm hungry."

"No, he doesn't!" Angela said, laughing.

I am, kind of.

Angela sighed. "Let's try this again. He looks into my eyes and says . . ."

Don't say, "You complete me," though it's true. "I love you."

"No."

No? "It's a romantic line."

" 'I love you' is not romantic," Angela said. "This is supposed to be a dream, man. I want a fiery, passionate, sweaty dream."

And I want her to have one of those instead of a nightmare. "Oh. How about . . . I want to make love to you, Angela."

"Better, but . . ."

She is so hard to please. "How's this: I want *you* to make love to *me*."

"Well, all you did was change the order of the words," Angela said.

She caught that. "Yeah, that was a little selfish. Oh, I have a good line."

"It better be," Angela said with a yawn. "My dream is becoming a bore. I may wake up."

No you won't. "Let's *do* it," Matthew growled.

Angela gasped. "That's . . . that's better. Go on."

"Get on me *now,*" he growled. "Rock my world. Grind me until I go off like a rocket."

"Like a rocket?" She laughed. "Really?"

A rocket is hot. What else is hot? "Like a . . . geyser. A *hot* geyser. A hot, thick, *steaming* geyser."

"Much better." Her hands strayed across his chest as she sat up, inching her booty lower and lower.

This is nice. "What do *you* do next in your dream?"

"I reach behind me and . . ."

We have a strong hand gripping my package.

"Already?" Angela said.

"Your dream is making me hard, and your whispers are making me harder," Matthew whispered. "You arouse me whenever you whisper. I think I have an antenna down there that amplifies your sexy whispers. Please. Finish your dream." *And don't let go!*

"You're my dream," Angela whispered.

"I'm just a guy from Williamsburg," Matthew whispered.

"You are so much more than a guy from Williamsburg," Angela said. "You're the only one I want."

"The feelings are supremely mutual." *And now she's moving that hand up and down.*

"Really?" she whispered. "You've never wanted anyone else?"

It's so hard to concentrate! "I thought I did. I just didn't know you were the only one at the time. Angela, I wasted my time with other women. I only want to spend my time with you."

"Okay," Angela whispered. "Let me finish my dream. I move lower . . ." She slid her booty closer to her hand. "And I guide him inside of me . . ."

Does she mean to do this? I'm inside of her. "Angela . . ."

"It's okay," she whispered. "I'm ready, Matthew."

She means to.

"I put him . . . wow . . . I put him deep inside me . . . as gently as I can . . . and I start . . . slowly . . ." Angela rose and plunged. "Oh." She pressed on his chest with her hands. "You're inside me, Matthew. Oh yes . . ." She arched her back and started to grind. "Please sit up and kiss me before I die."

Matthew shot up, grabbing her booty and kissing her neck as Angela rode him forcefully, her nails tearing at his chest.

"Angela . . . I'm about to . . . I shouldn't stay inside . . ."

Angela hugged him tight to her. "Stay inside me, Matthew. Stay inside me. Don't ever leave me . . ."

Matthew could contain himself no longer, thrusting up as Angela's legs quivered, sweat rolled off his body, and Angela broke into a glorious smile.

"Oh God, yes!" Matthew shouted. He fell back.

Angela fell forward. "Am I allowed to curse again?"

"Shit, yeah," Matthew said.

"Holy shit," she said. "Don't take this the wrong way. But we can't do that until I heal sometime this summer. Geez, what do you feed that thing?"

"Coffee and pastries," Matthew said.

She shook her head. "I'm cutting you back to half a cup and one pastry. Damn, you're good."

"I didn't do much, and I didn't last as long as I wanted to," Matthew said. "You were cooking. I was merely along for the ride."

"I had all the right ingredients." She eased off him, wincing. "Maybe we can do that again next . . . January. I will need some substantial recovery time."

"That long?" Matthew asked.

"I don't want you talking about *length* in this little bed at any time," she said. "I'll let you know, okay?"

Matthew held her close. "Is it okay if I tell you what's on my mind right this second?"

Angela sighed. "Yes."

"Whoo!" Matthew shouted.

Angela laughed. "Really? 'Whoo' is the only thing on your mind?"

"That, what we just did, was making love," Matthew said. "We made it right here in this bed made for much smaller people. We should be in a how-to video. *That's* how it's done, ladies and gentlemen. Try, if you dare, to top *that.*"

Angela pulled her hair off her face, resting her head on Matthew's chest. "Was it really that good?"

"You didn't feel the geyser?" Matthew asked.

"I felt it," Angela whispered.

"I felt that all the way from my toes to my nipples to just under my chin," Matthew said. "It was as if my entire soul was inside you. Angela, please believe me when I say that I have never let it all go like that before. I didn't hold back a thing. It wasn't just the act. It was . . ." *I have to say this word because it actually fits the freaking definition.* "It was amazing. I'm done looking. You're it. God, I want you so much, even now."

Angela raked his stomach with her fingers. "How faithful is that geyser of yours?"

"That's a loaded question," Matthew said.

"You have a loaded geyser," Angela said.

"From now on, until the day I die, I will only do this with you," Matthew said as he put his hand on his heart. "My geyser will be faithful to you, and to signify that I am totally, completely yours forever, I will do something I have never done before."

Matthew slipped out the bed and went to the window, opening it, a burst of icy wind screaming into the room. He stuck his head out the window and yelled, "Hey Billyburg! It's me, Matthew Mark McConnell!"

Angela laughed.

"I have met the love of my life, and her name is Angela Simone Smith!"

Angela huddled under the covers. "Close the window, man."

"And one day! One day soon!" Matthew shivered. "You're right. It's freaking cold." He closed the window, standing beside the bed. "One day soon, Miss Angela Simone Smith, I will make you my wife."

Angela threw back the covers. "Come here."

I am a Popsicle. He rolled into the bed, and Angela scrambled on top of him. "I don't want anyone but you, no one but you."

Angela rubbed his chest. "You got me, okay, you got me. Please don't die of frostbite." She blinked. "Is that . . ."

He nodded. *It has a mind of its own. It's bumping on her already.* "It's the, um, the change from cold to warm that's—"

"Shh," she whispered, her eyes welling with tears. "Nobody has ever wanted me as much as you have. And this proves it." She drifted her nipples across his chest. "I want you again." She sat back. "Damn, it's bigger." She eased onto him. "Matthew, I know what love is now . . ." She grabbed his hands and pulled him up, placing his hands on her breasts and locking her hands behind his head. "Love is never giving up."

He kissed her in time to her rhythm. "I like that definition."

"I am going to be so useless tomorrow," Angela said.

"It's already tomorrow," he whispered. "But only tomorrow?"

Angela threw back her head. "I'm going back to real coffee."

"Decaf has to be a plot to keep people from having amazing sex," Matthew whispered, thrusting up slightly.

"Shh, I'm working here." She removed his hands from her breasts and squeezed her breasts in front of him.

Matthew's hands cupped her booty. "I like when you do that."

She continued to knead her breasts. "It feels good. My nipples are almost as hard as you are."

I doubt it.

Angela ground her hips harder and faster. "I like how you touch me."

"I like how *you* touch you," Matthew whispered.

Angela slipped both hands between her legs. "Like this?" She started to stroke herself.

"Oh yeah." Matthew looked away.

"Why aren't you watching?" Angela moaned.

"If I do I'll come." *And I will. The show she's giving me is amazing. There's that word again.*

"Isn't that the point?" Angela whispered.

Matthew watched her fingers moving in circles. "Don't stop," he whispered. "Don't stop, Angela."

Angela's mouth opened wide. "Oh shit, oh shit . . ."

Matthew threw his hips up as Angela crashed down and howled, and Matthew joined her in a mutual "Whoo!"

They collapsed back together.

"You're amazing," Angela said, rubbing her sweaty forehead on Matthew's chest.

"We're amazing," Matthew said. *We're even iconic.*

Angela nestled her head into his neck, her hair tickling his chin. "I am going to think about this my every waking moment, you know that. I will be pouring coffee all over my counter."

"And I'll clean it up with a gleam in my eye." He kissed her. "Did you ever think *this* would happen?

"I knew it would happen eventually. You have no idea how often I woke up after a bad dream and just wanted to take you." She held his hand. "The next time it happens, I will." She squeezed. "And for some reason, I know you'll be ready."

"I'll be ready." He looked out the window. "That isn't the sun, is it?"

Angela sighed. "I don't want to get up." She turned his face to hers. "How soon will it be until this is legal, Mr. McConnell?"

"How soon do you want it to be?" Matthew asked.

"Yesterday."

I knew she'd say something like that. "Backdating a marriage license. I don't know if that's possible." *Or legal.* "Are you feeling better about us now?"

"I feel better than I've ever felt before," Angela said. "I feel so alive. But neither of us will straighten out our money if we're spending too much time in this bed when we should be opening the shop."

"So our daily schedule from now on will be to make money, then make love," Matthew said.

Angela nodded. "Oh yes."

"Life would be so much simpler if more people did that, don't you think?" Matthew asked.

"Of course," she said, hugging her Williamsburg man close, "it's *much* easier to make money just *after* you've made love."

"So the more love we make *before* we make money, the easier it will be to make that money," Matthew said.

"You are brilliant." She licked her lips. "Round three?"

Matthew nodded. "Three, they say, is a *magic* number . . ."

Chapter 30

For the next two weeks, Matthew and Angela flirted while working, traded hands in the kitchen, kissed often at the counter, cleaned up in record time, and shared blissful moments long into the night.

"We're drinking up our profits," Angela said one morning as she poured herself a second cup of house blend.

"We need the energy," Matthew said as he started his *third* cup. "And aren't our nights profitable, too?"

"Very," Angela said.

"I like your moneymaker," Matthew said.

"I like how often you make deposits," Angela said.

Gone unspoken but always under the surface was the idea that when Angela was better and their money was right, they would get married.

To that end, Matthew planned walks that would take them farther from the shop and closer to a jewelry store that stayed open late.

Angela has to help me pick out her ring. This is all new territory for me. Those "How to Pick Out an Engagement Ring" Web sites aren't helpful at all. They say I should be dropping one to two months' salary on the ring. What if I don't have a "normal" salary? What if I'm not sure how much money I'll be making in any given month? Who decided on that "rule" anyway? The jewelers?

There are too many things to decide. Choose metal: 14K gold, 18K gold, white gold, or platinum? Choose setting: bezel, pave, or channel? Choose cut: round, square, rectangular, oval, pear, heart, marquise, trilliant, or radiant? What degree of clarity and color? How many carats?

There are too many choices for one man to make!

If I could get Angela to close even an hour early, we'd be straight. We'd go to the store, browse the rings, and I'd watch her eyes light up when she saw the *ring. It would be easy.*

But she won't close early. We could "shop" online using my laptop, provided I can get a Wi-Fi signal, but where's the holding hands and gazing at rings with wide eyes and trying them on romance in that? Holding your finger up to a computer screen is silly.

Matthew couldn't wait for daylight saving time to give them an extra hour of daylight for their walks, but until then, he only planned short walks. They sauntered at a leisurely pace one block to Walter Foods to slurp oysters and little neck clams. They kept a reasonable pace for the two blocks to San Loco for a plate of Macho Nachos. The three-block trip to the W. E. Sheridan playground became a race there and back, because Angela's anxiety level was so high.

Matthew stared at the computer screen one Tuesday afternoon, thanks to animalcrack69, while Angela was putting away a delivery in the kitchen.

Jewelry stores sure have changed. They don't only *sell jewelry now, and they often don't have the word "jewelry" in the name of their store. Catbird, Bird, and fuego 718 all sell jewelry in Williamsburg. If I hadn't Googled them, I never would have known they sold jewelry.*

Catbird caught his eye because its Web site had plenty of wedding and engagement rings on display. Most of the rings, however, didn't quite look like traditional wedding or engagement rings. He saw rings in the shapes of fighting bears, deer, two-headed snakes, and dolphins. He saw double-finger rings, crescent-moon-shaped rings, and a ring in the shape of a tree trunk, complete with heart-enclosed, carved initials. He finally found one he liked by Conroy & Wilcox—gold band, round diamond, a classic, $4,500—but no matching wedding band. He found a "Conflict Free Eternity Band" that looked nice, and although it was silver, the name itself gave him hope. *Conflict free for an eternity. I know it's not made with "conflict" diamonds, but what if it was possible for a marriage to be eternally conflict free?*

He left the shop and called Catbird. "This will sound like a strange request, but could you stay open until nine o'clock tonight?"

"We're only open noon until eight," a woman said.

"I know that," Matthew said. "My girlfriend and I don't get off work until eight-fifteen or so, and we'd be there by eight-thirty at the latest. We work a couple blocks over on Driggs."

"I'm sorry, sir—"

"We're shopping for engagement rings and wedding bands," Matthew interrupted.

"Oh, *well,*" she said. "That's *different.* We'll be open for you, sir."

After cleaning up, Angela stood at the front door in her coat. "Where are we going tonight?"

"Bedford Avenue," Matthew said.

"That's a long street," Angela said.

"It's only about two and a half blocks from here," Matthew said.

Angela nodded. "Two and a half." She peered outside. "Is it raining?"

Matthew saw ice pellets bouncing off the sidewalk. "I think it's sleet. We'll have to hustle." *The weather in Brooklyn always has lousy timing.*

"It's so dark." She put her hand in his. "Couldn't we just go upstairs and snuggle?"

Later. "I want to get you something from Catbird." *Don't ruin the surprise. What else do they sell?* "I want to buy you a cashmere hat. It will look so good on you." *That was extremely lame.*

"You want to take me out in the cold and sleet to buy me an expensive hat," Angela said. "What sense does that make? I'm going out hatless to get a hat."

Matthew snatched one of the umbrellas left by customers from a box next to the first booth. "We will take an umbrella."

"Matthew, I really don't need a new hat," Angela said, "especially one made out of cashmere, and we need to be saving as much money as we can, right?"

Woman, I'm about to drop nearly five grand on you! Play right! "But you'll look so cute in the hat."

"Don't I look cute without the hat?" Angela asked.

"Yes, of course, but—"

"Look at the sidewalk," Angela interrupted. "It's looking more like hail than sleet now."

We're on a timetable here. "The umbrella will protect us."

"Couldn't we go on a night where there are at least some stars in the sky?" Angela asked.

Matthew looked at the sleet collecting on the sidewalk like hundreds of diamonds. "Sure. We can go another night." He pulled her close. "Let's go snuggle."

As they snuggled and Angela drowsed on top of him, Matthew lamented this wasted opportunity.

Catbird will most likely never stay open for me again. Unless I leave a substantial deposit. That might work. I could even go in and pick out the ring, but I don't know Angela's size. What if she doesn't like it? I don't want to pick out the wrong ring.

And suppose I do get a ring, where would I propose to her? Here, in her coffee shop? She'd get the ring, kiss me, show it off, and then go right back to work. I have to keep working on her to take a regular day off. Sundays would be perfect, but the before-and-after church crowd can be immensely profitable. Maybe I can convince her to close early on a slow night like Tuesday or Thursday.

He rubbed her warm back. *Someday we'll get you a ring fit for the queen you are.*

Matthew's legal work became steady, but it didn't fill up his bank account. He did simple wills. He looked over vendor contracts. He settled occasional disputes between landlords and tenants. He mediated an argument between neighboring business owners who both claimed the parking spaces out front as "their" loading zone.

He charged everyone a compromise between what they were willing to pay and what they actually could pay without breaking the bank. Matthew found it harder and harder, however, to gauge a client's ability to pay. Women carrying Coach bags and wearing designer clothes and heels often had to pay in installments. Men in work clothes had rolls of ready cash.

"You don't charge nearly enough," Angela told him.

"I charge what I think clients can afford," Matthew said.

"You have to charge enough to get their respect but not so much to hurt them," Angela said. "You need to make a price sheet."

"You could charge a dollar more for everything in this shop if you wanted to," Matthew said.

"And I'd lose customers left and right," Angela said. "They'd go across the street, and I'd go out of business."

"Your customers would understand," Matthew said.

"No, they wouldn't," she said. "Make a price sheet and stick to it."

Matthew made and posted a reasonable flat fee schedule:

Simple wills:	$75
Living trusts:	$250
Power of attorney:	$35
Bankruptcy:	$100
Name Change:	$150
Prenuptial Agreements:	$500
Simple Divorce:	$350
Limited Liability Company (LLC):	$100
Incorporation:	$200
Non-Profit:	$100
Tax advice:	A cup of coffee

"You're still not charging enough," Angela said, "A cup of coffee for tax advice?"

"I love your coffee," Matthew said.

"And only three-fifty for a divorce?"

"Provided both parties agree to everything," Matthew said, "I just fill out some paperwork."

"What does a divorce normally cost?" Angela asked.

"Anywhere from fifteen to thirty grand if it gets to court," Matthew said. "Mediation can run up to five grand, and some divorce lawyers charge up to a thousand bucks an hour."

Angela sighed heavily. "Then *you* need to charge more so people realize the *real* cost of divorce," Angela said. "Make getting a divorce more expensive, and the divorce rate will go down around here. It's far too easy and affordable to end a marriage these days."

Matthew agreed and raised his fee for divorce to $750.

He had no takers.

Angela is so very wise.

Matthew moved more of himself and his meager belongings to Angela's apartment. She marveled at his DVD collection, which included *My Cousin Vinny, The Verdict, Presumed Innocent, And Justice for All,* and *A Few Good Men.*

"Why do you own these movies?" she asked.

"These movies are great for research," Matthew said. "The courtroom is a stage, and these actors have helped me on that stage."

"So law school didn't adequately prepare you for the courtroom," Angela said.

"They tried," Matthew said, "but I learned most of what I know on the job."

She put *My Cousin Vinny* into the DVD. "What else are you going to bring up here?"

"I could bring my bed," Matthew said. "It's bigger than yours, and—"

"But I like being right on top of you," Angela interrupted.

Matthew left his bed at his apartment.

He didn't leave his chair at the apartment.

After turning off the heat and unplugging his empty refrigerator, he carried his easy chair through Williamsburg and into Angela's shop.

She didn't like it.

At all.

"But it's my thinking chair, Angela," Matthew said.

Angela walked around it several times. "This chair tells me a lot about how much or how well you think. This chair is telling me that you don't think much, and when you do think, you don't think that clearly."

"But it's a part of me," Matthew pleaded. "It has stuck with me through thick and thin."

"I'm surprised you don't get stuck *in* it," Angela said. She sighed. "I *suppose* we could get it re-covered."

"But it will lose its magic and its charm," Matthew said.

She pounded the seat with her fist, dust pluming into the air.

"That must be magic thinking dust, huh?" Angela quickly covered the easy chair with throw blankets, which blunted the effects of the springs and kept the dust from escaping. "How's that?"

Matthew sat. "Not bad." He opened his phone. "I want you to hear this." He turned on the speaker.

"Who are you calling?" Angela asked.

"My landlord."

"Hello?" Larry said.

"Larry, this is Matthew McConnell, and I have vacated my apartment."

Angela smiled.

"You already paid me this month," Larry said.

"I know," Matthew said. "I'm turning off my phone and the utilities on the fifteenth. I'll be cleaning it out soon."

"You already found another place?" Larry asked.

"Yes."

"May I ask how much you're paying at your new place?" Larry asked.

"You can ask."

"Okay," Larry said. "I'm asking."

Matthew shrugged at Angela, and Angela shrugged back. "A thousand for a two-bedroom, one-bath with living room, a kitchen from this century with a walk-in freezer, a huge refrigerator, a triple sink, two ovens, laundry room, and plenty of closets."

"How many roommates do you have?" Larry asked.

Larry isn't stupid. "You can start showing my apartment next week, and I'll want my deposit back."

"If it is clean and in good condition, you'll get your deposit back," Larry said.

"It will be. Bye, Larry." He closed his phone. "Want to help me clean my apartment? It will be the only time you'll ever be able to see my apartment."

"I'll pass," Angela said.

"It might be fun. That big ol' bed . . ."

"Where you and Joy slept together," Angela said.

Oh yeah. "You're right."

Later than night, Angela whispered, "You awake?"

"Yes."

"Do you ever miss your old life?" she asked.

"The security of it, yes," Matthew said. "There was always money."

"How much?" she asked.

"My best year I broke seven figures with bonuses." *I was once a millionaire, before taxes, but I wasn't happy at all.*

Angela was silent for quite a while. "And where is this money now?"

Dwindling. "I still have a decent chunk. I've been thrifty."

"You've been so thrifty that you moved in here and the apartment doesn't look any different to me," Angela said. "Could you be filthy rich right now?"

"If I had made partner, I could have easily broken eight figures with year-end bonuses." *And I used to want to make partner. That seems so far away and foolish right now.*

Angela grabbed his arms. "Go make partner."

"I'm done with all that foolishness," he said.

"I know you are." She propped her head up on her hands. "Tell me about your average date when you were really rolling."

"You sure you want to hear this?" Matthew asked.

"I want to know."

"Well," Matthew said, "first I'd call my driver."

"You had a driver?" she asked.

"At the pinnacle of my success, yes," Matthew said. "My BMW gathered dust in a garage because I had a driver. Max. Good guy. I'd tell Max to pick her up and bring her to my condo on Central Park West for some predinner drinking. Back then, I could mix a mean cocktail. Then we'd go to dinner at some new, overpriced, chic restaurant where the food was arranged on the plate and, gosh, it was a shame to eat all *four* bites, it was so pretty. We'd consume at least one bottle of wine or champagne with dinner, and then we'd sit drunkenly through a Broadway show, always sitting in the first few rows. After that, it was on to a nightclub for twenty-dollar drinks followed by a nightcap at my place."

"Did . . . did these dates always end with sex?" she asked softly.

"Yes. Pretty much." He felt Angela stiffen. "Do you forgive me?"

"Are you *sure* you don't miss it?" she asked.

She doesn't forgive me. I don't forgive me either. "I don't miss that life at all, Angela. It wasn't really life. It was all a show, one long buzz, an alcohol-fueled carnival ride, and I had nothing to show for it after eight years of excess. I'm finally liking what I do."

"You're finally working for a living, huh?" she whispered.

"Yeah."

"It's hard, isn't it?" she asked.

Yes. "But the rewards, meager as they are, are much greater."

"You appreciate money now," Angela asked.

Yes. "I appreciate it much more now that I don't have as much of it."

One day in early March, an elderly couple wearing vintage red 1970s tracksuits, came in, bought coffee, and stopped at Matthew's booth.

"We want a divorce," the man said. "You do them, right?"

Matthew looked at them. *White hair. Tracksuits straight out of* The Six Million Dollar Man *TV show. More wrinkles on their bodies than on my clothes.*

"I do simple divorces, yes," Matthew said. *Why are they holding hands? This has to be a setup.* "I will need seven hundred and fifty dollars up front to start."

The couple looked at each other. The woman scrounged up $750 from her purse and laid the bills on the table.

This isn't a setup, and old people carry far too much cash these days. "Please be seated."

They sat opposite Matthew, smiling at each other.

Why are they still *holding hands?* "I'm Matthew McConnell, and you are . . ."

"Joe and Donna Bauer," he said.

The obvious question. "How long have you two been married?"

Joe smiled. "Sixty-one years."

"Sixty-*two* years, dear," Donna said, also smiling. "Ike was president, remember?"

"Oh, right," Joe said. "Good ol' Ike. Now there was a president with integrity."

No anger. No hostility. What are they thinking? "Do you have any children?" Matthew asked.

"Four boys, eight grandchildren, and nine great-grandchildren so far," Donna said sweetly.

"I'm assuming you have a home," Matthew said.

"Paid off over twenty years ago," Joe said. "It's a six-bedroom on Greene Avenue in Bed-Stuy."

Matthew blinked. *They're white and live in Bed-Stuy. Wow. Bed-Stuy has been on the comeback, so their house could go for a half million or more now.* "Cars?"

"Oh, we don't drive anymore," Joe said. "We walk or take the bus. That's how we got here today."

"What other kinds of property do you have?" Matthew asked.

"Just a house full of furniture and memories," Donna said. "Framed photos as far as the eye can see on nearly every wall, and not the digital kind either. Real photographs. Some have faded, of course, but the memories haven't faded at all."

They're smiling, nice, kindly, not angry at each other, and they are still holding hands. "I have to ask. Why do you want a divorce?"

Joe squinted at Donna. "Why do we want a divorce again?"

Donna smiled at Matthew. "We want to play the field."

"Oh yeah," Joe said. "That's the reason. We want to sow our wild oats."

They have to be kidding.

"You see," Donna said, "we were eighteen when we married. Joe was going over to Korea, and we had been dating since we were in junior high, so we tied the knot. It was a beautiful wedding."

"It was," Joe said. "You looked so lovely."

"Thank you, Joe," Donna said. "He was the most handsome man I'd ever known."

Joe waved his free hand. "Oh, go on."

"You *were,* all spiffy in your uniform," Donna said. "You're still a handsome man."

"And you're still beautiful." He kissed her cheek. "So how soon can you divorce us?"

And he kisses her. "You two obviously still love each other."

"Oh yes," Donna said. "Joe is the only man I've ever loved."

"And yet you want a divorce," Matthew said.

"Right," Joe said.

"I don't think I understand," Matthew said.

Donna sighed. "We have only ever been with each other."

"Through thick and thin," Joe said.

"And we were thinking the other day," Donna said, "what it would be like to be with someone else."

"I was against the idea at first," Joe said. "I couldn't imagine being with anyone else."

"Oh, neither could I," Donna said. "Except for a few business trips Joe took over the years, I have gone to sleep with Joe by my side every night since he came back from Korea."

"I never could sleep on the road," Joe said. "We would talk on the phone for hours, and our phone bills! They were huge."

"I still don't understand why you want a divorce," Matthew said. "You two are obviously made for each other."

"But we really don't know that for sure," Donna said. "How can we know we're made for each other when we've only ever been with each other? We have no one else to compare each other to."

I can't fault her logic, but . . . "Did it occur to you that you might be soul mates? That you were destined to marry and grow old together?"

"Where's the fun in that?" Joe asked. He winked at Donna. "We want to take a walk on the wild side."

At your age? Just the walk could kill you. I can't take these people's money! And I can't believe I'm about to say this. "You don't have to get divorced to do that."

"Oh, we know that," Donna said. "But how would it look if I brought Larry Pearson home one night?"

"Larry?" Joe said. "You'd bring Larry Pearson to our house?"

"For the sake of argument, Joe," Donna said. "You know he has a bad back."

"Oh, right," Joe said.

"I don't want our neighbors to think we're swingers," Donna said.

How can I dissuade them? "Well, it would be a good idea for you to sell your house now that the market is coming back."

"Oh no," Joe said. "Donna would keep the house. It's her dream house."

"It really is," Donna said. "It's the prettiest house on the block. Joe painted all the shutters just last year. Burgundy."

"Her favorite color," Joe said.

"And where would you live, Joe?" Matthew said.

"I've already picked out the place," Joe said. "The SoHotel on the Bowery. Chinatown, Little Italy, and Soho are right there. It's a restaurant paradise."

"Joe likes to eat out," Donna said.

"Mrs. and Mrs. Bauer, I have to tell you," Matthew said, putting his legal pad away, "I don't think you should get a divorce."

Joe frowned. "You don't?"

"No," Matthew said. "You've been married for sixty-two years. You're still holding hands. You're still smiling at each other. You still kiss your wife, Joe, and you're still in love."

"What's your point?" Donna asked.

Matthew gave back the money. "If you really want to go through with this, I can't be your divorce lawyer."

Joe left the money on the table. "Why not?"

"Usually, but not always, there's a reason, a *cause* for the divorce," Matthew said. "You haven't provided me with one. For instance, has there been cruel and inhuman treatment in your marriage?"

"Oh, of course not," Donna said. "Joe is gentle as a lamb. He has been the perfect gentleman ever since I've known him."

"Have either of you abandoned the other or lived apart for a year or more?" Matthew asked.

"Except for my tour in Korea, no," Joe said.

"Have either of you been in prison for three years or more?" Matthew asked.

"Heavens, no," Donna said.

"Has there been any adultery?" Matthew asked.

"Not yet," Joe said.

I can't believe I'm hearing this. "Have you ever had an irretrievable breakdown in your relationship for at least six months?"

"No," Donna said. "We've had our spats, but we always agree to kiss and make up before the sun goes down."

These two have had the perfect marriage. "Mr. and Mrs. Bauer, you have no irreconcilable differences, neither of you has been unfaithful, and I doubt either of you has ever raised a hand to the other." Matthew shook his head. "There is no just cause or grounds for a divorce here."

"Even if we want to play the field for the first time in our lives?" Joe asked.

"I've played the field," Matthew said. "And trust me, what you two have is *golden,* a billion *billion* times better than anything else out there."

"It's easy for you to say," Donna said. "You've been out there. I've only ever been with Joe."

"As God intended marriage to be," Matthew said.

Joe turned to Donna. "You said lawyers weren't usually religious."

"That's what Joanie *told* us, Joe," Donna said. "Joanie's our oldest daughter. She's been divorced three times and is working on a fourth. She lives with us from time to time."

An opening! "And how has her life been?" Matthew asked.

"I love her to death," Joe said, "but she's always been a mess."

"There you go," Matthew said, sitting back. "Divorce is messy."

"Maybe our divorce will be like our marriage, Mr. McConnell," Donna said. "We've been friends for a long time, and we will continue to be friends until the day we die. Did you ever think of that?"

This would be the easiest money I've ever made, but I can't do this. "Won't you miss each other?"

"Oh, I'll still call her every day," Joe said. "I couldn't go a day without talking to Donna."

"Thank you, Joe," Donna said. "That means so much to me."

Now what? "I . . . I can't facilitate your divorce. You'll either have to find another lawyer, who will tell you the same things, or you two will have to stay together."

"Oh." Donna turned to Joe. "What do we do?"

"I don't know," Joe said. "What do we do, Mr. McConnell?"

You stay married!

"We need our space," Donna said.

"Right."

They need their space. Okay. I'll give them a way. "You know," Matthew said, "if you really want to spend some time apart, you could spend *weekends* at the SoHotel, Joe."

Joe nodded. "I could do that." He smiled at Donna. "Couldn't I?"

"And then we could be together during the week," Donna said.

"That's an idea," Joe said. "You won't get lonely without me?"

"I might," Donna said, "but you're only a phone call away, right?"

"Right," Joe said. He smiled sweetly at her. "This might work."

Unbelievable. "So you'll stay married, right?" Matthew asked.

"What do you think, Joe?" Donna asked. "Do you think we should?"

"I think he's right." Joe counted out five twenties and slid them across the table. "For your trouble."

Matthew slid back the money. "You'll need it for a night out in Little Italy, Joe."

"Oh, you have to have something," Joe said. "You've helped us. Take your girl out on us."

Matthew collected the money. "Thank you."

Joe and Donna left the booth, both of them shook Matthew's hand crisply, and they left Angela's shop hand in hand.

"Wow," Matthew whispered as Angela brought over a plate of cookies. "Were you listening?"

Angela sat next to him. "Yes."

He picked up a cookie. "Can you believe those two? Sixty-two years of marriage, and *now* they want to sleep around."

Angela rubbed his leg. "I'm glad you talked them out of it."

"I really shouldn't have taken any of their money," Matthew said.

Angela held out her hand.

Matthew put the money in her hand.

Angela folded the money. "You gave them a marriage counseling session. You earned this money. I read that some of these marriage counselors make up to one hundred thousand bucks a year. You need to add marriage counseling to your list."

A flat fee for counseling? "What if it takes five hours to counsel them?"

"You're right," Angela said. "Charge a hundred an hour."

Matthew added the fee to his list, but again he had no takers.

I charge too little for divorces and *too much for marriage counseling.*

He lowered the counseling fee to fifty dollars an hour.

He still had no takers.

Chapter 31

The second Sunday morning in March was Panic Day, and Matthew panicked the moment he started reading Friday's copy of the *Daily Eagle*.

The story started on the bottom of the front page with a headline ("Williamsburg Man Arrested in Blizzard Attacks") and the mug shot of a scruffy-looking man named Robert Warrick. Police had arrested him on suspicion of committing several assaults on women in Lindsay Park over a three-day period.

Lindsay Park is less than a mile away from here, and it's a block away from the 90th Precinct. Is the guy crazy? He was begging to be caught. Warrick could be any white man in Williamsburg. Slack face, somewhat shaved, dark eyes. They always have dark eyes. And he attacked women during the blizzard.

He looked over at Angela, who was staring out the front window at the last of the snow mounds glistening and melting in the sun.

This might be the same guy who attacked her four years ago. Do I show her? Should I show her?

He rose on unsteady legs and took the paper to the counter. "Did you see this story?"

Angela nodded.

Of course she did. "Do you think this might be the same guy?" Matthew whispered.

"I didn't see his face," Angela said. "He was wearing a ski mask."

This is the first time I've heard about a ski mask. "It might be worth talking to the police about."

"I've got nothing to tell them," Angela said.

"Maybe he left some DNA," Matthew said.

"I burned my clothes," Angela said.

More new information. "You burned . . . your clothes."

"Yes."

"Why would you do that if he only tried?" Matthew asked.

"He didn't rape me, Matthew," Angela whispered. "He . . . came *on* me just before I kicked him."

Even more new information. Either she's remembering more or she finally trusts me enough to reveal more. "What about the stairs? Those crime techs are very good. They might be able to find something on the stairs."

"I scrubbed the stairs and walls with bleach," Angela said, "and anything else he may have left behind I've already swept away."

She tried to make it all *disappear.* "Did he say anything to you?"

Angela left her stool, holding her hands in front of her. "I don't want to do this."

Matthew followed her to the kitchen. "Did he say anything?"

Angela washed her hands. "Yes, but I don't want to do this right now."

"What did he say, Angela?" Matthew asked.

Angela's body shook. " 'Dis da way you like it? You gonna like what I got to give you.' "

Wow. "He said it just like that?" Matthew asked.

Angela nodded.

"So he might be originally from Williamsburg," Matthew said. "You can't fake that accent."

Angela nodded.

"A white guy."

Angela nodded. "Yeah."

"And you kicked him in the balls," Matthew said. "I wonder if he still has some damage down there."

"I hope he does," Angela whispered.

"We might be able to check that," Matthew said.

Angela turned. "We?"

"I mean, that can be checked," Matthew said. "The police can check that."

Angela swallowed. "Matthew, what if it *is* him?"

Then you'll be able to confront him in court and really start to heal. "What if it is?"

"I mean, if it *is* him," Angela said, "and I had said something four years ago, those women wouldn't have gotten attacked."

Matthew held her close. "This guy may have been at it for many years. Your testimony now could be crucial in putting him away."

"I'm sure they have enough evidence." She stepped back and wiped her eyes. "They made an arrest, didn't they? They wouldn't have arrested him without evidence."

"You can never have too much evidence." He dug his phone out of his pocket and put it in her hand. "Call the Ninetieth Precinct." *I hope they answer today.* "Give your name and address, and then tell whoever answers that you have information on a similar attack that occurred during the 2010 blizzard."

Angela looked at the phone. "It might not be the same guy, Matthew. Maybe the guy who attacked me is already in jail somewhere. That's what I've always hoped."

"Whether he is or he isn't," Matthew said, "at least you can let them know what happened to you."

Angela gripped the phone. "Dr. Penn has wanted me to do this for years."

And so do I.

"I'm scared." She shuddered. "I'm really scared."

"And I'm still the only man behind you," Matthew said.

She looked into his eyes. "I know." She handed back the phone. "I don't know the number."

Matthew scrolled through his contact list, found the 90th, and hit SEND. He put the phone in her hand.

Angela took a deep breath and exhaled. "Yes, I'd like to speak to someone about . . . My name is Angela Smith, and I was attacked in my coffee shop on Driggs Avenue during the 2010 blizzard." She held her left hand out to him.

Matthew held it tightly with both of his hands.

"I read a story in the paper today," she continued. "Yes, I saw his picture in the paper, but I don't know if it's the same guy. He was wearing a black ski mask, so I couldn't see his face." She listened a moment then covered the phone. "They're transferring me to a detective."

The ski mask must have set off something over there. That information wasn't in the newspaper.

She uncovered the phone. "Hello." She closed her eyes. "Yes, it was a black knit ski mask with three holes, two for the eyes and one for the mouth." She opened her eyes. "Big, maybe . . . six-three, six-four, maybe close to two-fifty or more. He, um, attacked me from behind, so I didn't get a good look at him." She listened for a minute. "Smith's Sweet Treats and Coffee on Driggs." She sighed. "Right. The coffee shop across from La Estrella. Could you come over after I close at eight?" She nodded. "Okay, I'll see you at eight." She closed the phone and handed it to Matthew. "A detective will be here around eight. Could you watch things for a few minutes?"

"Sure," Matthew said.

She ran up the stairs.

Matthew served several customers, but he didn't wish them a Happy Panic Day. When Angela returned, she wore her signature smile.

"You okay?" Matthew whispered.

"I'm a little lighter," she said. "Can you take me out to dinner tonight?"

"I'd love to." He kissed her cheek. "You're doing the right thing, Angela."

"I know. I just wish I had done the right thing sooner." She looked at the tip jar. "Did you get some tips?"

"I hadn't noticed." *I was too busy watching the kitchen for your return.*

She peered into the tip jar. "You did."

And I wasn't even trying.

"What did you do differently?" she asked.

"I have no idea," Matthew said. "Maybe your customers are getting used to me."

She kissed his cheek. "It might be all our kissing. I think my customers are your customers now."

Matthew looked out into the dining area. "You think?"

She hugged him. "I *know.*"

"So I should keep flirting with you and kissing you and hugging you down here whenever I can," Matthew said.

"Yes."

Matthew smiled. "You may need to get a bigger tip jar."

Chapter 32

Detective Sidney Novak arrived alone before eight. Novak was in her mid-fifties, had reddish-gray hair, and wore black slacks and a brown leather jacket.

"We're almost closed, Detective," Matthew said. "Angela's finishing up the kitchen."

"And you are . . ." She took out a small notepad.

"Matthew McConnell," he said. "I'm Angela's business partner, lawyer, and boyfriend." Matthew seated Novak in his booth, then sat across from her.

"You're the infamous Matthew McConnell," Novak said. "Barbara doesn't like you very much, does she?"

"Nope," Matthew said.

Novak looked around. "The attack happened here in the dining area?"

"On the back stairs," Matthew said, "but I'll let Angela tell you about it."

Angela came out of the kitchen, poured Novak a tall cup of house blend, and brought the cup to her. "Hello," she said quietly.

Novak nodded and took a sip. "Thank you."

Angela locked the front door and joined them, taking Matthew's hand under the table.

"Miss Smith," Novak said, "thank you for calling."

"I don't know if I'll be any help," Angela said. "It happened four years ago."

Should I be here for this? "If you'd rather talk to Detective Novak alone, I can start mopping out here."

Angela gripped Matthew's hand. "I want you with me."

"I will stay then," Matthew said.

Novak took another sip of her coffee. "As her lawyer?"

"No," Matthew said. "As her friend."

"Okay," Novak said. "First, I need to see where the attack took place."

"It happened . . ." Angela slid out of the booth. "In the back."

They walked around the counter into the kitchen.

"I had different doors back here then," Angela said, pointing at the two steel doors.

"How were they different?" Novak asked.

"The back door had little glass inserts on the upper half, twelve, I think," Angela said. "It was all wood below."

"What kind of lock did you have on your old door?" Novak asked.

Angela sighed. "It was only a single deadbolt, and there was only one chain."

Novak wrote it down. "Take me through the attack."

Angela looked toward the stove. "I locked the front door and turned off the shop lights as I always do and came back here." She looked at the floor. "I saw broken glass here." She pointed to the floor near the door. "But since the deadbolt was still locked and the chain was up, I thought maybe a bird had knocked out a pane of glass. That had happened before. I keep my windows clean." She fumbled with her hands. "I was pretty tired that night. A lot of people were stocking up on coffee and sweets before and during the snowstorm. I got a broom and a dustpan and started sweeping up when the door going upstairs . . ." She pointed at the stairway door. "That one. It was a cheap wood door then, and it was never locked." She swallowed. "That door flew open . . . and he came out."

"Did he have a weapon?" Novak asked.

"No," Angela said.

Novak skipped back in her notes. "You described him as six-three, six-four, and maybe two-fifty, wearing a black ski mask. Can you describe what else he was wearing?"

"He was wearing dark jeans, snow boots, a big puffy jacket, and black leather gloves," Angela said.

More new information. I may get the whole story tonight for the first time. I don't know if I want to hear the whole story.

"Then what happened?" Novak asked.

"He dragged me by my hair and neck up the stairs to the landing and closed the door behind him," Angela said.

"Show me," Novak said.

She opened the stairway door, the light blinding. "I didn't have that light here then. It was pretty dark."

Novak shielded her eyes. "Go on."

"He . . . he pinned me into the corner of the landing with his body," Angela said. "He had one hand on the back of my neck, and he . . ." She closed her eyes. "He pulled down my pants."

"Did he say anything to you?" Novak asked.

Angela opened her eyes and started shaking. "He said, 'Dis da way you like it? You gonna like what I got to give you.' "

Novak wrote rapidly. "He said that exactly."

"I won't ever forget it," Angela whispered.

"You're absolutely sure," Novak said.

"Yes," Angela said.

Novak underlined the quote.

Novak jumped on that piece of information. Matthew had trouble feeling his hands. *Warrick had to have been here four years ago.*

Novak stepped around Angela and looked up the stairs, taking several more notes. "What happened next?"

"I felt him . . . I felt his penis against me," Angela said, her voice shaking. "He, um, he came before he could . . . before he could rape me."

"He didn't rape you," Novak said.

"No," Angela said. "He didn't."

"You're sure." Novak stared into Angela's eyes. "You're absolutely sure."

"I'm sure," Angela said, sighing. "Because that's when I kicked back with my right heel and hit him hard in the balls."

Novak blinked. "You're sure you kicked him there."

Angela nodded. "He dropped to the landing, screaming and

holding his . . . package, and that's when I pulled up my pants, kneed him in the nose, and ran out into the snow." She looked at Matthew. "I drove my knee into his face. I had forgotten that. I broke his nose. No wonder there was so much blood on the landing. All this time I thought it was mine."

"You broke his nose and you're just now remembering it?" Novak asked.

Angela focused on Novak. "I have PTSD because of the attack." She looked at Matthew. "It's about time I admitted it, huh?"

Matthew nodded. *She junked his junk* and *fractured his face. I love this woman! She doesn't need a Taser or a hammer.*

Novak wrote it down. "You've been diagnosed."

Angela nodded. "By Dr. Kenneth Penn. He comes to see me or I call him to come see me. I haven't been out of my shop much since the attack. Matthew has been helping me get outside again. I've been having flashbacks since the blizzard we had recently. I still don't remember everything that happened four years ago, but Dr. Penn says that eventually I will."

Novak tapped her notepad with her pen. "What happened next?"

Angela stepped off the landing into the kitchen. "I ran this way and tore open the back door. I broke the chain I pulled so hard. Then I ran out into the snow trying to find help, but I couldn't find anyone. I was outside for hours, I don't know how many. I watched from the back alley to see if he was still inside, and eventually I came back in."

Novak stepped into the kitchen. "We'll need to get some crime techs out here in the morning."

"I don't know if it will do any good," Angela said. "I scrubbed the landing with bleach."

"We might still be able to find some of his blood and maybe even some of his semen," Novak said. "It might have had time to soak into the wood before you cleaned it."

"Will they . . . will they disrupt my business?" Angela asked.

"I can meet you with the techs back here," Novak said. "We'll try to be discreet. Do you still have the clothes you were wearing?"

"No," Angela said. "I burned them all."

Novak nodded. "Did you burn your shoes, too?"

"I threw them out," Angela said. "They were ruined."

Novak shook her head slightly. "Why didn't you report this?"

"I was . . . I was ashamed," Angela said, pulling on her fingers. "I was afraid. I was angry for not protecting myself. And since I wasn't raped or really hurt, I tried to forget about it. When I read the story in the paper, I decided to let you know."

Novak closed her notepad. "You should have reported this four years ago."

Angela nodded. "I know. I . . . excuse me." She ran up the stairs, slamming the apartment door behind her.

What a rotten thing to say! I know she should have, and so does Angela. Some things should always go unspoken.

"Is she all right?" Novak asked.

"What do you think?" Matthew asked. "Of course she's not okay."

"Is she on any kind of medication?" Novak asked.

"No." He looked at the ceiling when he heard the toilet flushing upstairs.

"Should she be?" Novak asked.

He stared at Novak. "I'm not her psychiatrist."

"I know that," Novak said.

Matthew left the kitchen for the dining area.

Novak followed him to the booth. "Do you know if Dr. Penn prescribed anything for her?"

Matthew sat. "She's not taking anything."

Novak sat across from him. "We'll need her to come down to look at a lineup."

"I don't know if she's capable of that yet," Matthew said. "She won't close the shop, and she can barely walk three blocks away from here without panicking. But if Warrick was wearing a ski mask and attacked her from behind, a lineup would be useless."

"She obviously got at least a glimpse of him, right?" Novak said. "And if we *don't* have her do a lineup, the defense will say she never identified him in a lineup."

True. "She might recognize his voice."

"After four years? I doubt it." Novak sipped her coffee. "All the guys we had in the lineup were from Williamsburg, and they all sounded alike to me."

Matthew nodded. "Do you think this is the same guy?"

"I can't say for sure," Novak said, "but it's looking like it. The man hasn't changed his script. He waits for a snowstorm. He uses a similar method of entry, usually through an old back door. He breaks into a store, most often in a back alley, locks up behind him, and the victim thinks she's safe. He says almost the same exact words to each victim. We think he's been at it since 2006." She sipped some coffee. "But in these recent attacks, he only simulated the rapes."

Matthew blinked. "He didn't rape them?"

Novak shook her head.

"Because . . ." *Holy shit!* "Because Angela junked his junk."

"An interesting way to put it," Novak said. "It may be the reason, it may not be."

"Have you checked?" Matthew asked.

"I wouldn't touch Warrick if you paid me a billion dollars," Novak said. "He's slimy."

"You have to check," Matthew said. "Maybe some hospital has a record of his injury, or he has to take Viagra or something."

Novak nodded. "It's a possibility." She wrote down the information.

"What about his nose?" Matthew asked.

"That thing's been broken so many times he can probably fold it all the way to his ears," Novak said.

"Does Warrick have a public defender?" Matthew asked.

"You aren't thinking of defending him, are you?" Novak said.

"No, of course not." *What a stupid question to ask me!*

"Warrick has somehow retained Avery Filardi," Novak said. "He's taking Warrick's case pro bono."

She has to be kidding. Filardi normally represents a much higher class of thug, mostly corporate types. "Why would Filardi agree to represent Warrick?"

"Who knows?" Novak said. "Filardi loves the spotlight, and this could be a spotlight case. You know how he likes to put his Botoxed face on TV."

Why would any lawyer take a case he couldn't win unless he could *win it somehow?* "What did Warrick plead?"

"Not guilty," Novak said. "Filardi is already pushing to get Warrick's charges reduced to breaking and entering and *menacing* in the third degree."

"Menacing?" Matthew said. "That's bullshit."

"I know," Novak said.

Matthew shook his head, sighing. "Menacing, not rape."

"You're a lawyer," Novak said. "What's Filardi up to?"

"If I was him, and I'm not," Matthew said, "I'd probably push Warrick's inability to get it up. It would go something like this: How can my client be a rapist if he can't physically get it up?"

"He doesn't have to get it up for it to be considered rape," Novak said.

"I know that," Matthew said. "And you know no jury in Brooklyn will accept menacing after what he's done. If the other women were as shaken up as Angela still is, their testimonies should put him away for life."

"That's what we're hoping, provided we can keep these women interested in testifying," Novak said. "They each want to put it behind them, much like Angela has done. We had to dig one of the victim's clothing from her garbage, and she had already washed them. All of them are still scared of the guy. That's why we need as much physical evidence as we can find. When would be a good time for us to return tomorrow?"

"We open at six," Matthew said.

"We'll see you then," Novak said. "If she remembers anything else, let me know." She handed him her card.

"I will."

Matthew mopped the dining area, turned out all the lights, went up the apartment, and found Angela balled up on the couch. She stared blankly at the window, her arms grasping her knees. "Angela, none of the other women was raped."

Angela turned slowly from the window. "They weren't?"

"Nope." He sat in the chair and smiled. "He couldn't get it up."

"What?" Angela released her legs and sat up.

"Mr. Warrick did not have a working member, his soldier would not rise to attention, his John Thomas was asleep, he has a nonfunctioning penis," Matthew said. "I think you damaged his manhood beyond repair, Miss Smith."

"But he still tried to force himself on them," Angela said. "Isn't that still considered rape?"

Matthew nodded.

Angela bounced her head on the back of the couch. "I should have told somebody. The fear those women are feeling right now is because I was too afraid to tell anybody back then."

"You're telling people now, Angela." He left the chair and stood in front of her. "Feel like taking a walk?"

"I don't feel like walking tonight," Angela said.

"It's warmer out tonight," Matthew said. "Stars are shining everywhere."

"I'm tired," Angela whispered.

He knelt in front of her. "They *got* him, Angela. They *got* the man who attacked you. He's locked up. He's not out there anymore."

"How do you know?" Angela asked.

"Novak told me about the other attacks, and they follow the same script," Matthew said. "They've got him."

"I'm just . . . I'm just tired. Really. Aren't you?" She held out her hands. "Just hold me for a while, okay?"

"Okay."

He turned off lights and snuggled with Angela on the couch, rubbing her back until she fell asleep.

"You had a big, breakthrough day," he whispered. "Sleep well."

But when he woke several hours later, he couldn't find her in the apartment. He opened the stairway door, a wave of bleach assaulting his nose. He squinted through the blinding light and saw her.

Angela was scrubbing the landing with a brush and a bucket, a towel wrapped around her neck.

He crept down the stairs. "Angela, what are you doing?"

Angela kept scrubbing.

He sat two stairs up from her. "Angela."

She looked up briefly and continued to scrub.

"Angela, the crime techs are coming in the morning," Matthew said softly. "You might be destroying evidence."

She dipped the brush into the bucket then slapped the brush onto the landing.

"Why are you doing that?" Matthew whispered.

She scrubbed the baseboards. "Habit."

"It looks clean, Angela," Matthew said. "Come back to bed."

Angela slumped into the corner. "But I still see the blood, Matthew. I know it's not there, but I still see it."

"Angela, was any of it your blood?" Matthew asked.

"No," she said. "It was all his. I shattered his nose. Don't you believe me?"

"I believe you." *I have no other choice.*

"They're wasting their time here anyway," Angela said. "They won't find anything."

What else can they check? "Did you ever go to the doctor about your heel or your bruises?"

"No. I stopped going out, remember?" Angela said. "My heel only hurt for a day or two. I'm lucky I was wearing some pretty heavy boots that day."

Boots? She wore boots? "You wore boots, not shoes."

She dropped the brush into the bucket and started drying the landing. "It had been snowing, right? There was a blizzard going on outside. I wore boots. I had shoveled the sidewalk off and on all day when I could. I didn't want anyone tracking in snow." She stopped drying the landing. "I was wearing my daddy's boots all day that day."

"You said you threw out some *shoes,*" Matthew said.

She glanced into the corner of the landing. "I did throw out a pair of shoes. I kept them over there in the corner." She flattened her hand on the spot. "Here. They were white Nikes. They had blood on them."

"You threw *those* shoes away," Matthew said.

Angela nodded.

"But you didn't throw out the boots," Matthew said.

"No." She looked up at him. "I wouldn't have. They were my daddy's boots."

And they might be upstairs right now! "Where are the boots now?" Matthew asked.

Angela looked past Matthew. "I put them back in his closet."

In a room she never goes in. "Have you worn them since?"

Angela shook her head. "No. I haven't needed to wear them, right?"

Matthew remembered the layers of dust in her parents' room. "When's the last time you were in their room?"

Angela squinted. "Not since that night."

"Do you want to see if they're still there?"

Angela nodded. "Yes."

Angela rose, Matthew took her hand, and they went up the stairs and to her parents' door. He opened it, turned on the light, and only saw a few of his footprints in the doorway from when he had borrowed the mirror from the back of the door.

Angela pointed at the closet. "They should be in there."

If they're in there, and I'll bet they are, we can't disturb them. "We'll let the techs check tomorrow."

"Why?" Angela asked.

"There may be some of his blood or fluids on them," Matthew said, "and the amount of dust in here proves that you haven't been in this room for a long time. We have to preserve the evidence."

"There can't be anything on those boots," Angela said. "I ran around in the snow for hours. Whatever might have been on them washed off in the snow."

"Describe the boots," Matthew said.

"Green, rubber, black laces," Angela said. "They came up to my knees. My daddy's tall."

"Maybe some of Warrick's blood soaked into the laces," Matthew said. "How deep was the snow that night?"

"Deep. I was up to my knees." She shivered.

"There's always a chance," Matthew said, and he shut the door. "Let's get you to bed."

"It's almost time for me to get up anyway," Angela said.

"Just for a little while." He led her to the bed, letting her become his blanket.

"What do I say when Detective Novak asks me about the boots?" Angela asked.

"Tell the truth," Matthew whispered. "Tell her you just remembered."

"She won't believe that, Matthew," Angela said.

"She'll have to," Matthew said.

"I don't think she believed a word I said," Angela said.

He rubbed her back. "It's in her job description to be suspicious of everything. She'll believe you." *Eventually.*

Angela sighed. "I hope to God I don't have to testify."

"Why?" Matthew asked.

"Why? Because I'm crazy, Matthew." She held him more tightly. "I scrub a clean floor with bleach. I must have scrubbed that floor five hundred times. I avoid a room for four years for no reason, and now I know it's because of some boots. I don't go outside. I have more locks on my doors than most prisons do."

He held her face in his hands. "That's not crazy. You're protecting yourself from something you don't want to relive. That's nowhere near crazy. That's completely sane."

"Detective Novak thinks I'm crazy." She shrugged off the covers. "I'm getting up."

"Now *that's* crazy," Matthew said. "You just got warmed up."

"I smell like bleach," Angela said. "And it's almost four o'clock. I need my routines."

Matthew squeezed her hips. "What about this routine?"

"I have to warm up the ovens," she whispered.

"That's what I'm trying to do," he whispered.

Angela smiled. "And I appreciate it. I do." She slid out of the covers and stood.

"Could I help you?" Matthew asked.

"Do what?" Angela said.

"Get that bleach smell off you." He squeezed her booty.

Angela sighed.

"I'll soap myself up and let you use me as your washcloth," Matthew said.

"No thank you," Angela said.

She went into the bathroom and turned on the shower.

Matthew lay back on the bed. *I'd let her be* my *washcloth. Her soft, silken skin rubbing on me would definitely wake me up.* He got up and checked the bathroom door. *Locked.* He sighed. *God, help us get through this day.*

It might be a hard one.

Chapter 33

Two hours later, the crime techs arrived at the back door of the shop and immediately went to work, photographing the stairway and taking samples from the landing, the back stairs, the stairway walls, and both doorframes, all out of sight of any customers or Angela on her stool at the counter. They even pried up several boards on the landing to swab underneath.

Matthew beckoned Detective Novak to him after the floorboards were back in place. "Angela remembered something else last night."

"What?" Novak asked.

"They're upstairs," he said. "And bring someone with a camera."

"What's upstairs?" Novak asked.

"You'll see." He led her to Angela's parents' door.

"What's in there?" Novak asked.

"Evidence, I hope." Matthew opened the door. "First, take pictures of where my feet have been." He squatted and pointed. "I'm the only person who's been in this room in four years. Angela has avoided this room since the night of the attack."

The tech took several shots of Matthew's footprints.

"What evidence is in here, McConnell?" Novak asked.

"In the closet are the *boots* Angela was wearing that night," he said. "She wasn't wearing shoes. She was wearing her daddy's boots."

"She's sure?" Novak asked.

"Yes," Matthew said. "She threw out some shoes she had in the corner down there because they had his blood on them. She had been shoveling snow and wore the boots all day."

The techs put on booties and latex gloves before entering, taking pictures as they moved carefully toward the closet. While one opened the closet door, the other took pictures while another scanned the carpet behind them.

"They should be green," Matthew said.

"They're here," a tech said.

The other tech took several more close-ups of the boots and then bagged and sealed them.

A tech brought the boots to Novak.

"They fit her?" Novak asked.

"I'm sure she clunked around in them," Matthew said. "They belonged to her father."

"Get them analyzed," Novak said to the techs, and they left the apartment.

Matthew's phone buzzed. He heard the standard computerized jail recording and accepted the call. *Jade sure is persistent.* "This is Matthew McConnell. How may I help you?"

"You da coffeehouse lawyer dat lives at Smith's Sweet Treats on Driggs, right?" asked a gravelly voice.

That's definitely not Jade. "I do business at Smith's Sweet Treats, yes. Who is this, and how can I—"

"Business," the man interrupted. "Right. Third booth. You sure do like your pastries and turnovers. You oughta lay off the coffee. It'll rot your stomach."

Someone has been watching me. "How may I help you?"

"How's your girlfriend doing?" the man asked. "Haven't seen her go outside much in a coupla years. Four years, right? She afraid of her own shadow or what?"

Warrick. Matthew motioned Novak into the bedroom and turned on the speaker. "Please state your business, Mr. Warrick."

"You recognized me," Warrick said. "Yeah, dey tell me you're real sharp."

Novak nodded, checked her watch, and began taking notes

"It was stupid of you to give up all dat money with Schwartz, Yevgeny, and Ginsberg, but to each his own," Warrick said. "I also hear you and Angie are shacking up. What are you, her guard dog?"

"State your business, Mr. Warrick," Matthew said through gritted teeth.

"Have da techies left yet?" Warrick asked. "I'll bet dey haven't. Dey ain't gonna find nothing. My date with Angie was a long time ago."

Warrick admits he was here. What a fool! "It wasn't a date, Mr. Warrick. You broke in and attacked her."

"Angie is a little firecracker," Warrick said with a low laugh. "She liked it rough, the rougher the better. But you should know dat, right? I heard you shouting up a storm da other night."

The footprints in the snow.

Warrick came here after the storm, and he was down there the first night I was up here in the apartment. He wrote a note on Novak's notepad: "He was in alley during/after storm."

"You know, it's kinda funny," Warrick said. "I coulda got *her* for assault. My poor nose."

"Which she broke *after* you assaulted her," Matthew said.

"Angie told you she invited me in, right?" Warrick asked.

Not in a million years. "You broke a window to get inside, Mr. Warrick."

"I don't remember it dat way," Warrick said. "I remember her opening da door for me with a big smile on her face, kinda like she used to do for you every morning before you two started playing house."

He's been spying on us for weeks! "What do you want, Mr. Warrick?"

"Angie sure walks fast, don't she?" Warrick asked. "I've had trouble keeping up."

And he's been following us. Angela was right to be paranoid.

"I just wanted to talk to you about our date," Warrick said. "Yeah, it was some date. We started out okay. Angie dropped dem panties in a flash. Angie got a nice ass, don't she? Nice and round and brown. But den she changed her mind and somehow da window got broke. I'm pretty sure she broke it with her hand. And, man, did she want me, oh yeah, she *wanted* me, and den . . . she didn't. Angie knew she couldn't handle me. There she was, open for business, if you get my drift, and den suddenly she was closed for da night."

I'm getting tired of this bullshit! "You're going to get life," Matthew said, "and I hope they put you in with the general population."

"You know I won't get life, Matty-boy," Warrick said. "I may get a few years, three or four tops, and my lawyer will make sure I'm in protective custody da entire time. I can do four years standing on my head. Bet Angie won't even be able to go outside for the next ten years." Warrick laughed. "I'll be out before she will!"

Matthew bit back a string of curses. "You're out of your mind."

"Angie's the one seeing that doctor, not me," Warrick said. "At first I thought he was her boyfriend, but he's too old for her. He got some cool snowshoes, though. I gotta get me some of dem. It'd make it easier to cover my tracks."

Warrick has been everywhere and watching everybody. He's beyond obsessed with Angela. "You're insane."

"Nah," Warrick said. "We thought about using dat defense, but I won't need it. Filardi says it's important da jury sees me as an ordinary, normal guy. Filardi says I'm da victim in all dis." Warrick laughed. "Dat's right, *I'm* da victim. The DA needed a scapegoat, so dey arrested me. Filardi says we're gonna embarrass a lot of people. I can't wait for dat to happen. Hey, my time's almost up. In more ways dan one. You know Filardi is gonna get my bail reduced, and I'll be out looking for a good cup of Angela's coffee in no time."

I wouldn't mind him showing up here. Angela has lots of weapons now, and I'm one of them. "You do that. I'll be here."

"You ain't nothing, Matty-boy," Warrick said.

"Test me," Matthew said.

Novak shook her head.

Matthew turned away from her. "I look forward to meeting you face-to-face, or are you too much of a coward? You like hiding in alleys and preying on defenseless women. Really, Warrick. Calling you a pussy would be a compliment."

"It's been real good talking with you, *Matthew*. Dat's what she calls you, right? *Matthew. Oh, Matthew.* Say hello to Angie for me. You know, if you weren't banging the hell out of Angie, I mighta asked you to be my lawyer."

"I would *never* represent you, *Robbie,*" Matthew said.

"Hey, anything can be arranged, right?" Warrick said. "I think I'll tell this to Filardi, see if he can get you to join my defense team. Gotta go. Oh yeah, one more thing. Ask Angie what she said to me dat night. She was sure talking up a storm. Get it? A snowstorm outside, and your little girlfriend couldn't stop talking up a storm to me. 'Give me what you got, big boy,' Angie said. 'Don't keep me waiting all night.' "

Click.

Matthew turned to Novak. "She would never have said that."

Novak checked her watch and wrote down the time. "We'll have to ask her."

"You believe him?" Matthew asked.

"It adds to his admission that he was here that night," Novak said. "If she corroborates what he said *she* said, then—"

"She didn't say it," Matthew interrupted.

"We still have to ask her." She closed her notepad. "What I can't understand is why Warrick would call you."

"To taunt me," Matthew said. "That's how he gets off."

"Or to put doubt in *your* mind in case you were called to testify," Novak said.

"I have no doubts," Matthew said. "But why would I ever be called? I wasn't there, right?"

"If this PTSD thing is for real," Novak said, "you could be called—"

"It *is* real," Matthew interrupted. "And Dr. Penn would testify to that, not me."

"You don't want to help her?" Novak asked.

"Of course I do," Matthew said. "I could talk about the phone call I just got from Warrick."

Novak pocketed her notepad. "And you wouldn't even have to do that. We record all inmate calls. All we have to do is play it in court. And if we find his blood or DNA anywhere, especially on those boots, we've got him."

Or do we? Warrick had to know the call was being taped. I'll bet Filardi told him to call me so he could establish the idea of a date. "His DNA or blood will only prove Angela busted his nose or that he prematurely ejaculated. It won't prove he attacked her. And Filardi will make everything sound consensual. It's ultimately Warrick's word against Angela's."

"We have evidence from the other attacks," Novak said. "We have eyewitnesses. We have a pattern."

"But you have no evidence that Angela *didn't* invite Warrick inside the shop and later changed her mind," Matthew said.

"Whose side are you on, McConnell?" Novak asked.

"Yours and Angela's, of course, but even a rookie public defender could poke holes in Angela's story," Matthew said.

"We might even have evidence outside waiting to be found right now." She walked to the window. "The techs are in the alley now."

"What could they find?" Matthew asked. "It's been weeks since the blizzard."

"Warrick chain-smokes," Novak said. "Pall Malls exclusively. We might get lucky and find one of his cigarette butts."

"And what will that prove?" Matthew asked. "That he's a peeping Tom?"

Novak shrugged. "Juries don't like peeping Tom's, do they? Or stalkers. Let's go talk to Angela again."

Matthew blocked the doorway. "She had a rough night. Could you talk to her some other time?"

"I have other cases I'm working, McConnell," Novak said. "How rough a night did she have?"

"She was cleaning the landing with bleach early this morning," Matthew said. "It's part of her routine. It keeps her sane. She says she can still see the blood."

Novak frowned. "What is she trying to hide? I'm beginning to think that maybe something more happened on that back stairway than she's telling us."

"I believe what she told me." *I have to. That belief keeps* me *sane.*

"McConnell, I've been doing this a long time," Novak said. "Rape victims don't always tell the whole truth, to protect their reputations. It's still possible she was raped, and from what we know of these recent attacks, she might be the *only* woman Warrick *ever* raped. We need her testimony to be solid."

I don't want to think about it. "Angela says she wasn't raped. That's enough for me."

"She's obviously not one hundred percent sure what happened that night," Novak said. "She was sure she threw out shoes but forgot she was wearing boots too big for her on one of the snowiest days in the history of New York City. If she forgot *that* key point, she may be blocking out—"

"Stop, just stop," Matthew interrupted. "She's the victim. Don't forget that. Angela is the victim."

"I know that," Novak said. "But Filardi wouldn't dream of letting her be the victim on the stand, would he?"

Matthew sighed. "No. He'd probably make her the aggressor." *He'd torture her.*

"We have to ask her what she said to Warrick that night," Novak said.

She's right. As distasteful as the question will be, we have to ask. Matthew stepped aside. "Don't be surprised if she doesn't remember."

They waited in the kitchen doorway until Angela wasn't busy. When Angela entered the kitchen, she looked through the window over the sink. "Why are they in the alley?"

"Warrick may have been back there recently," Novak said.

Angela turned to Matthew. "He was?"

"He's been watching us," Matthew said. "He just called me from the jail."

Angela wheeled on Novak. "They let him do that?"

"He has the right to make phone calls," Novak said, "even if we don't think he deserves to have that right."

"Angela," Matthew said, "he knows quite a bit about us. He's been watching us for weeks, and he may have been in the alley the other night during or just after the storm."

Angela held her elbows tightly. "He was coming back to finish the job."

I don't even want to consider that possibility. "He didn't, did he?" Matthew asked.

Angela breathed heavily.

"He didn't, *did* he?" Matthew repeated.

"No." She looked at Matthew. "No, he didn't."

"He's too much of a coward anyway," Matthew said. "The techs are out there hoping to find something he may have left behind."

"Like what?" Angela asked.

"Cigarettes," Novak said. "Pall Malls."

"He smoked a lot," Angela said.

Novak took out her notepad. "How do you know this?"

Angela leaned back on the sink. "I smelled like smoke afterward. My clothes smelled like smoke. That's one reason I burned them."

Novak jotted a few notes. "Warrick says you talked to him during the attack."

Angela's eyes widened. "I was screaming at him, that's for sure."

"What did you say to Warrick that night?" Novak asked.

"Why does that matter?" Angela asked. "I was screaming and cursing."

Matthew moved closer. "He says you—and please understand I'm telling you what he told me; I don't believe it—he says you encouraged him with what you said."

"He says I . . ." Angela pushed off the sink. "I didn't. Why would I encourage him to try to rape me?"

Novak flipped back in her notes. "Did you say, 'Give me what you got, big boy. I ain't waiting all night'?"

Angela looked into Matthew's eyes. "Does that even sound like me?"

"No," Matthew said. "It doesn't."

"But maybe you said something *like* that," Novak said.

Angela shook her head repeatedly. "Why would I say anything like that? I was being attacked!"

"What *did* you say to him?" Novak asked.

Angela closed her eyes. "I don't remember."

"Maybe you said something to set him up, you know, to lure him into a false sense of security before you fought back," Novak said.

"I fought back the *entire* time!" Angela shouted. "I had bruises all over me afterward! I thought he was going to *kill* me!" She threw a towel into the sink, then rubbed the back of her neck, staring into the alley. "He wouldn't *do* anything. He just kept pressing on me, pushing me, pinning my head into the corner. All he did was talk, talk, talk. He kept threatening and threatening. 'You want dis, don't you, bitch? You never had nothing like dis. You're gonna wish you had some of dis every night.' He wouldn't shut up!"

Did Angela grow impatient? His taunting was part of the torture. Did she want the torture to end? "Did you say *anything* to him, Angela?"

"He was pressing up on me so hard." She dropped her head, tears spilling into the sink. "He told me to say, 'Give me what you got, big boy,' and he said he'd let me go. I wouldn't say it. I cursed him, and he pressed up on me harder. I could barely breathe." She turned. "Matthew, I didn't want to say it."

"He *made* you say it," Matthew said. "I know you didn't want to."

"I *had* to," Angela pleaded. "I was afraid I'd pass out. He was squeezing the back of my neck and crushing me. That's when I finally said it. And that's also when I got angry. I cursed him again and I said, 'I ain't waiting all night, motherfucker! You gonna do it or jack off in your pants? Give me what you got, big boy!' "

Novak wrote furiously. "You said those exact words."

Angela nodded.

"Did you relax?" Novak asked.

"What do you mean?" Angela shouted.

"Did you quit fighting him?" Novak asked.

Angela balled up her hands into fists. "Just long enough for him to think he was going to succeed. That's when he came all over my back and I kicked the living shit out his balls. As soon as that motherfucker hit the ground, he starting crying like a bitch, and I kneed him so hard in the nose I thought I killed him. I wished I had." She blinked rapidly. "Oh shit. I'm sorry. I, um . . . I don't normally talk like that."

Novak put her notepad away. "You were angry. I would have said a lot worse."

Angela looked briefly at Matthew. "But I encouraged him."

"*After* he tortured and threatened you," Novak said.

"But I still let him think he could have me," Angela said.

"You survived, Angela," Novak said. "You did what you had to do to survive."

Angela ran to Matthew and held him, weeping and shaking. "I'm sorry."

"You have nothing to be sorry for," Matthew said, rubbing her back. "You did the only thing you could do. No one on earth can ever blame you." He lifted her chin. "You hurt him for life. You took away his manhood. You're a hero, Angela. And when they convict the motherfucker . . ."

Angela wiped her eyes. "You never use that word."

"That's what Warrick is," Matthew said. "When they convict him and send him away for a long, long time, you *will* be there to see it."

Chapter 34

So that Angela would not have to appear in front of a grand jury, Novak arranged for a video team to come to the shop the next night after closing to tape Angela telling her story.

Her testimony was a carbon copy of her statement to Novak and Matthew, only without most of the cursing.

When it was all over, Matthew asked, "Do you feel better?"

"Some," Angela said quietly.

"You know daylight saving time began over the weekend," he said. "You can still see the sunset."

"I feel like walking tonight," she said. "I feel like going for a long walk."

Yes! "Where do you want to go?" Matthew asked.

"Wherever you take me," she said.

Shoot. It's too late for Catbird to be open. "Do you mind if we wander?"

"I don't mind at all," Angela said.

They wandered six full blocks north to 6th Street and The Cove as the sunset painted the western sky every shade of the rainbow.

"I have never danced with you, Angela," Matthew said. "Want to dance a little?"

She peered at the crowd inside. "It looks so crowded."

"I'm only going to focus on you," Matthew said. "Those people don't exist. But if you say the word, we'll leave immediately."

She took his hand. "Promise?"

"I promise."

While the hip and trendy crowd bounced off the ceilings, the walls, and each other at The Cove, Angela and Matthew stayed locked together in a less crowded, somewhat quieter space, embracing, kissing, and sighing while the lights bathed them in green.

"I don't really think we're dancing," Angela said during a rare slow song, Keith Sweat's "Nobody."

"What are we doing, then?" Matthew whispered, sucking on her earlobe.

"Grinding," Angela said, squeezing his left thigh with her legs. "I don't know about you, but I'm doing some serious foreplay." She slid her hands into his back pockets. "I'm imagining you inside me."

"You are?" Matthew whispered. "Where are your legs?"

"Up on your shoulders," Angela whispered, squeezing his booty.

"Way up there, huh?" He kissed her neck. "And what am I doing?"

"You're making love to me." She bit her lower lip. "And I'm about to come."

"Yeah?" Matthew whispered.

She squeezed his booty hard. "I'm about to come right now."

Matthew smiled. "Really?"

She arched her back away from him, her legs squeezing on his left thigh. "I am so wet," she whispered. "Oh shit." She snatched her hands from his pockets, pulled down his head, and tried to suck Matthew's tongue out of his head.

"Did you just . . ."

Angela nodded. "We have to go home now, okay?"

Matthew nodded and took her hand.

Matthew didn't mind the race back to Angela's apartment, and he certainly didn't mind when Angela disrobed and hopped up onto the back of the couch. She guided him inside her, resting her legs on his shoulders while gripping the couch with her hands.

"Make love to me," she whispered.

"This couch is exactly the right height," Matthew whispered, plunging in and out.

"I feel weightless," Angela whispered. "Go deeper."

Matthew ground as deeply as he dared, pulling on her booty. "Damn, you feel nice."

"Harder," she panted. "Harder."

Matthew threw his hips into her again and again. Angela's mouth was open, her eyes rolling back.

"I don't want this to end," Matthew whispered.

Angela pushed him back, turning and resting her stomach on the back of the couch.

"Are you sure?" Matthew asked.

She looked back. "Yes."

Matthew kissed both her cheeks, straightened, and entered her, holding her hips lightly. "You okay?"

Angela didn't look back. "Yes." She reached back and squeezed his booty. "Don't be shy. I won't break."

He squeezed her hips as she slammed her booty back into him repeatedly.

"Yes," Angela panted. "Yes!"

A few thrusts later, Matthew lifted Angela into the air and carried her back to the bed, sitting opposite the mirror as Angela rose and fell in front of him, his hands squeezing her breasts, her hands busy below.

"I'm close," he whispered, looking at Angela's eyes in the mirror.

"Me, too," she whispered.

"Let's do this together then," Matthew whispered. "Angela . . ."

They came together, finding each other's hands, rocking back and forth.

Angela smiled.

Matthew smiled.

There was nothing left to say except . . .

"I love you, Angela."

"I love you, Matthew."

Angela slept beside him through the night.

She didn't have a single nightmare.

Chapter 35

Matthew and Angela fell into a blissful routine that left them both exhausted, yet content. After working all day, they walked into the night as far as Angela wanted to go. They went fifteen blocks north to Vinnie's to eat some pizza. They bowled a few games at The Gutter before watching an entire game of kickball at McCarren Park more than half a mile away from the shop. They walked west, hand-in-hand, to eat salmon mozzarella rolls at One or Eight and to sip mai tais at a midnight showing of *Big Trouble in Little China* at indieScreen. They even walked halfway across the Williamsburg Bridge to watch the boats and bathe in the lights of Manhattan.

If I had the ring, I would have proposed there. But who proposes on the Williamsburg Bridge? The Brooklyn Bridge, maybe.

Whenever they finally returned to Angela's apartment, they reinvented the *Kama Sutra,* adding a few more positions they practiced in front of the mirror long into the night and early morning. They were very good at practicing. It reminded Matthew of a never-ending game of Twister.

They did lots of laundry together.

They even shared the hot water in the shower.

Angela was a *very* good washcloth.

When La Estrella began offering coupons on the first day of spring, Angela was ecstatic. "Coupons are the last act of desperation before a business closes for good," she said. "I am winning this coffee war."

As the weather changed and Williamsburg warmed and turned green, Matthew's caseload picked up.

Unfortunately, most of his cases involved divorce.

I thought spring was the time of year for love. Evidently, people are tired of old love and want new love in springtime.

A couple straight out of *The Sopranos* came into Angela's shop one day, the woman dressed in too-high heels and too-tight jeans, her jet-black eyebrows visible under stacked blond hair, the man wearing a long, black-leather jacket and sporting an Elvis pompadour.

"You the marriage counselor?" he asked Matthew.

"I don't want counseling," the woman said. "I want a divorce."

"Let's see what he says first," the man said.

Is it my turn to speak? "Please be seated."

The man sat opposite Matthew, and the woman reluctantly slid in beside the man, saying, "Move over."

The man didn't move.

The woman sat on the edge of the seat rolling her eyes.

Nice guy. "What are your names?" Matthew asked.

"Jacobo and Sandy Antonelli," Jacobo said. "We drove all the way up from Dyker Heights to see you."

Was that a challenge? Matthew slid over two copies of his fee schedule. "Here are my fees." He let them look at the prices before asking, "Mr. Antonelli, what makes you think you two need counseling?"

Jacobo straightened his jacket. "We just hit a glitch in our marriage, nothing major. A glitch."

"You fucked Lorena!" Sandy shouted.

Jacobo turned his head to Sandy. "You fucked Rolando!"

Oh boy. "Please keep the language civil. We're in a public place." *Though these two would probably curse each other during Mass.*

"My apologies," Jacobo said, scowling. "But it's what happened."

"Who's Lorena?" Matthew asked.

"My sister," Sandy said. "My *youngest* sister, barely twenty-one."

Nice. "And who is Rolando?"

"My cousin," Jacobo said.

Family affairs. "And how long have these affairs been going on?" Matthew asked.

"It only happened once, I swear," Sandy said.

"Same here," Jacobo said. "So, one time." He shrugged. "That makes it a glitch. Can you fix us?"

"Jacobo, I want a divorce," Sandy said. "I don't want counseling."

I could charge Jacobo the hourly for the counseling and Sandy the full seven-fifty for the divorce. It would be a package deal. "I'll start with Sandy. Sandy, what led up to the affair?"

"He fu . . ." She looked around. "He *slept* with my sister."

"So as a result," Matthew said, "you slept with Rolando to get back at Jacobo."

"Yeah," Sandy said. "Jacobo doesn't have any brothers I'd sleep with. They ain't handsome at all."

Jacobo shot his cuffs, dropping his arms to the table. "You *wish* you could sleep with my brothers. They would *never* sleep with you. They got character. So who did you end up with? Rolando, a second cousin on my mama's side."

"He's more of a man than you are!" Sandy shouted, waving her long fingernails in Jacobo's face.

"Please, quiet down," Matthew said.

Sandy turned away from Jacobo, crossing her arms. "He started it."

These are grown children. He looked over at Angela, and Angela shook her head sadly.

"Jacobo," Matthew asked calmly, "why do you think the marriage can be saved?"

"It was a one-time deal," Jacobo said. "We both messed up. Water under the bridge. Let bygones be bygones, right? One glitch shouldn't end a marriage."

If only it were that easy. "Sandy, why do you think the marriage *can't* be saved?"

"I can never trust Jacobo again," Sandy said. "He did my sister! In our bed at our house!"

"I told you I thought she was you!" Jacobo shouted.

"She looks nothing like me!" Sandy yelled. "And everybody in *his* family and everybody in *my* family knows he did her. I can't face anyone anymore."

These two need something to keep their hands busy so they don't put their hands on each other. "Want some coffee?"

"Yeah, I guess," Jacobo said.

"Sandy?" Matthew asked.

"Decaf if you got it," Sandy said.

Both of you are getting decaf whether you like it or not. "One moment." Matthew went to the counter, where Angela was already pouring their coffees. "What do you think?"

"They never should have gotten married in the first place," Angela whispered.

"I kind of agree," he said, sighing. "I can't please both of them, though."

"Then don't please *either* of them," Angela said.

Matthew nodded. "That could work. I like that idea." He picked up their cups and put them on the table. He sat and watched them sipping their coffee.

"Good coffee," Sandy said.

"It's all right," Jacobo said. "So, what are we gonna do?"

"Nothing," Matthew said. "Sandy, you don't deserve a divorce."

"What?" Sandy said.

"And Jacobo," Matthew said, "you don't deserve your marriage."

Jacobo slammed down his cup. "What?"

"After what I've heard," Matthew said, "you two should *never* have gotten married in the first place. Never. What were you two thinking?"

"Hey, now," Jacobo said, "at the beginning—"

"As far as I can tell," Matthew interrupted, "you two have absolutely *nothing* in common other than sleeping with family members to get your revenge on each other. You could have done that without a ring and a marriage, right?"

"Jacobo, you gonna let him say that about us?" Sandy asked.

Ah, the protective instinct is kicking in. "Really, what were you thinking, Jacobo? I think I know. On the day you got married, you looked into Sandy's eyes and thought, you know, I think I'll bang her younger sister one day."

Jacobo leaned forward. "I did no such thing!"

"And Sandy, the second after the kiss, you were already lusting for Rolando, weren't you?" Matthew asked.

"Rolando wasn't even at the wedding!" Sandy snapped.

"Hey now, you got no right to say these things about us," Jacobo said. "You hardly know us."

"You cheated on her, right?" Matthew asked.

Jacobo only blinked.

"Right?" Matthew said.

Jacobo nodded.

"She can't trust you," Matthew said. He turned to Sandy. "Sandy, you cheated back. He can't trust you. This is no glitch, Jacobo. This is serious because it involves trust. There is *no* way that either of you can get that trust back, so why even try? This conversation we're having is a waste of time. If I could, I'd dissolve your marriage this second." He opened his briefcase and looked through some papers. "I'll try to find the quickest way to get you two away from each other. Now, are you going to split the cost of the annulment?"

"The what?" Jacobo said.

"The annulment," Matthew repeated.

"It's not on this sheet," Sandy said, tapping on the fee schedule with her nails.

"You weren't listening to me," Matthew said. "I said you two should *never* have been married. Therefore, you should get an annulment instead of a divorce."

"How is that different?" Sandy asked.

"An annulment makes it seem as if the marriage never took place," Matthew said. "It erases everything between you. Each of you goes away with nothing but what you had before the wedding. Your marriage will cease to exist permanently. My annulment fee is two thousand dollars."

"But it's not on the sheet!" Sandy shouted.

"It doesn't happen that often that two people, such as yourselves, are so ill-suited for marriage," Matthew said. "There's nothing left to save, so let's make it go away forever. Two thousand dollars, please."

Jacobo shot a look at Sandy. "But we have two kids. Jacobo Junior and Silvia. Who gets them?"

I will pray for them every night for the rest of my life. "You'll have to put them up for adoption or turn them over to child protective services," Matthew said quickly.

Angela coughed and turned away.

I knew that would get to her. I almost made myself laugh.

"What?" Jacobo shouted.

"Jacobo, if the marriage no longer exists, the children can no longer exist either," Matthew said. "If you want a full annulment, they have to vanish, too."

"Are you crazy?" Sandy shouted.

"No crazier than either of you for getting married in the first place," Matthew said. "Two thousand dollars, please."

Sandy turned out of the booth and jumped to her feet. "Come on, Jacobo! This man is out of his mind!"

Jacobo slid out of the booth and swaggered to the door. "You gotta be the *worst* marriage counselor on earth!"

Matthew stood. "Are you two going to stay married?" he shouted.

Several customers turned from Matthew to Jacobo.

We are so entertaining.

"We *have* to stay married for the kids," Sandy pleaded. She stepped close to Jacobo. "They need their father." She grasped the front of Jacobo's jacket. "I need you, too."

Jacobo put his hands on her shoulders. "I couldn't live without you, Sandy."

Matthew smiled and checked the clock. "That session only lasted fifteen minutes. The charge is twelve-fifty."

A few customers smiled and nodded at Matthew.

Jacobo blinked. "What?"

"The marriage counseling session is over," Matthew said. "Twelve-fifty, please. You can put it in the tip jar."

Sandy pulled Jacobo close. "Pay him, and let's go."

Jacobo put three fives into the tip jar.

Angela gave him two-fifty in change.

Jacobo and Sandy left the shop holding hands.

A few customers clapped.

Matthew bowed slightly and went to the counter. "I heard you coughing during my session, Miss Smith."

Angela laughed. "When you brought up the adoption, I nearly lost it."

"I don't think we'll ever see them again," Matthew said.

"I would have charged them two hundred on principle," Angela said. "I have never had to give out change for money in my tip jar."

"They have kids," Matthew said. "Maybe they'll do something nice for Jacobo Junior and Silvia."

"The way they were looking at each other, I think they're going home to work on child number three," Angela said.

Thanks for the opening. "What about you? Think you should be having a baby?"

"I'm, hmm," Angela said. "I'm not even married, Matthew."

"Do you want to be?" Matthew asked.

Angela rolled her eyes. "Of course."

"Just checking." *I need to make another call to Catbird.*

After the "Antonelli Miracle," word raced through Brooklyn and beyond that a lawyer at Smith's Sweet Treats and Coffee could save anyone's marriage for twelve-fifty over a cup of coffee. Many couples came in skeptical and left holding hands. Several couples returned to thank Matthew; a few even became regular customers.

One couple, Richard and Colleen O'Hara, came for a session that tested Matthew's abilities and tried Matthew's patience. After an hour of forward and reverse psychology, sound arguments and illogical threats, Matthew gave up.

"I think it's hopeless," Matthew said.

"That's what we thought about our marriage, too," Richard said. "You're good, though, Mr. McConnell. You were very convincing. I wish we had used your services earlier."

"Earlier?" Matthew said.

"*Before* our divorce," Colleen said. "It's too late for us. We're already divorced and engaged to other people."

"Nice try, though," Richard said.

"So why did you come?" Matthew asked.

"Just to see," Colleen said. "You actually reinforced all the reasons we got divorced."

"You put everything in perspective," Richard said. "I think I now truly understand the divorce. I didn't understand much of anything while I was going through it."

I made it all clear? I was trying to confuse them into staying together! "You're here together now."

"True." Colleen smiled at Richard. "One of the rare times we actually agreed on something, huh?"

"Yes," Richard said. "You have your fifty?"

"Yes," Colleen said.

Matthew collected the money reluctantly.

"You tried, Mr. McConnell," Colleen said. "But some marriages are simply past saving."

"And you proved it again for us today," Richard said. "Thank you."

I can't admit defeat yet. "You say you're both engaged. Colleen, why isn't your fiancé here, too?"

Colleen looked at her hands. "He doesn't know I'm doing this."

"My fiancée would never understand any of this," Richard said.

Aha! "She's the jealous type, huh?" Matthew asked.

"Very," Richard said.

"And not the brightest bulb either," Colleen said.

Richard didn't disagree with her.

He must be engaged to someone like Joy. "What is she jealous of?" Matthew asked Richard.

"Isn't it obvious?" Richard said. "Colleen is exquisitely beautiful, incredibly intelligent, and infinitely classy."

"Thank you, Richard," Colleen said.

"It's true," Richard said.

Colleen smiled.

I knew there was still something here. "Is your fiancé jealous of Richard?"

Colleen nodded. "Terribly and to the point of irrationality. My fiancé isn't nearly the businessman or the man Richard is. He thinks I compare him to Richard whenever we have sex."

"Do you?" Matthew asked.

Richard smiled. "Yes, Colleen, do you?"

Colleen turned crimson. "Well, I don't *tell* him I'm comparing him to Richard. That would be rude. I only think it."

Richard nudged her with his shoulder. "You still think about me that way."

"Yes," Colleen said, her eyes shining.

"I think about you that way all the time," Richard said. "That's one thing we didn't mess up, huh?"

"No," Colleen said. "We never had any trouble in that department."

Matthew smiled at both of them.

Colleen blinked. "Wait a minute. Mr. McConnell, what are you trying to do here?"

Play dumb. "Do? Here?"

Richard leaned forward, raising his eyebrows. "Yes, what trick is this?"

"There's no trick here," Matthew said. "I'm listening to you two talk. I wouldn't even charge you. It's just three people drinking coffee and talking at a booth in a coffee shop."

"What are you saying?" Richard asked.

"I'm not saying anything," Matthew said. "I'm listening. This is a fascinating conversation you're having. You two are divorced, and yet you're on each other's minds. It's kind of romantic. No, it's *very* romantic. I'm learning a lot from you two about romance."

Richard looked shyly at Colleen. "It *is* kind of romantic when you think about it."

"A little." Colleen glanced at Richard. "It's actually *quite* romantic. I think about you all the time."

"I go to sleep wondering about you every night," Richard said. "Perhaps we could continue this conversation elsewhere."

"I'd like that, Richard." She touched Richard's hand. "I'd really like that." She looked at Matthew. "You may have started something here."

"I didn't start anything," Matthew said. "You two have never ended."

Colleen smiled, resting her hand on Richard's wrist. "He's right. We're not finished."

Richard turned his hand palm up and held Colleen's hand. "No, we're not." He dug out his wallet. "What else do we owe you?" He pulled out another fifty.

I deserve this one. "This will cover it." He took the money.

As they stood beside the booth, Colleen said, "Thank you. I don't know how you did that, but thank you."

"Yeah," Richard said. "How'd you do that?"

"I gave up," Matthew said. "I stopped trying to convince you two to stay together, and you convinced each other."

"It worked," Richard said. "Thank you."

After they left, Angela beckoned Matthew into the kitchen, where she laid a long, hot kiss on him. "Is there any relationship problem you can't solve?" she asked. "I thought you had met your match. How do you do it?"

"I'm not sure," Matthew said. "I guess it's because of all the dysfunctional relationships I've had."

"Including ours?" Angela asked.

"We're not dysfunctional." He kissed her.

"I want you right now," she whispered.

"Now? Here? You may have customers waiting."

Angela glanced into the dining room. "You'll have to be quick then."

Matthew looked around the kitchen. "Where?"

Angela pulled him near the refrigerator, yanking down her pants and unzipping his jeans. "Go into the corner."

Matthew backed into the corner as Angela backed onto him.

"I won't last long," she whispered.

"Neither will I," Matthew said. "You're already wet."

Angela bounced furiously against him. "I think about this all the time."

So do I.

"Faster," she panted. "Faster!"

I hope the customers out there think we're hammering something back here.

"Oh . . . yes!" Angela shouted.

Matthew joined her, trying not to shout.

Angela pulled up her pants.

Matthew zipped up his zipper.

"Back to work," Angela said, and she washed her hands, threw water on her face, dried off, and went into the dining room.

Matthew recovered for several minutes in the corner.

I have met my match. Angela is my spiritual, intellectual, and physical match. We have to get engaged, and soon. I can't get enough of my future . . . wife.

He closed his eyes.

Angela will be my wife, and I will be her husband, and we will work here, especially in this corner, for the rest of our days. I may have to put some padding on the wall, though. She was trying to push me through the wall and into the alley.

He smiled.

I tried women everywhere else.

I'm done trying.

This is my home.

I am going to marry a Billyburg babe.

He washed his hands and face, checked his zipper, and walked up behind Angela. "Thank you," he whispered.

"Thank *you,*" she whispered back.

"I need to make a phone call," he whispered. *To Catbird.*

"Go ahead," she said, cutting her eyes to the shop phone.

"It's a secret," Matthew whispered.

"Does it involve me?" Angela asked.

"It involves *us,*" Matthew said. He squeezed her left hand, rubbing her ring finger.

"Oh," Angela said. "Matthew, don't go to any trouble."

"I thought we could go look at rings tonight," he said.

"Rings." She sighed. "Could we talk about this some more first?"

"What's to talk about?" Matthew asked. "I want to marry you."

Angela picked up a towel with her right hand and wiped the counter. "I know you do, it's just that the time isn't right."

After some miraculous, powerful sex in the kitchen? What time could be better? "What are you worried about?"

She looked through the front window. "I heard La Estrella is cutting two baristas and all of their prices ten percent and changing their hours from seven to seven to six to eight. *My* hours. They're even adding Wi-Fi, and I swear they sent a guy over here the other day to write down my prices. They're trying to put me out of business."

It sure sounds like it. "That only means they're getting even more desperate, Angela. Their coupons are littering Driggs from one end to the other, and their coupon prices are still fifty cents higher that yours, and for inferior coffee."

"I've been pacing back here all day," Angela said.

She didn't even hear me.

"And I've been staring at all the people going in there," Angela said. "I wish I had the power to make all their red and orange lights explode."

"Is that why you dragged me back there?" Matthew asked.

"It certainly broke some of the tension," Angela said.

Matthew let his hand slip from hers. "So I'm a tension breaker."

"You're more than that, Matthew," Angela said. "You are. I'm just worried about money, okay?"

"Aren't we doing okay financially?" Matthew asked. "I'm pulling in a lot more now that spring has arrived."

"I know, I know," Angela said. "You're making more than I am now. But I still worry, and I'm still worried about me. The trial starts at the end of June, and the closer that day comes, the more anxious I get." She faced him and held his hands. "I want to wait until after the trial, okay?"

Until Warrick is officially gone for a long time, hopefully forever. "You want to wait that long to get engaged? Angela, we can make this official tonight. And we can change the tip jar to read: 'Angela and Matthew's Wedding Fund.' "

"I'm not ready," she whispered.

Don't rush her. She loves you, and she wants everything to be perfect. "I can wait." He kissed her.

"You're not angry?" she asked.

He looked into her soft brown eyes. "I can never be angry with you. And you can break any tension you have with me anytime. Are you feeling tense now?"

Angela smiled and turned away.

There's my shy girl.

"I know I'll feel tense later tonight," she said.

Matthew sighed. "I will be ready, willing, and able to break your tension." He stared at La Estrella. "What about iced coffee?"

"What?" Angela said.

"I know, bad transition," Matthew said. "Iced coffee is something La Estrella has that you don't have."

"Because it's sacrilege," Angela said. "My daddy would be foaming at the mouth if I put iced coffee on the menu."

"If you were to make it better, and cheaper . . ." Matthew said. "They're stealing your hours from you. Why not steal something back?"

Angela narrowed her eyes and nodded. "And strawberry shortcake."

"With lots of whipped cream," Matthew said, holding her close.

"Whipped cream, yes," she said.

"We'll get through this."

"I hope so," she said.

A customer cleared her throat. "Could I get some coffee now?"

Angela hugged Matthew first. "Get some ice." She turned to the customer. "Would you like to try some iced coffee today?"

"I want a large house blend," the woman said.

"Try it with ice and I'll only charge you half price," Angela said.

"Okay," the woman said with a smile.

Iced house blend was an instant hit, as was the strawberry shortcake. Matthew enjoyed taking trips to HOD Fruit & Vegetable Market on Roebling to get fresh strawberries, and he spent many hours removing stems and washing strawberries in the kitchen while Angela tried to keep up with the orders out front.

No matter how often Matthew tried to reassure her, however, Angela still worried about money and the upcoming trial. In the bedroom, the love they made was miraculous but only occasionally healing, Angela crawling on top of him for protection from dreadful memories that would not let her sleep through the night without sobbing.

Matthew was at a loss as he held her in the darkness. *I should ask her to marry me anyway. I should propose. Yes. That's what I'll do. I'll pop the question, and she'll remove some more of her armor. She'll see I'm her knight in shining armor and that no one could ever hurt her again. Every time she sees her ring, she'll think of something permanent, lasting, and safe.*

But what if she says no? What if she still isn't sure? Would anything ever be the same again? I have to be sure. I have learned never to ask a question I don't know the answer to, and right now, I really don't know what Angela's answer will be.

Angela stirred and opened one sleepy eye. "Am I keeping you up?"

"No," Matthew whispered. "Go back to sleep."

Angela nestled her head on his chest and was purring moments later.

She wants to wait until after the trial.

I don't.

I can't.

I won't.

I'm getting Angela a ring tomorrow.

And I'll propose to her . . .

When the moment's right.

Whenever that is.

Chapter 36

"Do you know her ring size?" the woman at Catbird asked the next morning.

Matthew had already picked out the ring, the classic solitaire he had seen online, and he now looked for a place to put a box of seriously ripe strawberries so he could hold the ring in his hand. *This shop has too many displays and no floor, table, or shelf space.*

"She's kind of petite," Matthew said. He balanced the box on his knee and felt the fingers of a plastic hand holding several other rings. "The pinkie feels right, but I'm not sure."

The woman slid the ring down the pinkie. "It's a little big, but we can resize it later," she said. She turned the ring over and looked at the tag. "This is a seven. Maybe she takes a six and a half."

"Maybe," Matthew said. He sighed and put the box of strawberries on the counter. "Sorry." He pulled out his wallet and handed his Visa to her. "I'm kind of in a hurry." *I don't want Angela to ask why it took so long.*

The woman swiped the card. "Those strawberries smell wonderful."

"You should get some strawberry shortcake at Smith's Sweet Treats and Coffee sometime," Matthew said.

"They're still open?" the woman asked. "I thought La Estrella put them out of business."

"It's almost the other way around," Matthew said, signing the credit slip. "And on such a hot day, a large iced coffee and some strawberry shortcake will cool you off."

"Sounds good," she said, beginning to bag the fuzzy black box.

"No bag," Matthew said. "And no box." *I don't want her seeing a different kind of bulge in my pants.*

She removed the ring from the box, slipping it into a smaller drawstring pouch. "You're giving it to her now, huh?" She held out the pouch.

I have no idea when. He took the pouch and slipped it carefully into his pocket. "Soon." He picked up the box of strawberries. "Thank you, and we'll be sure to come back for wedding bands."

"Great," she said.

Great. I have an engagement ring in my pocket for the first time in my life, it's eighty degrees, I'm carrying a box of overripe strawberries, and Angela is going to wonder why a half hour trip to get strawberries took more than an hour.

Unless she's busy. I hope she's busy. That way I can sneak by her to the back and start washing these. Maybe she won't notice . . .

Angela noticed.

The second Matthew walked in, she asked, "Where have you been?" A half dozen customers were waiting in line.

Matthew zipped by her to the kitchen. "These are very ripe," he said. "I have to wash 'em."

Angela gave him a few minutes' peace with the strawberries before entering the kitchen. "You didn't answer my question."

He stuck a ripe strawberry in her mouth. "Aren't they good?"

"They are," Angela said. "Now answer my question."

He dried his hands on a towel. *This is not what I envisioned, but . . .* He took the little drawstring bag from his pocket. "Angela."

She focused on the bag. "Yes?" she said in a soft voice.

She's half smiling. Okay, I can do this. "Angela . . ."

She bit her lower lip. "Yes?"

This is going nowhere. I should have practiced this. "Angela . . ."

"You already said that." She looked into the dining room. "Hold on a sec. I have a few customers."

Thank God for customers. I am botching this up so badly. She's efficient, so I have to think fast. He looked at the floor. *Clean as always. I know. I'll kneel in front of her, tell her I love her, and ask her to join me on a lifetime adventure. No, not an adventure, a journey.*

A lifetime journey. No, that sounds lame. A lifetime of happiness? I plan to give her happiness, of course, I mean, that's expected. What guy wouldn't promise that?

He looked at the bag. "I give you this ring because . . ." he whispered. "Because I can think of no one else I would want to give it to." *That wasn't bad. A little vague, though. I can think of no one else? Well, I can't. I could say—*

"Who are you talking to?" Angela asked.

Matthew whirled around, palming the bag. "To myself."

Her eyes searched for the bag. "Where's the bag?"

He opened his hand.

"Is that for me?" she asked.

"Yeah."

"I've always wanted a little bag like that," she said.

Funny. He knelt in front of her. "I know you said to wait, but I can't wait any longer, Angela."

"Since when have you ever listened to me?" she asked.

"I listen to you all the time," Matthew said. "And I want to hear your voice and see your eyes for the rest of my life." He took the ring from the bag and held it up. "You give me peace. I hope I can give you peace for the rest of our lives."

Angela shot out her left hand.

Matthew slipped on the ring.

"It's a little big," she said.

"I guessed at your size," Matthew said. "We can get it resized."

Angela shook her head. "It's okay. Don't you have something else to say?"

I thought I said everything. "I love you, Angela."

"I love you, too," she said, ruffling his hair. "But there's something you're supposed to ask, isn't there?"

I didn't ask her to marry me! Wow. "Angela Simone Smith, will you marry me?"

She looked up and sighed. "I guess I'll have to. You're a good worker. I need those strawberries now, by the way. There are ten people waiting for shortcake."

Matthew stood. "I'll get right on it." He turned to the sink and ran cold water over a colander full of strawberries.

"Hey," Angela whispered.

He turned around.

Angela's eyes were full of tears. "Thank you." She hugged him. "I'm glad you didn't listen to me. It proves you really want me."

"I do want you," Matthew said.

She dried her eyes on his shirt. "Make sure you get all the stems, okay?"

He nodded. "I really messed up my proposal, didn't I?"

"You didn't," she said, backing away. She looked at the ring. "I'll never be able to forget it. Hurry up with those strawberries, Mr. McConnell."

Matthew smiled. "Yes, Miss Smith."

Angela left the kitchen.

That wasn't so bad. I'm glad I only have to do that once.

Matthew worked feverously removing stems, rinsing and pouring the strawberries into a large silver bowl dusted with powdered sugar. As he was sprinkling a fine layer of powdered sugar on top of them, he heard people clapping. When he stuck his head out of the kitchen, the ovation grew louder.

"*There* he is!" someone shouted, and the ovation grew even louder.

"Come here," Angela mouthed.

He picked up the bowl of strawberries and took it to a side counter before standing behind Angela, wrapping his arms around her stomach. "I take it they know."

Angela nodded. "Look at the tip jar, Matthew."

On the jar was a new sign: "Our wedding jar."

"And *you* knew," Matthew whispered.

"I knew something was up when you were half an hour late," Angela said. "It doesn't take an hour to walk from here to Division Avenue and back."

"Congratulations," the customer at the front of the line said. "Now could I please have my strawberry shortcake?"

Angela kissed Matthew to more applause and then pushed him to the side table. "I'll need at least twelve, chop chop."

"Coming right up, Mrs. McConnell," Matthew said.

Angela smiled. "Not yet."

Matthew could contain his joy anymore. He picked Angela up

and carried her around the dining room, shouting, "Free strawberry shortcake today!"

"*Half price* on strawberry shortcake, today!" Angela shouted. "*Half* price!"

Matthew kissed her shouting away. "*Free.*"

"Kiss me like that again," she said.

Matthew dipped her almost to the floor.

"Okay," she said breathlessly. "Free."

"Because," Matthew said to the crowd, "that's what I am when I am with this woman. I'm free. And feel *free* to add to our wedding fund."

Angela had to empty the tip jar twice that day.

After closing, they raced upstairs, closed all the windows, turned off Angela's window air conditioner, and enjoyed a sizzling night of sweat and sighs, moans and groans.

As Angela rose and fell on Matthew as they sat in his "thinking" chair, she planned their wedding.

"We're not separating the bride's and groom's families," she moaned, grinding her booty into him.

"Do we have to plan this *now?*" Matthew asked, nibbling on her shoulders and massaging her back. "I'm trying to concentrate."

"This is *our* thinking chair now," she whispered.

"How can you think at a time like this?" Matthew asked.

"I can multitask." She rose up and held her booty still. "And at the wedding reception," she said as she dropped, "we're not announcing everyone. That takes entirely too long. People are hungry. That's why half of them come to the wedding in the first place."

Matthew reached around and teased her nipples.

"Pinch them," Angela moaned, "pinch them hard."

Matthew twisted her nipples.

"Oh shit, oh shit." She rested. "I'm up to three."

I have some catching up to do.

She spun around and rested her head on the footrest while Matthew continued to fill her. "I am *not* catering my own wedding, though I guess I could."

"Angela, please, I'm trying to catch up with you."

She laughed. "You'll never catch up with me, so why even try? Oh, and we can't do that first traditional dance. I'll only start grinding on you like I did at The Cove."

Matthew massaged her stomach. "We can't have that." *Now hush so I can—*

"And that garter tradition is just plain dumb," Angela said. She pulled herself up using the arms of the chair. "I mean, who wears a garter anymore?" She licked and nibbled his nipples.

Matthew pushed Angela back gently and inhaled most of her right breast into his mouth.

"No bouquet," she wheezed. "No throwing of anything, not even rice or birdseed. Damn, are you trying to eat my breast?"

"It tastes good." Matthew pulled back and licked both nipples.

"It tastes like sweat," she said. "We are definitely not having a traditional wedding."

Matthew guided Angela's hands between her legs. "I'm close. Show me something."

Angela's fingers tapped her clitoris repeatedly.

He thrust up and held it. "Here comes number two. Kiss me."

Angela kissed him until his spasms subsided. "And I don't want to get married in the summer. I'd rather get married in the fall when the trees are colorful."

I have an orgasm, and she talks about colorful trees. He moved his hands down her sweaty back. "What about our honeymoon?"

"What about it?" she asked.

"Are we going to have one?" he asked. "We're barely having a wedding."

"You're right," she said. "We might as well skip the wedding and go straight to the honeymoon, somewhere hot and sweaty like this."

"Can we bring this chair?" Matthew asked.

Angela smiled. "Okay, I'll admit. This chair has its uses." She bounced up and down. "You're still hard."

"I can't help it," Matthew said. "You keep it hard."

She began a slow grind, rising and falling. "And you keep me wet. We have to meet each other's parents, too."

"From 'you keep me wet' to meeting the parents," Matthew said.

She sped up her grinding. "Don't go away now."

"I won't." *I can't. Not when she does that.*

"You told your parents we'd come down to visit," Angela said, holding his hands to her breasts. "And we haven't even called them. When are we going to do that?"

"We'll figure something out," Matthew said.

"We're good at that," Angela said.

"We're good at this, too," Matthew said. "We really should make a how-to video."

"I'm too shy to do that," Angela said.

"You're not too shy when we do this," Matthew said, kissing her ring. "Now lean back."

She leaned back, resting her head on the footrest.

"Keep touching your breasts," he whispered. "You know I like that."

Angela pulled her breasts up by her nipples.

"Doesn't that hurt?" Matthew asked.

She licked her lips. "So good."

He pulled her legs out from around him, placing them on his shoulders. "I wish I could lick you and do this at the same time."

"So do I." Angela closed her eyes. "Use both of your thumbs on me down there."

A few moments later, Angela shook, shouted, and sighed. "Four."

No fair.

"I intend," she said, wiping sweat off her chest, "to always be one step, one orgasm, and one thought ahead of you."

I can live with that, though it is inherently unfair, for the rest of my natural life.

Chapter 37

Engaged life began in earnest the next morning with two phone calls at five AM.

Since both sets of parents were early risers, Matthew put his cell phone on speaker on the shelf of the prep table as he and Angela prepared for the day.

"Daddy, it's me, Angela."

"Is everything okay?" her father asked.

"Everything's fine," Angela said, sifting flour. "I just wanted you and mama to know that I'm engaged."

"Engaged?" her father said. "I didn't even know you were dating."

Angela cringed. "Yeah, I guess I should have told you about that."

"When have you found the time?" her father asked.

Angela smiled at Matthew. "He just sort of appeared in my life one morning."

"When's the last time we talked?" her father asked.

"Easter, I think," Angela said.

I don't feel as bad about calling my mother now, Matthew thought.

"Were you dating him then?" her father asked.

"Yes," Angela said. "We've been seeing each other since the second of February."

Groundhog Day. I'm glad old Phil saw his shadow.

"You could have told us sooner." Her father sighed. "Well, who's the lucky man?"

"He's right here helping me make pastries," Angela said. "His name is Matthew McConnell. He's not only my fiancé, but he's also my business partner."

"Hello, Mr. Smith," Matthew said, rolling out some dough. "You have an incredible daughter."

"Your *business* partner?" her father said. "Since when do you have a business partner, Angela? Don't you think you should run something like that by the *founder* of that coffee shop and your mama first?"

Angela has kept her parents deep, *deep in the dark about me.*

"Daddy, I . . . a lot has happened that I haven't told you or Mama," Angela said, "things I should have told you a long time ago."

Matthew picked up the phone and turned off the speaker, handing it to Angela. He kissed her cheek, whispered, "Tell them," and went out into the dining area, wiping a few tables and polishing the display case. *She has so much to tell them. I hope they can handle it.* He poured himself a cup of house blend and sipped it, watching the lights come on inside La Estrella.

Thirty minutes later, Angela signaled him back to the kitchen.

She turned on the speaker. "He's back."

"Matthew, I owe you an apology," her father said. "I'm already proud to know you and I haven't even met you. Angela has told us how much you've helped her, and I want to say thank you."

"Hello, Matthew," a female voice said.

Angela's mama. "Hello, Mrs. Smith."

"Thank you for keeping our daughter safe," she said. "Angela had me look at your picture on the Internet, so I am looking at you now. You are a handsome man."

"Thank you," Matthew said. *And* they *have Internet in* their *home.* "I've seen your picture, too, Mrs. Smith. Angela has your smile."

"Yes, she does," her mother said. "So when are you two getting married? And where? We will be there no matter what."

"Mama, we're still working that out," Angela said. "But you'll be the first to know. We need to talk to Matthew's parents now, so . . ."

"Good-bye, Angel," her mother said.

"Good-bye," her father said. "And call us the second you know when and where, okay?"

"Okay, Daddy," Angela said. "I will. Good-bye." She turned off the phone. "They know everything now."

"How do you feel?" Matthew asked.

"I feel bad," Angela said. "I should have told them a long time ago."

"What would they have done?" Matthew asked.

Angela rolled her eyes. "They would have come back to Williamsburg to rescue me. Either that or they would have flown me down there."

And we might never have met. I don't want to think about that.

Matthew dialed his parents. "This will be a shorter call." He turned on the speaker. The call went directly to voice mail. *That's strange. Someone's usually up by now.* "Hey Dad, Mom, Angela and I are engaged. I'll call you later today with the details. Just wanted you to know before anyone else. Bye." He closed the phone. "Ready to make some money?"

"You left them a *voice mail* to announce your engagement," Angela said.

"I'll call them later," Matthew said.

"You better." Angela opened the refrigerator. "Is it supposed to be hot again today?"

"Mid-eighties, I think," Matthew said.

"We'll need more strawberries then," she said. "And I want you to call your parents back."

He kissed her forehead. "I will."

After opening the shop, Matthew finished his coffee before walking down to HOD Fruit & Vegetable. Along the way, an idea struck him that made him smile.

Angela's parents want to know where and when. I know my parents will want the same information.

I think I know the exact *date and place.*

He first called his parents.

"We got your message," his father said. "When's the date?"

Matthew told him the date and why.

His father liked the idea.

His mother complained initially, but she agreed. "Have I told you how hard you've been on me, Matthew? You're pushing me into an early grave."

"You'll outlive us all, Mom," Matthew said.

"No thanks to you," she said.

He called Mr. and Mrs. Smith, and they were overjoyed, giving Matthew a few more ideas.

"How are you going to keep this a secret from Angela?" Angela's mother asked.

"I have learned a great deal from your daughter about keeping secrets, Mrs. Smith," Matthew said. "I think I'll do okay."

Matthew bought two boxes of fresh strawberries, and as he walked, his phone buzzed. "This is Matthew McConnell."

"McConnell, this is Paddy."

What does O'Day want? "What can I do for you, Paddy?"

"You know I'm lead on the Warrick case, right?" O'Day said.

"I'm sure I read it somewhere," Matthew said. "How's your case going?"

"Not good," O'Day said. "Our eyewitnesses are getting cold feet, and the two that are prepped and ready are going to get hammered by Filardi on the stand because they're scared shitless of the guy. I can't get one of them to speak louder than a whisper."

I don't like where this is leading. "What about all the evidence Novak said she had?"

"We didn't get any DNA or prints from *any* crime scene," O'Day said. "None. Warrick covered his tracks well."

And without snowshoes. "There was nothing on the boots Angela wore?"

"Nothing but dust," O'Day said. "We found some cigarette butts in the alley behind her place, including Warrick's brand, but they couldn't pull any DNA from them."

"What about the phone call he made to me?" Matthew asked. "He admitted being at Angela's during the last blizzard."

"And that's the only indisputable evidence we have right now," O'Day said. "If he hadn't called you, we would have had to drop the attempted rape charge for lack of evidence because Miss Smith destroyed all the evidence. Right now, it's back to his word against hers, and we need her words. We have to have her testimony. Live."

Matthew's heart sank. "I was hoping she wouldn't have to testify. I was hoping you were going to use the tape of her grand jury testimony."

"It's great testimony, don't get me wrong," O'Day said, "but Angela isn't exactly the most reliable witness because of her condition, and Filardi knows she has PTSD."

"How?" Matthew asked.

"I don't know how he knows," O'Day said. "He only threw it in my face the other day."

Why is this happening now? "We both know Angela's *memory* is unreliable. *She's* not unreliable."

"It will be the same difference to Filardi, McConnell," O'Day said.

"So why put her on the stand at all?" Matthew asked. "Run the tape and hope for the best."

"Look, McConnell, I don't want to call her as a material witness," O'Day said, "but if I have to, I will."

From eyewitness to material witness. They could arrest and detain Angela until the trial. Why is this shit happening? I finally have Angela back!

No, I can't say I have her "back." She's not all the way back yet.

"We're up against it, McConnell," O'Day said. "We believe Warrick attacked five women, and we charged him with five counts of attempted rape, but the man was smart. He didn't leave a trace behind."

"What about the things he said?" Matthew asked. "Didn't he repeat the same words to each victim?"

"And how would you as his defense attorney attack those repeated words?" O'Day asked.

Matthew nodded. "I'd say the witnesses had been coached by the district attorney, but as a prosecutor, I'd damn sure get those words into evidence."

"We will, we will," O'Day said. "We aren't as dumb as you think we are, but Filardi is trouble. You know that. He's in the news today chirping and creating a media circus saying his usual bullshit. 'My client is innocent, this is a vendetta, the five women accusing my client have been misled and brainwashed by the police, they have no physical evidence whatsoever.' It makes me sick."

"So what exactly do you need?" Matthew asked.

"We need Angela," O'Day said, "and since you're her lawyer, we expect you to advise her to do the right thing."

Matthew stopped in the shade a block from Angela's, setting the strawberry boxes beside him. "Or what?"

"McConnell, you know we'd rather have her as a cooperative eyewitness," O'Day said, "but if we have to issue a warrant to get her to appear, we will. Talk to her, okay? The trial starts next week. I'll be in touch."

Matthew closed his phone. *Now what? Why does this have to happen today? Life is finally coming together for Angela and me. What do I do now?*

Call the doctor.

Call Dr. Penn. He'll know what to do.

He dialed Dr. Penn. "Sorry to bother you, Dr. Penn, but I may need your help." He explained what O'Day wanted Angela to do.

"Is she stronger now than she was three months ago?" Dr. Penn asked.

"I think so," Matthew said. "But she's been having nightmares more often as the trial approaches. I don't think she's slept more than a few hours a night for the last month."

"As might anyone who has been through what she's been through," Dr. Penn said. "But I think I've told you this before. Angela is *much* tougher than she appears to be."

"I know that," Matthew said.

"And this will give her the opportunity to face her attacker," Dr. Penn said. "Many people never get this chance. This might be the best possible therapy for her."

"I thought love was the best therapy, Doc," Matthew said.

"It still is," Dr. Penn said. "Love will always be the best therapy. But in Angela's case, confrontation may be her ultimate cure."

He's right. He has always been right. "By the way, we're engaged."

"That's wonderful," Dr. Penn said. "But why don't you sound happier?"

"We're engaged as of yesterday, and now this."

"Why should this diminish your happiness?" Dr. Penn asked. "Facing Warrick will only help Angela, I assure you. When's the happy event?"

I thought I had some idea an hour ago. "We haven't set a date."

"Did she accept your proposal without any reservations?" Dr. Penn asked.

"Yes," Matthew said.

"No hesitation whatsoever," Dr. Penn said.

"None," Matthew said. "Is that significant?"

Dr. Penn laughed. "Go tell Angela she's going to testify against Warrick, and don't wait another minute."

"I don't know if that's a good idea," Matthew said. "She told her parents what happened to her only a few hours ago, we got engaged only yesterday, and she's still not sleeping well."

"Ask her right now," Dr. Penn said. "I'm not a betting man, but I bet she says she can't wait to testify."

"Is that your considered opinion as a man or a psychiatrist?" Matthew asked.

"It's my considered opinion as *me* this time," Dr. Penn said. "I have seen remarkable changes in Angela. She is by far the toughest person I've ever met, and remember, I served in Vietnam with the toughest of men. I believe Angela has been waiting four long years to confront this man, and here's the golden opportunity. Go ask her."

"Just go up to her and say, 'You're going to testify in open court against the man who attacked and ruined your life four years ago,' " Matthew said.

"If that's the way you want to say it, sure," Dr. Penn said. "She's going to surprise you, Matthew, and you won't need to call me back, probably ever. I'll read her testimony in the newspaper."

"I wish I had your confidence," Matthew said.

"Oh, but you do," Dr. Penn said. "You had the confidence to ask Angela to marry you, knowing that her past may never be completely behind her. That takes toughness and resolve. You're almost the second-toughest person I've ever met."

"Who was the second-toughest?" Matthew asked.

"My wife," Dr. Penn said. "Go ask Angela right now."

Matthew exhaled. "I hope you're right."

"Good-bye, Matthew," Dr. Penn said. "Give my best to Angela, and be sure to send me a wedding invitation."

"I will."

Matthew closed his phone. *Just tell her. Is it going to be that easy?*

He backed into the shop and took the boxes of strawberries directly to the prep table in the kitchen, only nodding at Angela as she put a tray of cookies into the oven.

"Everything okay?" she asked.

Here we go. "Paddy O'Day is lead prosecutor on the Warrick case, and he wants you to testify."

"When?" Angela asked.

Matthew blinked. *She didn't ask why or curse or cry or fall to pieces.* "If I were him, I'd save you for the end of the trial since your testimony should be most damaging to Warrick."

Angela nodded. "Okay. Why'd you get two boxes?"

I am in awe of this woman. Can't she see I'm trying not to cry? "It's going to be really hot today, and the strawberry shortcake was such a hit yesterday, I thought why not two?"

"Good idea." Angela squinted. "You okay?"

I'm better than okay. "Yeah."

"Allergies again?" she asked.

"Yeah." He nodded. "Allergies."

And my love for the toughest woman who ever lived on planet Earth.

Chapter 38

For the next six days, Matthew prepped Angela to testify long into the night, peppering her with questions he thought Filardi might ask her.

For the first four days and nights, Angela did well, answering each question directly and calmly. "He attacked me from behind . . . He wore a black knit ski mask . . . I didn't report the incident because he didn't rape me."

The last two days, Angela wasn't cooperating, and she couldn't keep her feet still.

"When did you begin getting psychological counseling from Dr. Kenneth Penn?" Matthew asked, trying to recreate Filardi's nasal tone.

"Two years after the attack," Angela said.

"Two years," Matthew said. "So for two years, you didn't think *anything* was wrong with you, did you, Miss Smith?"

"I knew something was wrong," Angela said.

"But you *didn't* seek help for two *long* years," Matthew said. "Wasn't your encounter with my client just another date gone *bad* for you, not that you've had many dates in your life, am I right, Miss Smith? What are you, thirty-five and unmarried?"

"Fuck you," Angela said.

"Angela, you can't say that in court," Matthew said.

"Why not?" Angela asked. "That man knows nothing about me or my relationships. How can he say that about me?"

"He'll probably say far worse to set you off," Matthew said. "It's his job to make you look completely unstable and unreliable as a witness. He's going to pick at you relentlessly, hoping you'll lose control. Remember: you're the victim here. You have to stay in control."

"Why? Why can't I show some anger? A man stole four years of my life from me. I'm angry. The jury should feel my anger."

"But if you curse Filardi," Matthew said, "the judge can hold you in contempt."

"Let him," Angela said. "I don't give a shit."

"You have to care, Angela," Matthew said. "Your testimony will be crucial in putting this guy away for life."

"I can't hold back, Matthew," Angela said. "I will not play the sniveling victim. I am a survivor. I want the jury to see the real me, the powerful woman who survived, and if I go off, I go off. I want them to know how truly pissed off I am. I want them to see me fight."

She's right. Her testimony isn't the time to be quiet. She has to roar. She needs to create some fireworks. Juries expect to see cowering, frightened witnesses in sexual assault cases. What if the jury sees a powerful woman, a fighter who refuses to yield any point the defense has?

"I'm not a victim anymore, Matthew," Angela said.

"You're right," Matthew said. "You're the predator now, and Warrick is the prey."

Angela blinked. "You agree with me?"

"Yes, and I don't know why I didn't realize this before," Matthew said. "Angela, forget what I've said to you for the past week. Answer any question you get the way *you* feel it at the moment. If Filardi pisses you off, I want you to spit fire. If he attacks you, fire back. It would be great if you could set Warrick off, too, but I don't want you to let your guard down for a second."

Angela smiled. "I don't intend to. I also intend to ignore Warrick for as long as I can. I won't even dignify his presence in the courtroom."

"But the jury might see that and think you're afraid of him," Matthew said.

"Oh, I'll look at him," Angela said, "but only when the time is right. And I won't be smiling at his sorry ass. Until then, I don't want the jury to think I give a shit about him."

This could work. "I have to call O'Day."

"Why?" Angela asked. "This is *my* case now, not his."

"You're right," Matthew said. "He needs to know that it isn't his case anymore, right?" He called O'Day. "Paddy, I need you to do something for us."

"What?" O'Day asked.

"I don't want you to ask Angela any questions about what she did with her clothes or shoes or her cleanup after the attack," Matthew said.

Angela blinked rapidly.

"It's okay," Matthew mouthed. "I got this."

"What?" O'Day yelled. "That's evidence vital to our case, McConnell."

"And I don't want you to even mention PTSD or Dr. Penn," Matthew said.

"We already decided to bring that up first, didn't we?" O'Day asked. "To beat Filardi to the punch."

"Change of plan," Matthew said. "Trust me, Paddy. Let Filardi bring all that into evidence. Let him throw his jabs. Angela's going to drop him with some wicked hooks."

"But he'll be able to prove Angela is hiding something!" O'Day shouted. "He'll be able to prove she's unreliable!"

Matthew smiled. "Trust me. If Filardi even mentions any of it, he'll be sorry. We have to let Filardi open Pandora's Box, and once he does, all hell will break loose."

"I don't know, McConnell," O'Day said. "That's taking a huge risk."

"Only a slight risk," Matthew said. "And we also don't want you to make any objections to any question Filardi asks or any snide comments he makes."

"What, I'm just supposed to sit on my thumbs?" O'Day asked.

"Yes," Matthew said. "Do as much nothing as you can once you've led Angela through her testimony. Make *no* objections. We've got this." He smiled at Angela. "Angela's got this. She will be in total control. *She* will win you your case. You've got to trust us on this."

"Oh man, McConnell," O'Day said. "If this backfires . . ."

"It won't," Matthew said. "I guarantee it. Your star witness is going to blaze brightly in that courtroom tomorrow, and all you have to do is sit back and enjoy the show."

Smith's Sweet Treats and Coffee was closed for the first time in forty years. Angela wore a white blouse and stylish black skirt as O'Day gently led her through her night from hell. Angela delivered her testimony flawlessly in front of a packed courtroom in the Kings County Supreme Court building on Jay Street in downtown Brooklyn on a hot and humid June morning. Matthew knew Angela's feet were still most likely dancing in place behind the wooden wall of the witness stand, but that was all right.

She's just warming up for the fight.

Matthew stared at the back of Warrick's head. *Warrick looked so smug when he came in, dressed in a suit Filardi probably bought for him. It looks better than the one I'm wearing, but I'll bet it's the only suit Warrick has ever worn. If all goes as it should, that will be the* last *nice suit Warrick ever wears.*

"No further questions at this time," O'Day said.

"Your witness, Mr. Filardi," Judge Pedroia said.

Filardi, wearing a $25,000 Ermenegildo Zegna suit and $1,500 New & Lingman Russian calf shoes, didn't leave his seat. "Thank you, your honor." He stared at Angela for a full ten seconds.

As if you could ever scare her, Filardi. And it is so disrespectful not to stand in the presence of a lady.

"Miss Smith, I understand that you've been under a psychiatrist's care," Filardi said. "Would you care to elaborate?"

Just as I expected. Filardi is trying to put the idea of "crazy witness" into the jury's minds with his first question. He has no idea how this line of questioning is going to backfire on him. Matthew looked at his feet. *Hey, now my feet are dancing! Let's box!*

"I have been receiving counseling from Dr. Kenneth Penn about once or twice a week for the last two years," Angela said. "I've also received extensive therapy from my fiancé, Matthew McConnell."

Both Filardi and Warrick swiveled in their seats to look in Matthew's direction.

Hi, Robbie. Remember me? You are going down *today. Dude, is that your nose, or do you have an eggplant growing on your face?*

Warrick winked and turned away.

Yeah, practice that wink, Robbie. You'll have to make friends quickly in prison.

Filardi swiveled toward Angela. "Isn't Matthew McConnell a lawyer and not a psychiatrist?"

"Yes, but you don't need to be a psychiatrist to help people get better, do you, Mr. Filardi?" Angela asked.

Nice touch, Angela. He can't disagree or he'll look like a bigger ass than he already is.

"Oh, I agree," Filardi said. "So you've been a patient of Dr. Penn for *two* years. Didn't the alleged attack happen *four* years ago?"

"Yes," Angela said.

"Why did you wait two years to begin intensive therapy with a psychiatrist?" Filardi asked.

"I thought I could get by on my own," Angela said. "It's not in my nature to ask anyone for help."

"It's not in your nature," Filardi repeated. "Tell us about your therapy. It sounds intense. How intense is your therapy?"

"It's not very intense," Angela said. "Dr. Penn asks questions, and I answer. I ask him questions, and he answers. It's kind of like a court case." She smiled. "Only in my particular case, the verdict may never be handed down."

I couldn't have reeled him in any better! Take the bait, Filardi. She's dangling it right in front of your hooked nose.

"Please elaborate, Miss Smith," Filardi said.

He took the bait! Yes!

"I may never be cured," Angela said. "I suffer from PTSD, post-traumatic stress disorder."

Filardi flipped hurriedly through a few pages of a legal pad.

She beat you to it, didn't she, Filardi? You wanted to spring that on the jury, and she beat you to it. Angela stole your thunder, and you're about to be lit up by her lightning.

"Were you ever in the military, Miss Smith?" Filardi asked.

"No," Angela said, turning slowly to her right.

This is the moment she has chosen to face Warrick. I'm getting goose bumps.

"I had a different kind of battle, one I believe that I will win." She stared directly at Warrick for the first time. "Yes, I am *definitely* going to win this battle."

Angela timed that perfectly. She's setting her jaw. I'll bet her hands are fists. God help you both now. The battle has begun, and you have no idea how many weapons she has in her arsenal.

"Oh?" Filardi finally stood, all five-feet-five of him. "You may *never* be cured?" he said to the jury.

"No," Angela said, "but I get stronger and stronger every passing second as I confront my past."

Good! Challenge the man to ask you the wrong question. If Filardi is wise, he'll change directions in a hurry.

"Miss Smith, do you recognize the defendant?" Filardi asked.

Filardi changed directions. It's okay. He'll mess up eventually. He's too cocky.

"No," Angela said, "I do *not* recognize the defendant."

Filardi shook his head and sighed in front of the jury. "How then do you know without a shadow of a doubt that he's the one who attacked you?"

"I don't," Angela said.

Whispers flowed around Matthew, and Judge Pedroia cleared his throat. The whispers died down.

"You don't?" Filardi asked.

"No," Angela said.

"Did you ever do a police lineup?" Filardi asked.

"No," Angela said.

"Why, then, are you on the stand as a witness against my client in this trial?" Filardi asked.

Angela smiled. "Good question."

If Filardi is wise, he'll say, "No further questions" and sit down. If he's the fool I know he is, he'll use this moment to gloat and badmouth the state's case.

Filardi shook his head at the jury. "A good question indeed. The police found no DNA evidence of his presence at your apartment, is that correct?"

"Yes," Angela said, "not that they didn't do a thorough job.

They were at my apartment and shop for about three hours. They even pulled up a few floorboards."

"And they still found none of my client's DNA," Filardi said. "I wonder why that was. Do you have any idea why none of Mr. Warrick's DNA was found at your apartment?"

What a monumental blunder! Angela can talk for days *now, and I'm glad O'Day is sitting on his thumbs. Paddy could be saying, "Calls for a conclusion."*

O'Day turned to look at Matthew. He nodded once and smiled.

Yes, Paddy, Filardi is an idiot! He asked Angela a vague question to elicit an opinion *from Angela, so now Angela can say whatever she wants to say for as long as the judge allows her to say it.*

"I think I have an idea," Angela said.

"Won't you please enlighten us?" Filardi asked.

You're about to be enlightened, and you've just lost this case. You just don't know it yet.

"I think they didn't find any of the cowardly Mr. Warrick's DNA," Angela said, "because I burned my clothes, which had his smoky stench and his semen on them."

"Objection!" Filardi shouted.

Yep. You're screwed now, Filardi. Duh! You can't object to the answer to your own *question!*

Judge Pedroia stared at Filardi. "You asked her to enlighten us, Mr. Filardi. That's what she's doing."

Filardi looked lost. "Your honor, I *disapprove* of her calling Mr. Warrick 'cowardly.' "

"Oh, I'm sorry," Angela said. "Did I call Mr. Warrick 'cowardly'? I won't call Mr. Warrick 'cowardly' again. I don't know why I said the word 'cowardly' in reference to Mr. Warrick. 'Cowardly' isn't a word I even use that often, and here I am applying it to Mr. Warrick. I wonder what made me say it today." She glared at Warrick.

And the word "cowardly" will echo in the jury's mind for days. Ooh, that punch had to hurt!

Filardi blinked several times.

Angela looked up at Judge Pedroia. "May I continue my answer?"

Filardi rushed back to his legal pad and lifted it up. "You had never seen Mr. Warrick until you saw his picture in the paper. Is this correct?"

Angela sighed. "Your honor, I wasn't done with my previous answer. I wasn't through enlightening the court about why Mr. Warrick's cowardly DNA wasn't found at my shop or apartment."

"She used the word again!" Filardi shouted.

"I referred to his *DNA* as being cowardly," Angela said. "I didn't say Mr. *Warrick* was cowardly this time."

I wish I could see Warrick's face. I'll bet he's ready to foam at the mouth. Keep swinging, Angela. Don't stop now.

"Your honor," Filardi pleaded.

Judge Pedroia looked down at Angela. "Miss Smith, I don't think DNA can be considered cowardly. It is what it is."

"Oh, I agree, your honor," Angela said. "I was just considering the *source* of that DNA."

"Your honor!" Filardi shouted loudly.

That was definitely a head shot. Wow!

Judge Pedroia leaned his considerable bulk to his left. "Miss Smith, continue your explanation, but please avoid the use of the word 'cowardly.' "

"I will." Angela faced Warrick again. "Another reason no DNA was found at my place was that I used bleach to scrub my stairway landing, which had his blood all over it."

"No blood was ever found!" Filardi shouted.

"Because I cleaned it up," Angela said. "I run a coffee shop in Williamsburg. I have to keep the place clean at all times or the health department will shut me down. Besides, I wasn't going to track his gutless, spineless blood up my stairs into my apartment."

"Your honor!" Filardi shouted.

I wish I had some popcorn. This is a great show!

Judge Pedroia sighed. "Miss Smith, please avoid using language of an inflammatory nature."

"I didn't think I did," Angela said. "Blood doesn't have guts or a spine, so therefore, it's gutless and spineless. *Especially* his."

I love this woman! Go . . . go . . . go!

"Your honor, I want her testimony stricken from the record," Filardi said.

"You originally opened this can of worms by asking for her

opinion, Mr. Filardi," Judge Pedroia said. "Miss Smith, I warned you not to use inflammatory language."

"I'm sorry, your honor," Angela said. "I'm sure Mr. Warrick's blood is *extremely* courageous and *extremely* brave."

Sarcasm has many uses, especially in a courtroom.

"Your honor, I disapprove of her sarcasm," Filardi said.

"You'd be sarcastic, too," Angela said, "if you had a man pinning you into a corner and trying to put his microscopic penis inside you."

And this *is what is called an uproar! Yes! Oh, listen to the gallery! Even the jury is laughing!*

Judge Pedroia banged his gavel. "Miss Smith, if you continue to use such language, I will hold you in contempt of court."

"Then that *wasn't* his penis?" Angela asked. "I wonder what it was." She looked at her pinkie.

The courtroom exploded in noise and laughter again, and Judge Pedroia had to bang his gavel repeatedly until the crowd quieted down.

"Miss Smith," Judge Pedroia said. "You *will* be civil. This is your last warning."

"Yes, your honor," Angela said. "I'm sorry."

"Mr. Filardi," Judge Pedroia said, "please continue."

Filardi approached the jury, his face significantly redder. "Let's get back to the evidence. Where is there *any* evidence that my client was even in your shop that night?"

"He called Matthew from the jail the day the crime tech team was there, and in that conversation he admitted being there," Angela said.

Filardi smiled. "Yes, we've all heard that tape, and in that tape, my client insisted it was a date gone bad. Wasn't it a date, Miss Smith?"

"No," Angela said. "It wasn't a date."

Filardi walked across to Warrick. "You *didn't* have a date with my client?"

"No," Angela said. "In fact, I had to remove two doors from my shop and replace them with steel security doors after what you and Mr. Warrick call a 'date.' There's less light in my kitchen because of that. I like lots of light in my kitchen. I wish I could spend more time in the light. But my condition keeps me inside."

Angela is a genius! She answered and deflected his question by baiting him to ask another question.

"Ah, yes," Filardi said. "I understand you haven't left your apartment in, how long has it been?"

"Until I met Matthew McConnell," Angela said, "I hadn't left my apartment in four years, ever since that gutless, spineless attack during the blizzard."

Filardi threw up his hands. "She did it again, your honor!"

"I called the *attack* gutless and spineless, Mr. Filardi," Angela said. "I didn't refer in any way to your client."

Filardi started to speak and stopped.

"You agree that the attack was gutless and spineless, don't you, Mr. Filardi?" Angela asked.

"I want those words stricken from the record," Filardi said.

"You're the one calling attention to them," Angela said.

"Your honor," Filardi said.

Judge Pedroia hesitated. "Overruled. Please continue, Mr. Filardi."

Filardi returned to his table and pulled out another legal pad. "Miss Smith, did you report this alleged incident?"

"No," Angela said.

"Why didn't you report this alleged incident?" Filardi asked.

"I wasn't raped," Angela said. "My attacker couldn't finish the job. He failed. He came up short. And there was a blizzard outside. No one could get to me anyway, not for a few days. The police had so many other worries that night."

"But what about your alleged injuries?" Filardi asked. "Didn't you seek medical treatment?"

"No," Angela said, "but they were only bruises that healed eventually. The bruise on my knee took about a week to heal. I got that one when I kneed Mr. Warrick in the face."

Filardi's body shook. "Do you have any *proof* you did this?"

Angela pointed at Warrick. "Look at his nose. That has to be the most crooked nose I've ever seen."

The jury's eyes are glued to Warrick's nose. I hope some of them are thinking, "Yep, she splattered that man's nose all over his face."

"The police found no blood of *any* kind where you said it would be, not even under the floorboards," Filardi said quickly. "Where was all this alleged blood?"

"I cleaned it up," Angela said, "but I already told you about that, and it really hurt to clean up because I had a nasty bruise on my heel."

She's amazing again. I'll guarantee Filardi wasn't going to ask about her heel. Now it's in the court transcript.

"I'm looking at a list of your alleged injuries, Miss Smith," Filardi said. "Aren't these injuries consistent with a fall of some kind? Did you perhaps slip and fall down your stairs that evening? It was an awfully icy, snowy day, and you *were* wearing your father's boots, which were five sizes too big for you."

I would have objected on the grounds that Filardi was being argumentative, but what an opening he's given Angela. Within every lawyer is a fool who can't stop talking.

"Outside later a couple of times, yes, I slipped and fell," Angela said. "I slipped and fell trying to escape my attacker, but my injuries weren't consistent with a fall, Mr. Filardi. They were consistent with an *attempted* rape. Mr. Warrick had a little premature ejaculation, nothing to be ashamed of, happens to the best of men."

"Your honor!" Filardi shouted.

"Miss Smith," Judge Pedroia said, "I'm almost at the end of my patience."

"I'm sorry," Angela said.

No she isn't!

"Proceed, Mr. Filardi," Judge Pedroia said.

"Miss Smith, didn't you fail to report this attack because there *was* no attack?" Filardi asked.

"There was an attack," Angela said.

"Didn't you fail to report this attack because you and the defendant had a *date* that evening," Filardi said, "and you led him to believe the date would end with sexual intercourse, and when the time came, you changed your mind?"

"Well, if it was a date, and I'm *not* saying it was," Angela said, "it ended very badly for Mr. Warrick."

Filardi scowled. "You mean the broken nose you *allegedly* gave him."

"No, it ended badly for Mr. Warrick," Angela said, "because of the heel I kicked up into Mr. Warrick's balls."

And we have another uproar! Oh, it's even louder than the last one! I hope Judge Pedroia doesn't cite Angela for contempt. He has every right to do so. Please let her keep talking!

Judge Pedroia banged his gavel, and the tumult died down. "Miss Smith, I have been very patient—"

"I'm *so* sorry, your honor," Angela interrupted. "I didn't know what else to call them. Should I have said scrotal sac? Testicles? Where I come from, they're balls, and either you have them . . ." She stared hard at Mr. Warrick. "Or . . . you . . . *don't.*"

Warrick is turning in his seat, and that isn't a smile on his ugly mug anymore. She's getting to him. I have never heard a quieter courtroom.

Judge Pedroia shook his head. "Miss Smith, please respect the decorum of this courtroom."

"I was just telling you how I injured my heel, that's all," Angela said. "I feel bad about it. I hope your limp isn't too noticeable, Mr. Warrick. With a little surgery, you can be up and about in maybe a year."

Warrick jumped out of his chair and shouted, "You *bitch!*"

Yes! She got him out of his seat!

"I'm sorry if I ruined you for life down there, I really am," Angela said quickly. "Did you want to have children?"

Warrick leaped away from his chair and shuffled awkwardly toward Angela shouting, "You *bitch!* I *hate* you! You *bitch!*"

Two bailiffs intercepted Warrick before he could get within six feet of Angela, escorting him roughly back to his chair.

Angela turned to the jury. "He *does* limp, doesn't he?"

Yep. The man's junk has been junked, and now he's headed to jail. No jury on earth could ever forget this moment.

"Your honor!" Filardi screamed.

Judge Pedroia stood to bang his gavel this time. "Order, order in the court!"

Keep going, Angela! Now, *when there's chaos everywhere!*

"I am so sorry, Mr. Warrick," Angela said. "I'm sorry I hurt you. I don't know if there are any words I can say to return your manhood to you, if you ever had any, that is."

Judge Pedroia pointed at Angela with his gavel. "Miss Smith, that is *enough.* Mr. Filardi, anything further?"

Filardi shook his head. "No, your honor."

O'Day jumped to his feet, his fat face one big smile. "Redirect, your honor?"

Judge Pedroia sat in a heap. "Keep it brief."

"Miss Smith," O'Day said, "please describe the last four years of your life for the jury."

Angela looked at Matthew. "I have suffered." She sighed. "I have suffered four years of self-lockdown, four years of guilt, four years of pain, self-hate, fear, nightmares, and grief. The attack changed my life for the worse. But you know what? It didn't ruin my life or even cut it short. I'm free now. I'm *free.* And after this moment, my attacker, Mr. Warrick, will be nothing to me." She turned to stare down Warrick. "You . . . are . . . *nothing.*"

O'Day looked at Filardi for an objection.

The jury looked at Filardi for an objection.

Matthew looked at Filardi for an objection.

Judge Pedroia looked at Filardi for an objection.

Filardi kept his seat and his silence.

"Nothing further, your honor," O'Day said.

"The witness may step down," Judge Pedroia said.

Angela stood tall, left the witness stand, eased through the double half-doors, and sat next to Matthew, grabbing his hand.

"You were amazing," Matthew whispered.

"I know," Angela whispered. "I amazed myself."

"Mr. Filardi, is the defense prepared to present its case?" Judge Pedroia asked.

Filardi didn't move. He didn't seem to be breathing.

"Mr. Filardi?" Judge Pedroia asked.

"The defense requests an adjournment until tomorrow, your honor," Filardi barely whispered.

"Court is adjourned until nine tomorrow morning," Judge Pedroia said. He banged his gavel, the courtroom erupted in noise, and reporters streamed quickly toward the exit.

Matthew stood, pulled Angela to her feet, and hugged her. "You did it!"

She kissed him tenderly. "*We* did it. I couldn't have done any of it without your coaching."

"You did most of it on your own," Matthew said.

"So I improvised a little," Angela said. "You do it all the time. Let's go celebrate. I want some pizza, and I'm buying."

After wading through a massive throng of reporters and cameras, Matthew saying, "No comment" every two steps, he and Angela took the slowest walk in the history of Brooklyn from the courthouse in downtown Brooklyn more than two miles to Mezza Luna on Havemeyer.

"Look at you," Matthew said. "You're practically dancing as you walk."

"I have lots of reasons to dance, Mr. McConnell," she said, smiling in the sunlight. "I'm in the sunlight for the first time in four years."

While they waited for their pizza at Mezza Luna, Matthew pointed out the "Breaking News" line moving across the bottom of a little TV. " 'Bombshell Testimony in Blizzard Rapist Case,' " he said. "That makes you the bombshell."

"I dropped a few bombs in there, didn't I?" Angela said.

"You sure did," Matthew said.

"And not one of them was an F-bomb," Angela said.

"Because you're a lady," Matthew said.

"I *can* be," Angela said.

As a "Breaking News" banner sped across the screen, the scene on the TV shifted from the studio to a bank of microphones on stands in front of the Kings County Supreme Court building.

"Oh look," Angela said. "Isn't that Filardi?"

"Yes," Matthew said, "and he's looking green."

Angela smiled. "Green is *not* his color."

"Mr. Filardi! Mr. Filardi" several reporters shouted.

"Why did Warrick change his plea to guilty?" a reporter asked.

"We *got* him," Matthew said. "Yes!"

Only Filardi's eyebrows, forehead, and receding hairline were visible above the microphones. "My client has changed his plea, *not* because of the flimsy evidence against him, but because the media have already convicted him of crimes he could *not* have committed, and I've said all along that my client could *never* get a fair trial in Brooklyn . . ."

"He never said that," Angela said.

"It's damage control," Matthew said. "Filardi blew the case so he has to hand out the blame to save face."

"So," Angela said, "what do you think Warrick will get?"

Matthew shrugged. "I'm sure Warrick made a deal, but if the judge sticks to the guidelines, he should get a *minimum* of twenty-five years."

"Sounds good to me," Angela said.

The second the pizza arrived, Angela tore into a slice, the sauce dripping from the corners of her mouth. "I'm so hungry," she said.

"I can see that," Matthew said.

She put her finger on a slice. "You want that slice?"

"No." He smiled. "It's yours."

Angela folded it, biting off nearly a third. "We need to go on power walks often. I don't want to get too big."

"You'll never get too big, Angela," Matthew said. "In fact, I think you could use a few more pounds."

She sipped from her Coke. "I hope it's not too cold next March."

"Yeah." *She's certainly being random today. It must be the stress.*

"You know, we should have had sausage and anchovies on this pizza," Angela said.

Matthew blinked. "I didn't think you liked sausage or anchovies."

Angela smiled. "I *know.* But I suddenly *do.* Isn't that amazing?" She picked up, folded, and bit into another slice.

"Yeah, it's amazing." Matthew started his second slice.

"I like Angel for a name, don't you?" Angela asked. "It's what my mama calls me sometimes. I think it would be the perfect name for our daughter, don't you?"

"I like it," Matthew said. "But what if we have a son?"

"Oh, I'm pretty sure we'll have a daughter first," Angela said. "But Angel would be a good name for a boy, too, right?" She sat back and patted her stomach.

"Angela, are you all right?" Matthew asked.

Angela wiped her mouth with a napkin. "No. I'm afraid I've developed another condition."

Oh no!

She smiled. "This condition has a pretty quick cure, though."

"What condition?" Matthew asked.

"I'll be healed of this condition in March, Matthew," Angela said. "I only hope I don't have to close the shop for more than a few days."

Matthew blinked. *She's eating voraciously, yet she's worried she'll get big. She told me her future daughter's name. She keeps mentioning March, which is about . . . nine months away!* "Angela, are you . . ."

"Due in March? Yes." She smiled. "We're going to have a baby, Matthew."

Matthew stumbled out of his chair, helped Angela to her feet, and hugged her. "We're going to have a baby!"

Angela pushed him away and sat. "Hey, I'm not done eating. Get me a slice with anchovies and sausage on it. Oh, and banana peppers and pineapple if they have it."

Matthew couldn't eat another slice, but he watched Angela eat three more. *There's a little angel named Angel inside her right now. I hope she likes anchovies.*

"When did you find out?" Matthew asked.

Angela looked up. "I think I knew a few days ago," she said. "You thought I was throwing up because I was nervous about the trial. I wasn't nervous about the trial at all. And my period's been late, so . . ." She sipped her Coke. "What do you think?"

"I think it's amazing," Matthew said. *Well, it is.*

"I hope she doesn't come out weighing twenty pounds," Angela said. "Are you happy?"

Matthew nodded. "I don't know if I've ever been happier." *Wow. I'm going to be a father. But first I have to be a husband.* "I hope you don't mind if I planned something for later."

"What are you planning?" Angela asked, grabbing his hand. "I hope it involves whipped cream."

"I planned a little trip," Matthew said.

"Where?" Angela asked.

"To visit your parents," Matthew said.

"To visit . . ." Angela blinked. "That's not a little trip, Matthew."

"I know," Matthew said. "Our plane leaves from JFK tomorrow at seven AM. I booked the Presidential Suite at Barcelo Punta Cana. Your parents are meeting us there."

Angela dropped her current slice. "What about the shop?"

"We'll have to close for a week," Matthew said.

"A *week?* What about my customers?"

"They'll understand," Matthew said, "and so will you if you let me tell you the rest. *My* parents are already down there."

Angela squinted. "Why are you parents in the Dominican Republic, Matthew?"

"They'd like us to get married in their presence," Matthew said. "If it's okay with you. On the beach at Punta Cana. It's all set up. All we have to do is get there. What do you say?"

Angela smiled. "You're marrying me on the beach?"

"Yeah," Matthew said. "Outside in the sunlight. Is that okay?"

Angela's eyes filled with tears. "Okay? Of course it's okay." She leaned across the table and kissed him. "When?"

"We'll arrive at Punta Cana around noon tomorrow, so by three o'clock tomorrow, we'll be married. Unless you want to wait a few days."

Angela shook her head. "No, tomorrow will be fine." She squeezed his hand. "You planned all this for me?"

"I planned all this for us," Matthew said.

Angela rubbed her stomach. "And Angel will be there with us." She leaped to her feet. "We have to go make a sign for the shop."

"Okay," Matthew said. "What will it say?"

A few hours later, the sign was complete. Angela and Matthew stood on the sidewalk looking at their handiwork: WE ARE ON OUR HONEYMOON! SEE YOU ON THE 7TH!

"Do you think we should have included the date?" Angela asked. "That might give people some bad ideas."

"The shop will be fine," Matthew said. "The good people at the Ninetieth have promised to roll by and check out the shop a couple times a day."

Angela headed to the door, but Matthew pulled her back, holding her close. "Stay out here in the sunset with me. We have to practice for when we get to the beach. I want to watch all the sunrises and sunsets with you while we're down there."

"I can't wait to get to the beach," Angela said. "I wish I could walk on the water in all directions at once."

I'd love to see that. Walking in all directions at once has to be the greatest freedom imaginable.

She looked into his eyes. "Thank you for freeing me, Matthew."

"You were always free, Angela." *Always.*

"You provided the key," she whispered. "You gave me love."

And you, my sweet, tough woman, turned my love into peace.

Chapter 39

The four-year-old girl slid into the middle booth as Christmas music filled the coffee shop. "Daddy," she said, her big brown eyes and tan-as-sand skin shining, "why do you sit way back here? You can see the snow *much* better from the big window."

"I have a nicer view from here, Angel." Matthew winked at the love of his life serving coffee at the counter, as the line of customers snaked around tables all the way to the door.

"Isn't the snow pretty, Mommy?" Angel asked.

"It's beautiful, Angel," Angela said.

"Can I go play in it?" Angel asked. "*Please?*"

"We'll all go out and play in it later," Angela said, ringing up another order. "We'll make snow angels and build a snow family on the sidewalk."

"When?" Angel asked.

"Tonight after we close," Angela said.

"Oh, I think we can go out as soon as I finish my breakfast." Matthew ate his third apple turnover. "And now I have finished my breakfast. Go get your coat."

Angel scooted to the kitchen.

Matthew peered through the backward letters of Smith's Sweet Treats and Coffee Shop at the faded "For Sale or Lease" sign on the empty red and yellow building across the street, its taped-up front window disappearing as the snow thickened.

He smiled at Angela, the woman who smelled like coffee, pastries, and lemons. "Should we put the baby in the snowwoman's arms or let him stand alone?"

Angela rubbed her stomach. "At the rate he's growing, he's going to be born standing up." She helped Angel with her coat and hat. "I wouldn't be surprised if he came out of me and started running."

Matthew left the booth as Angel scampered to the front door.

"Come on, Daddy!" she cried.

"One sec," Matthew said. He approached Angela and kissed her. Then he knelt in front of her. "Matthew Mark Junior, I have so many stories to tell you about women, and I pray that one day you will find yourself a woman who will give you the kind of love that sets you free."

Postscript

As you have probably noticed, I am not an expert in the law, so I offer my deepest apologies to purists of that noble profession.

I grew up watching *Perry Mason, Night Court, Matlock, Ally McBeal, and L.A. Law,* and now I enjoy *Harry's Law* and *Law & Order* and all its many acronyms. Any mistakes I've made in courtroom procedures and various points of the law are entirely my own. I doubt any judge would have allowed much of Angela's testimony, no matter how dramatic or entertaining it may have been.

It was, however, an *extremely* enjoyable scene to write.